Jimmy Bass

Howard Weider

ISBN: 9781079740134

DEDICATION

This book is dedicated to

all who want to follow God

and love high school basketball,

but have been bullied and tortured

by the pain of depression.

I pray you will realize that everyone,

even those considered nerds,

can learn to follow

the love, joy, peace,

and the adventure of

working with God.

Let God lead in your life!

CONTENTS

The best way to overcome

the pain you suffer from bullying

is to get counseling

and turn your life

to the Lord, Jesus Christ.

He is love and

wants to give you peace.

ACKNOWLEDGMENTS

I would like to express my gratitude to the many people who saw me through this book; to all those who provided support, talked things over, read, wrote, offered comments, assisted in the editing, proofreading, and design.

First and foremost, I would like to thank my Lord and Savior, Jesus Christ, for showing me His love and inspiring me to write this book for Him.

I would also like to thank my friend, Vaughn Jennings, for helping me in the process of editing spelling, punctuation, and grammar.

I beg forgiveness of anyone who has assisted me over the course of the years and whose names I failed to mention.

The future is for you, not the past.

Chapter One

Monday, the last week of August, 1962, I was in my Uncle Walter's home in the country outside Nashville, Tennessee. The farm has a small orchard which is mostly Aunt Helen's project. I worked it for her. They have no children, so I am their hired hand from early spring through summer. I've lived with them ever since I left St. Luke Hospital, where I was under the care of Doctor Walter Bass, my uncle, and my Psychiatrist.

My name is Jimmy Bass. Uncle Walter and Aunt Hellen were discussing my situation in his home office. He's about six-foot-one, slim and in his early fifties. When I came here in the middle of May 1961, I was around five-foot-eight. Now I'm six-foot-two, pushing six-foot-three. The pushing is almost gone. I believe I'm more like six-foot-three pushing six-foot-four. The taller I am, the better. Being taller makes me feel better. I think that will make me a better basketball player and that's my goal.

I have blond hair, and I'm no weakling. I have a muscular build from working out in an area gym. Plus, I have worked hard in the orchard for the last two summers.

I also shoot hoops at the gym with kids in the neighborhood or sometimes alone on an outside basket that Uncle Walter has. I couldn't make an outside jump shot until Uncle Walter trained me. At first, with my growth to over six-feet tall, I learned to post-up inside. I've been a guard most of my life. Uncle Walter convinced me I should stay a guard, or maybe a small forward. He told me that if he couldn't teach me to shoot the outside shot, he would work with me inside.

I have always wanted to be an inside player. But I could never hit the outside shots. I knew that shooting was critical in playing. You could conquer every other ability in basketball. But from what I have learned from past coaches, if you don't shoot well, you don't play. So Uncle Walter worked with me religiously on my shooting. Now I make shots all around the court.

Why all this commotion about learning the game when I am only six months from being nineteen? I am still eligible to play high school sports at my home in northern Ohio.

Oh, I'm eligible here in Tennessee, too, but I have my senior year to finish. I missed a year of school when my life went blank, and I didn't finish my Junior year. But I was able to complete the required credit hours in the right subjects with the help of Aunt Helen, is a certified teacher, and Cutler Ridge School, my school in Ohio. So now I'm qualified to enter my senior year.

Memories of my Junior year are mostly gone, and memories of my sophomore year aren't good. The memories are so fuzzy that I wonder if they were real or fantasies.

My father and mother have come to take me back to Ohio. Was predestined? Did I decide, or was I ordered?

Father talked with me, telling me all the right things I needed to hear. He said this was probably my last counseling session with Uncle Walter.

How do I know if this what I wanted? I felt I was a man now.

People back home would look at me differently. I was little and must have stunk at basketball before, but I know that I am an outstanding player now. That is very important to me.

"Jimmy, before we talk about you going back to Ohio, let's talk about how you feel about going back to school, period?" remarked Uncle Walter.

"I want to go to school for two reasons. I want to learn, and I want to play basketball," I replied. "That's my dream. You taught me how to act around people. I believe I was an extrovert before, but now I'm working on being an introvert. I need to remember when to keep my mouth shut and not put my foot in it."

"That is good advice, Jimmy. But being an introvert or an extrovert is not as important as thinking about what you are going to say before you speak. Then you will be able to talk to anybody."

"I don't want to put my foot into my mouth," I said to please my uncle. "I think I should be modest, quiet, and act like I am important. I act that way here, but can I get away with it at home? I want to act like I'm important because I think it is probably the best way to act. And I need to blend in so nobody will bug me."

"That is good, Jimmy. You're working on your self-esteem, believing in yourself. If piers hurt your feelings, don't let your emotions make you feel like you're worthless. You are Jimmy Bass, a whole human being. Nobody can take that away from you. We have been working on that a lot, Jimmy. I hope you remember what Aunt Hellen and I taught you!"

"Yes, Uncle Walter."

"What if basketball doesn't work out for you and you end up sitting on the bench like before? Remember, you have bad memories about this."

"I still don't remember the team. All I remember is the horror of sitting on the bench. But I know that was Cutler Ridge. Those fears were then, and I don't want to think about them or discuss them, now!"

"I want you to have positive thoughts about yourself."

"I know, and that's what I have to do. Thanks to you, I am a better player. I believe what people told me. If I stay here or if I go home, I have a chance. I have confidence, and if I am not playing, I'll quit. I won't go through sitting on the bench again. Never!"

"I understand, Jimmy, but first, if you believe you should play, talk it out with your coach before quitting."

"I will, Uncle Walter."

"Let's talk about the incident."

"I still don't remember it. All I remember is waking up at St Luke's and talking to you. You said it was months after what you call 'the incident.' But I don't know what the incident is. What is it?"

"I promised your father I wouldn't tell you anything about the incident. All I'll say is that it was an event in which your father finally realized you needed to see me."

"You mean I was going crazy?" I asked, then raised my hand to stop Uncle Walter from saying what I knew what he was going to say. "I mean, I needed help, and I couldn't remember my past?"

"No, you had a traumatic psychotic event that took your memory away. Some will call it a nervous breakdown. When somebody asks you what happened, that is what happened."

So I tell people I had a nervous breakdown?"
"Yes, and that is all!"

Pausing for a few seconds before continuing, Uncle Walter said, "You haven't lost all your memory, just faces, and people. Those will probably come back slowly. But situations and some events will probably take a little longer. The fear of sitting on the bench and not playing may always be with you. You remember, we talked about this before."

"Yes, I agree. It's the people. I remember the school, the town, and everything else, but not faces,"

"I believe that will come in time. We talked about kids teasing you in school and calling you names. Do you remember any particular time or name that bothered you?"

I have told you many times, No, I do not remember! I've thought a lot about it, but I can't remember. I don't even remember the names they called me in my Sophomore year."

"How are you going to handle it if they tease you and have a name for you that you don't like."

I wanted to say, "I'll beat them to a pulp!? I'm sure I could do it now, but I knew Uncle Walter would be upset. So I responded, "I don't know what I'll do. Maybe I should try to ignore them. I have good self-esteem. The names can't hurt me as long as I believe in myself. Which I do, Uncle Walter."

"You understand the meaning, and I hope you use this belief in life. Don't let anyone push you backward. Self-esteem is essential in how you live the rest of your life, Okay?"

I nodded my head in approval. "I think I can follow this belief."

One thing I know for sure; nobody is pushing me around again. Joe Cline, one of Uncle Walter's neighbors, taught me how to fight and put me through training for self-defense in the gym in his basement evenings when I wasn't playing basketball. Uncle Walter knew nothing about it. Joe told me to keep it quiet because Uncle Walter would never approve. That was fine with me. The training made me feel tough, not weak as I was before, or how I thought I was.

Since I lost my memory, I am not sure what I was like before. I could have been a bully, but I doubt it. I must have been a weakling. Uncle Walter taught me about self-esteem and self-love. He made me think I had been weak, though he never actually told me I was.

"Are you ready to go back to your home?" Uncle Walter asked.

"I know your father wants you at home and claims everything will be different. He insists he has a qualified counselor to see you weekly. He is a minister in a church at Cutler Ridge, but that is not the church where your family attends. He is also a part-time teacher in the junior high."

He paused, looking at Jimmy sternly. "If you go home, you have to promise me never to miss seeing your counselor."

Nodding my head, I agreed with him.

"Well, are you ready to leave, or do you think you should stay here? It is a small school here, and I know, from talking to adults who have seen you play, you will be successful on the basketball team. You're a shoo-in for being a forward. Some of the kids you know from playing basketball at the gym play for the high school. We had to hire students during the picking season, and from what your Aunt Helen and I have seen, you seemed to get along with them. You won't feel like your going to a new school, some of the kids going there will be familiar to you."

After a pause, he continued. "Be truthful and tell me how you feel. Don't worry about your father; I'll handle him if you want to stay."

Giving it more thought, no matter how much I loved it here, I knew the answer.

"Maybe it would be safe to stay here and go to a new school, but there is a mystery back home. I feel I have to find out what it is and not run away from it."

I thought for a while before I continued. "Fear makes it easy to stay away from home. Deep down, I know I have to face it."

"Are you afraid to go home?"

"In some ways, I am, and in some ways, I'm not. I don't think there's anybody at home that wants to hurt me. But there is some doubt about that. That's an unknown factor. I've told you this before."

"You have, but you also said it could be your imagination."
"That is right. I know part of the problem is not playing on the

basketball team, but I believe I wasn't a good player. You know how I played when you first saw me."

"You weren't that bad. You just needed a shot. Another thing, you didn't have back then, your height. And you're still growing."

"I had no confidence in myself, either. Now I feel I do. I just thought of something else. I'll hardly know anybody if I play here. Even though I lost some of my memory, I remember some of the people in my town. Clyde Carl, who owns the local Gas station and Mr. and Mrs. Keller who operate the local restaurant were always nice to me. If I'm as good as everyone says, I want to play for them."

There was a long pause. Finally, Uncle Walter announced. "Okay, I guess you have decided."

"Yes, I've decided, and that's my final answer.

It felt exciting to go back home and show those people I wasn't a nobody. I was going to take on the whole town and show them how tough I was. I knew that wasn't right. I was merely a good kid, and that's all.

I remember Mrs. Sears, who lives across the street. She's a widow in her seventies and is always kind to me. So was Mrs. Kokel, another widow who lived a few doors down from us. When I thought of them, I missed them.

Uncle Walter was waiting for an answer. "What is your answer?" he asked.

"I'm going home!"

Chapter Two

Tuesday, at seven in the morning, my family and I loaded our suitcases into the trunk of Dad's car. I had only two bags because I didn't accumulate much while staying here. However, I wasn't the only one with luggage. It took my family a couple of days coming to Tennessee then they spent last night at Uncle Walter's home. When all the baggage was in Dad's big, blue, 1960 Buick, we headed for home. It took us two days, with a layover in Lexington, Kentucky.

We got home Thursday afternoon. Next week, after Labor Day weekend, I would become a student at Cutler Ridge School on Tuesday morning.

~~~~~~~~~

My father is Arnold James Bass, born and raised in Tiffin, Ohio. He has black hair and a muscular build. He keeps in shape with the help of a gym in Tiffin. At forty-two he's considered a good looking man for his age. Dad went to Bowling Green, a state college, forty miles west of Tiffin, where he earned a degree in business. He came back home where he worked in the accounting department of a factory. Now he's an assistant manager and gets a high salary.

People say my mother has the same build she had as a teenager.

She's five-foot-three and beautiful. That's something a son doesn't want to admit. It's like telling my sister she is gorgeous because she looks like Mother.

About three o'clock on Thursday afternoon, we entered Cutler Ridge, a small town with forty or fifty houses, not counting the buildings in the downtown area, and four and a half miles northeast of Tiffin.

The downtown area is the middle of the town. The first business is Clyde's Gas Station on the south side of the street. Across from Clyde' is a small Library. Next is Keller's Restaurant. Back across the street, beside Clyde's is Walls' Bar. Stalling's Barber Shop sits directly across from Jean's Grocery store. It's a small store, not like those big grocery stores in Tiffin, where most people go weekly. But it serves a purpose. If you forget to get something in the big store, or Jean's can't come up with sale prices as low as the big stores can, and if Jean's doesn't carry some items the big stores do, the trip to Tiffin makes it affordable.

That's all there is to the business area. Next to the grocery store is a brick building which covers most of the block. The auditorium or gymnasium is the first part of the building. During game nights, the doors in front of the gymnasium are the way to enter from the sidewalk on Main Street. The rest of the building extends down to the end all the block, with areas alongside the building for parking as well as in the back of the building. Our school is one of the smaller ones in Ohio.

Part of the mystery was the joy of coming home and not knowing whether the incident was in the school, or not. Somehow I could feel the school represented the evil that hurt me. A fear was defiantly there. My eyes were glued on the school as we passed and I kept looking at it through the back seat window.

When Father turned down the next street, we rode with the school's parking lot on our left. To the right, it was all residential. Traveling half a block further we passed the school grounds and entered

17

an all residential area. Then the street came to a dead-end with our driveway straight ahead. Father had built our house on the backside of Uncle Fred's farm. If you came down our street too fast and lost control, you could drive straight into our home. But Father put in large posts, so cars would have to get through them before they hit our house.

We drove past the house and turned left onto another part of the driveway where our garage sat in the back corner of our property. If you went straight, instead of turning behind the house, the road leads to a one-story barn where Father has a workshop. He restored old cars and stored them there. I remember helping my father when he worked on cars. I hated it because I wanted to play with my friends. I have always enjoyed working with vehicles but was afraid to act like it. I believed my father would have me working with him more.

Another reason for not wanting to help him was a fearful hidden memory that was coming back to me. Maybe it was memories I had never lost. Now that I'm home, the memories are returning.

Father was okay until I made a mistake. I don't want to think about that anymore. I have a fear that I need to walk error-free around my perfect father. I don't want this fear. If I have to live with it, I'm gone! And he can't stop me.

I remembered him talking about how he had to be more patient with me when he was trying to convince me to come home. He had to be more understanding, especially if I helped him do things around the house and the yard. He said nothing about his shop.

I remember something happened in the shop that brought up the feeling of fear. It's something horrible, but it won't come out. It's hidden deep in my memories. No matter how hard I try, I can't make it out. Did I make a mistake coming back here? No! I am stronger than I was. If the big bad wolf comes after me, I can take him down.

Father built the house and barn on the edge of my uncle's farm.

I should say my Great Uncle's farm. He's dead, and his wife is, too. Dad and Uncle Walter inherited this one-hundred-fifty-acre farm after their Uncle Fred died.

They were Uncle Fred's only heirs. My father told me on one of his visits to Tennessee that he bought out Uncle Walter. Uncle Walter never said anything about it. I wonder why. Was there a disagreement between the two of them? I know there was a disagreement over me after my comma. Instead of going to a mental institution, I came to live with Uncles Walter. I overheard my father, saying I belonged in a mental institution. Uncle Walter got pretty adamant about that with my father.

"You're not putting him in a mental institution, even though you're the father. I am the psychiatrist, and I'm taking him home to my place. I will take care of him."

That's how I ended up at Uncle Walter's place, and I'm glad. I'm not sure why I feel that my father was mean to me, except that he wanted to put me in a nuthouse. From that day on, even though I had no memory of what he did, I painted my father with fear. That's all I remember of him.

I was living with Uncle Walter when Uncle Fred died. I wanted to go to the funeral, but Uncle Walter thought I wasn't ready for a funeral. I loved my Great Uncle Fred. And I enjoyed helping him on his farm and used it as an excuse to get away from my father and working in his shop.

Where did that memory come from?

I remember working on the farm, but not to get away from my father. The house and barn were on another road about a half a mile north of town.

Dad parked the car in front of the garage, and everyone piled out. Taking my two suitcases, I went to my room. I entered the back door into a small hallway that led to another hall and steps leading to the basement. Walking down the short hallway, I could see an opening to the kitchen on my left. Straight ahead, through an archway, was the living room and the dining room. To the right, the hallway led to a utility room and four bedrooms. There were two average-sized bedrooms at the end of the hall. To the right was my room. At the end of the hallway was a door leading to a guest room.

Looking back toward the kitchen, I could see a big bathroom with two doors, one leading to the hallway and one leading to my parents' bedroom. The second bathroom was in the guest bedroom. That's the bathroom I use.

I hurried to my room and entered as if I had never gone. There is a double bed which has the headboard attached to the back wall, the same wall which connects to the garage. To my left is a window. That's the only place there could be a window in my room. The guest room was an add-on five or six years ago and covered over half of that wall. Sandy is unlucky. There's no window in her room.

To my right is a walk-in closet. A dresser where I put most of my underclothes stands against the wall in front of my bed. The first thing I did was unload my suitcases and put the clothes I had in their proper place. When done I sat down on the bed.

On the walls, my mother had hung the pictures of events I did in school. I never had posters of athletes. I admired superstars as all kids do, but I wasn't into that.

I felt fear when I saw the school, but I didn't know why? I should be happy and wanted to see friends, if I had friends and if I could remember them.

There are blank spots where there should be memories in my mind. Trying to think of kids, I would have graduated with last year draws a blank. I can't even recall the girls. I might have liked the pretty ones. Forget it! I never had a girlfriend or even a date. I believe that's true.

Memories come to me, but they come with fear. I wish I had a girlfriend, but I never had one. It seems nobody wanted anything to do with me. Surely someone would have, but I guess not.

Suddenly there is a memory of an attractive, brunette, a little over five feet tall with a cute face. I know I had a powerful feeling for this girl, and she did for me, too, at one time. Or I thought she did. No, she left me for somebody big in the school. Probably he was the most popular kid in school.

He had an unusual name, and so did she. Maybe they were nicknames. Everybody has one. Their names had something to do with their popularity in school. I tried to remember what their names were, but I couldn't do it.

Why try to remember them? They're probably married, or she has gone off to some state college. I remember she was smart.

Where did this memory come from? Did I love her?

Yes, I did, but she hurt me badly, and I can't remember how. Oh, how I wish my memories would resurface. In time I guess they will. Uncle Walter said, maybe there are some I don't want to remember. Perhaps even her name could bring back bad memories.

My father opened my bedroom door, came in, and stood in front of my bed. "Jimmy, why don't you change into some jeans and a tee-shirt?" he suggested. I was wearing dress pants and a collared shirt. "I want to show you something at Uncle Fred's farm. I'll meet you in front of the shop. We'll take my truck." Then he left.

I wondered, was this a summons or an order? Father had promised he would try to stop commanding, and he acted excited, so it must be a good thing. I quickly changed and met him at his truck; a 1960 one-ton Ford pickup painted red. It has a four-speed transmission with a powerful V-eight engine. It had to be a reliable vehicle to pull his trailer and haul cars he picks up when he goes south.

Dad came down to see me several times and brought the truck and trailer and, if he found one, hauled an old car or pickup truck back home. Sometimes Father told me he was looking for a vehicle for a friend. There must have been more cars then I imagined in his shop. I know he took home a lot of autos. I wondered where he stored them. Were they in Uncle Fred's barn? Maybe that is what he wants to show me.

We went down our driveway and into the street, then turned east. After going one block, we were in the country. We turned north on the next crossroad; then took the next road left. After about a mile, we arrived at Uncle Fred's farm. Of course, it's father's farm, now.

Turning down a small lane, we came to a big white two-story house, with a front porch that ran the length of the front of the house. Like most houses with a porch, it has a roof. A couple of big oak trees in the front yard give the porch plenty of shade.

Good memories come from that porch. At times, Uncle Fred and I sat there and discussed events of the world, and sports, especially if the Detroit Tigers won the pennant. Most people in our neighborhood were Cleveland Indians' fans, but Uncle Fred was a die-hard Tiger's fan. Many discussions exploded between him and the Indian followers. They were fun to listen too. When he asked me who I rooted for, I would say, "Both teams!" I didn't want to hurt anybody's feelings. By his facial expressions, I knew he didn't like the answer, but he accepted it. I always have good memories of Uncle Fred.

Remembering the farm was always there and what kind of baseball fan he was, made for a lot of good memories that never left me. Maybe I forgot only the terrible things. Perhaps it would be best if I never remembered them.

When we came to the barn, a hundred yards or so behind the house, I could see the front door of the barn was different. Instead of the tall sliding doors to accommodate large farm machinery, there were two garage-style doors with overhead tracks. Above the doors, where the top half of the old doors had been, there was now a solid wall.

Father pulled his truck in front of the right door. Without saying a word, he left the pickup, and I followed him. He went to the second door, unlocked it, and slid it up. I could see my father had turned two sections of the barn into a shop with a cement floor, plywood walls, and a plywood ceiling. I guessed it was twelve feet high. Lights on the ceiling glowed brightly when father flipped the switch.

What could be a shop, looked more like a storage area. There were a couple old Model T Fords and an old pickup truck that Dad had restored. A 1947 Chevy two-door sedan he hadn't yet returned to its original look sat with the others. I also saw a 1950 Yellow Ford convertible that he had acquired from Uncle Walter. It barely ran.

There was a lot of space left for more projects. Then I saw a beautiful two-tone car with blue on the bottom and white on the top. It was Uncle Fred's 1957 Chevy, and it still looked to be in excellent shape.

As I looked the car over, I couldn't find any rust. I remember when Uncle Fred bought this car. He had undercoating sprayed on it. Then before winter came, he would jack the car up and spread grease all over the under-body. Looking underneath the car, I couldn't see any rust.

In Ohio, as in most northern states, the road crews use salt on the road to melt the ice and snow. When the snow gets thrown on the under-body, the snow melts, but the salt finds nicks and crannies. If it's not washed off, it will cause rust.

I raised the hood and saw the clean, 283 cubic-inch, V-eight, with a four-barrel carburetor. The engine compartment and the underside of the hood had been painted stock black. Closing the hood and opening the driver's door, I slide in behind the steering wheel sitting on the bench seat. There was a three-speed stick on the column, no automatic for Uncle Fred, and the speedometer showed only twenty-three hundred miles. That is very low.

My father stood beside me with the door still open. Arnold Bass crouched down and said to his son, "Do you like it?"

"Yes, Dad. Uncle Fred's fifty-seven is an excellent set of wheels."

"Well, these wheels are yours. Your Uncle Fred gave them to you in his will."

I was shocked. Never in my wildest dreams had I thought I would own this car. I never expected Uncle Fred to will it to me. This gift was a great surprise, a great surprise indeed.

"It's yours, but I had it put in my name until you graduate. Then I'll sign it over to you. It is all according to the will. While you're in school, the insurance will be lower if it's in my name."

"Okay! I understand." I cried excitingly. I couldn't wait to get it on the road. All the girls will love me now, I thought.

Stupid! Stupid! Stupid! What girls? If there were girls or even a girl in my life, I couldn't remember. I was feeling so good right now that all I wanted to drive around the neighborhood. Maybe I would recognize something.

"Promise me one thing, Jimmy. Don't drive this car in the snow." my father proclaimed.

"I know, Father. I don't want any rust on this car. I'll walk when there is snow. I will never drive this car to school. We live to close."

Wouldn't kids get a kick out of me driving this to school? Then I thought, "What kids?"

"When there is snow, you can drive Uncle Fred's Ford truck, stored in his shop."

"Okay, Father." I agreed.

Uncle Fred's shop is only a few hundred feet in front of the barn, by the driveway. When we came in, I didn't pay much attention to it, but now, as I looked at it through the windshield, I could see it was still in good shape, and the truck was inside.

"Start it up and drive it, Son. It's 3:30. I'll meet you at home by five o'clock."

"Okay, Father. Thanks," I replied deep in shock.

He nodded his head and stepped back so I could shut the door and start the car. The engine purred like a kitten. The Chevy was parked about twenty-five feet from the open door. I pushed in the clutch, shifted into first gear, slowly left the barn, and headed down the driveway.

I knew how to drive a stick shift. That's what I used when I learned to drive. Driving Uncle Walter's truck in the orchard gave me plenty of practice, too.

At first, I wondered where I should drive. Then I thought of driving around the county and Cutler Ridge school district. That is if I could remember the roads. I had no particular direction or destination. I just drove. Some of the farmland looked familiar, but I still couldn't remember the names of the folks who lived there. Then, to my surprise some, I remembered a place. I could even recall the faces of kids who lived there. They were all at least a couple of years older than me. And that is all I remembered. I wondered if this was a real memory or a fantasy.

I realized that most of the kids I would have been close to in school had probably graduated. The kids who would be in my class this year would have been Sophomores when I was in school. I felt I wasn't close to that class. I was closer to the Seniors when I was a Junior.

Where did I get that memory? Was it true?

Then I saw a farm that rang some bells. Someone who lived there was very close to me at one time. I had driven past the farm so at the next crossroad I turned the car around and headed back the way I had come. When I saw the farm again, I looked at the mailbox for a name. No such luck! Nothing was on the mailbox. Another look at the house triggered another memory. I felt it was a girl.

Oh, how I wished I could remember! I wanted to drive up the driveway and say, "Hi." The people there had to recognize me. But I couldn't find the courage. I didn't have the guts, will power, or whatever it was I lacked. So I kept driving.

Then I noticed the gas gauge showed the tank was almost empty. I headed for town and Clyde's, a typical gas station. It is only one building with two stalls to work on cars and an office. One side of the office held a cash register on a bench that was almost the length of the room. It had glass in the front so you could see things displayed in it. Three selves held an assortment of candy, potato chips, and other snacks.

I told the attendant to fill the gas tank. I didn't recognize the attendant who looked to be close to my age, but I did remember Clyde, a husky man behind the counter. Another big man who seemed to be close to my age was in front of Clyde. I didn't recognize him, but the two men were having a conversation. I went to the Coke machine, put in the proper change, opened a small door to pull out a glass bottle of Coke, and opened it with the opener on the side. Just as I was taking a drink, a voice called "Jimmy Bass!"

"Hello, Mr. Carl," I replied.

I said nothing to the younger man because I didn't recognize him. I wondered if he was an enemy. Thoughts of fear suddenly attacked me. If enemies came up to me, I wouldn't know them. This big guy could be one of my tormentors! But I don't remember. By the way I felt and the things Uncle Walter taught me about self-esteem, I decided I had to have been a nerd, and this was one of my tormentors.

"No mister to me, Jimmy. When did you get home? Look how

26

tall you are! You were just a little guy when you left."

"I wasn't that small. The last time you saw me, I was around five-feet-nine pushing close to five-foot-ten. It's in my genes to be tall. Uncle Walter is six-foot-two. My father's close to six-foot-one. I guess I'm a late bloomer."

"How tall are you, now?" asked the young guy I didn't recognize.

"I'm six-foot-three."

The stranger just gave me a weird look, like he couldn't believe his eyes. It felt like he was thinking. "I can't push this kid around anymore."

Am I overreacting? This guy might be a friend, but I doubt it.

"So, Jimmy, when did you get home?" asked Clyde.

"About an hour or so ago," I answered.

Shaking his head, he remarked, "Jimmy, it's unbelievable how you have changed. I don't mean just the height. You seem calmer, too."

Clyde pointed at my car and said, "I see you're driving your Uncle Fred's old fifty-seven. Your father told me you inherited it. He told me you were coming back. If you've only been here a little over an hour, you got your car pretty quick!"

How did my father know I was coming back? I just decided a couple of days ago. Father must've been sure I was coming back here.

I answered Clyde, "As soon as we got home, Father took me to my uncle's farm and gave me the car. He told me it was mine and I love it! It's an awesome gift. When I heard UncleFred died, it pained me greatly. We were very close."

"I know. Fred used to talk about you a lot when he came here. When you left, it hurt him. He talked about going down to Tennessee and visiting you. But he never made it. He was too sick to go."

"They never told me what killed him and wouldn't let me come to the funeral. Could you tell me, Clyde, what he died from?"

"It was cancer. It was all through your uncle's body, Jimmy. He was very sick towards the end. That's all I'm going to tell you because I want you to remember your uncle the way he was. So, how are you doing? What has happened about your problem?"

He shook his head and then said, "I should've kept my mouth shut. I'm sorry!"

I didn't know how to answer him, but I didn't feel embarrassed either. So I said, "I'm doing fine. I'm starting back to school next week for my Senior year."

"Too bad, you can't play sports. They need players on the basketball team, especially some with your height. They didn't even have enough for a baseball team. Pat, here, tells me most of the boys in the Junior and Senior classes are into farming, not athletics."

"I can play."

"How is that?" asked the younger man.

"I only missed one year. I finished my Junior year in Tennessee."

"He is right. That is the law, Pat. Remember last year they figured out Weider had missed only one year."

"Now that I think about it, Joey Bell flunked our class. Remember, Jimmy? Oh, he is going to be surprised how tall you are."

I looked at Pat. There was some recognition, but that was all. I couldn't remember if I knew him or not. How should I react? Did I remember Joey Bell? The name sounded familiar, but that was all. I was confused about what to say to this big man standing there. I was dumbfounded and couldn't say a word. He was heavier than me, but not much taller.

"Pat, you don't remember, do you? "Clyde stated. "Jimmy's

father said there was some trouble with his memory."

"You don't remember me, do you, Jimmy?"

Shaking my head, as if I was ashamed, I said, "Sorry, I don't know who you are."

I just stared at him for a few seconds, then continued, "Due to the incident, I lost some memory. Mostly I don't recall people I knew before. I think you may be from my class or maybe the class ahead of mine."

Then I added, "I'm sorry."

"I'm Pat Enders. I was in your class; maybe I should say your old class. You will now be in the same class as my brother, Tim."

Pausing for a few seconds he smiled, "I was a good friend of yours. At least I thought I was."

Pat look as if he was disappointed that I didn't recognize him.

I didn't know what to say. It was an awkward moment.

The attendant came in and told me the cost of the gas, and I pulled out my billfold, handed the money to Clyde, and he rang it up. I took my change and said good-bye.

I wanted to say more to Pat, but my new introvert personality kicked in. I hurried out of the station and to my car.

~~~~~~~~~~

Pat looked at Clyde and shook his head. "I can't believe he couldn't remember me. We were close friends. Yeah, we picked on him and teased him, but he didn't act as if it bothered him. He was always friendly to me. I thought he looked up to me. Some kids put him down, but I stood up for him. It didn't seem to bother him. We were always joking around."

Pat thought for a while before going on. "I know the basketball season of our Junior year bothered him. Summerall never played him. I remember Jimmy asked if he could play Junior Varsity. Summerall laughed at him. During basketball season and afterward, he changed.

Sometimes Jimmy seemed to be in a daze. He defiantly became strange after that and hardly wanted to speak to anyone. He was obsessed with Elisabeth Hasselback, who was dating Jake. She completely ignored him, and that hurt Jimmy pretty bad. Jake Bickhart and his buddies, Singer and Alter, were hard on him. Not just hard on him, but downright mean to him."

Pat looked troubled. "Clyde, talk about a coward, I'm a big one. I watched what Jake and his buddies did to Jimmy, and I did nothing about it."

"I heard that Jake and his buddies controlled the school," Clyde remarked, shaking his head.

"They had Summerall under there thumb. If there was a prank or someone who got in trouble, it wasn't them."

"You spoke up when you had to, Pat. That was how we got the discipline cleared up for your Senior year."

"I know, but that was after what they called 'the incident' at the skating rink."

"Arnold is trying to keep his son from knowing about the incident. I guess Jimmy doesn't remember a thing. His father says he should forget the past and concentrate on the future. I guess that's what everybody should do. Remember, Jimmy is part of this community, and we should try to protect him, so don't say a word about it to him and let the other kids that will be around him know to do the same thing. Tell Tim and maybe have him tell the rest of the kids he will be around."

"I will, but I feel sorry for Jimmy. There were only a few of us around that night when it happened, and it wasn't an incident."

Pat tried to come up with the proper words. Finally, he said, "It was like he left this world."

~~~~~~~~~~

I drove home, knowing it was close to supper time. I parked the car in front of our house, but my thoughts were on how I disappointed the guy called Pat Ender. He claimed he was a close friend, but I couldn't remember him, that hurt. I needed friends. I needed close friends that cared about me. It seemed that wasn't possible. Wanting to be an introvert looked like it wasn't the best option.

Do I want that to be my way of life? I didn't think so. Being an introvert doesn't seem like the right choice. I want friends. Yes, I do!

I guess I'll have to act like I'm going to a new school as if I had stayed down in Tennessee. But it isn't fair. People here know me. Since I didn't know what kind of person I was before, they have an advantage.

Then a negative thought came to me. Father said that people might think I was in a mental hospital and suggested I keep that fact quiet. I wonder why. After saying that, his next comment was, "Think of the future!"

People will think I went off the deep end, and that is how they will look at me. So I'm an introvert because people won't want to be friends with a person like me. Girls won't want me. Their parents won't want a crazy man to date their daughters.

"You're a loser, Jimmy Bass, and you'll always be a loser.

I tried to push these thoughts away as I left my car and walked toward the house, then I saw a strange car in the driveway. It made me wonder who was here. When I entered the back door, into the kitchen, Grandmother Linbreck, my mother's, mother, gave me a big hug and kissed me on the cheek.

She broke away, saying, "Welcome home, Jimmy."

Then Grandfather Linbreck, or Pete like he wanted everybody to call him, shook my hand and welcomed me home.

Pete and Judy Linbreck were in their middle sixties. Grandfather is about five-foot-six, and Grandmother is five-foot-four, rather short for a woman. They live a good life, and both are considered chubby.

Pete was a retired school teacher from the Tiffin Public School District. He has always taught Junior High. For a few years, Grandfather was a Junior High principal but didn't like it, and went back to being a teacher.

They stayed for supper and into the evening. The conversation was about everything in my grandparents' lives, and no one mentioned a word about my hospitalization or my problem. Father's idea was to be carried out. My past was over, and we were to think only of the future. I hope it'll works. What will happen if my horrible past returns? It must have been terrible. It put me in never-never-land. How would I handle it?

Uncle Walter kept reminding me, "Think positive! Having self-esteem is going to help you. No matter how bad your past was, you should ignore it and think about the future."

"The future is for you, Jimmy, not the past."

Chapter Three

I remember sitting on the bench during a game. Every player on the team got to play, except me. The whole team was laughing. I don't remember their faces; but I do remember their laughter, their name-calling, and that much of it was due to the coach.

The pain was horrible, but I didn't cry. I held my feelings inside, trying to act like a man. But the torture kept pushing at me. As soon as the game was over, I ran away.

I was in a lonely place, trying to get away and screaming for mercy until I stumbled and fell to the ground. The pain was terrible. There was no sympathy, just never-ending misery. Every living thing seemed to scream that I was worthless.

I heard voices around me screeching "Worthless! Worthless! Nobody cares about you! You want to have love, but who would love a person like you? No one will even like you. You are worthless, worthless, worthless!"

When I awakened, I sat upright and shouted, "That's not real! It was a dream!"

My emotions were surging, and I was soaking wet. Tears rolled down my cheeks. The pain of depression pushed me into a hole from which it would be difficult to return.

I remember this type of pain was common in my past. It was something I wanted to eradicate from my life. But it kept pushing and pushing, telling me I was crazy. A voice kept pounding at me, telling me how worthless I was.

I almost bought into the claims of the voices, but Uncle Walter's words kept pounding at me, trying to drown out the evil voices. "You are a new, fully self-esteemed person."

I held onto that thought, and the pain subsided. Feeling I needed exercise.

The clock on my nightstand said it was six-thirty so I got out of bed and put on a tee-shirt and sweatpants. I grabbed my tennis shoes and thought, "Where is my basketball."

After a few seconds, I remembered I had put it in the hallway closet by the back door. If it was there, would it still have air in it?

Stopping in the kitchen, I left a note under the salt shaker on the table so my family would know where I had gone.

My old basketball wasn't in the closet, but I found a new one. Dad was again trying to make up for my past and the way he had treated me. I didn't remember very much about the treatment I'd received, only the impatience Father had with me in the shop. At least I had a new basketball!

Outside I thought about my car, but I wasn't going back to my room to get my keys. I decided to run. That would help me.

~~~~~~~~~~

Carolyn Bass awoke when she heard the sound of the back door slam, and screamed, "What was that, Arnold? Did somebody come into our house?"

Arnold, in his pajamas, quickly climbed out of bed, and hurried out of the bedroom door running down the hall to the kitchen. When he saw the back door was unlocked, he began to worry. Carolyn had followed her husband, and as she entered the kitchen, she saw a note on the table, picked it up, and began reading it.

"Did you lock the back door last night? It's unlocked! Arnold demanded as he entered the kitchen.

"Yes, I did. The sound we heard was Jimmy leaving," Carolyn answered, showing her husband the note.

"He went to play basketball this early in the morning?"

"I wonder if this is a common thing or if something has happened to cause him to feel he needs physical exercise. Your brother said if he gets depressed, activity can help relieve the pain that depression causes."

"Yes, Walter did say that! I sure hope Jimmy isn't depressed. I thought he was completely over all his problems. Should we take him back to my brother?"

"No, but we have to encourage him to not to let his depression bother him. Maybe I'm jumping to a conclusion."

Arnold went to the front window with Carolyn right beside him. Then he turned around and went back to the kitchen and into the hallway. Opening the closet, Arnold saw the new basketball was gone. Turning to his wife, he said, "He didn't take his car, and the basketball is gone. I bet he's at the outside gym behind the school. Do you think I should go and find him?"

"I would feel better if you did."

Arnold quickly dressed and left the house. He walked down the sidewalk. Then turned onto the street that went behind the school. A small walkway led between two houses and continued to the school's baseball field.

There were a few stands along the first baseline, and more were along the third baseline. Behind these stands was the outside basketball court. Regular nets hung on each basket. At times, that was a problem. Vandals stole them. But the athletic department kept replacing them to encourage kids to use the court. Some had suggested using chain nets, but the idea got squashed for fear that players might get their hand caught in the chain links, causing severe injury. During the winter, the nets they removed because nobody would want to use the court when it was cold.

As he rounded the backstop to the baseball field, the sun was peaking over the horizon. In the partial darkness, Arnold saw someone shooting baskets on the court and was sure it was his son. Staying close to the backstop so Jimmy couldn't see him, Arnold wondered how his son could see ten or fifteen minutes ago when he had first arrived. Then he remembered the full moon last night and decided it must have given enough light.

By the way the young man was shooting, Arnold was sure it was Jimmy. He shot the way Walter had taught him, and he was just as good a shot as his brother. Arnold couldn't wait for his son to play on the team. Shooting like that, in a game, would make him proud, not the disappointment he went through before.

Why hadn't Jimmy been a strong lad? When somebody messed with him, he should have punched there lights out! Instead, he took the constant teasing that drove to, what Walter called depression and was so discouraged he became a zombie.

In his worst nightmares, Arnold didn't want to relive that horrible time. People were asking all kinds of questions about Jimmy, but he didn't know how to answer them.

Arnold was ashamed that Jimmy was his son. He wished his son was a star, not just a player who could score a few points. Yes, that's what he wanted to make him proud.

"I wish Jimmy would make up for all the shame I had to face," Arnold dreamed. "I hope it wasn't a mistake bringing him home. Maybe I should have left him in Tennessee. If his memory comes back, all hell could break loose. But it can't! Walter said it couldn't, wouldn't. It simply can't!"

Watching his son practice for a few minutes, Arnold enjoyed seeing those great shots. "It's going to be wonderful seeing the Bass name in glory! Jimmy will provide that, and will make everything worth it."

Feeling his son was okay, Arnold headed back home. Suddenly he was surprised when Jimmy dunked the ball on a drive to the basket. Dunking the ball was a remarkable feat for a man Jimmy's size.

"My son is unreal!" Arnold smiled, full of pride as he hurried home.

~~~~~~~~~

In my mind, I was playing a game. Every shot I made was helping my team win the game, and I was on fire. I couldn't miss a shot. One after another, the ball went in as I continually took outside shots. If I missed the basket, I rebounded it and shot again. When I was anywhere close to the basket, I used my backboard shot. If I made the outside shot, I retrieved the ball and dribbled for a close backboard shot. No matter what, I shot an outside-shot and then a short-shot. After I did this for a while, I started doing lay-ups, and a dunk once in a while. I learned I could do that in my last week in Tennessee. I never thought I would conquer it, but when I did, it was almost unreal.

I also mastered a shot for when a player was going to block me, I twisted my body to the right or left, away from the block, and handed it to the backboard. Whether it was left-handed or right-handed, made no difference. As long as I used the backboard, I could make the shot. I didn't drive to the basket unless I had a clear path. When a person got

37

my way, I took a quick shot, surprising many defenders who thought I would go all the way to the basket. I believed offensive rebounding would be a great plus for me. I could follow a shot off the rim, whether it was mine or someone else's shot.

The depression went away, but I knew it was lurking nearby, ready to pounce on me again. Depression was familiar territory, but I had not recalled these feeling since I came out of my comma in the hospital. The responses to depression must have come from my past, a past I barely remember.

I had dreams of sitting on the bench but not to the extent of those I had last night, and I was confused about how to handle this situation.

A thought came to me, something Uncle Walter taught me, "I am full of self-esteem, and I can handle depression. Depression does not exist. No, it doesn't! I won't let it! By thinking positively, I'll be okay.

After the sun was fully up, I played for another half an hour, hoping I could find some kids who would like to play a pick-up game. I guess most of the athletes in Cutler Ridge were on the baseball team. Basketball was the farthest thing from their thoughts.

~~~~~~~~~~

The next morning I woke refreshed, around seven o'clock. Quickly dressing in shorts and a tee-shirt, I left my room and started down the hall. My parents were in the kitchen, eating breakfast. I stopped in the kitchen and told my parents I was going to shoot hoops.

Mother wanted to make breakfast for me. I declined at first, but she finally convinced me that I had to eat, so I sat at the table beside my father, who tried to start a conversation by asking what classes I had signed up to take that semester. I told him, and he seemed to agree. Then, trying not to counsel me, Father casually asked me how I felt. I was tempted to tell him about my dream the night before, but I was afraid of how he would react. I chose not to say anything about it. After

Father decided I was alright, the conversation became awkward for both of us.

I felt that deep inside; it was an act. I was a basketball player, and I was going to make him proud. Sometimes it seemed that he never got away from the old me. I knew it was true, but there was something else missing, and I couldn't remember what it was. One thing I knew, I would try to be his obedient son, but he had better not cross the line.

What am I saying? What am I thinking? Fathers and sons love and care for each other! Would that ever be us?

Carolyn always said that one of the problems Arnold had with Jimmy was not being able to talk to him as a father to his son. Maybe they could speak as friends, but Arnold felt awkward and always wanted to be in control.

By law, Jimmy was an adult. He would be nineteen next February the second and didn't want to give in. Arnold presumed that since he was the father, he was the boss. Jimmy was the son and needed to accept his father's control. Didn't it say that in the Bible?

He still thought that he had the right to cut Jimmy off, even if he was an adult. A father had to keep his control. The kid had been a problem, a big problem, and couldn't he be trusted. Could Arnold believe in Jimmy now?

For now, his parents didn't have to worry about him. Jimmy was listening to his father. At least he didn't do anything unless he asked his parents first.

One thing always worried Arnold. If Jimmy's memory came back, what would he remember? Walter had said he didn't know if it would ever come back. But if it did, how would Jimmy react? That was a huge obstacle. Would being the father of a basketball star be enough reward for the pain he had experienced with his son?

~~~~~~~~~

Before Father went to the shop to work on one of his cars, he reminded me that if I shot hoops, I need to remember my appointment with Reverend Wood at ten o'clock. I nodded my head and started eating my bacon and eggs.

Mother's attempt at conversation was the same as Dad's. She wondered how I felt. I didn't tell her about my wild dream, just like I didn't with Father. I was trying to convince her everything was okay, but she wasn't buying it. I acted like I didn't understand what she was asking, so she gave up the interrogation.

I finished eating, quickly said good-bye, and headed for the basketball court. I planned to shoot hoops for about an hour then off to St. Matthew's to talk with Reverend John Wood.

Chapter Four

Ten years ago, St Mathew's was a small Baptist church then it had been abandoned until seven years ago when some people in our town turned it into a nondenominational church. A few people gave their time to fix it up, make it presentable for worship, and began searching for a pastor. John Wood fit the bill because he was looking for a part-time position, and the church could afford him. More importantly, he went along with their beliefs.

The unwanted parish house had fallen into decay, and eventually, the people demolished it. John Wood and his wife lived in a house a block south of the church. The church office was half of the front part of their home with the other half left for the living room.

The office included a small desk sitting in the corner with a swivel chair in the front, two comfortable chairs in the middle of the room, and plenty of books in bookcases along the wall.

~~~~~~~~~

Pastor John knew little about me, so when we met, he was surprised by my height. "Somebody told me you were a little guy. That sure isn't true," he laughed. Then he said, "My records on you say that on April the fourth, 1961, you went into a psychotic induced coma, and now you can't remember much of your past."

I nodded my head.

"Tell me about what you remember or don't remember."

I thought about this for a few minutes, then answered, "I don't know. Before I came home, I thought I would recall things, but I still have no memory of most people. I remembered some people when I was in Tennessee. I've been here a little over a day so, hopefully, when I see more people, I'll remember more."

"Does it bother you that you can't remember more people?"

I explained about my meeting with Pat Ender and how he said we were good friends. "Here is the funny part," I smiled, "I think I remember his brother, James. He's tall, like his brother, but not as heavy and he has blond hair."

"That describes James Ender, alright. Who else do you remember?"

"Joey Bell, I heard his name mentioned at the gas station when I met Pat Ender."

"Describe Joey."

"He's small like me, or like I used to be. I'm not good at describing faces, but I know he is good looking and has brown hair."

"What do you mean small like you used to be?"

"Before, I was close to his height. Now I am six-foot-three. If Joey is the same height, I'd say he is five-foot-seven. I was a little taller than him. I think at the time I left; I was around five-foot-ten."

"That's a good description of Joey. He goes to our church, and he is an outstanding Christian."

"I remember that he didn't like it when kids swore."

"Do you swear?"

"I don't know if I swore before, but I don't, now." I shook my head. "I don't even think about swearing." After a quick pause, I declared, "I remember that if my father heard of me swearing, I would get my butt kicked. Sorry, I mean I'd be punished. I shouldn't use the word 'butt' when I'm talking to a preacher. No swearing for me! I don't think so. I hope Joey will be my friend."

"I think he'll be your friend, but you seem to have a friend in Pat Ender."

"I don't think my father wants me to be friends with Pat. Father doesn't think we were friends. Of course, he's out of school, so I probably won't run into him much."

"That is true. But I'm sure Joey will be your friend. Were you close to him before?"

"I think so, somewhere in my past, but I don't know." After another pause, I continued, "I also heard at the gas station that Joey flunked a year. So maybe we were classmates."

"That could be. But I'm sure there will be other guys who will be your friend."

"I hope so, but my past might push people away. Maybe I did something horrible so nobody will like me. And I'm sure no parents would want their daughter to be friends with me."

"Don't be so negative about your self."

"I'm not negative. I'm realistic. You say 'mental problems' and people think I'm a crazy man. They think I'm some rapist that will ravage their daughters. I don't think people know I never was in a mental institution. I guess the only reason I wasn't is that Uncle Walter is a psychiatrist. But they'll assume I was. I might be a problem. They'll have to watch me closely."

I knew I was coming on strong to my counselor, but it was the truth. That's what Uncle Walter said could happen.

"If a stranger came into this community, that might be true," John acknowledged, "But you're not a stranger! People know you from your past. You were harmless; at least I don't remember hearing about you being mean or anything like that."

"What was I like before I lost my memory?"

"Hasn't your father or your uncle told you?"

"No. Father doesn't want me to know the past. He says, 'Forget the past. Think about the future.'"

"How about your uncle?"

"I think my father has convinced him about the same thing. It seems my father has some control over him."

"What do you want, Jimmy?"

"I want to know about my past, even though I may never remember it. If I knew what happened in the past, I wouldn't be so shocked if I remember it."

"That makes sense, Jimmy. What I remember about you, or heard about you, wasn't anything terrible. I teach Junior High. When you were in school, it was my first year here. You know Junior High and High School are in different sections all the building. We are in the elementary school section. So I don't get to see the High School students. I probably never knew you. But I was at the hearing after the incident where the community was in an uproar over what caused your problem. There were many disturbing rumors and complaints in the community. That's where the principal, the head basketball coach, and the superintendent got fired. After the hearing, people in the community feel sorry for you and accept you back."

"That answers one question. I wasn't a mean kid."

"No, you weren't mean that I know of. If you were, Jimmy, people wouldn't feel sorry for you."

"I didn't understand. I had the idea that everyone picked on me, even some of the adults. Everybody knew about me. That's what my thoughts are telling me. Weren't they?"

I wondered if I should tell my counselor about my dreams. If I did, people would send me back to Uncle Walter. But I want a shot at being normal and playing basketball. If the depression gets so strong that I might explode in front of people, I won't let that happen! I have it under control. I do, I know I do! I want to be open and share my feelings. But how do I do that? I still have to figure that out.

"So, Jimmy, how are you feeling now that your back?"

"I feel okay." That was a lie, but I can't tell him I'm scared. I want to be a real man, a strong man, a man who can handle life.

"What do you mean by 'okay?'"

"Well, except for not remembering people or events in my last year in school, I'm okay."

"You don't have problems with depression or dreams as your Uncle Walter wrote in your medical record?"

Busted! He knows my past. Should I play dumb? No, I ought to tell him something. There is no memory, only dreams. I can change the subject. Yes, that's what I'll do. Wait, no, I can't do that.

John could see Jimmy was struggling over the question. He knew this was something the boy had to tell in my own time, so John changed the subject.

"With your new height, I bet you're a better basketball player?"

"I think so. Uncle Walter was a good player in his days, and he taught me how to shoot, especially from the outside. Uncle Walter taught me other shots on the court in his back yard. We played one-on-

one a lot. I got into some pickup games with kids that played at the local school as well as some black kids from a big city school. Their competition taught me a lot."

"Really? That had to be a great game, and it's good to hear. I help Jerry Chumbly coach basketball. If I didn't, I would ask you to go with me to the court behind the school and play me one on one. I was pretty good in high school. But if I'm caught with players before the season starts it could cause trouble. Of course, your height will be a big help to you and the team."

After thinking about what Jimmy had said, John continued. "Did you say you could shoot outside like a guard?"

"When my uncle started training me, I was small, like a guard. I was never taught to post up. If I have to play that position, I can play it. But I think when you see me play, you will see I do better as a guard or a small forward in shooting, ball-handling, and everything else. I'm not a point guard. I can help on offensive boards."

"I understand," John replied, then paused to gather his thoughts before he asked, "Do you have any thoughts or dreams about the last season you had here? A lot of the kids close to you think that was the reason for what happened to you. Even some of the teachers said that you started leaving this world spontaneously."

"I don't remember any of that, but I guess it must be true." then without another thought, I continued, "I have dreams of sitting on the bench and everyone laughing at me."

Now that I've told him, I'm probably in trouble. I know I should man-up and tell him, even if Uncle Walter may want me back in Tennessee. No, I'm safe. Father controls Uncle Walter, and Father wants me here.

"That's normal. It may be the start of you remembering things. Don't be ashamed. You weren't the only one that had that happen. Some of the kids quit."

"I remember I wanted to quit. But my father wouldn't let me. He said, 'Bass's aren't quitters!'"

Suddenly I blurted out, "That's a new memory! It just popped right out."

"That might be the way other memories will come. Can you remember what happened to you during this bad time? Did you have to spend a lot of time sitting on the bench?"

"I can barely remember that horrible time. I remember leaving school as fast as I could to be alone so I could scream and yell."

It was so awful that I didn't want to talk about it. "That's all I want to say," I said. "My memories are so foggy when I think about it, all I can feel is the pain, and I don't want to go there if I can help it."

"I understand, Jimmy. The secret is between you and me.

John gave me his business card. "This has my telephone number and the number at the church. Don't be afraid to call and talk any time. If I'm not home, talk to my wife. She is a counselor, too. Now I need to ask you one more question. Do you believe in God?"

I felt this was a weird question, so I answered, "Sure, like most of the people around me."

"Who are these people?"

"You've got me there. There are probably people I don't remember. My parents and sister believe but not my Uncle Walter, though. If he did, he never mentioned it to me. Now that I think about it, Uncle Walter never mentioned God in his counseling."

"Okay. What about you? What do you believe about God?"

"He is the Supreme Being of the world, and we are supposed to worship Him. In Tennessee, I tried to go to church every Sunday. Sometimes I missed and felt bad about it."

"Why?"

"Because if you don't go to church, God will be mad at you."

A lot of churches teach Hellfire and damnation. That's something John despised. He knew that now was not the time to discuss this, so he said, "Do you pray to God, especially when you are depressed? You don't have to admit it to me, but God loves you, and he wants you to pray to Him when you're in trouble."

"Okay, I will."

"You are invited to attend our church tomorrow morning."

"My parents are strict Lutheran. I'm sure the whole family will go to the Lutheran church tomorrow."

"I don't think so, Jimmy. Your sister comes here to church."

I was shocked. There was no way my parents didn't go to the Lutheran Church, a few miles out of town. If what John said is true, I'd prefer to attend John's church then that hard-nosed Lutheran Church.

John said that was the end of our counseling session for today and ended it with prayer. When I left, he reminded me to pray when I was hurting. That's something I'll remember. I will!

Chapter Five

The Ender's home was a large white house with five bedrooms, four upstairs, and one downstairs. It had a regular kitchen, spacious dining room, and a comfortable living room, as well as a huge front porch. A three-car garage sat at the side of the house with a driveway that went straight from the street to the garage and a cement parking lot where you could park three or four cars. An abundance of trees filled the front yard.

~~~~~~~~~~

Saturday, around ten-thirty, Carolyn went shopping in Tiffin. Arnold was working in his shop. Jimmy was counseling with Pastor John Wood, and her daughter was at home doing housework, as she did every Saturday, to earn her allowance. Carolyn planned to stop at the Ender's home before shopping.

She knew Hazel Ender didn't work in their hardware store in Tiffin on Saturdays. Her husband had died recently, so Hazel ran the store with her sons, Pat and Tim, during the week. Tim ran the store on Saturdays, closing it at noon.

Today's visit was for Jimmy, and if Arnold knew she was visiting the Enders, he would have a fit. He didn't like them, but she didn't know why. Arnold's dislike for the Enders was even worse after Jimmy's incident, and people in the community shunned them, believing the way their family treated Jimmy caused his problem.

Arnold was hard on Jimmy, possibly too hard and Carolyn played the subservient wife, turning a blind eye like she had learned to do from the church's teaching that the husband is the head of the household, and that's all there is to it.

Jimmy had returned, with a new future, and Carolyn wasn't turning a blind eye anymore. Arnold didn't care if his son had friends, only that Jimmy was quiet as a church mouse and didn't make waves. But he was to be the star on the basketball team and get good grades in school.

Carolyn realized Jimmy needed friends who knew the circumstances of his life and his lost memory, so she knocked on the Ender's front door. After a few minutes, the door opened, and Hazel Ender stood in the doorway looking down at Carolyn's five-foot-four frame. Hazel was five-foot-ten, a tall, lanky woman in her fifties. Carolyn was just over forty.

Hazel greeted Carolyn, saying, "Hello, Mrs. Bass, what can I do for you?"

Carolyn wasn't close friends with Hazel. They casually greeted each other and usually talked only at school functions. She had never gone to Hazel's house, but she knew Jimmy had come to this house and knew Hazel and her sons well. She put on her best smile and said, "I would like to talk to you about my son, Jimmy."

Hazel's eyes lit up. "Sure, come into the living room."

When they were seated, Carolyn noticed how clean and well-arranged the room was. A long plaid couch with lamps and shades on wood end tables at each end sat across from two comfortable chairs. The coffee table held 'Post' and 'Look' magazines as well as the local paper. Carolyn sat on one of the chairs, and Hazel sat across from her on the couch.

"I have always liked your son. He was a polite and considerate little guy."

"Wait until you see him. He isn't that 'little guy' anymore."

"Well, that little guy you knew is six-foot-three, now, and still growing."

"Good for him! It's amazing how quickly some kids grow in a short time. It's been a little over a year since he had that problem at the skating rink."

Hazel stopped suddenly with an embarrassed look on her face. "Oh, I'm sorry. Maybe I shouldn't have said anything about that."

"That's fine," Carolyn responded. "That's why I'm here. Jimmy has recuperated but has a memory loss of the last year he was here. Everything seems to be gone. He has no memory of people, mostly classmates and other students in the class before him. Pat, your son, and his classmates were Jimmy's former classmates, but he has no memory of them. Strangely, he remembers your younger son, Tim, and Joey Bell, as well as some of their classmates. They will be his classmates this year. Perhaps this will be helpful.

"Really? Pat said that Jimmy didn't remember him when he met him at the gas station. Is his memory loss going to be forever?" Hellen asked.

"No one knows. Jimmy's doctor, Arnold's brother, doesn't know if his memory will ever come back. It may never return at least not all at once. I'm asking you to tell your sons about Jimmy's memory. Right now, he needs friends that will accept him and know he might never remember them from the past."

"I understand, Carolyn. I'll help you any way I can. Did you say he is going back to school here? Oh, wait; I remember Pat told me he is eligible to play sports."

"That is correct, and with his added height, he should do well."

"I would think so!"

"My brother-in-law, Jimmy's doctor, taught him how to shoot, too. I must say he has quite an outside shot. I hope he does well, after everything that has happened to him. He needs another chance, and he loves basketball."

"I hope he succeeds, Carolyn. Coach Summerall was not a good coach and very unfair to the kids. Coach Chumbly is completely different."

After a quick pause, Hazel added, "He will be fair to Jimmy."

"I certainly pray he will," Carolyn smiled.

~~~~~~~~~~

After seeing John, I drove around for a while, not wanting to face Father. He might be mad since I didn't come home right after my session, but I didn't care. Maybe I would run into someone I knew. That didn't happen, so a little after Noon, I went home.

I drove into the driveway and parked in front of Dad's shop. The door was open, and he was working on a car. I assumed he would want me to help, so I walked toward him.

When he saw me coming, he stood up. I expected him to ask where I had been, but he said nothing, so I asked him a question that was bothering me. "Do you still go to Grace Lutheran Church?"

"No, we don't go to church there," he answered, shaking his head. After a short pause, he continued, "Following your incident, the members shunned our family. No one would talk to us, and people began gossiping behind our backs. So we just slipped away, and don't attend anymore."

"Where do you go to church? Do you go to Tiffin?"

Bowing his head, Father thought for a minute before he continued, "Your Mother and I go to St John's in Fremont once in a while, but I'm ashamed to say, most of the time we don't go to church anywhere."

He hung his head in shame, something I had never seen him do before. Was it an act, or was it real? Did he believe in God? He had to! He raised Sandy and me in the church.

Then he perked up and asked, "Do you remember Grace Lutheran?"

"I don't know why, but I do," I replied, then I paused for a bit before asking the next question.

"Is it true that Sandy goes to St. Matthew's?"

"Yes, it is. It was your sister's choice. Where you want to go to tomorrow is your choice, but I think you should stay away from Grace Lutheran."

"That's okay. My choice for where I attend church is St. Matthew."

"I figured that would be your choice since John is your counselor. I guess you like him?"

"I do."

"Are you hungry? If you are, why don't you take Sandy to Keller's for lunch? Your mother is shopping in Tiffin and probably won't be home until late afternoon."

"Okay," I said and headed toward the house to talk to Sandy.

"Sandy has money for you two to eat out," Father yelled.

Sure enough, Sandy had money and was dressed in a skirt and blouse to go out.

Keller's restaurant has two sections. We sat in the first section because the second section opened only for private parties or when an excessive amount of patrons were in the restaurant. There is a big table in the middle for when thee are large parties.

As we entered the restaurant, I could see that the layout is the same as I remembered. Some booths could accommodate four people, or five if you squeeze in.

The front windows provide a view of the sidewalk and street and booths are on each side, against the East and West walls.

The middle section of the restaurant has small tables for four people. Each table had an ashtray, and you could smell cigarette smoke as soon as you entered.

A bar is in the back with stools in front of it. Coffee and soda machines are behind the bar along with coolers for ice cream. Towards the end, on the west side, there is a large serving window where the waitresses deliver and receive orders. Behind this window is the kitchen.

The restaurant was a little over half full. We saw an empty booth on the west side and walked toward it. People began to stare at us. They must know who I am, even with my new height. I am sure they were thinking, "How do you talk to a person who had a mental health condition?"

Maybe they thought I didn't belong here. I imagined all sorts of things people were saying behind my back. Most of these people believed I had been in a mental hospital. I had decided to keep the truth a secret but wasn't sure why. Maybe it was Father's pride. I'm glad I wasn't in a mental institution. Uncle Walter and Aunt Helen gave me wise counseling. Would the people believe me if I told them?

"The less said, the better," was what Father always said. This time, I agreed with him.

We ordered our food, then Sandy and I talked about the coming school year. When the food came, and we started to eat, and three guys came towards our booth. One was the guy I had met at Clyde's. I remember he said his name was Pat Ender. Behind him was his brother, Tim, whom I recognized, and Joey Bell was with them.

I stood up and greeted Pat, saying, "I still don't remember you, but I know who you are." Then I shook his hand and looked at Tim.

"Somehow, I remember you. You're Tim Ender." I shook his hand.

"Are you sure your Jimmy Bass?" Joey Bell thundered, "What happened to little Jimmy, who was my size."

Most of the people in the restaurant turned and looked at me. Maybe they didn't know who I was when we walked in. I grinned at Joey. "I grew!"

Tim, who was standing beside me, and a little shorter than me, said jokingly, "It's better than being shrimp like you, Joey."

Everybody laughed, then Joey asked if he could sit beside Sandy. She agreed. Tim sat beside me, and Pat got a chair from one of the empty tables and sat at the end of the booth. They said they had ordered and were waiting for there food.

"Will you be able to play basketball with us this year? With your height and the way you handle the ball, you should be a big help to us," Tim grinned at me.

"I hope so! My Uncle Walter taught me how to shoot an outside shot."

"An outside shot is what we need!" Joey exclaimed. "I can hit a little."

"You sure can!" Pat declared. "I think we have a better team this year. Maybe the same as last year, when we won nine games."

"That had to be something. Cutler Ridge won nine games?" I blurted.

"We don't have Summerall any more. Chumbly teaches defense. It's all man to man for him. You guys will win some games, this year, just using defense." Pat stated.

I thought that was great. Man-to-man was a defense I liked.

"I don't think there is a lot of talent on the team this year," Pat continued, "But maybe I shouldn't say that. We haven't seen Jimmy play.

Then he looked directly at me and said, "Here are your teammates, Jimmy. First is my brother, Tim, Then there is Weiden, an inside man, mostly low post. He makes good rebounds and can score there, even shoot some at high-post. The other big man is a kid who came from Chicago last year. His mother died, and now he's living with his grandparents. Do you remember the Oaks? They own a farm out by your Uncle Fred's place."

I nodded my head in acknowledgment.

Pat went on, "His name is Brad Weiden, and he's around six feet tall, but he jumps like a guy six-foot-three or four. Give him a running start, and he can stuff it. He never played organized ball before, but he played pick-up games on the street. He learned quickly last year and will be hard to beat inside."

I nodded my head again before Pat continued.

"Then there is Glen Carl, a Junior who is a little shorter than you. He's a good defender and can score inside. He'll be a back-up to Tim and Brad."

"There must be a couple more," I grinned.

"Well, you are correct," Pat declared. "We have two other guards to go along with Joey. They are Sam Sessions and Jack Rendles. Both of them are Juniors. They are quick, great defense, and have high-grade ball handling averages. But they are not good shots, except in a fast break. That's about what we have for our team. The rest are Freshmen and

Sophomores who play Junior Varsity.

"Now we have you, Jimmy, and your height!" Joey yelled.

After a quick pause, he continued, "This afternoon, at three, we have a pick-up game in the court behind the school. Will you be there, Jimmy?"

I agreed that I would. It was my chance to see how good I was with these players. For the rest of the conversation, we tried to figure out who I remembered. I remembered some of the names and some I didn't. At least I had three friends, and they would let other kids know about my memory.

There were ten players, and they had picked teams before I got there. Two guys that graduated with Pat were the extra players. One was my former classmate, Bill Kumer and the other was Glen Hass.

Bill was a five-foot-ten guy with a good build and a face that seemed always to have a smile. As we played, I got chances to talk to him and discovered he was the most popular kid in class.

Glen was a tall, thin guy, around six-foot-two, and had blond hair. When we weren't playing, he talked about our past, like Bill did. They both acted like we were good friends and had seen each other a lot. However, I couldn't remember them, the events, or the situations they talked about. I learned later; these two guys were part of the reason they won nine games last year.

Joey was the final player on our team.

Our opponents had Tim Ender and Sam Sessions, a Junior at around five-foot-ten. As the game progressed, I saw that he was quick and fast but only an average shot. Jack Rendles was a junior and a little smaller. He was fast and quick but didn't have the driving skills that Sessions did. I could see Sessions probably would average in the double figures, even though he didn't have the best shot. But when driving to the basket, his quickness gave him a chance other players couldn't handle, and he would score.

Brad Weiden was a jumping-jack and could score inside.

As the game began, my team was leading. It was a very close game. Our quickness and speed matched our strength inside. Since I was a guard with Joey, we could get back and stop some of the fast breaks. I had some excellent blocks that surprised a lot of the players. My team slowly got behind; nobody could hit their shots. At first, I didn't shoot much, but with our team down, I figured, "Why not?"

From then on, everybody was surprised at what I could do. I was hot as I drained the outside shots. I didn't want to be a gunner, but my teammates encouraged me to shoot.

Since both teams were playing man-to-man, my teammates set picks for me.

Sessions and Rendles tried to stop me when a pick didn't work to get me open; I'd start to drive as they back-peddled. Then I'd shoot, releasing the ball before they could recover. Sometimes I faked a shot. When they moved to block my shoot, which they didn't come close to doing, I drove around them for a closer backboard shot. But most of the time, on this move, some other player would try to stop me, leaving a teammate open for a good shot.

Sometimes they stopped me; then I'd merely pass to a teammate. I also got some offensive rebounds. There wasn't anybody who could block my shots. I went up so quickly that nobody had time to stop me. Uncle Walters had made me understand that quickness is the answer. That's the way I practiced.

What my uncle in Tennessee didn't teach me, I learned by observing my teammates. I wasn't the quickest player, but certain moves would always work. When I'm alone, I shot while going straight up, a picture form shot, my right hand pointed towards the basket when I released the ball. According to Uncle Walter, this is the way to shoot.

When the game was over, everybody congratulated me on the way I could shoot. It felt good to have this much praise, something I never felt before. It was gratifying, especially the approval from players I knew I had played with before. It felt like a coming-out party, even though I couldn't remember which players I played with previously.

Pat Ender's mother was there to watch the game. She came to me and introduced herself. She hugged me and said she was glad I was back.

Everybody gradually left, except Hazel and her two sons. I remembered her as a charming woman. Hazel asked me how I got along with my father, and I told her he seemed fine to me. She didn't seem to buy it entirely but didn't press me for more information.

Some of my early memories and feelings made me believe my father was strict, even downright hard on me. He apologized when I was at Uncle Walter's and promised he would treat me better. As for him being the cause of my—What should I call it?—"My problem," I wasn't sure.

Our relationship was okay now. Why wasn't it like that before? I don't know? I must have known previously.

I always ask him for permission when I want to go somewhere or do something. Usually, he says, yes, and I'm smart enough not to ask him for something stupid.

I believe I used to help him with his cars in his shop. I know how to do a lot of things with cars and can do some things by myself. But my father didn't trust me. I don't trust him either, and sometimes I think he had something to do with my problem.

~~~~~~~~~

In a room that overlooked the outside basketball court on the second floor of the school, two men watched the scrimmage. Though the room was hot and the windows were not open, they were glued to the game and were amazed at what they saw. Not a word was said until the scrimmage was over. John Wood and Coach Jerry Chumbly knew they would have the best playing team in the League.

Jerry Chumbly was excited and wanted basketball to start tomorrow. "That Jimmy Bass is one fine player. I never dreamed I would find a player who was that good in a country school. Everyone says he wasn't much of a player before he left quickly, over a year ago. Clyde told me that boy was a lot shorter, close to 5-foot-10, and never got to play in a game. He sat on the bench the whole time, even as a JV player."

"Clyde felt that Summerall hated him," John Woods disclosed. "He was a good kid. Sometimes helped Clyde in the gas station. He knows his way around cars, but that's all Clyde could say about Jimmy. I am going to talk to Pat Enders. He could give me more information on the kid."

Chumbly agreed and stated, "The way he's playing now, he plays more like a guard. Even though he's a changed person, who has learned how to be a better player with his shots, his quickness, drilling skills, and passing skills tell me he must have had that talent before.

~~~~~~~~~~

Arnold watched the game in the distance. He could see that Jimmy was the best player. No doubt about it, his son was a star. There would be no shame for the Bass family now.

Every time Jimmy made a basket, his father cheered quietly. His son's defense was great. Watching Jimmy rebounding and blocking shots, Arnold thought Jimmy could jump as high a Weiden. It was this going to be a great year!

Arnold didn't like Hazel Ender greeting and hugging his son. She had caused a lot of his trouble by saying evil things about the way he handled Jimmy. She even told people that he beat Jimmy. Things like that were none of her business! Jimmy was his son, and he had a right to discipline him any way he felt. He had that right as the father. Arnold knew he had never beat Jimmy as severely as someone had when he saw his son at the hospital and had a nervous breakdown in the skating rink. It looked as if someone had beat him with a whip. Why had Jimmy had let somebody do that terrible thing to him. Well, he is no weakling now!

Then came the nagging thought that his son had grown to be a big, healthy adult. Maybe Jimmy could beat him if he tried to be too forceful.

"No, Jimmy will listen to me without force," Arnold reasoned. "He respects me as his father. If I have to, I'll remind him that I expect that respect. Since he goes to St. Matthew's and gets closer to God, I will tell him as many times as I have to about honoring the father. I can use that fear that he has to have for my benefit. As long as he fears me, I have no problem."

Chapter Six

Tim, Pat, Sam Session, and Joey sat at the kitchen table, talking about the scrimmage, and drinking Cokes.

"Bass is perfect. He can do everything!" Pat gushed.

"Did you see him shoot from outside?" Joey commented. "I guess his uncle taught him correctly. All I saw was net."

"And he can score inside," added Tim as he looked at his brother sitting across the table from him.

"What are you thinking, Brother?"

"I was thinking about how Jimmy played before...You know, before he had his problem, 'the incident.'"

"He was horrible; plain and simple!" Sam declared.

"No, he wasn't Sam. That was how Summerall projected him. Jimmy could handle the ball well, both dribbling and passing. He could handle himself inside, too. Jimmy was just too small to do anything about it. He had all the right ingredients. Now he can shoot, plus he has height. And we have a new and improved Jimmy Bass."

"How does that happen? Once he was a nerd, now he's a..." Sam paused as he shook his head. "He's someone we don't know. He could have turned into anything weird or evil."

"Why are you talking about Jimmy like that?" Joey asked.

"You sound like you were good friends with him. Did you know him before he went crazy? If you did, maybe you should have stopped him. Now he's back, but he's a person with no memory, and you are going to accept him as an old buddy?"

"Yes!" Tim said with authority. "Some of us knew what he was going through and didn't do anything about it. If anybody deserves a second chance, he does. I, for one, am going to be his close friend."

"Okay, Tim, since you knew of his trouble before, why didn't you do anything about it?"

"Because I was scared, we were all scared, of Jake Bickhard and his gang. They made Jimmy's life miserable as well as intimidating most of us, and I stood around and did nothing about it." Pat exploded.

Then pointing his finger at Sam, he stated bitterly, "If I were you, I wouldn't say a word about Jimmy until I learned about all the circumstances of his situation. If you or anybody else tries to hurt him, you will go through me."

Pat stood up, towering over Sam, waiting for him to make another comment. He was angry enough to tear into Sam, and Sam knew it so he lowered his head, hoping all this anger would go away.

Hazel came running into the room, grabbed Pat, and slowly lead him out of there.

As soon as they left, Sam looked at Tim and demanded, "What did I say?"

"Sam, you don't understand the situation with Jimmy. We all hurt when we heard what happened to him. Pat was there and saw it all. As Pat said, 'We all turned a blind eye to the people who were hurting him.' Now Jimmy's back, and it's time for him to have a good life, and you act like you're jealous!" Tim answered with authority.

"What do you mean, jealous?" Sam snapped back.

"We all know the way you talk about people. You want to be the star this year, and Jimmy threatens your chance. I can see that with him on our team and all of us working with him, with no jealousy, we can have an awesome team."

"How do we know he won't be cocky and think he's the greatest since he can shoot like that?" Tim scoffed.

"Like you?" Sam snapped back. "That sounds like the way I thought you'd act, cocky as all get out, just like you were last year. And you know what? We don't need you!"

"You don't know Jimmy. He's nothing like you!" Joey declared.

"He could have changed."

"No! Never! Not like you. We talked to him at Keller's for close to an hour, and he is the same person, but with more confidence, good confidence, not cockiness!"

Sam had heard enough. He finished his Coke and abruptly left without saying another word.

As soon as he was gone, Joey said, "Sam's going to be a problem."

"I believe so. But Sam won't hurt Jimmy. No way, Joey. No way!"

~~~~~~~~~~

When I arrived home, I parked in front of the shop where my father was working. I felt an urge to help him, so I asked if I could do something.

"I could use help to put a front end on this forty-seven Ford truck I'm rebuilding," he answered.

I went into the house to change into work clothes.

Dad needed assistance in putting inner-fenders on the truck. First, we had to attach the front radiator support, then the fenders and the hood. Father had everything painted except the outside of the fenders and the top of the hood.

There was over-spray on the edge of the outer part of the panel. Father always says never to paint the outside until everything gets bolted together. It's to easy to scratch.

While we worked together, the main topic was the scrimmage I had played.

"Who was there? Who was on your team? Who impressed you? How did you play?" Father asked.

The way I played seemed to be the most important question to him. I could feel the pride emanating from him, and this made me happy. Then he asked if I talked to Hazel. I wondered why he asked all these questions because he was there and saw everything. Weird, I thought.

"Yes, I did?"

"What did she talk about?"

"She just welcomed me home." I left out the part where she asked about him.

"You should stay away from her. She could be trouble for you!"

I was shocked but didn't comment. That was all I said, and Father went on to the next subject.

Then out of the blue, he asked, "Jimmy, do you think you could take one of these old vehicles and restore it from scratch?"

Could I remember all of the things I learned in his garage? We had just bolted the hood to the hinges, and now he was adjusting it.

"I think so, Father. I believe I helped you with a lot of those old cars. The knowledge came from you. I could restore a vehicle, but I wonder if my memory loss will give me trouble. I don't know if all the concepts are back."

"I understand about your memory loss. But you have helped me many times. Maybe, someday, you will restore a vehicle of your own. What do you want to do with your life after you graduate?"

"I have no inkling of what I want to do. All I want is to get through school and basketball season."

"That makes sense, Jimmy. That makes sense."

~~~~~~~~~

I was back in the gym, and our team was getting buried. Coach Summerall was emptying the bench. I watched the time as another player went in. Everyone was in the game except me, and only a minute and a half remained. I watched the seconds tick away, hoping my name would get called, but knowing it wouldn't. I always had a little hope. As the seconds ticked away, my heartbeat went with them. The pain increased with each tick. I wanted to scream but knew I shouldn't do that in public. The pain pounded more and more until I was about to lose control. I realized a scene would not please anyone, especially my father. He would be ashamed.

I wished the game would end so I could disappear into a fantasy world where there is no pain. I assumed the pain would never cease, and the suffering was eternal.

"No!" I cried as I awoke in a daze and went to my bedroom closet. Putting on sweatpants, tee-shirt, socks, and sneakers, I quickly sneaked out of the house so I could run.

I had no idea what time it was; only that darkness still controlled the sky. As I ran, the pain started to ease. There was no desire to scream as I had thought, but tears flowed down my cheeks and dissipated as I ran.

~~~~~~~~~~

Pat Ender had his usual nightmare about Jimmy Bass and the incident. He was there that night and saw Jimmy staring into space like he was in another world. No matter what anyone said to him, there was no answer.

Pat had tried unsuccessfully that night to bring Jimmy out of his despair. But Jimmy was locked in fantasy, and he couldn't leave.

Blood began forming on Jimmy's back. Pat didn't touch him but wanted to see how bad it was. The more he stood there looking at Jimmy; the more blood oozed out. The blood from Jimmy's back had to be from beatings that Jake and his buddies had given him.

For a second, Pat froze, then he began screaming, "We need an ambulance! Jimmy's bleeding!"

Soon the ambulance arrived and took Jimmy to the hospital. That was the last time Pat saw him until this week when he saw him at Clyde's.

After the incident, Pat had many nightmares about witnessing Jimmy staring into space with blood flowing everywhere. People teased him to no end, and the guilt stayed with him. He had teased Jimmy, not to put him down or hurt him. He thought it was friendly teasing like friends do. Nothing was meant to hurt Jimmy, not at all.

But Jimmy didn't have a strong spirit and was always trying to make friends. He would never hurt anybody, or call them names but was merely trying to please everyone. When something embarrassing happened, either in actions or words, people teased him about what he had done. Sometimes he reacted poorly and more or less crawled into a hole.

Jimmy acted like he was—what should he say? Arrogant, no, in control. Pat ignored the responses Jimmy made. Why should Pat Ender concern himself with a nerd like Jimmy? He was a friend, but friends don't let things happen the way Jake Bickhart and his gang tormented him to no end.

Basketball practice was the place Jake seemed to like putting him down the worst, and Coach Summerall did nothing. If he blamed anybody, Summerall blamed Jimmy. It was disgusting that nobody did anything about it. Pat knew that it was the least he should do.

~~~~~~~~~~

Counseling had helped Pat overcome the guilt he felt. But now that Jimmy was back, the blame returned along with it his nightmares. He got up from bed, dressed only in his underwear and put on a pair of shorts and a Tee shirt. Even this early in the morning, he guessed it to be around six o'clock. The August temperature was warm.

Soon he had a cup of instant coffee and was sitting at the kitchen table. Everyone else in the house, Tim, his brother, Kathy, his sister, and his mother was asleep. His father had died suddenly from a heart attack, six months ago. With father gone, He and his mother ran his father's hardware store.

Pat planned to take morning classes two days a week at Tiffin University, a business school. Then he would spend the rest of his time at the store.

When his father died, it made a lot of things more complicated, especially his plans for going to Ohio State, but working and helping run the hardware store wasn't that bad.

Of course, He wished his father hadn't died, he missed him very much, but why did his father's death hurt him less than Jimmy's return?

Pat knew that Jimmy went through hell and probably still was, but what about himself? The nightmares were back, and so were the guilt and the pain. How could he fight it? Should he go back to the shrink? "No!" he screamed. "I'm a man, and I am strong. I can handle it!"

If only Jimmy could remember him and the past, then the things he had done to him could be released. He could apologize to Jimmy, but for now, an apology would be worthless, and he still had with those miserable nightmares.

Pat wanted to be Jimmy's friend again. He tried to tell Tim and Joey to keep an eye on Jimmy at school. They could make sure no one gave him a hard time. They had to!

Pat certainly didn't want to see Jimmy go off the deep end again. Never! Not on his watch! Then he thought, "What am I thinking? No one in school is big enough to mess with Jimmy. He won't get teased now. Most of the students would be terrified to harass him, even those who had taunted him, before. Jimmy would be okay in school.

Sam seemed to have some animosity, but Pat was sure it was all about Jimmy becoming a star. He couldn't remember much about him now. Sam had been a freshman when Jimmy left. No, Sam won't go after Jimmy, but he may talk behind his back. That wouldn't be good.

Jimmy needed to watch out for his father. If Arnold went back to his old ways, the way he had treated Jimmy, he could move in with our family, and his father couldn't do a thing about it. Jimmy was legally an adult, and Arnold couldn't stop him.

Pat wanted to hate Arnold, but he and his family were Christians who believed in grace and forgiveness. He couldn't hate, because the Bible tells God's followers to pray for their enemies, and Arnold was one of them.

~~~~~~~~~

When I came home from running, it was about seven o'clock. My parents were up and dressed. They told me they were leaving to spend a day at Lake Erie and maybe go to the islands. Saying they would be back later tonight, they asked me to take Sandy to church and left money on the kitchen table for me to take my sister out to eat in Tiffin after church. I agreed, and out the door, they went.

St. Matthew's was different from Grace Lutheran. John's wife, Kathy, taught Sunday School. She was attractive, tall, slender, and pregnant. Sandy told me John's wife was carrying their first child.

All high school students were in her class, but the only one I knew, other than Sandy, was Joey. I should have known the others, but I had no memory of them. Everybody was friendly to me, even the girls.

The class was studying a series about King David. Mrs. Wood did most of the talking. I knew most of what she talked about, so, in my opinion, the class was boring. However, John's sermon wasn't. He preached about God's love and the sacrifice Christ made for us. It was very touching and was the first time I realized that God loved me. There was an altar call asking for people to go to the front of the church and give their life to Jesus.

Strong desires pushed me forward, but I couldn't understand why. I've always believed in God and tried to follow the way He wants us to live. So why did I have to give my life to God? I felt He already had it. I believe that when I do something wrong, God punishes me.

What about the pain? That thought disturbed me. Either it was part of life, or God was punishing me. Maybe it could be a trial, used by Satan to draw me away from God. But I didn't know which. I guess I should be strong enough to fight it off. That's what God probably wants me to do. John said God loves me. I need to fight for the great love God has for me.

~~~~~~~~~

It was a hot Memorial Day. Pat Ender, his brother Tim, Joey Bell, and Jack Reynolds were relaxing with a cold Coke in the shade on the front porch. Pat sat on one of the wooden outdoor chairs, and Tim sat on another one. Joey was on the porch swing with Rendles beside him.

They ate at noon, and then at one o'clock, they played a game of three-on-three at the school with Jimmy Bass and Brad Weiden. They scrimmaged for an hour and a half. Then out of the blue, Pat announced, "You guys need to do me a favor and watch over Jimmy very carefully.

"What are you talking about Pat?" Jack asked

"Pat was there and saw the incident that drove Jimmy into the hospital. He used to have nightmares because of it. With Jimmy back, the nightmares are back." Tim replied.

"Oh, I'm sorry, Pat. He seemed normal to me, today and Saturday."

"Ya, I know, but is he? He can't remember me or any of my classmates he has known since kindergarten. Now he doesn't remember any of us. When will his memory come back? What will happen?"

"I don't think it's something you have to worry about."

Pat stared at Jack thoughtfully. "You weren't there, Jack. You didn't see him. It was like he was in another world. I tried to talk to him and tell him it was okay and whatever happened, we could work it out. All he did was stare at me as if he couldn't see me, and I was right in front of him."

Everybody was silent, not knowing what to say. Joey knew the torment Pat went through over Jimmy's incident. To comfort Pat, Joey said, "I'll keep a close eye on him, Pat. I mean it. Jimmy was my friend, too. When I was in your class, we were close. When I flunked seventh grade, we drifted apart.

"I'll hold you to that, Joey."

"I will too, Brother," Tim answered.

"Guys, I'm not trying to be weird or anything, but I have a lot of guilt over the way I treated him before the incident," Pat stated.

"Forget the guilt. I can't remember you treating Jimmy that badly," Tim protested loudly.

"Maybe you're right. I keep trying to tell myself that. I pray a lot about it, too. But I keep seeing him staring into space making me think I helped cause him to act that way. Somehow I want to make up for it, but I can't be around him like you guys can. Please don't think I'm weird."

There was a pause, then to change the subject, Jack said, "Sam talked to me this morning. I asked him about the afternoon scrimmage, and he's angry about the way you guys treated him. Sam hates him, and you guys, too. What did you say to him?"

"Sam said some inappropriate things about Jimmy and Pat lost it. Then I told him he was jealous of Jimmy because he thinks he is the star," Tim explained.

"That's true. Jimmy wants to be the star, but he doesn't put any work into it, and Jimmy can play circles around him. Jimmy Bass can play circles around everybody!"

They all agreed. "Since this is the way you guys feel about him, I'll be his friend and watch out for him."

~~~~~~~~~~

I figured that the first day in school everybody would be staring at me. School started the day after Memorial Day, and I neither knew nor remembered very many students. They looked at me but seemed afraid to say anything. Some classmates acted like they wanted to talk with me, but were worried. Maybe they had heard some of the nasty stories told about me and thought I had been in a mental institution.

Perhaps it was my height. I was the tallest guy in school. Whatever the reason, I knew it was going to take time for my classmates to open up to me, but Joey and Tim were always friendly. Even Brad

Weiden would say Hi when I met him scrimmaging in basketball.

Friday, at noon, I was sitting in the lunchroom by myself, when a guy came over and sat down. I had seen him before and knew he wanted to sit by me. For some reason, he had always changed his mind, but this time, he didn't. He introduced himself as Jack Victory.

"I'm sorry I don't recognize you, I explained.

'That's okay, but I used to be a good friend of yours. I have an old Ford coupe, and you helped me put a 283 engine and a four-speed transmission in it," he said. "You showed me how to get the right rear end to match the engine and transmission. After we got it running, you showed me how to do bodywork on the car. It had been in a barn for years, so there wasn't much rust on it, just a little surface rust. You helped me get it ready for paint. It isn't quite ready yet. You told me you would paint it for me with acrylic lacquer just before you left the community."

It surprised me that Jack hadn't said anything about the incident.

"Another friend painted it dark blue for me when I finished with the bodywork. We had a whole lot of fun working on in my garage."

"Several of my friends are from Tiffin. I work there in a grocery store. You tuned up a lot of their cars and helped them with other repairs, like brakes. And you never charged them for the work," he smiled as he continued.

The more Jack talked, the more I realized I had lots of friends.

"Some men in the community left their family cars with you to be fixed up. You would help them do it. But you weren't always around because you liked sports. Sometimes your father wouldn't let you come to my place."

"Where do you live?" I asked.

"It isn't very far from where you live," Jack answered. "All you have to do is go east along the edge of your uncle's farm. My parents' barn is about a block away."

"I think I know where you live. I have to see that car!" I replied. "But I don't remember you or the Ford coup we worked on. I'm sorry, but I still hope you will be my friend."

Jack invited me to come down to his place after work and said he could show it to me. I agreed. We set a time that I could see him at his family's barn, where he had to go to work right after school.

My first week in school came to an end, and the second week promised to be even better. Jack was becoming a better friend. He had friends in school that knew me from before, but they were farmers and didn't play sports. Sometimes Joey, Tim, and Brad Weiden hung out with me in school. That weekend, my father asked me what friends I met at school. When I told him about Jack Victory, he told me to stay away from him because he was a problem.

Why would my father say that? Jack seems like a great guy to know. But I won't mention his name around my father again. That didn't make me want to give Jack up as a friend.

I bet if I asked my father to list the boys, I shouldn't hang with, or even girls, he wouldn't name one. But I wondered if this list would be for him or me. He didn't want kids who had anything to do with my past, or the "incident" to tell me about my history. He always said people don't take in the past; they get the future.

I knew he was hiding something, but I never asked Mother or Sandy. I knew they'd be too scared to tell me. Father rules the house with an iron fist. I know that for sure.

I'd do what he wants, but if he ever crosses the line, things will change. One thing for sure, he will never touch me. I don't care what the Bible says about honoring the father. I would obey him to a certain point, and that's all.

Chapter Seven

John Wood and I were at his house on the last Saturday of September, discussing how school was going. "I have friends with four guys: Joey, Tim, Brad Weiden, and Jack Rendles," I reported. "We are all tight, even at lunch when Tim and Joey are with their girlfriends."

After eating, students socialize and walk around outside, but most don't stray from school property. Businesses in town play by the school's rules and don't permit kids to patronize their shops during school hours. On cold days everybody goes to the auditorium. Either way, this is the time when kids meet up as boyfriends and girlfriends.

I told Pastor John about Jack Vickery and how he is a friend of mine because I was good with cars. I told him about how I fixed Jack's Ford coup and how I helped his friends with their cars. Some were from our school, and I knew and their parents.

"I figure I learned this talent from my father. It makes me feel good to know I had friends, but I knew most of them through my mechanical ability. When I told my father about my friends, he said to stay away from them because they're evil. I don't believe they're bad, but Father says they are. There is something in the past; he doesn't want me to remember, John. I believe he doesn't want me to have friends, just be a star on the basketball team. That's cruel!"

"Does he demand that you not see these people?"

"No, he just 'suggests' I don't see them, no anger or madness, just a friendly gesture."

"What do you do about it? Do you ignore these people?"

"No they're my friends, and he isn't going to deny me friendship. But he doesn't like what I'm doing by not listening to him. He told me the Bible says I should honor him as the father. It seems funny since he doesn't even go to church. But still, John, am I dishonoring him? I feel guilty when I think about it that way, and I dread he'll turn out to be whatever he was before."

"He is treating you well now, so don't worry about how to solve that problem until it comes."

John knew, from what he had heard about Jimmy's past, that Arnold had been cruel to his son. He wished Jimmy would give his life to Jesus and trust in the Lord. It would make it easier for Jimmy to handle his father.

"You're right, John, while things are good, I need to accept life and not worry."

"You can take every problem to Jesus, and I mean everything, Jimmy! He will guide you. Do you read the Bible, especially the New Testament? The four Gospels tell us the words that Jesus said. I'm not trying to make you feel guilty for not reading the Bible. I'm trying to encourage you."

"I've been reading the Bible, mostly the new testament, before I go to bed. As you said, I feel that reading the words of Jesus does encourage me."

"If your father gets mad at you and says, 'I am the father, you have to listen to me,' quote Ephesians six, verses two through four. The command says, 'You must respect your father and mother. This is the first command that has a promise with it.' And notice this is the promise, 'Then all will go well with you, and you will have a long life on the earth.' Then it ends with these words, 'Fathers, don't make your children angry but raise them with the kind of teaching and training you learn from the Lord.'"

Pastor John gave me the scripture, written on a piece of paper, and I tucked it into my billfold.

"Are you saying you have a lot of friends in school, friends you never knew you had when you first came here? You must have been an awesome person, and people liked you. That must make you feel great."

"It does. Now I know I wasn't mean to people, and that makes me feel better."

"What about girls, do they like you, and would you try to date one?

"My Uncle and my father warned me about the girls. Parents don't want their daughters going out with a conceivably crazy person."

"I don't like to think people in this town would have that attitude. Maybe some would, but not all of them."

"Well, it seems like they do, but maybe I'm just shy. Anyways, I'm not interested in girls right now. If I were dating a girl, it would have to be with her parents' approval since I'm of age. In a few months, I'll be nineteen. Of course, I have forgotten which girls knew me before and are afraid to talk to me for fear that I wouldn't remember them."

"That could be true, Jimmy."

"Well, I'm not interested in girls, just basketball and school work. There is one guy who acts like he downright hates me. He says cruel things about me, behind my back and when he looks at me in school, he gives me dirty, evil looks. One time when he was alone with me, he told me he was going to kick my butt. That is something he will not do!" I said seriously.

"Who is it?"

"Sam Session."

"I understand. I bet Sam doesn't play basketball with you guys."

"He did at first, but not now. Maybe it's his way of intimidating me. He probably knows that in the past, I was a weakling. Even though I am big and strong now, he looks at me as if I am the same as I was. He might believe that if I fear him, I'll leave him alone. A bullies biggest legacy is fear. That's how he's acting towards me. I know how bullies act, and he seems to be one."

"He might be trying to act like a bully to you, but there may be another reason. He may have thought this year he would be the star on the team and now he has seen you play. You threaten the status he wants, Jimmy. Don't get worked up over the star struggle. You have told me, over and over, that you want to be a teammate. But he doesn't look at it that way. He is afraid he isn't good enough to be a star."

"I understand. Sam won't intimidate me anymore, and I won't cause him any trouble. I'll try to ignore him at all circumstances. I don't want to fight. But if he attacks me, John, I believe I should defend myself."

"I agree, Jimmy, but you don't have to beat him. As big as you are, you can restrain him."

"I never told you this before, but I know martial arts, and I know how to restrain people without hurting them."

"That's good to know, Jimmy. He probably won't try to push you around, because it might jeopardize his chances on the team. I often see him practicing alone on the outdoor gym in the back of the school. When the season starts, we'll handle him.

"How do you feel about being alone, for instance, when you talk to people you don't remember them?" John asked.

"I'm okay," I paused for a second before I added, "It doesn't bother me. As I told you before, at school, I'm rarely alone. After school, I help Clyde at the gas station. I'm volunteering for something to do. He appreciates what I'm doing, and Randy Driller, the mechanic, and I are becoming good friends. He's another person who says he knew me from before and says I helped him work on his hot rod. He showed me the Ford coup he has in his Mother's garage. It's close to being finished, and he claims he's going to drive it next summer. So that's two people I helped build hot rods, and I'm friends with both of them.

"I spend a lot of time at the Ender's home, even though Father frowns on me being there. He has never told me why. It's like he has something against the Enders."

"So everything is great?"

"Yes."

Out of the blue, John asked, "Do you believe God loves you and is with you, Jimmy?"

His question didn't surprise me because when we were winding down our sessions, he usually brought God into our time. It made me feel it was time to open up to John. The depression and pain hadn't left me. I was trying to be positive like Uncle Walter taught me to do, but it didn't seem to be working.

"If God loves me, why is he punishing me?"

"Whoa, there! How is God punishing you?"

"I guess you could call it depression. I get these bad dreams. I think I told you about them before. They leave me depressed, sometimes for hours. But here is the weird part, I just figured out, when I was living with my Uncle, most of the time this depression wasn't there. Why is that?"

"Satan knows when to fight his battles. That may seem strange to you, but not to me. Let me ask you something. When you were living in Tennessee, if your Uncle wasn't around was your Aunt?

"Yes."

"Even if you were not with them, were you still under there influence."

"Whenever I felt depressed, I would go home and tell Uncle Walter and or Aunt Helen."

"And as soon as you got close to them, the depression left?"

"Yes, you're right."

"See, Satan knew he didn't have a chance with you when you were around your aunt and uncle because they were teaching you how to fight it." John paused for a minute, then continued. "Now let me ask you, did you have a nightmare this morning?"

"No. And as I remember, it never comes on the mornings I am scheduled to see you, but I always get this nagging feeling that I should skip seeing you. It tells me I shouldn't talk about what we are talking about."

"Again, that's Satan. I might be able to give you some ideas on how to fight your problem. One thing he does not want you to know or understand is that every time you feel this depression, you say, 'In the name of Jesus Christ, my savior, I rebuke you.' Satan can't stand those words. He flees from the name of Jesus."

"So you are saying the depression is not a punishment from God? It's Satan trying to draw me away from God?"

Yes, God loves you, and He doesn't want you to hurt."
"But doesn't He punish us?"

"Discipline is what the Bible calls it, not punishment. When He does, it's a way of guiding you. If you sin and realize it, then you ask for forgiveness, and He will forgive and forget."

What about Job?"

"Job wasn't being punished. His faith was strong. God was showing Satan that Job had a strong faith."

"Then, this depression isn't a punishment from God? All this pain that happens to me and me losing my memory isn't from God?"

John paused for a few seconds, then he smiled and said, "I don't know about your memory going away. It might have been the best for you. If it didn't happen something worst might of happened to you."

I thought over the last statement; it made sense to me. It did! But I had one more question.

"What is an altar call, and what does being born again mean? I have been struggling with this since our first counseling session, and the first time I attended your church. I know in John, three, it talks about being born again. But I don't understand what that means. Sandy says it's giving your life to Jesus and letting Him guild you through life. Being raised in the Lutheran church, I believe I was born with God, and if I follow God's laws and worship Him, I'm walking with God."

I paused, and John was about to speak, but I said. "I always thought God was in control of my life."

"You also think God is punishing you with depression. How can you follow all of His rules? Are you without sin?"

"No, but when I sin, I ask forgiveness."

"Okay, that's good. Do you believe the only way to have salvation is through behaving and good works?"

"Yeah, I suppose I do."

"Actually, salvation is a gift to you, and there is nothing you can do to earn. It's called a gift through grace, and our sins are taken away through the death of our savior." Pausing to let it sink in, John continued, "It sounds like you are reading the Bible. The four Gospels have all that I've told you. And walking with Jesus is a better life than trying to struggle alone by your self."

"As I said earlier, I read the Bible every night before I go to bed."

"I forgot about that. That's great. But think about being born again, Jimmy. Giving all your problems and all your pain to Jesus. Walk with him, and he will guide you through life."

"I'll think and pray about it, John. Maybe I'll make my decision tomorrow."

John thought he could do it right now, but something guided him gently away from that decision. The Holy Spirit spoke to him, telling him to be patient.

It was time for me to go, so we had prayer before I left.

Chapter Eight

On Saturday, September the twenty-ninth, Pat's mother, Hazel, called to ask if John would counsel her son, even though Pat went to another church, the Methodist church in Tiffin, but it didn't matter to John where Pat attended church.

Hazel asked what the cost would be and John said, "You can donate to the church if you want if not, that's fine. I'm don't counsel kids for money."

Hazel insisted on paying and said she would send a check. By two o'clock that afternoon, Pat was in Pastor John's office.

"Your mother tells me you're having nightmares over the incident that caused Jimmy's problem."

"You mean when he had to go to a mental hospital," Pat emphasized.

"I was told not to probe Jimmy about the incident," John stated.

"This meeting is different; you can't mention any of our conversations to Jimmy!" Pat begged.

John wanted to tell Pat that Jimmy was never in a mental

hospital, but felt it wasn't his responsibility.

"Who won't let Jimmy know about the incident, his father?"

"His doctor."

"Do you know who Jimmy's doctor was?"

"Yes. It was his Uncle. Now that's all I can say." John said, trying to be evasive.

"Okay, I won't ask any more questions about what Jimmy should know or not know. I could have told him because I was there."

"That is gracious of you, Pat, thinking of the family's request."

Pastor John paused for a few seconds before he continued. "Now, I take it the dreams are about the incident."

"Yeah. It was Tuesday, April the fourth, and the skating party at Tiffin Skating rink was ending. The party was put on by the Juniors for the Seniors. Very few Sophomores were there and then only if they were with a date. It was around ten in the evening, and most of the people from the Junior and Senior classes were gone.

Jimmy was skating around the rink by himself when somebody who worked at the rink went up to him and said it was closing time. Instead of leaving the rink, he started skating in small circles until he came to a stop in the middle of the rink. Then he sat down, crossed his legs, and just stared into space. I went up to him, knelt in front of him, and told him we had to go."

Pat stopped for a couple of seconds and stared at the floor, deciding what he should say next. When he looked up, he and stared at John and said, "I never saw anything like it, before. It was like he was staring into space. Anything I said to him got no response. I don't know how long I knelt in front of him and tried to talk to him, but it was to no avail. Then I saw the blood. It was soaking through his shirt. His whole back had blood seeping out of his shirt. I yelled for the manager

84

of the skating rink to get an ambulance because Jimmy was bleeding. I knew Jimmy had to be in pain, both physically and mentally. He didn't move until the ambulance came. First, they checked where the blood was coming from and gave him first aid. Even when they were giving him first aid, Jimmy had no reactions. He just kept staring into space. When they put him on the stretcher, there was no reaction. He didn't fight the EMT's. He was like a zombie."

"Were there any other students there?"

"A few. Jake Bickhart thought it was funny. His girlfriend, Elisabeth Hasselback, didn't. Jake kept calling Jimmy a slave. I knew what he meant by that. Jake called Jimmy his slave all the time and claimed he was king of the school, and most of the students were his slaves. But Jimmy was treated worse than anyone else and was continually tormenting Jimmy; so what did I do? I stood by and watched Jack and his buddies torture Jimmy. Jimmy's father was no better. I want to hate them, but as a Christian, I can't do that."

"Do you feel guilty that you didn't try to protect Jimmy?"

"Yes!"

"Were you afraid of Jake?"

"Yes, it was a fear I couldn't shake. I'm not afraid of Jake, now. But in school, I was."

"You were just a kid, and bullies have ways to control people. We call that intimidation. That's the reason Coach Summerall, who was also the principal, and the superintendent got fired. They were intimidated didn't control the kids; especially Jake and his gang. The blame doesn't go to you. It goes to the teachers. If you tried to do something, you would have been in trouble. I heard that after Jimmy's incident, you were one of the students who had the guts to go to the school board at the public hearing and tell them the truth. That could have backfired on you if the school board hadn't fired the teachers. So I say you are the hero."

"But it's too late for Jimmy."

"No, it isn't. Look at Jimmy now; he's a better kid than he was. He's more confident than he was. And I heard he is a fine basketball player, too."

"That's true!" After a pause, Pat admitted, "Okay, it seems like this shouldn't bother me, but it does. Because I thought I was Jimmy's friend. That night, when I tried to talk him out of whatever was making him freak out, it was weird. It was something I'll never forget. And the blood, he had to have been beaten badly. He had tape all over his back, but it wasn't holding the blood back. I knew who did it, and I wanted to go up to him and beat on him. But I was terrified. Now I feel guilty. In my nightmares, Jimmy is blaming me for the way I acted toward him. It feels like he is punishing me. Oh, I teased him, but it was all in good fun. I didn't mean to harm him. Maybe I wasn't all, but, for some reason, part of his problem."

"Pat, if you were, it wasn't much. You couldn't help Jimmy that night. He was out of it, and in a psychotic comma, and he didn't even know where his mind was. I believe he was in God's hands, and God was safely guiding him to where he is now. I think if Jimmy's memory comes back, he will look at you as a friend."

"Then, I could apologize, and I would feel better. But how can I now when Jimmy doesn't remember me."

"I understand, but he may never remember, and you have to ask for God's forgiveness then forgive yourself if you think the guilt is warranted."

After a long pause, John asked, "Are you a Christian, Pat?"
"Yes, very much so."

"But, your letting Satan get under your skin and cause you pain. Rebuke him in the name of our Lord Jesus Christ and get on with your life."

~~~~~~~~~

I woke up on Monday morning, and for the first time in a few days, I hadn't had a nightmare. But the depression was pounding at me like a hammer. As I rose from the bed, thinking of going for another long run, I looked at the small alarm clock on my nightstand next to my bed. It read 4:10. Dad would freak out if I left the house at this time in the morning. He had a long talk with me the first Sunday morning I was here.

Although he didn't say anything that morning, when they came back in the evening, we talked. I didn't tell him why I went out. I just said I was nervous and needed to run. He didn't go any deeper, but I felt he was afraid that my problems might reoccur. He asked me not to do that again, and if I wanted to run, I should wait until daylight and tell him or Mother.

But what could I do? The pain was getting worse, and the voices claimed I was worthless, deserving only pain. I got down on my knees beside my bed and started to cry. The pain began to get worse with every tick of the clock. The pain shot through me, growing worse and worse. I knew it could push me to the point of no return, like what happened when I was in the Hospital.

Before, running or shooting hoops would slowly drive the pain away. But I couldn't go out now, and I felt trapped.

Then Pastor John's voice came to me, "Rebuke Satan in the name of our Lord Jesus Christ." A force pressed me down, so actively it wouldn't let me say those words. No matter how I tried, that force wouldn't let me move. I couldn't understand what was going on or why. It was like I wanted the pain and where it might take me.

Then I was back on the bench in my Junior year, and everybody was playing except me. The pain was horrible, and I had no control, none at all. I cried out to God, saying, "I rebuke you, Satan, in the name of my Lord, Jesus Christ."

The pain was gone! There was no anxiety, no depression, nothing, and I couldn't feel the hurt lurking in my surroundings. All I felt was this beautiful peace engulfing me. I looked to the ceiling like I was gazing into the heavens and started praising God.

In another bedroom, across town, another young man was doing the same thing. He was battling the same battle as Jimmy. Maybe not as severe, but now the pain was gone after he rebuked Satan in the name of his Lord, Jesus Christ. Pat began praising God, just like Jimmy.

~~~~~~~~~~

The following Sunday, I didn't hesitate. I went up front for the altar call and gave my life to Jesus with tears flowing as I felt the pain drain entirely away. Now I knew God loved me, even if nobody else did, God did. I was so glad I had finally given my life to Him and that I was safe in His hands. I would diligently read His book, as I had been doing since that attack on Monday morning.

Sandy had followed me, and as I bowed at the altar, she put her hand on my back as if she understood my pain, and was with me as I gave my life to Jesus. It was time to stand up, and Sandy helped me up from my feeble knees. Even though I was so much larger than her, Sandy had the strength to help me stand.

That day, Sandy and I became closer than ever before. Many times after that, we talked about Jesus together. She would tell me Scriptures to read to help me in my walk with Jesus. It was true. She was there, and I had a good friend.

Chapter Nine

Friday, November twenty-three, was Cutler Ridge's first game of the season. We had practiced six weeks for this day. The Seneca County League is composed of small schools with graduating classes between thirty to forty students. None of the schools had a football team. They had baseball teams that played into September with a season that started in June. The tournament was late September, but there were no more games until middle October when the first practice was allowed by the state.

With no football, the basketball season started a lot earlier than schools that had football; our schedule was all-league games until after the first of the year. The league consisted of nine teams that played each one twice, giving each us sixteen league games. There were four games for each team to play out of the league. Teams were allowed to play only twenty games in the regular season, followed by the league tournament which started the last week in February or the first weekend of March.

Our first game was against Hopewell Loudon, about fifteen miles away. Their school was northwest of Tiffin, and we were northeast of Tiffin.

Hopewell Loudon was the dominant team in the league, and we were the cellar dwellers. Hopefully this year it would be different.

Sam Session's hatred toward me had settled down. But he fought with Coach Chumbly and threatened to quit. I heard that Sam felt I was crazy and didn't belong on the team. His father talked to Coach. I heard, although John wouldn't say anything to me, that Coach had a long talk with Sam's father, and after that talk, Sam started changing his attitude towards me. That meant more team ball.

I was the starting small forward, and Coach set up an offense that had a lot of picks and cuts. There was no center on the team. After a player picked and set, one guy would go inside, and one would go outside. If the inside players were not open for a shot, they would crossover and pick with the other inside player.

When the outside player was open, the point guard threw him the ball, and the point guard would break down the middle, hoping to be open for a layup. If he weren't open, he would go to the side opposite to the wing-man with the ball. Then the other wing-man would go inside and set a pick with the point guard. The inside player would suddenly break out to the wing. That was our all-against-a-man-to-man defense, and we would continue the motion until somebody got open.

Session was five-ten, with inaccurate outside shooting skills, and his dribbling skills were strictly power-right, meaning he could only dribble successfully with his right hand. With his quickness, he could get away with driving right. Also, in the fast break, he could get down the floor very quickly. In a scrimmage, in practice on defense, if I rebounded the ball or got a steal, Weiden or Tim passed the ball to me from a rebound, the team would try to fast break with Joey or me running it.

If I saw Sam breaking down the floor and I could pass the ball to him, his speed would take him past the defenders for an easy two points. His defense was tremendous and could create steals.

Sometimes being overly aggressive got him in foul troubles and his outside shooting was also a drawback.

Weiden is six-foot-one, quick, and could jump. His dribbling skills were the same as Session. He was an inside man all the way, mostly using offensive rebounding and a ten to fifteen-foot backboard shot. They said he had it last year, but now, with his jumping ability, that was a plus. Also, anytime I could penetrate towards the basket, drawing attention to me, from a defender in his area, whether it was man-to-man or zone, he was the best to work alley-oops, too.

I told John that my uncle taught me to tunnel vision in the game. "Don't let any outside influence bother you, except listening to the coach from the bench," he repeated over and over." I paid no attention to what an opponent said, and John agreed.

John was my counselor and my private coach, so I could feel him showing me how to be successful. He kept reminding me, "Be a team player, but take shots when they come because the success of this team will be with you scoring."

I understood what he said, but I wasn't going to be a gunner. As John told me, I had to shoot.

Another one who hoped I would be successful was my father. I recognized he wanted to brag about me. He was disappointed when he was voted off the school board earlier this month. I heard rumors that members disliked him because he was harsh. They defiantly didn't want him to have authority in the community or town. If his son became the star of the team, maybe steadiness and peace would come over him.

Father never told me directly, but somehow I knew, the incident had pushed people away from him. I didn't understand it and hoped I could fulfill his wishes, but I wanted no part of being a star, but I knew my job, and scoring was part of it.

Carl Glenn was a back-up for Weiden and Tim. He could box out and rebound, but stick-backs were where his points came. Jack

Reynold was the back-up to Joey and Sam. He was the bag-guard, but he wasn't as quick as Joey or Sam. He could handle the ball well and could shoot from the outside.

We were mostly a seven-man-team with the rest of the bench Sophomores. Varsity seniors are Joey, Tim, Brad, Sam, Jack, Glen Juniors, and me.

Hopewell Loudon had a stage for their gym, as most small schools do. The locker rooms were on the upper level. Players had to come out of the locker room and go down a few steps that led to the doorway of the gym. The floor and the auditorium were more massive than most of the gyms in the league, although ours was close in size.

I am nervous when I enter a gym. It may be familiar to me, but not for playing a game. The memories of this gym were strong. As good as Hopewell Loudon was in the past, with some of the greatest players that performed in this gym. I felt it an honor to be part of a game here. I'm not sure why I was nervous, but after a few warm-up shots, I calmed down.

When the buzzer sounded the players huddled for their last instructions from the coach. Then the National Anthem was played, and the announcer gave the starting line-up.

When they announced my name, excitement, and fear blasted through me. There was one last huddle where we all got in a circle, and each put one of our hands into the center, touching the rest of the team members. Then we yelled, "Go Indians!"

As we lined up for the starting jump ball, I thought, "This is the first time I get to play in a varsity game!" My nerves were tight. I remembered the great players I played back in Tennessee. I recollected how good they were, and how playing against them gave me courage. I don't think the players in this league aren't as good, but I could be surprised.

The coach couldn't decide if Brad or I should make the center jump, so we had tryouts, and I out jumped Brad. The coach was amazed. He declared, "I assume you could easily stuff the ball; you have an incredible jumping ability."

When he told me that, I realized I should have no fears of someone blocking my shots. I praised God for the abilities I had as an athlete and my skills in basketball.

I tipped the ball to Tim, and he passed the ball to Joey to set up the offense. Our offense players were getting open, but that's when nerves cause us to miss shots, especially open layouts where Sam would break loose in the offense and could make a shot.

In the first quarter, I had six points, all sticklebacks. I didn't take a shot in the first quarter. I guess it was my nerves.

With our dismal shooting in the first quarter, we stayed even with Hopewell Loudon due to our superior defense. Brad and I got a few blocked shots, and our guards got some steals that turned into layouts. A few of those layups we made were the reason we stayed in the game. It was all created by our defense.

In the second quarter, I got the ball and drove towards the basket. About ten feet out, I stopped and took a backboard jump shot. I was successful and scored eight points. When I found Brad or Tim open underneath for shots, we went ahead by five points. The coach of Hopewell Loudon got angry and called a timeout.

After the timeout, they started sagging on us trying to make us shoot outside. That's when I took my first outside shot and missed. The next time Joey got a chance from outside, he made it. Sam tried to drive against their sagging defense, but they stripped the ball from him.

Hopewell pulled ahead of us by four points, then through our offense, I started taking outside shots and hit four in a row. We pulled ahead of Hopewell by two points with another outside shot. Sam wasn't in the game because he made too many turnovers, and was getting too aggressive, trying to steal the ball and got in trouble.

Oh, he was mad when he got taken out of the game. I knew he would hate me even more, now. But I told myself to concentrate on the game, and that's what I did. I made another outside shot giving us a twenty-five to twenty-two lead.

As the second half started, I noticed they pulled out of their sagging defense. I was full of confidence and ran roughshod over Hopewell. With my past and scoring all over, a lot of inside jump shots off the backboard, Hopewell had no one to stop me, except to foul me and they did that a lot until we were in the one-and-one. Then I beat them on the foul line.

My passing was excellent, especially when they tried to double-team me. So I was the one who scored the most, even more than Sam. Amazingly we scored seventy-five points to the home team's sixty points. I was on the bench the last thirty seconds of the game. Once the game was over, Coach told us to head straight for the locker room. I was on the floor heading for the locker room when the Hopewell Loudon head coach, Jerry Crum, stopped me.

"Where did you come from? You look like you might be twenty-five years old." he asserted.

He wanted to check me out to make sure I wasn't cheating. But I froze not knowing what to tell him.

The assistant coach saw Crum confronting me and ran over telling me to go to the locker room. "He has to be a ringer," Crum accused. "He looks like he's at least twenty-two or twenty-three years old. I heard you had a pretty good player, but he can't be that good!"

"Are you saying that Cutler Ridge can't win a game against you unless we cheat? Well, I'll tell you, Mr. Crum, you check with the County School Board and the State School Board. They know all about Jimmy Bass, and they will tell you he is legal."

"I know your a preacher, a teacher, and the assistant coach of Cutler Ridge and you wouldn't lie, so tell me where he came from!"

"You may not believe this, but he's from Cutler Ridge. He didn't go to school last year because his doctor wouldn't let him. He lived with his uncle in Tennessee and had a growth spurt. When he came back, in late summer, nobody could believe his height. He's between six-foot-three and six-foot-four. I'm not going to tell you any more about it. You can check out everything, and you will find out he's legal."

John stepped away from Crum and went to the locker room.

~~~~~~~~~~

Allen Jamison, the sportswriter for the Advertising Tribune, was surprised at the performance of Cutler Ridge's team. Beating Hopewell Loudon was shocking, and one player had done it, not by scoring, but by passing and rebounding. On the record, he was a small forward, but he was the tallest one on the floor, and could out jump everybody. He played any position on the floor that offense let him play. He got outside shots, sick backs, and primarily short jump shots. No one in the league was going to stop him. If they double or triple-teamed him, other players had easy shots. Knowing how to stop him would be a nightmare.

Jamison saw Jerry Crum confront him at the end of the game. It looked like Jerry was about to lose it, but John Woodcut Jerry from his player. He must have told Crum something right, for it calmed Jerry down. Who would want to yell at a preacher?   Everybody thought Hopewell Loudon would have a down year, but who would have thought Cutler Ridge would beat them by fifteen points on Hopewell's floor? Perhaps Cutler Ridge caught them off guard. Maybe Cutler Ridge has a good team. Whatever it is, I wouldn't want to be in Jerry Crum's locker room. What a surprise! He would have to look into the record book to find out the last time Cutler Ridge beat Hopewell. It looked like Cutler Ridge would be an exciting team to watch this year.

"I'd sure like to see that Bass kid play again. I know some people, like Jerry Crum, might think he's illegal. I had heard about the player Cutler Ridge had. I also checked all the records to make sure he was legal. I could tell Jerry everything was legit. Tomorrow he will probably be calling the league president to what the State Athletic Department says. He will find out more then what John Wood told him."

"I've got to see him play more, especially the teams that play strictly man-to-man. I bet none of those teams have a player to stop him one-on-one. New Riegel, who they play next, is purely a zone team. Thompson, their next game, used to be a zone team, but with there new coach, who knows? No matter wherever this season takes him, I don't think anyone could match Bass."

~~~~~~~~~~

Arnold was proud as he walked out of the gym. Other than his good friend, Clyde Carl, nobody congratulated him on his son's playing. Most ignored him, but he got the last laugh. It was his son who created the greatest upset in school history! His son, Arnold Bass's son!

"Weep and cry for your sons. I have the best, The best!" he grinned.

~~~~~~~~~~

Hazel had gone to the game with Pat and Emily, Pat's new girlfriend. He had met in his morning classes. She was slender and about five-foot-eight, a perfect match in size and they clicked in personality, too.

Hazel didn't think Arnold deserved a kid like Jimmy. She wished he was her son. She was happy with how Tim played. He had over ten rebounds and made eleven points, but the game Jimmy played was remarkable. It was fantastic. If he kept performing at this level, the town would embrace him. Or would his bragging, arrogant father ruin everything for his boy? It was a good sign when the fans all cheered his performance. Most of the fans around her were excited about Jimmy's game. Some were shocked, even though the story around the town was that he was perfect. Some had watched the students play in the outdoor gym. Now they saw his performance against a team. That had to be the greatest upset in school history.

~~~~~~~~~~

There was chaos in the locker room, with everybody cheering excitedly about their win over Hopewell. Coach and John were giving everyone high fives. Coach Chumbly gave a speech on playing good defense and good teamwork.

I quietly told everybody, "Good game!" and slide into my quiet mode. "The less said, the better," and I returned to being an introvert.

Players who had cheerleader girlfriends sat with them on the bus, and some of my memory came back to me. I recalled the terrible experience I had playing in my Junior year, riding home on the bus after an away game. Going to the game, I had hope and coming home; I thought I was a failure again. I went to the back of the bus to get away from the coach, who always sat in the front. I got stuck behind a couple who were making out, and I remembered the pain I felt.

I must not have had a girlfriend. I probably never felt the joy of female companionship.

Memories began to come back piece by piece. What brought on this new memory? I guess it was the first bus ride home after the game that brought on my memories. It seems they were always bad ones.

Joey broke into my thoughts, saying, "Jimmy, I am very proud of you. That was a great game you played tonight."

"Thank you, Joey. You played a good game as well."

Joey's girlfriend wasn't a cheerleader, so he was sitting with me. "Think about it. We upset Hopewell! At the end of the game, I kept looking at the scoreboard, and I couldn't believe my eyes," he shouted.

"Ya, it was amazing."

"It was all because of you, Jimmy. You're the best player around. With you on our team, who knows what we can do? I'm glad you came back to finish school here instead of in Tennessee. But, I didn't know you were going to come home as a giant!"

He was going to say more, but I cut him off with a question. "What do you mean?"

"Rumors were you were never coming back."

"What other rumors were spread about me?"

"That you were in a state mental hospital and so far gone that you couldn't come back. There were a lot of rumors like that. I'm sorry, Jimmy."

"No problem, and I mean it, Joey. I figured if I came back, I would hear things like that. Most of those rumors are lies, Joey, mostly lies."

After a pause, I said, "A lot of people are not going to believe what I'm going to tell you. John Wood and my family are the only people in our community that know this. Even my father wants to keep it a secret, and he tells me nobody would believe it. But Joey here is the truth. I was never in a mental institution. I was in a regular hospital while I was in a coma. I don't remember what happened during that time. When I came out of the stupor, I went to Uncle Walter's home, and he was my psychiatrist. I'm so glad that happened to me. Not only did I get the mental help that I needed, but my uncle taught me how to shoot. He was a great player in Tiffin Columbia."

Joey didn't know what to say and just nodded his head in agreement. Then out of the blue, he said, "That's strange. It was your father who told us you were in a state hospital. I heard him say it, myself."

I lowered my head as if I were depressed. I couldn't believe Father would lie about something like that and want to make me look bad. Now, I'm his hero. Or am I? I don't know. It could be that he thought I would end in a state mental hospital until Uncle Walter brought me to his home. Maybe he thought I belonged there. Whatever the reason, he lied to everybody, and now wants to keep it quiet, so he doesn't look like a fool. That made me angry, but what could I do?

"I'm sorry I told you that, Jimmy. It's none of my business."

I turned and looked at Joey. I was sure he was someone I could trust. "Joey, it's okay. I'm asking you one thing, try to keep what I said to yourself. That is all I'm saying about this subject."

Changing the subject, I questioned, "What about Sessions? Does he still dislike me?"

"No, he's happy. He was part of the greatest win in Cutler Ridge history. He's even saying good things about you. Mostly he's bragging about his great defense and his driving skills that were a big part in the win. He had fourteen points, but he'll never say how we set him up for those drives."

"I know, but he can drive! He got in trouble when he tried to drive through a double-team."

I'm not sure why I said that. Am I jealous of Sam? No, I can't be that way. I have to be humble like Jesus wants. He gave me the talent and the height, why should I brag about what I did? Although I was amazed at the things I did tonight, it was like I was in a daze and the reactions were all automatic. I enjoyed it, and I can't wait to play again. I know I am going to get a lot of praise. People are coming out of the woodwork to congratulate me.

"Jesus, guide me through this. Even though this is something I wanted and I enjoy getting all this praise, I want people to look up to me, not as that person I was before, who I think I was."

When the bus pulled into Cutler Ridge, I grew excited. I knew the praise was coming.

Chapter Ten

As the bus drove into Cutler Ridge, people lined the street, especially in the downtown area. Bedlam broke out on the bus as it parked in front of the auditorium. The players were mobbed with fans as they disembarked. Although usually closed on Friday nights, Keller's restaurant opened both sides of their establishment to celebrate the big win and probably be open every Friday or Saturday night there was a game. The team ate free cheeseburgers, fries, and Coke.

As I got off the bus, people crowded around me, congratulating me on my great game and walked towards Keller's. I saw a man in front of Wall Bar watching me and taking everything in with a big smile. I wondered if he was friend or foe.

The man turned out to be Arnold Bass. I was making him a hero by being his son. I began to think about the rumor he had spread about me; or did he? I started to realize that he didn't want me back here unless I could make him famous.

Although my anger wanted me to confront him, he was my father and deserved my respect, I guess. He had told people I was going to the State Hospital until Uncle Walter pulled the rug out from under him. What did that mean? It didn't feel like love.

~~~~~~~~~~

Men who wanted to talk about the Friday night game crowded Fred Stiller's Barbershop late Saturday morning. Everyone was excited about the team, especially that kid, Jimmy Bass. They were sure they had a great team this year. How could anything go wrong?

Jen Stiller, a seventy-five-year-old pessimist, claimed he had seen every basketball game played in this town. He reminded them that it been a long time since Cutler Ridge had a winning season. Last year they almost won, but they failed in the end.

"Don't count your chickens before they're hatched! Even with that big fellow, strange things can happen. So don't get too excited. Just wait and see; we will fail!" Stiller told the men,

Nobody in the barbershop wanted to listen to his perspective. "We'll win!" they shouted.

"You have to think positive." someone barked.

"Out of the last several games, this is the biggest upset ever." another man stated.

"This was the best game any of us can remember."

"Tonight will be another game and this one is at home!"

"Just wait!"

"We can't wait to see it!

~~~~~~~~~~

At ten o'clock, Saturday morning, Jimmy was in John Wood's office. John started the session with a prayer, thanking the Lord for the game they had last night, as well as the way Jimmy and the other players played.

"Well," he grinned. "How do you feel about your first game?"

"First of all, John, how many points did I make last night? I've had several numbers thrown at me. My mother thought it was close to thirty points, but I'm not sure."

John opened one of the drawers in his desk and pulled out a notebook. "You had twenty-nine points, thirteen rebounds, and eight assists. The next scorer was Sam Session with fourteen points. Hopewell couldn't stop him when he was racing down the floor. He got quite a few layouts from the long passes from you, Brad and Tim. Joey was next with thirteen points, and three steals and Brad was right behind him with eleven points and nine rebounds. Tim made seven points and had ten rebounds. Jack made one point. So there it is Jimmy, four guys in double figures. I think that was good for our team."

John had a big smile on his face when he asked, "How do you feel about the game you played?"

I thought before I spoke, then replied, "I'm a new Christian, but I praise God that He did what I hoped. Maybe not as much success as I had, but God gave me the ability and the height to reach my dream. I'm sure I had the ability for a long time, but I got the chance to do it. I accept the blessings, and I will play as hard as I can. The win is not for me, but for the school, the team, and most importantly for Jesus."

I looked directly into John's eyes and stated, "If I ever get cocky, kick me in the butt."

"I won't kick you in the butt, Jimmy," he laughed. "But I will remind you."

Suddenly, John's smile dissolved into a grave expression, and he continued, "Jimmy, enjoy this gift God has given you. Don't let guilt, shame, or fear take that enjoyment away from you. Teammates, opposing players, and even fans will put you down at one time or another. Usually, it will be when you have something they want. Opponents may call you ugly words, and make mean comments about you or your girlfriend."

"I know you don't have a girlfriend right now," John grinned.

Then, becoming serious again, he declared, "You will have to deal with roughness on the floor. Coaches will tell their players to intimidate you, especially when you go inside. Some will double-team you or triple-team you to stop you."

"That doesn't bother me, Coach." I interrupted. "When they double team or triple-team me, that means somebody else is open. I love to pass. I only score because the team wants to win. I may score a lot, but it won't become an obsession with me."

I enjoyed the conversation with John as we talked about my walk with God. Our time ended with prayer, and I went home.

~~~~~~~~~~

On Saturday night, November twenty-four, the Cutler Ridge Indians played the New Reigal Blue Jackets in our gym. The Blue Jackets had lost their first game to Old Fort by eight points and were considered to be like us, bottom feeders of the league, along with Thompson, Republic, and Bettsville. The top teams were Hopewell Loudon, Old Fort, Bloomville, and Attica. At least that was what everybody thought until our upset last night. Nobody knew where we stood. The Advertising Tribune call our game "the upset of the year."

The article told about me and my performance, too. So our auditorium was packed. It seemed the whole town wanted to see the nerd play and I didn't want to disappoint them.

Our game, from start to finish, was the defense. The players on the opposing team were taller than us, but we were quicker and could out jump them. Sometimes it surprised me how high I jumped, so I got some great blocked shots, just like I did against Hopewell. I was fairly successful.

I hit my first four shots from the outside in the first quarter and made some offensive rebounds to give us an eighteen to nine lead. They went into a box-in-one defense in the second quarter. Coach called time out and put in an offense he designed in practice in case this happened. He had me running the baseline with no wing-man. Joey and Sam split out front to pick for me.

It became a grind of a game with Coach telling the guards to slow the game down, looking for me to break loose in the corner or one of our big men would come open because the defense was worried about me. It worked. I didn't get the ball much, but Tim, Brad, Glen Carl, when he was in, got some easy baskets. Then they tried to stop me from the outside for a natural basket from inside. We played a good team game.

Session got in trouble with fouls because he was impatient. He thought his points should come quickly. But after he missed two layups on fast breaks, he went down the floor slowly on defense, disappointed in himself for missing a shot. Maybe he felt everybody ought to feel sorry for him, but it was too late for our defense. That caused New Reigel to try a five-on-four, giving him a good shot which they missed because of the protection of the four players.

When he got to his man on defense, who was driving the ball, he tried to steal the ball but got caught with his third foul.

Jerry told Jack, "Get him out of there!" but before Jack got into the game, Sam had a technical called on him.

Sam ran off the floor to get back to the bench before the ref called another technical, but it was too late. Not only did he get a technical foul, he got ejected from the game and John took him to the locker room.

In the locker room, Sam sat on one of the benches and stared into space.

"What is the matter with you, Sam? Why did you lose it as quickly as you did? You need patience. If you relax, points will come to you because you're quick."

"The nerd won't pass to me, John. He wants all the points to himself."

"That's not right, Sam, and you know it. He is passing the ball when you are open on a fast-break, or just breaking to the basket. I hate for you have it in for him, the way you talked about him in school, saying he's crazy and doesn't belong here. He has just as much right to be here as you do. If you work with him and have patience with him, you could average around fifteen points a game, but you want more. All you care about is yourself, not the team. What your answer to that?"

"You say he is all about the team, but he wants to break Jake Birkart's record. He doesn't care about the team! His father is pushing him to be a star. He should've left him wherever he was. That's all I have to say! If you want to kick me off the team, so be it. I hate him and will never quit hating him! I know you're a preacher, and you say it's wrong to hate, but I don't care what you think!"

"I'm not going to say anything else. Take your shower and get dressed. You can't play anymore because the referees ejected you from the game."

"What are you going to do?"

"I have to stay here and watch you, so you don't do anything to the locker room."

Sam was about to make a comment when a voice said, "I'll watch over him and take him home."

John turned around and saw Sam's father glaring at his son. Sam said no more, so John left the locker room.

~~~~~~~~~~

We had a ten-point lead, but it was cut down to four points by the time John got back to the floor. There were four minutes left in the first half when he got back to the bench, and Jerry had the team in a timeout. Nobody had to tell John what happened; the opposing team had made the foul shots and a basket when they got the ball on the rebound. It was part of the technical call.

With three minutes left, we had an eighteen to fourteen lead. The Sessions explosion seemed to fire the team up, and we exploded for ten more points, allowing the visitors only four. Now we had twenty-eight points to the visitors eighteen. When we made it down to the locker room at halftime, Sessions father and his son were gone.

~~~~~~~~~~

In the second half, New Reigel went back to the to-three-zone and packed it in trying to force us to take only outside shots. The box-one was killing them. They were concentrating too much on stopping me. New Reigal gave up a lot of easy inside baskets. They did everything to slow the game down everything they could to stop the fast breaks. I only had six points from the first half, but with me on the wing now and in the zone, they played, I knew I had to shoot from outside, so I did. That gave us a fourteen point lead in the third quarter.

In the fourth quarter, the opposing players started double-teaming me. If I was on the right-wing or the left-wing, it was a double team. Every time I got the ball, they surrounded me. Even the center on the defense would come to help stop me leaving several of our players open for good shots. My passes reached my open teammates' good shots, and we blew them out with seventy-four to fifty-six. I had twenty-three points, most of them from the third quarter.

Chapter Eleven

The gymnasium and auditorium were quiet. Except for the New Reigal fans, everyone was celebrating in the town. John Wood and Coach Jerry Chumbly sat in the coach's office, just off the gym next to the locker room. There was only enough room for a desk and chair with a couple of extra chairs in the front. Coach Chumbly sat behind the desk, and John Wood sat in one of the chairs. John, the only assistant, was in charge of the Junior Varsity. Most of the time, they worked together. The final say always went to Jerry Chumbly. The agenda for tonight's meeting was how to give suggestions and criticisms on how to improve the team and the development of Sam Session.

"What do you think about Session? Do you think we should suspend him? "Jerry asked.

"Jerry, I'm always for forgiveness, but what he said in the locker room about Jimmy Bass was based on fear and hatred. I don't know if he wants to come back. If he does, I would suggest he sets out two games but doesn't miss practice."

Jerry looked at John and shook his head. "Your right. Sam can't have his hatred against Jimmy Bass and be on the same team. A two-week suspension sounds good, and he has to practice. We need to give him a good lecture on Monday, then watch him closely. I'll keep a close eye on Jimmy. If I see Sam harassing him, Sam is gone!"

John nodded his head in agreement.

"Are you sure Bass doesn't have mental problems?" Jerry questioned. "Your his counselor, John, so keep an eye on him. Should I watch for anything? He is not only the best player but the smartest?"

"Your right. Do you know what Jimmy told me after the game? He wasn't cocky, but he said New Reigal Coaches were stupid because they did everything they could to stop him from shooting outside shots, leaving the other players wide open for an easy shot! Then he added, and I quote, 'I still scored in the twenties.'"

"He's right, they were stupid, playing there regular two-three might have made the game closer, but still I believe we have the better team and the best player in the league, maybe even in all of northern Ohio."

"Maybe, but don't forget Weiden and Ender are two good players and work well with Bass. Our point guard isn't a bad player, either."

"I agree, John. Sam would add a nice piece of the puzzle, but his whole attitude has to change. Jimmy was a solid kid in town before, and the way he acts now is no different, except he is a little more introverted, quieter. So most the people in town are behind him, especially when they see how good a basketball player he is. As for Jimmy, the only problem is his memory. Will he get it back?"

"His uncle, a psychiatrist, doesn't think it will come back. But who knows? If it does come back, I hope it's a little at a time. As it is now, Jerry, it comes back to him in bits and pieces. I think something terrible happened to him right before he left. If his memory returns, I hope I'm around him."

"You think he will get violent?"

"I don't think so, but we won't know until it happens. I know it won't happen in practice or on the basketball floor. In practice, the boy's mind is concentrating on helping make the team, and himself get better. In a game, he is trying to help the team win. If we punish him, something like that might happen."

"You're right, John. You're right."

~~~~~~~~~~

I was lying in bed, thinking about the celebration at Keller's after the game. It had been fun, especially all the compliments I got, just like the night before. Appreciation for something you've accomplished is satisfying. But I didn't want to get a big head, never. Uncle Walter had warned me about it. It was something I never believed I would have to worry about. I figured I might score a little over double figures and no one would get excited about that. But thirty-one points one night and then twenty-three the next was remarkable. Uncle Walter must have realized how good I am.

How should I handle it? I know I'll always be humble on the outside; it's just me. But what about my inner feelings? Do I think I'm better than everyone else? Maybe I am, I have to accept that. But I want to be humble. Yes, I always want to be humble, inside, and out. If I stick to those principals, everyone will like me. Isn't that the principal part? There will be no arrogant walking around like I'm the greatest. I can't stand people like that, especially people like Jake.

The thought made me sit up. Who is Jake? Was he an enemy I had in the past? Why did this memory arise?

I tried to think about my past, but no Jake came to mind. Whoever he was, I have no memory of him, except the thought that he was a very arrogant person. Maybe I should ask somebody.

My father says to leave the past where it is. I can't understand why he would keep saying that. There must be something horrible in my history that he doesn't want me to remember. Father's continually warning me about my past, makes me want to remember it. Maybe I should suppress it if it tries to come out.

I know Father tells lies. He lied to Joey about me being in a state mental hospital. What other lies did he say about me? I could confront him, but it would probably be more lies, and it might get Joey in trouble. That couldn't happen unless Father went after Joey. That would never happen, I thought, shaking my head. Father wasn't that big a fool.

He may have told people I was in the State Hospital, thinking that was where I was going. But why not tell the truth now? It was probably his pride, having to be right all the time. It had to be that. If I confronted him, he would counter with the future thing again. "Nobody needs to know our business," he would remind me.

Father is probably right. I am leaving the past alone even if I remember it. Keeping it quiet might be a good idea. My life is good. Why do I want to go back to the past? The past is over, and what I remember of it tells me it had to be a terrible thing. No, I don't want to go there, and I pray God won't let the past come knocking.

Here's a thought, maybe God wants me to know my past. I hope not! Because every memory I have of my past seems to have negativity around it. Why don't people tell me about the incident? Pat and other people were there. They know what happened.

"Forget it, Jimmy," I tell myself. "Leave the past alone!"

I know my father has a lot to hide and a lot of stuff he was afraid I would know, things like I told John. But what can I do? The past is past, and I have to accept it.

~~~~~~~~~

Allen Jamison, a writer for the paper on the weekend, sat at his desk writing a story about the Saturday night games in the Seneca County league. Another writer reported on the City Schools, but Allen had two different columns during this time of the year. One was about the Seneca County League players. The other was about a team he felt the subscribers would interested in.

Jimmy Bass, a player from Cutler Ridge, caught Jamison's attention last night when he saw him play against Hopewell Loudon. The kid was impressive, and his team had a big upset, showing how good he was.

Tonight's game against New Reigal promised to be as exciting; however, there was one teammate in the box who was against Bass. Session's actions were stupid. Jamison wished he could put that in the article. But if he did, he wouldn't be a writer for the paper anymore. It was something you didn't do.

Session's attitude could hurt this team. They played better without him in the second half. If he had a better attitude, he could have helped his team.

Was Bass as good as Jamison thought he was, or would good competition put him down? Time would tell, but he hoped the kid would succeed.

Where had this kid come from? He couldn't remember seeing him play before, but he had heard from Cutler Ridge fans that he grew up there. The facts didn't make sense. He had kept careful records of the teams and players in the league. That was his job. So if he is from Cutler Ridge, how did he get these skills all at once.

Then he remembered that the superintendent of the Ridge had sent him a list of the names of the players who would be on the team, along with there ages and birthdays. He remembered seeing a new name, Jimmy Bass. Jamison checked everyone's age and realized they were all legal, but still, this player's story would be interesting. Where had Bass been last year?

~~~~~~~~~

Going back to school on Monday morning was exciting. Everybody in our High School seemed to be a lot friendlier. Students, especially girls, congratulated me on the game over the weekend.

After eating lunch, I went to the auditorium and sat in the middle row of the seating. Usually, I was alone. I used to hang with the team, but most of the team members had girlfriends, and I felt like a fifth wheel. I was comfortable being alone. Sometimes I read a book for one of my classes or just a fiction story. I assume this wasn't the norm before when I would be attempting to make friends or trying to avoid the bullies. Was this memory just a feeling. I have these thoughts a lot. But my memories stayed away, making me frustrated.

Out of nowhere, two girls came and sat beside me. One came from one side, and the other came from the opposite direction, then they sat down with me in the middle.

The one on the left was Marsha James, a five-foot-four girl with a well-curved body, an attractive face, and long black hair. She is the Senior class president, a cheerleader, and considered the most popular girl in school. With her sitting beside me, my heart pumped a little faster.

The girl on the other side was a little taller, slender, had blond hair, and was quite attractive. Her name was Ginger Tillman, a close friend of Marsha. They were always together, and both were cheerleaders.

They were in a flirting mood, and I didn't know what to think. I was thrilled, but my principals were solid. Neither was eighteen, meaning they were underage. They started with praises for the great game I played over the weekend, and I complimented them on their cheer-leading.

The conversation turned to things happening in school. Then we started to talk about some boring stuff when Marsha asked me,

"Why haven't you been interested in us girls?"

She pouted as she asked the question, and I felt it was part of the flirting. But how would I know? I hadn't dated any girls. It seemed this was forward for a girl. Things like this didn't usually happen, most girls wouldn't walk over and sit beside a boy, but I was a man, would she be thought of as being fresh?

Next, she seemed to be asking me for a date. I had never heard of such a thing! How did I know this? Maybe she was asking for someone else who wanted to date me.

No, Marsha was flirting with me! Wasn't she? I didn't know. Again, why would she ask me? Am I that good looking?

Anyway, these girls could get away with this encounter, I guess. Other girls would be looked down on, but these girls were popular.

Maybe, this was a joke to try and make me look like a fool. How would I know? Had that happened to me before? Was this a game, popular girls played? I was sure they were the queens of the school.

Fear overtook me, and I became cautious of what I should say. I didn't want to look like a fool!

Instead of answering with words that might sound like I was flirting with her, I told her the truth. "I can't date if that's what you want. I'm of age, and most of the girls in our high school aren't."

Man, was I forward! They probably never wanted to date me in the first place and were playing with me. But I got a surprising answer.

"That doesn't matter! I'm seventeen and girls my age date men of your age all the time. Our parents don't care, as long as they know the guy."

"Another thing is my problem and where I just came from."

Why did I say that?

"You don't act like that kid you were before. I've heard you can't remember that kid, but he was nice. I hated to see him get teased and pushed around by the bullies, and I want to know, who you are now?"

Marsha had given me a lot of information. I imagine I was a

nerd just as I always suspected. I didn't know how to answer her. Maybe it wasn't a joke.

After giving it some deep thought, I came up with an answer that wouldn't be a flirt or sound like I was trying to act like somebody I wasn't. It would be the truth.

"Marsha, I'm trying to learn about myself, one day at a time. I know I'm different in appearance with my growth since I was here before and am a better basketball player. I'm sure I never had a girlfriend before, and I wouldn't know what to do to have one now or even how to go on a date."

"What about Elisabeth Hasselback?"

"I've heard about her, but I have no memory of her."

"I know you were friends. I thought you dated until Jake came into the picture. I know that hurt you very much. Other than that, I don't know."

I didn't remember Jake, but his name has come up several times. I guessed he was the top bully, so I answered. "I don't think we ever dated."

I thought about it then continued. "I'm confident with myself. I'm no psycho ready to explode, a sex pervert, or any other kind of weirdo as people may think. The only problem I had was low self-esteem. I lacked confidence in myself

Marsha seemed to understand what I was explaining to her and accepted it. We talked until the bell rang, telling us it was time to go back to class. Ginger had lost interest in me when a couple of other boys came over to talk to her, flirt, and try to get a date.

~~~~~~~~~

Wednesday night, the 28th of November, Allen wanted to see

114

the game at Thompson, one of the northern schools in the league. He knew it was one of the worst teams in the league. They were probably no better this year than Thompson, but they may be somewhat improved.

With Cutler Ridge's history of bad teams, could it be this is a good team? Well, they had upset Hopewell Loudon.

A call to John Shumer, Cutler Ridge's superintendent, garnered some information. First of all, Bass was legal; of course, he knew that. Jimmy Bass had missed last year because he was under a doctor's care.

The superintendent said, "For the sake of the family, I will not tell you any more about him. Except he was only around five-foot-ten when he left and never played. He's had a growth spurt and is almost six-foot-four now. His dad's family has a lot of tall men, so it must be in the genes. I'll leave it at that."

Could he do that? Allen was a reporter and had to seek the truth. Sometimes the truth hurt people, as the information given by Shumer. Still, he was a reporter, and people should know the truth. He had to find out then he would be the judge. That's just the way it had to be.

~~~~~~~~~~

The Junior Varsity won their game, and now it's time for us to win ours. I got a chill down my back when the announcer said my name. The visiting team is named first, then the home team. After a short huddle, the referee blows his whistle. Then the starters head to the center to jump, and the game begins. Brad, who is doing the center jump tonight, out jumped Thompson's center and tipped the ball to Tim, who passed the ball to me, and I set up the offense.

Thompson played a two-three zone, and the first half was a grind out game, both teams played a half-court game. We had a fast-break, if it was there, then the same happened with Thompson. Both had been bottom feeders in the league for many years and had experience beating each other in the past. Neither team wanted to give an inch. Their defense was as tough as we were. We had an offense that had me rotating around, sometimes leaving Tim at the wing. The coach put this play because scouting showed they had some powerful inside guys. We would have a hard time getting anything inside.

Thompson beat Attica the same night we beat Hopewell. The following night Old Fort beat them by two points, so they thought they were pretty tough as we did. But our points inside weren't coming, and I had to shoot. Our coach stressed keeping the game slow and no over the back fouls, trying to get an offensive rebound. We were playing it safe.

Coach also stressed watching how we guard their big men and not getting in foul trouble. He meant that for Brad, Tim, and Glen.

The players he had me guarding where shorter than me. Coach's theory was that I could dominate these players and not get in foul trouble. I was usually taller and usually quicker. Sometimes a switch would put me on a big man, but I never fouled him when they went up for a shot. I went straight for the ball, trying not to touch the player; that way, I avoided foul trouble.

I was hitting the outside shot, and so was Joey. With a couple of deep rebound shots and a basket, we made several points the first half.

The shot that was going for me was the deep corner. I was playing team ball all the way, and we passed around the zone a lot. Everybody was afraid to shoot, but the only thing we got was outside shots. Thompson was doing so well inside on defense that we had to score from outside, except for a few fast breaks we created.

On offense, Thompson ran a pick-off, same as we did. Their scoring came from all over, their big guys could get some inside shots, and they got some from outside. But we led twenty-eight to twenty-two at the end of the half. I felt I had close to sixteen points.

As the writer for the weekend paper, I sat in the Cutler Ridge section with my eyes mostly on their team, especially Jimmy Bass. I was surprised by the way they played as a team. The wing-men were always trying to set Bass up for a shot. He was almost perfect with the outside shots tonight. Their center, Ender, was on the right-wing at times which surprised me and their rotating offense was a ploy to get the ball to Bass in the corner. Ender never shot out from there and played some high post.

It was unbelievable how the team wanted Bass to shoot the majority of the shots, but I understand why. Thompson's big men were impressive, but Bass's shooting was too remarkable for Thompson to overcome in the first half.

At halftime, I asked some fans about Bass's history. A couple of them asked me if I was trying to ruin there star. They said this was their first time, in a long time, for a chance to be a winning team. That shocked me, but I wondered why it should. Bass was providing them something no other player gave them. He was their only hope. I hope nothing illegal is happening here. I got some information from fans, who said he had been gone from school for a year under a doctor's care. They told me he was of legal age because he flunked a year in school. Some told me he was a good kid with a horrible father, who probably caused his problems but that was all they would say to me; it seemed the whole community was protecting him, and I understood why. I noticed, for the first time, Sam Sessions wasn't on the team.

~~~~~~~~~

Thompson pushed around Cutler Ridge's six-point half time lead and led by four points at the end of the third quarter. They were hot, and it seemed like everything they shot went in.

I realized we had to play better defense, and we were on guard at the start of the fourth quarter. Thompson missed their shot. Brad got a rebound and sent the ball to me at the top of the key. I gathered the ball at the half-court line, catching everybody by surprise. I was all alone. A quick drive to the basket took me in and a dunk. That woke up our crowd and they rose to their feet cheering wildly.

Then Joey stole a layup, tying the game at forty-five. Now, our fans were rocking, and our team was fired up.

As the game went on, the lead was back and forth. I calmed down and pushed the fear of shooting that Sam had started. The layup broke me of my anxiety, which had pounded me in the third quarter, making me think I was shooting too much, but we would lose if I didn't start shooting again. We began running our offense, and I started hitting shots. Then Thompson's defense made a great effort to stop me, opening shots for the inside guy, especially Brad.

Surprisingly, some missed shots from Thompson in the last couple of minutes left turned into some fast break points. At the time we were ahead by two points and pushed the lead to eight points. Thompson made a basket, and we started to stall with a six-point lead.

Thompson began aggressively double-teaming anyone who had the ball. But good inside passes gave us a few points that countered with more points, and we stayed with our team having a six to eight-point lead, and we ended up winning sixty-four to fifty-six. We were now three and zero.

Riding home on the bus, I was basking in the glory, but I stayed humble. For the first time, I had over thirty points. I had thirty-four points out of sixty-four with eleven rebounds and five assists.

Joey had the most assists, seven, along with fifteen points. Brad got ten rebounds and made eight points. Tim was able to get two assists and ten rebounds. Jack earned a point and got a couple of steals as well as a couple of rebounds. Glen had five rebounds and made four points, all inside from good passes when they tried to double-team me.

Joey, sitting in the seat I had started in, began to draw me up. Even Tim, behind us, leaned up to get into the conversation and said the same things Joey did. I enjoyed the compliments but tried to wave them off, saying, "You're making me feel like I am a star, and that is the furthest thing from my mind."

"Jimmy, you don't like to have us brag about you, but what happened to you in the past, is why you deserve our praise," Tim yelled. Then he added, "I don't care if you scored fifty points or if you earned twenty. We won the game, and that's all it matters! If you were an arrogant, cocky guy like Jake Bickhart, I wouldn't give you the time of day. But we're a team, Jimmy, and you're one of us. We want to work with you to get the ball so that you can score. You score almost anywhere on the floor, but we can't. So keep scoring, Jimmy. That's a gift you have given us and everybody in the community!"

I shook my head, not believing what I was hearing, and said, "I can't believe I can score that many points in a game. I understand scoring in the middle twenties, but not the middle thirties!"

"If you hadn't scored those points, we would have lost. Thompson's big men are too hard for us to handle us. I believe the bottom feeder teams will control the league this year," Joey added.

"That could be. And I hope we are the ones on the top," Tim continued.

When there was a pause, I asked Joey for some advice. "Monday, at our noon hour in the auditorium, I was sitting alone where I usually sit."

"I know, why aren't you hanging with us like you used to?"

"I feel like a fifth wheel. You guys all have girlfriends, and I don't."

"I don't think you can claim that with Marsha sitting by you."

"There is nothing between Marsha and me. I know she has been sitting beside me at lunch, but I don't know why."

I didn't want to tell him I thought she had been hinting for a date, so I asked, "You think she wants to date me?"

"Very much so!"

"But why me?"

"You're the most popular guy in school, especially how well you play basketball. Most of the girls in school have a crush on you."

"Girls are attracted to me because of the way I play basketball?"

"That's part of it. Before you were that mysterious guy that hardly spoke to anybody except your teammates, all the girls think you're handsome, with that blond hair. They all know you lost your memory, and nobody knows how to approach you, so Marsha and Ginger approached you on a dare from the popular section of girls. That's what my girlfriend told me. Now it seems Marsha likes you at least she acts as if she does. It's all about popularity. You're the most popular boy in school, and Marsha is almost the most popular girl. With you as her boyfriend, she would be the top girl."

I looked at Joey with a shocked expression. "Am I the most popular boy in school?" I never thought that would happen. I played the introvert, not to avoid popularity, but to avoid people thinking I was a crazy man. Joey's words couldn't be correct.

"Their parents wouldn't be pleased to know that I'm popular. I'm the former nut case in school," I asserted.

"Don't talk like that, Jimmy, most people don't think of you that way. They think you're a nice guy. The reason a lot of people don't approach you is they feel awkward about your memory loss."

I thought about popularity and dating a popular girl. That might be fun. It's something I had never done before. I just thought, "Me, King of the school?"

Then I began to feel fear. Being the king of the school was

terrible. I don't know where that came from, but it scared me. What if I wasn't humble? But humble was what I wanted. Being popular would be scary. Dating Marsha would put me in a situation I don't want to think about, but being king was even worse!

"Joey, I just can't have this!" I blurted out. "This scares me. No, No, No! I want to go to school, get good grades, and play basketball, and that's all!"

"Okay, Jimmy, but don't lose it. I don't think Marsha is the girl for you, anyway. There must be some nice Christian girl in our church who would like to date you."

"No, Joey, I'm not ready. When I think about all the mess I went through; I'm not ready until more memories come back, showing me what happened and how I felt. My feelings are the biggest part, Joey." I said with emphasis. "I can't have a relationship, and I can't be the most popular boy in school."

Joey nodded his head as if he understood. Just then, the bus pulled up in front of the school. There were only a few people uptown to celebrate our win. Thankfully, people had other things to do. Even Keller's wasn't open. The town was pretty dead, except for Walls Bar and I bet my father was in there. I went straight home after I got off the bus. When I got home, Mother congratulated me on my game. My father wasn't there. He was at Walls bar, drinking and bragging about me. I hoped he didn't come home drunk again.

Mother made me a couple of hamburgers. As I ate, I listened to the local Tiffin radio station. It was mostly music until the eleven o'clock sports report. I wanted to know how the teams in our league were doing. There were a lot of surprises. Old Fort had won their first two games, and Republic knocked them off. Another win for a bottom feeder. Hopewell lost another game, this time it was to New Reigal.

I heard all the scores, and we were the only undefeated team. That was great. I hoped we could keep going.

After announcing our score, they said something about me scoring thirty-four points and I was, by far, the league-leading scorer, averaging twenty-eight points in every game.

That made me feel proud. Who would have thought I could score that many points in three games? Not Summerall. For some reason, I could remember him from my past. If he could see me playing, would he be ashamed? Come on, to give him credit, I wasn't as tall back then, and I surely wasn't a shooter. And that's the truth!

After I ate, I asked Mother to check my height. She measured me on the wall leading to the back door there where several marks. She had to stand on a stool to get the line correct. When this process was over, I stepped away, and she measured it, proving what I expected, I was close to six-foot-four. I thanked Mother and praised God for my height and the game I played as I went to bed.

Sandy was coming out of the bathroom, and stopped. So did I.

"Great game, Brother," she grinned.

"Thank you, "I answered with a smile on my face.

We started to move to our separate bedrooms when a thought came to me. "Am I the most popular boy in school? Somebody told me that, today, and I can't believe it."

She smiled and told me something I didn't want to hear. "You are, Brother. My shy, older brother is the most popular boy in school. Who would have believed it, but you are, especially after they've seen you play a game. Oh, by the way, did mother recheck your height?"

"Yes, she did. I'm close to six-foot-four."

"Unbelievable. I have to strain my neck to look up at you. Sometimes, I think I'm in a fantasy world seeing a giant in our house. Oh, Jimmy, you've changed so much, physically."

"I know, Sandy, and I have a hard time believing it too. But I am, and I'm glad I am. Thank you, Lord."

"Now, before I go to bed, Jimmy, please don't get involved with Marsha James. She made a challenge with some of the other popular girls, to see who would be the first to date you."

"You must be kidding me. I want no part of that."

"They only want to date you for popularity. The popular girls think they control any guy who dates them. So, Jimmy, stay away from her."

"I will, Sis. Anyway, I feel like I'm too old for her. I know eighteen-year-old boys do date sixteen, and seventeen-year-old girls. But I've never dated before, have I, Sandy?"

"Not that I remember, except you had a big crush on Elizabeth Hasselback, a cute little blonde that you knew when you were younger. You were close friends. But when she got in High School, she wanted popularity and dated Jake Bickhart. He made a fool of her. It made you very sad, Jimmy. If you don't date, it's probably best for you."

I nodded my head in agreement, said good night, and we both went to bed.

As I lay in my bed, I pushed the word "popularity" away from me. I still didn't believe it and didn't want it. I didn't know why, but it scared me. Dating the most popular girl seemed wrong. I would make a fool of myself, and that is something I wanted to avoid. I know she might get me into trouble. But I was attracted to her, and she was beautiful. I can't dwell on her. She is trouble, trouble, trouble.

Suddenly another thought came to me; I felt good that Sessions wasn't on the team, tonight. After his double technical, the coach suspended him for two games. Then when the coach told him, Sam shouted, "I quit! I wouldn't play with that Crazy Freak!"

I knew he meant me.

Then Sessions yelled, "The only way I will come back, is if Bass gets kicked off the team! He doesn't deserve to be on the team!"

In school, he put me down, but not to my face. What would I do if he did? I couldn't beat him up. Oh, I would if it wasn't against the school's rules or God's requirements for a Christian. If he attacks me, should I have a right to defend myself? I wouldn't punish him; I would only restrain him as Joe Cline taught me.

Who is Elizabeth Hasselback? Did I love her and she rejected me? Sandy said we were friends at one time. I need to meet her. I was trying to remember what she looked like as I drifted off to sleep.

~~~~~~~~~~

Thanksgiving Day started well, but Father ruined it. The celebrating began with a feast at my grandparents' place. Mother's sister, Jean, was there with her husband, Joe. They have a son a grade below me and a daughter who was a sophomore. Their boy plays football but doesn't play basketball, except in the recreation league. The School in Tiffin is enormous, compared to our little country school. He would probably make our team if he tried, but there was no chance at their school.

Uncle Joe told me I could be a starter at the Tiffin School. He had seen me play my last two games. That made me feel good, and I could see my father's pride was apparent, he wanted to talk only about me. It was the general topic while we were eating until Aunt Jean asked how I was feeling since my hospitalization, and if my problems were over.

I could understand why she asked the question, this was the first she had seen me since I got back, but she knew the family wanted to keep it hush-hush. Her husband gave her a dirty look, like "What are you doing?"

The question put the final nail in the coffin of the conversation around the table for the rest of the meal and the rest of the time spent at my Grandparents' house.

I was willing to answer Aunt Jean's question. I had no qualms about my mental health. But Father felt completely different. He cut her off by telling her outright that we don't talk about that. Aunt Jean was embarrassed, and her expression proved it. I felt sorry for her, but the look I got from Father told me to keep my mouth shut. Then Aunt Jean got up from the table, crying, and ran off to her old bedroom.

It wasn't long before we headed home. As soon as we were out of my Grandparents driveway, Father started to lecture me. "Your problem is nobody's business, and you shouldn't talk about it except to John Wood and Uncle Walter."

Father's declaration wasn't a suggestion; it was an order that a king gives, commanding a peasant in his kingdom. The way he had been treating me was gone, and the king was giving a warning, "Don't cross this line!"

I was angry; this was the way he had treated me before. I couldn't remember, but the feelings were there, and I wanted to lash out at him. I was about to rebuke his request by informing the king he didn't own me. His fear wasn't going to control me, but something held me back. It wasn't fear; I knew I wasn't afraid of him. Maybe I respected him; I hoped that was it. No, I have chosen to believe in God, and I have been born again. I need to act with reason and kindness. I won't talk back to my father. I will be the perfect child who makes his father proud. I will not give a nasty response.

My father was still angry and began tearing into Mother about her sister, but Mom won't argue with him. In her eyes, that was a no-no. Arnold could vent, and when he calmed down, everything would be fine. I sure didn't want a marriage like that. Women should have a say and not feel the man was right, all the time.

When we got home, I went to my room. I had bought a desk at a yard sale and put it in my bedroom. The temperature was in the thirties and dropping as the day progressed. I felt venturing outside on any activity wasn't inviting so I decided to stay in my room and read. I began studying some of my books from school, but the Bible was more appealing to me. Father started watching a football game and calmed down, he even invited me to join him, but I told him I was reading. He seemed to accept that and didn't push me to watch with him.

I started thinking of my relationship with my father, and I knew someday it would come to a head. He would explode, and I would tell him I had had enough. The more I reflected on my memory, the more of today's outburst seemed to be part of my past. Maybe the incident had a lot to do with him. Perhaps he drove me to it. My father had to be part of the incident, but it can't come out because it would be a final blow to his pride.

The more I think about my problem, the more I realize Father has to keep this hidden. The blowup today tells me he keeps a close guard on it. Even though Aunt Jean's question had nothing to do with the incident, there was something in her question that shows she knew what happened to me and maybe a conversation would tell me things Father never wanted me to realize.

A thought occurred to me that secrets always find a way to come out, but not always at the right time. What was the right time? I knew that whatever the mystery, I would have to face it. More thoughts of my father erupting today made me realize it would be a lot worse the next time. Maybe he would become violent. I ran this thought over in my mind, and somehow, I knew I would have to protect myself from him.

I had to stop these thoughts. I chose to play basketball because it would get my mind on other things and keep my grades up as consecrate it.

That had to be the answer. Those other thoughts scared me. The rest of the weekend, I either stayed in my room or practiced basketball. We had a long practice on Friday afternoon and worked on me, driving towards the basket. When I was double-teamed or picked up by another player there were plays, picks set by one player and another player, cutting to the basket for a layup. It wasn't always a specific offense, but the plan was to react to what the defender was doing. The crucial part was me scoring and the opponents trying to stop me.

If I could penetrate to the basket and score with either a short jump shot or a layup, the defense had to stop me by collapsing on me opening a shot for a teammate. But the coach still pushed teamwork, so we ran the offense. He told me privately that he didn't want me to dribble down the floor and shoot unless I had an open layup. He claimed the more people touch the ball, the better they felt like they were in the game. If they could set me up for a shot, that would make them feel good. They knew I had to score, but they wanted to be part of it.

I completely agreed with him, and I felt selfish if the ball wasn't passed around. I knew sometimes it was helpful, but as the ball was passed around and got to me, I was relaxed when I shot the ball. Playing team ball maybe feel good.

The coach also told my teammates, "If Jimmy is double- teamed and stopped, that's when a good pick and a break to the basket would leave an open player for a layup."

Coach was altering the concept of our defense. Instead of me being a small forward, he wanted me to be a center. I don't know why he changed, but I liked it. The centers on teams were usually not quick, and I could easily block their shots without fouling them.

Our next two games were against teams that played man to man. At first, I didn't mind being the primary scorer, but double-teaming allowed me to set teammates up for shots, and I liked passing as much as scoring. And all was not lost, if they couldn't get the ball from their picks, the offense was set for other players on the team. Joey could drive anytime he felt he could, or take outside shots when he was open. A lot of cuts to the basket from the picks were set for me, leaving others on our team open for an easy shot. Everyone on the team got passes from other teammates.

The offense was set around me, causing the opposing teams to try to stop me, thus leaving other players open. Without this play, Session's quickness and driving ability was a loss for our team.

After practice on Friday, Father was working, but Mother, Sandy, and I went to Tiffin for a little Christmas shopping. I was able to purchase most of the gifts I was giving to my family. Early in the evening, we ate at a restaurant. It was enjoyable spending time with Mother and Sandy, with no fear lurking around to spoil the moment.

The team had a short shoot-around on Saturday afternoon, and afterward, the starting five went to Enders. Glen couldn't come because he had chores to do on the farm. Other than that, I was mostly at home reading. My friends all had girlfriends, and Saturday night they spent time with them. I stayed at home.

I went to church and Sunday school as well as the youth group that met on Sunday night. I could see Brad Weiden liked my sister. They were together mostly during our youth session, and he sat beside her in church. I knew Father wouldn't approve. He didn't want any boys around Sandy, especially one who was a former hood, no matter what the circumstances were.

The more I thought about my father's strict dictatorship and the atmosphere of fear he created around himself to make people fear him, the more I hated it, I just hated it!

I wasn't spending time with my friends at lunch when we had free time because I didn't want to intrude with their time with there girlfriends. I was alone, except when Marsha sat by me and talked. There was no flirting, only a conversation about school. She's a friend, and that's the way I like it.

I wanted to ask her if I was the most popular boy in school, but I was sure Joey and my sister had to be wrong. The most popular guy had to be on the school council and be involved in other activities. Then I remembered that before I started playing basketball, those positions were determined. The thought was confusing, and I wanted no part of it.

Lately, when Marsha wasn't around, a couple of pretty Juniors were friendly to me, and our conversations were fun with no sparks for romance. If romance came, I hoped it would be with Marsha, but I felt a special woman was coming my way. I didn't know who it was, but I was sure it wasn't Marsha. The two Juniors talking to me also made me think it was only due to my popularity, but I had decided to accept it and enjoy it, and I refused to think about it anymore.

Chapter Twelve

On Friday night, December 7, 1962, Bettville, considered a below-average team, came to our gym to play against us. Old Fort had beat them, but they beat Republic, another team who, like us, was considered a bottom feeder, so it was predicted to be a close game.

~~~~~~~~~~

Elisabeth Hasselback pulled her Buick beside the pumps at Clyde's gas station. The petite young lady jumped out, and Clyde came to her car. "I was about to close up, but I'll make you my last customer."

Elisabeth was barely five-foot-two, and her body was almost perfect, short hair framed her pretty lightly freckled face, and two dimples appeared on her cheek when she smiled.

"I know it's a high school basketball game, but it looks like there's a larger crowd than I ever remembered," she commented as she stood a few feet from Clyde while he filled her car's gas tank.

The stop was a quick fuel up before she headed to her parents' farm. It was actually her mother's farm because her dad died last year. All she was thinking about was a warm house and hitting the books. She had eaten in at a restaurant in town.

"We have a star, Elisabeth. Do you remember Jimmy Bass?"

After a pause, while she seemed to be thinking of what to say, Clyde smiled, "I know you do, Elisabeth. I remember the two of you being friends."

She stood there with a shocked expression on her face, not believing what she had just heard. Then with her voice showing her excitement, she asked, "Did you say Jimmy Bass is back?"

"He sure is, Elisabeth, and he's the star of our team. Where have you been?"

"I, I.." she stuttered. "I don't know. I guess mostly at Heidelberg. Let me get this straight. Are you telling me Jimmy Bass is back? When?"

Clyde finished filling her car's fuel tank, and she handed him a twenty.

"Follow me to the office so I can get your change."

As they were walking side by side to the office, the conversation continued, "Yes, Elisabeth, he came back just before school started, but you probably wouldn't recognize him. He looks the same in the face, but he is close to six-foot-four now."

"Jimmy must have returned the same time I came home from Chicago." Then it dawned on her what Clyde had said. "Six foot four? You mean he's that tall?"

"Yes, he's that tall."

"He must be too old to play on the school's team?"

"That is where you are wrong. Jimmy missed only one year of school, and everybody is allowed to miss one year because of bad grades or being under a doctor's care."

131

Elizabeth followed Clyde into his office as he continued to talk. "Elisabeth, he doesn't remember a lot of his past. If you were to run into him, I doubt he would remember you. Remember that Pat Ender was a good friend of his? Jimmy saw Pat the first week he was back and still doesn't remember him. And that goes for a lot of other people he knew."

He handed her the change adding, "I need to close up."

Pausing for a few seconds, he went on. "Elisabeth, you can leave your car set if you want to go to the game. See?" he pointed out to his parking area around the garage. "Friends are already filling up my parking area. If you leave where you're parked, someone will take your spot. It's past the tip-off of the Junior Varsity game."

"I'll think about it," Elizabeth answered as she left the office and walked towards her car. The lights to the pumps went off, meaning the gas pumps were shut down for the night. She got into her 57 Blue Buick and sat there, her thoughts totally on Jimmy. She had cared for him at one time, then came, that horrible night that she tried to forget. But now, he was back. Would the memories of that night give her nightmares? Memories of when they were young and Jimmy worked for his Uncle Fred and farmed their farm.

~~~~~~~~~

Jimmy spent a lot of time on my family's farm, and we became friends. We were close in school, too, but only talking friends, nothing romantic. It wasn't until our Junior High when our special friendship started. Jimmy worked in our fields with a tractor and other equipment. I never could understand what to call each piece of equipment or what it did.

Mother was always sending me out with some lemonade or a Coke. Jimmy would shut the tractor off, and we would sit in the shade, on the ground, leaning against the tractor wheel and talk. That's when we became friends.

In high school, we continued to be friends, just friends, never boyfriend and girlfriend. I had enough credits to skip my Junior year, and people said I had a great brain. I can't remember ever getting anything but an "A" in high school.

Jimmy and I stayed close friends, but from February on, he started acting weird. I knew that part of the problem was the fact the coach didn't play him, and it made him upset.

Then came the letters about how I hurt him in what they called "the incident."

No, I won't go there. I'll only think of Jimmy the way he was before that time. We were friends, and that's it. But, now I want to see him play basketball. Yes, I do!

I walked towards the gym and found a seat close to the front with a couple who went to school with me. Beverly would have graduated with me if I hadn't skipped. She was in love with a guy named Ben, who graduated with me, and they were engaged.

During the Junior Varsity game, our conversation was mostly girl stuff and her upcoming wedding. Then we got on the topic of Jimmy. Beverly told me that what Clyde said was true about Jimmy, he didn't remember much about the past, he was tall, and he could shoot. We stopped talking when the Varsity came on the floor to warm up, and the home crowd stood up to cheer.

When I saw Jimmy, I was shocked, even though people told me how tall he was. It was unbelievable a little Jimmy grew up to be a giant. Oh, not a giant, but it was a great big leap in his height. Mostly I watched Jimmy. I was mesmerized by him. Again, I thought about how I had hurt him. If he remembered me, he would probably hate me for what I did to him.

~~~~~~~~~

After the warm-ups, it was time to announce the starting line ups, and old memories streamed in as I stood beside the bench. Even

133

though the announcer called the names of the other starting players; I felt he would never get to mine. I waited for him to say my name ao I could run onto the floor and receive the applause. Usually, I was the third called, being a small forward, but tonight it seemed I would be called last.

The announcer shouted, "Last but not least, Jimmy Bass."

My body tingled with excitement every time this happened, giving me a thrill I had never expected in my lifetime. As if a reminder from John, I thanked God for this moment. When I entered the floor for the game to start, things came into focus.

~~~~~~~~~

I felt a familiar tingle when the announcer called Jimmy's name. I remembered all those years he wanted to play, especially his Junior year, and how disappointed he was. At the time, I paid little attention. My thoughts were on other things, mostly on other boys. I remembered those times, but now it was different; Now, Jimmy was the star.

Cutler Ridge got the tip, and our offense started successfully. Brad tipped to Jimmy, and he drove toward the basket, passing the man guarding him, for an uncontested layup.

I watched a close match, but it was mostly the "Jimmy Bass game." My former friend did everything he could to help Cutler Ridge win; from shooting the long shot, rebounding missed shots, and scoring layups. His passing was setting up teammates for the ball. Joel Bell and Tim Ender had a good game.

~~~~~~~~~

It was a close game down to the wire. I kept my focus on the game as pressure built that we might lose. With a minute and a half to go, the score was fifty-eight to sixty, Bettville.

We had the ball, and my teammates were looking for me to score. Before scoring was okay, but now each shot meant a win, and the pressure was intense.

I put all fear behind me thinking this was why I had received my training. I concentrated on dribbling the ball and made a move as if I was going to drive. Then I stepped back and shot my outside shot. It went into the basket, and we tied the game.

I was relieved since I had missed the last two shots I had taken. I knew the pressure wasn't off because the team expected me to shoot in these situations.

Our defense held, and with less than a minute to go, we got the ball back. As I dribbled over the timeline, I tried to penetrate down the left side. Joey, the point guard, who had a good game, wanted nothing to do with these shots, so he stayed out of my way. I saw Brad's man slacking off of him along the baseline. He knew what I was trying to do, and he broke to the basket from the corner. A perfect bounce pass caught Brad's defender off guard and Brad had a layup that made two points.

Now the score was sixty-two to sixty with forty seconds left. The pressure was on Bettville, and they called a time out. Chumbly stressed defense and showed some plays designed to guard if they ran them. But he emphasized to look out for anything. His last words were, "Our team is out of time outs, so don't call any; And don't foul!

We played a tight defense as time ran off the clock. With only fifteen-seconds left, Bettville's guard took an outside shot, with Joey's hand almost in his face, and made it. That tied the game. Now, with close to ten seconds left, I had to take my last shot, and we had no timeouts!

Brad in-bounded the ball to me, and I drove quickly to the timeline with my defender tight on me. I promptly maneuvered to get the room so I could shoot but saw another player coming towards me. I wasn't even close to the proper range, just a couple of steps across the timeline. It was now or never. I took my outside shot, a defender went with me, but I knew I could out jump him. As I landed on the floor, my hand still pointed in a pose toward the baskets wish. We won sixty-four to sixty-two.

I stood there with my same pose, shocked that it went in the basket. Or was I relieved? Anyway, I was motionless until some of my teammates grabbed me with excitement.

Some of the fans with Pat Ender and his brother hoisted me up on their shoulders and ran around the floor then continued to the locker room. When I entered, everybody screamed and yelled about the game. I gave a silent prayer of thanks to God.

~~~~~~~~~~

I jumped and screamed when Jimmy made that last basket and, like other fans, I wanted to run onto the floor and congratulate him. But I remembered he wouldn't recognize me. That knocked the excitement out of me; I couldn't celebrate with one of my best friends. Does he remember what I did to him in his last days leading up to the incident? I felt hurt, but this memory was the truth. If he did remember me, he would probably hate me.

I remember the letter that Jimmy sent on February 12, 1961.

~~~~~~~~~~

Dear Elisabeth,

Why won't Summerall play me? We got buried twice this weekend, and everybody played except me. As soon as I got home, both nights, my father was on me, blaming me because I didn't play. He said I created shame for him, and I was a disappointment to him. He said people were talking about how pathetic I looked, the only one on the team who didn't play. Then he slapped me across the face several times saying how ashamed he was.

I escaped to my room and cried myself to sleep. I know you told me to leave you alone. We are in different classes, and you have other interests than a lonely, pathetic person like me. But, Elisabeth, I need your friendship. You're the only one to whom I can talk. I know I'm not good enough to be your boyfriend,

136

but you told me when we made a vow behind the barn on your farm, we would be friends forever. You even kissed me.

I thought, after that moment, you would like me forever. But I was wrong because a loser is always a loser. No one will ever love me. Most girls think the old slave is a loser. I never thought you would forsake me. But you have, and I'm all alone.

Your friend, Jimmy

~~~~~~~~~~

I folded the letter and put it back in the envelope. I felt terrible that I had treated an old friend like that. At the time, all I thought of was popularity and dating Jake Bickhart, the basketball star. He was the only thing on my mind. But all Jake wanted was to do me, and that was what he did.

Oh, what a fool I was. Jake, that charming snake, got what he wanted. It's a wonder I didn't get pregnant. How could a girl only five foot two with freckles attract the best looking, and the most popular guy in school? I gave him what he wanted and went along for the popularity.

"Stupid, Stupid, Stupid!" I cried, alone in my bedroom, sitting cross-legged in my pajamas on my bed. I didn't want to take the letters out. They have been in the back of the right lower desk drawer since the time I got them. Now something drew me to them. I grabbed another one, and it turned out to be the first one Jimmy wrote, the first of five. This one was enough. The pain of what I did to Jimmy was so intense after I got the letter, that I avoided him even more. He got my message and stayed away, too.

"I'm very sorry, Jimmy. I wish I could have a do-over. I would dump Jake and run to you," I breathed. I put the letter back into the drawer, closed it, and went to bed, but all I could do was cry.

Even though Jimmy stayed away, I watched from a distance. I could see the misery he was going through. I had talked to him many times about my problems and Jimmy always listened and was concerned. Why couldn't I do the same for him? Jake, the snake, was why! I cried myself to sleep.

~~~~~~~~~

I had a good time celebrating our win at Keller's. I had made twenty-seven points and seven assists, along with thirteen rebounds. Joey had a good game, scoring fourteen points and four assists. Tim earned twelve points, Brad got eight points, and Glen secured three points.

Everybody was patting me on the back. My teammates kept saying it was a great victory. As I was leaving through the front door of Miller's, Pat and his fiance Emily, walked with me since Pat had parked at the end of my street. I said good-bye to Pat, and Emily then walked to my house.

~~~~~~~~~

It was Saturday night, and I wasn't going to do anything, but I remained hooked on the game. A little later, I went to the balcony of the Old Fort gym and sat in the first row. The guy beside me was a man in his middle thirties with a large notebook sitting on his lap. I figured he might be a scout for another school, possibly a future school Cutler Ridge would play.

I had a small notebook and planned on using it to keep track of how many points Jimmy made. As the Cutler Ridge starting players were announced I stood up and cheered for them, especially when they announced Jimmy's name. As I sat down, the announcer called out the Old Fort starters, and I realized that most of the fans around me were for the home team. That wouldn't bother me, or prevent me from cheering with enthusiasm.

It was a close game at the start. Jimmy missed a few shots from the outside, but when he got going, it was good-by for Old Fort. He got the majority of the points for Cutler Ridge in the first half, mostly from the outside with a few rebounds from them fouling his shots. Having two older brothers who both played basketball, and started, I knew a thing or two about the sport.

Dad had built an outdoor basketball court, and I played with my brothers. I wish they had girls basketball, but there are no sports for girls, except volleyball and that was more recreational. No one came to see the games.

I remembered that when we were close friends, Jimmy talked about his dream, not as a big scorer, but as a starter playing, what he called, "team ball," and that's what they're playing now. There were a lot of picks and cuts until Jimmy had a shot. I learned all about picks and cuts from my brothers. Our team was scoring points, but they were going for Jimmy. Joey was cold except for a couple of driving layups and Weiden wouldn't shoot. It seemed the whole team wanted to let Jimmy do all the shooting, and he did.

I cheered for Jimmy, but the older man beside me didn't like it, especially when we went ahead. It's seemed the coach of Cutler Ridge wanted Jimmy to take most of the shots, and he got them mostly from outside. If he drove to the basket, the defense would cut him off. A pass to another teammate was mainly to a player called Weiden.

Jimmy's long shots were a thing of beauty, a perfect arch that hit nothing but net. He made twenty points in the first half while Cutler Ridge made thirty-five points, bringing the halftime score to thirty-five and twenty-five. Jimmy and his team were kicking the home team's butt.

The man sitting beside me leaned over and asked me, "Do you think your team has a chance to win? I know they have the lead, and Bass has put on quite a show, but I doubt that Old Fort will let him continue to shoot."

Looking at the man, I answered. "I hope you're wrong. We haven't beat Old Fort in a long time."

139

After pausing for a few seconds to think, I went on, "I can't remember the last time we won."

"I see you're keeping track of Bass' points. Are you a friend of his?"

"We used to be."

"When was that?"

The question caught me off guard. Nobody needed to know that, especially somebody from another school. Jimmy's secret was nobody's business, particularly things between the two of us.

I countered, "Why do you want to know?"

"Well, he comes out of nowhere and is this big star. As a sportswriter for the Advertising Tribune and one who covers the Seneca Country Schools, I know every player, except him. Wouldn't you be curious?"

"Maybe, but it is a story nobody should know. I guarantee that he was born and raised in Cutler Ridge, and that is the only school he ever attended."

An Old Fort fan sitting beside me cut in stating, "I'm almost fifty, and I know a lot of people from Cutler Ridge. If he's from there, who are his parents and what does his father do?

I turned to the fan and said, "His father works at ITF, and I think he's a big shot there."

"I'm a foreman at ITF. Who are you talking about, Miss?"

I looked him square in the face. I hate to be called Miss, so I retorted," My name is Elizabeth and Jimmy's father is Arnold Bass!"

The expression on the guy's face was one of surprise. "Did you say that player that scored most of the points against us is my boss, Arnold Bass's son?"

A couple of guys behind him said in surprise, "What are you talking about, Joe? Who is Arnold Bass's son?"

Joe quickly turned around, looked at them, and said, "The player who's beating us, the big kid who could shoot all over. According to this woman, he is Arnold Bass's son."

The word spread quickly around in the balcony. Most of the fans must have been workers from ITF.

"There's a year missing. Where was Bass for the last year?"

I stared at him and thought of what I should say. "A simple answer is Jimmy was gone last year, and he came back as a good player. What else do you need to know? I'm sure the State School Board knows all about him for him to be eligible."

"I checked with them, and all they told me was that the records had been sealed. They said Bass was under a doctor's care."

"There you have it. I can't tell you any more. If I knew something, I wouldn't be able to tell you because it's a private matter. If you want that kind of information talk to Jimmy or his parents."

Down in the locker room, Coach Chumbly was having a serious talk about why the other players weren't shooting when they had a good chance. Old Fort has begun to double-team and triple-team Jimmy so he can't score. He is our leading scorer, but he can't do it all by himself. He continued to stress teamwork until the players went out on the floor to warm up for the second half.

~~~~~~~~~~

We had an excellent first half, especially me, but that all ended when the third quarter began. What coach stressed was right. My teammates couldn't expect me to do all the scoring. I wanted to say something, but it wasn't for me to say.

The second half, they were more physical primarily towards me. Old Fort's defender guarded me carefully and would foul me

141

rather than let me shoot, and they were hard fouls, sometimes knocking me to the floor. I knew they were trying to intimidate me so that I would be afraid of them, and when I shot, fear of them hitting me would make me shoot differently, but that wouldn't get me. I played rough in Tennessee, and that didn't scare me.

Suddenly another thought came to me. I've been beaten so severely in the past that these players don't bother me. I knew this had to be correct, but I had no memory of it.

The referees called a lot of fouls, and we were one-on-one. Every time I went shoot a one-on-one foul, I got points. The rest the players were following the coaches orders. When they had a chance, they shot it. Some helped us keep our lead. Old Fort cut our lead down to six points.

The fourth quarter started with Old Fort double-teaming me, determined I wasn't going to get the ball, leaving Joey or Rendles open. They were successful, mostly driving and drawing one of the prominent defenders to them and leaving Tim or Brad for an inside shot. Old fort stayed close throughout the quarter and took the lead, sixty to fifty-nine at the last minute.

They always had a man guarding me when we took the ball out of bounds on the home team's court, fronting so I couldn't get the ball. This time I got loose, but the double-team caught me before I could do anything. But I wanted the ball, so I broke the baseline as I had before. But this time, after a few steps, I broke up the middle.

Tim, who was taking the ball out of bounds, got me the ball. The next obstacle was the defender at half court. A couple of fancy moves with my dribbling and I was around him. There were two big men to the left, so I went between them for a shot. I pushed the shot just over the basket to the backboard, and it went in. As soon as I released the ball, I got clobbered.

I expected it, but I wanted to get the shot off before anyone hit me, I crumbled backward to the floor. Quickly moving my body around, I got one hand behind me to break my fall. I landed lightly, then jumped to my feet. There was no pain because I was too pumped up to feel it.

I was trying to get a one-and-one but feared it wouldn't work. Then the referee surprised me by saying I was fouled after the shot, giving me a one-and-one off of the foul line.

With absolute concentration to keep the pressure from getting to me, I made both shots. That gave us a three-point lead with a score of sixty-three to sixty.

~~~~~~~~~~

Sitting in the balcony, I saw Jimmy shoot the two foul shots. Old Fort, on offense, couldn't score and Jimmy got the rebound with twenty seconds to go. He dribbled down the court, trying to avoid getting fouled, but they hit him and pushed him to the floor. I hoped he wasn't hurt and to my relief, he got up quickly and went to the foul line making both shots. Old Fort called time out with ten seconds to go, and Glen came in for Jimmy to roaring applause.

After the time out, Old Fort got two shots off, but both missed, and the game came to an end. The coach rushed his players off the court for fear there would be a fight.

The final score was sixty-five to sixty. Jimmy had made thirty-two of the points. According to Allen Jamison, the stats said Jimmy had twelve rebounds and five assists. Joey had made twelve points, Weiden scored twelve, Ender got six, Glen made two, and Rendles made one point.

The Old Fort fans around me were upset, but they were gracious to me. They gave a standing ovation to Jimmy when he came out of the game. Was it because of the game he played or were they trying to make points with their boss? I bet they will remind their boss about his son and the game he played when they see Arnold Monday.

~~~~~~~~~

In the locker room, Coach told us why he wanted to get to the locker room so quickly. He thought there might be a fight. When he came to me, he stopped and asked, "Jimmy, how are you? You took quite a beating in the game. It looked like one or two of Old Fort's players might start a fight with you at the end of the game. They were calling you all kinds of names. That's why I took you out of the game when I did."

"I didn't hear a thing, Coach. I block out everything except your voice. What were they saying to me?"

"Really, Jimmy?" Coach asked with a surprised look.

"That's right, Jerry," John added.

"What were they saying?" I asked.

"They said you were a psycho and belonged in a nuthouse. They called you a crazy man. Things like that. But you know the reason they hate you is because of the points you scored."

"Has this happened before? Have they called me psycho and things like that?"

"No," Tim put in.

I was angry. "John, what should I do? They got it all wrong. I had low self-esteem and felt worthless, not crazy. Should I talk to the Old Fort team and set them straight?"

"No, Jimmy, let it go. I'll write a letter to the coach and the principle to set them straight." John answered.

I nodded my head at John, then said to Coach Chumbly, "I'm okay. I can take a beating. There are scars all over my body showing I've received several. They played a rough game in Tennessee. I might

144

have a few new bruises, but that's okay. We won, and that is all that counts. We beat Old Fort, and we are still undefeated. The whole locker room erupted in a cheer.

~~~~~~~~~~

Outside of Old Fort's gym, a man Allen didn't recognize came up to him as he was walking to his car. Allen stopped when the man asked him to.

"You don't know me, but I know you, Mr. Jamison? I've got something to tell you about the Bass kid. He was locked up in a State Mental Intuition in Nashville, Tennessee. They say he was psycho, crazy, out of his mind, and he shouldn't be playing high school basketball. What if he freaks out on the floor and hurts someone? He belongs in an insane asylum, not on a basketball floor. Check it out!" Then he turned and left before Allen could ask any questions.

He figured something like this was the reason Bass' absence for the year. The State Athletic department had listed "doctor's care" to explain his missing year.

"So, he had a mental problem. Don't a lot of people in the world?" Jamison reasoned. "No matter what happens to the kid, people don't need to know about his mental health. There would be no more inquiries with Cutler Ridge fans.

There would be no write up on him that would bring more attention to him unless I have some real evidence he is a danger to others.

Chapter Thirteen

The number of points I made this weekend was unreal! There were twenty-seven points against Bettsville and thirty-two more tonight against Old Fort. Uncle Walter taught me a lot of ways to shoot and how to make the almost perfect shot from the outside. There seemed to be no competition to stop me unless they doubled teamed me.

Some people might call me a gunner, but that kind of person is out to shoot for himself. I don't shoot for myself. I shoot for the team. I loved setting up a teammate for a shot, and so far, we were successful. Joey Bell had a big game tonight, and so did the big men. Without their scoring, we probably would have lost. It was a team effort!

Maybe I could have scored forty or forty-five points, but would we still would have won. The rest of the year, I may have to score the most significant part of the points, but with the rest of the team scoring and good defense, it's a team effort.

What I learned in the locker room had me scared, or at least it disturbed me. Why were players saying things like that to me? Was it because I was their enemy on the basketball floor, or was it something else? Their hits on me were unusually rough. Were they trying to hurt me?

I know the referees were not calling many fouls. The way I looked at it, the refs were letting us play. But they called the rough fouls on me. I made at least seven points on the foul line in the third quarter. Even after all the foul shots I made, from Old Fort fouling me, they kept being rough with me, and sometimes the referees let the fouls go. I suppose what they said to me was to make me angry and start a fight and get me thrown out of the game. Of course, an Old Fort player would have to go out, too. But their player wouldn't be as good as me, so with me out of the game they would win. They are used to easily beating Cutler Ridge regularly. That could be why they were so rough.

~~~~~~~~~~

Joey and I were sitting on the bus back to Cutler Ridge. Since his girlfriend wasn't a cheerleader, Joey liked to sit with me and encourage me on how I played the game. He was co-captain with Tim and seemed to believe it was his duty to do this.

Tonight, after a silent period, he said. "Jimmy, how are you doing after hearing what the Old Fort said to you?"

"Somebody told them some lies, Joey. Think about it. How would they know that I had, mental problems? Only the people in our community know or care about my problem. An enemy, someone who hates me and wants to hurt me got to the Old Fort players and told these lies to them."

"You have a point, Jimmy, but don't worry about it. This incident is probably isolated and the team, along with a lot of people in town. have your back."

Nothing more was said as we entered Cutler Ridge and came to the downtown area. People were waiting for us and milling around us on the sidewalk.

147

"Can you believe that?" Joey cried out." The welcoming crowd is the biggest, so far. I think everyone from Cutler Ridge is here. It's a lot bigger than last nights crowd!"

"Unbelievable!" Tim cried out. "And we've won only five games."

"It's beating Old Fort!" Rendles yelled.

It was wild as we left the bus. There was a celebration at Keller's, and everybody on the team enjoyed it.

I remembered coming home on the bus on another weekend. It was horrible. Jude Simpson and his girlfriend, Janet, were making out in front of me. Oh, how I wished I had a girlfriend, but no one wanted me.

Elisabeth wasn't a cheerleader at least I didn't have to watch her make out with Jake. I wish she loved me, or at least we were friends like she had promised.

~~~~~~~~~~

Dear Elisabeth,

You said we were young and didn't know what we were doing, but I am in pain, and you are happy. That wasn't fair. We used to be friends, and you always seemed to understand what I was going through. I need someone to listen to me, to hear me, to care about me. I thought you would always be that person, but I guess not.

I cry all the time. The pain pounds me so hard that I don't know where to turn. I want the basketball season to be over.

I asked Summerall why he didn't play me as my father told me to do, but Summerall didn't pay any attention to me. It was like he didn't hear me or care. No one seems to care. My father claims it is all my fault, and if I were a man, things would be better for me. What is going to happen to me? I seem to keep going under more and more.

I thought you would be the one person who would be concerned, but I guess I am wrong. You don't care. You have Jake, and everybody is happy, except me.

Jimmy Bass

~~~~~~~~~

I sat on my bed, reading Jimmy's second letter to me before the incident. He certainly experienced pain, and I could have helped him, but I chose not to. I don't know why I didn't. Jimmy's second letter showed me he was in pain, but I ignored him thinking he was stupid. He didn't have to act or feel like that.

Tonight's celebration should make Jimmy happy. Everybody in town was proud of him. I wish he remembered me. I was close enough to him for me to tell him it was a good game, but he didn't recognize me. I wish he would. Maybe it's better that he doesn't remember the way I treated him before he went off into his silent world in the skating rink. He was in a different world and didn't know anyone around him. He just stared into space, and I caused that.

Jake called him all kinds of names while Jimmy sat on the floor and cried. I thought Jake was heartless that night, but Jake thought he was going to get in my pants that night, he had before. He was surprised. That was the night I broke up with him.

~~~~~~~~~

On Friday, December 14, I was on a bus for a game in Republic. I felt this should be an easy game, but Coach had been pounding into our heads, "Sometimes, these are the hardest games to win! They might play a box-in-one, one defender guarding and the rest of the team playing a two-two defense and me, two players in front, between the foul line and the top of the key and two people close to the basket. If they played this defense, our offense would be the same as we did against New Reigal."

149

All week long, the paper had something in it about how we beat Old Fort and won our whole season, so far. Old Fort was supposed to be the best team in the league, and the experts were still predicting them to win the league. Some fans believed that our bubble would burst, and we would end up one of the worst teams in the league. The experts said the wins over Old Fort and Hopewell were flukes and soon I would be shut down because I couldn't keep the same pace I'd been going. That gave me an incentive to prove those experts wrong. I hoped the team felt the same way.

Republic has a weird little gym. One side has regular seats with a three-foot wall in front of them. The benches and scoring table are directly behind the wall. To get onto the floor, you have to go through a gate. On the opposite side is a stage almost as long as the floor, with a big set of bleachers, like those used at a football or baseball field. The playing area has three-foot-high walls like the stage and the other seating. The end of the gym is a regular wall.

At first, the game was close. Both teams played excellent defense. Republic's defense was a regular two-three zone; there was no box-in-one on me. I played on the wing, but with our switching offense again, sometimes in the corner. At first, I didn't shoot, trying to get in the flow with the rest of the team. But with Joey not hitting from the point guard position and Brad and Tim pretty boxed in underneath, Republic earned an eleven to six lead at the halfway point of the quarter. Up to this point, I had taken no shots and kept trying to find other players open for shots. None was, and when they were, they missed.

I knew I had to shoot, but when I did, I missed because I wasn't following through correctly. On defense I got some steals to score and one stick-back to give me six points in the first quarter to pull us closer to Republic. At the end of the first quarter, Republic's lead was thirteen to twelve.

In the second quarter, I missed my first two outside shots but got a rebound from ten feet. I wasn't the only one missing shots. The rest of the team was missing, too. Brad and Tim were now playing high post, there was no switching, and I was on the left wing. We did a lot of passing, looking for the perfect shot, and I was frustrated about what was happening. Why couldn't I hit the outside shots? The team needed my shots if we were going to win. Then I remembered what the experts said about me being shut down. I played a lousy game, and no matter what I did, I would miss.

These thoughts stayed with me for a while and almost had me convinced. Then an idea came to me from out of the blue, "Backboard shot from the deep wing."

I had the ball, shot it, it kissed the backboard then went in. I made three more in a row. Their defense couldn't stop me. If I had the ball, I could out jump any of their players.

Joey determined I was to be doing the shooting even if he was open. A high pass got me the ball, but Republic stopped me and fouled me before I could make the shot.

No one-on-one foul shots yet, so an out of bounds pass from Joey to me brought a double team on me around the top of the key and a pass to Tim at high-post. He shot and made it.

The rest of the quarter went to the team. Republic was bound to stop me by denying me the ball, by overplaying a defense with one defensive guard and defensive wingman. Both defensive men were out of position, creating open shots for my teammates with quick sharp passes.

We cruised to a twenty-eight to eighteen halftime lead. Believe it or not, I made only twelve points.

The second half, Republic played their regular defense. I hit some outside points and some offensive rebounds, along with the rest of the team. We cruised to a sixty-seven to fifty-one win. I made twenty-eight points in the game.

151

Celebrating at Keller's was relaxing as I sat with two of the cheerleaders, both of whom were Juniors and wanted me to sit with them. Other guys who were out of school were hitting on them, but the girls wanted no part of them. I had become relatively good friends with them at school and had discussed reasons we couldn't date. Lois was a tall, thin Redhead who was good looking, in my opinion. So was Ruth, a five-foot-three brunette.

Lois liked me but agreed we couldn't date. Her father didn't trust me, but that was all she would say. I knew the reason was my former mental condition.

I wanted to sit with Marsha, but she was with a couple of guys she knew. I didn't know who they were, but I was sure they were out of school and seemed to be very close friends. I shouldn't be jealous, but I was, even though I knew better.

Our conversation wasn't about school or the game. Lois was giving Ruth advice about which boy she should like, who was good looking, and who was not. I thought it was funny that I sat with two attractive girls who were talking about other boys.

I notice Sandy was with a group of girls, and Brad was with a Senior girl who went to our church. I wondered what happened to Sandy and Brad. Maybe it was for a good reason.

Sandy saw me and came over to ask me if she could walk with me when I went home. I told her, yes, and she smiled. Then she left.

I was eating a hamburger and drinking a Coke when I saw a woman across the room. I knew she didn't go to our school. She introduced herself to me through Pat as a former friend. But I couldn't remember her.

She was a small woman, about the size of Ruth and she had the cutest face I could remember seeing and wore her brunette hair short.

152

Suddenly I remembered that I was in love with her. Or was I?

The memory was hazy, but It made me want to know more.

When she started to leave, Lois began talking strangely to me. Was she flirting with me? No, that couldn't be.

I had finished eating and was ready to leave, but I didn't want to be rude to Lois, so I got into a conversation with her about school. She leaned closer to me. I couldn't believe it. Was she was flirting or merely being friendly and got carried away? Lots of guys would say go with the flow. I was a Christian and couldn't get in a situation by going with the flow.

Maybe I was wrong about the whole situation, but I didn't want to take a chance, especially after seeing the woman I am sure I loved at one time. I tried to talk to her, but my opportunity was gone.

I had to talk to Pat and learn more about her and not go with the flow with the minor I was sitting beside. If I dated anybody in school, I would try for Marsha.

So I quickly excused myself and told the girls I had to go home. I motioned to Sandy, letting her know I was leaving. Lois asked me if she could drive me home. The girls paid for their meals and left the table when I did following me out. Was Sandy behind me?

Outside, Lois again asked about driving me home. I said no. Meanwhile, fans all around were congratulating me over my game. Some wanted to talk with me, and I was willing, but the girls grabbed my arms, one on each side, and said he is with us. I shrugged my shoulders and smiled at my fans. I didn't want to be in this situation, but what could I do? They couldn't do anything to me. Sandy was right behind me, and I wasn't sure if the girls knew that.

~~~~~~~~~~

My brother sure is in trouble, Lois and Ruth are going after him. I know it's mainly Lois, she's always talking about him, but I know my brother doesn't want to go with either of them. That's why he keeps looking at back at me. I'm going to stay with him, and I'll even but in if the girls get too crazy. So I walked with them and hardly said a thing.

~~~~~~~~~

Lois walked close to me, and I could tell she wanted me to hold her hand. Her presence tempted me, but she's a minor and her father doesn't trust me. I said good-bye when we got to their car at the end of the street. They started to protest, but just then Sandy walked up to me and said, "You ready to go home?"

I nodded yes and started walking with her, then asked, "Did you and Brad break up?"

"I had to, Jimmy, if dad found out he would have killed me. Besides, Brad's too old for me. If I have a boyfriend, I want one from my grade in school."

"I understand, it was probably for the best. Now I want to ask you a question. Did you see that short brunette girl? She's the girl that Pat had introduced me to. I think she said her name was Elizabeth Hasselback."

Sandy laughed and said. "That's a girl you had a crush on, Jimmy, but she dumped you for Jake."

"How would you know? You were in eighth grade."

"I know a lot about you, Jimmy. You were mad at Jake because she was dating him."

"So she's out of school. Would she have graduated with me?"

"No, well, she would have if she hadn't skipped a grade. She graduated with Jake, skipping her junior year. I heard she left town, but I guess she didn't. I think she went to some musical college in Chicago. Maybe she's back or on holiday vacation. But I don't know.

154

I don't think she's married. If she were, it would be spread all over town by her mother. If she wanted you, she would be right down your alley, Brother. She's probably close your age or maybe a little older.

~~~~~~~~~

Elisabeth sat in her pajamas on her bed, holding Jimmy's third letter. She had never read it. The envelope remained sealed. She opened it and began reading:

March 2, 1961

Dear Elisabeth,

Friday is our last game. I know I won't play, but I have to finish because Father says Bass's aren't quitters. However, that isn't the reason I'm writing to you. God is punishing me, Elisabeth. The pain I'm suffering has to come from God. I must be so worthless that even God doesn't want me, or He loves punishing me.

Maybe, I did a horrible sin, and I need this punishment.
Whatever it is, it hurts. The pain is so severe that I want to crawl into a hole and die. I can't talk about death. Suicide is wrong, for I would automatically go to Hell, a place I do not want to go!

Why is God punishing me with this unbearable pain? What have I done to deserve this? All I want is love. That is all I want, but I'm not allowed. All I get is punishment, punishment, and more punishment. I hurt and cry, wondering if this is the way my life will always be.

Elisabeth, help me. You are the only friend I have. It doesn't have to be romance, just friendship. Maybe you can direct me to a girl who might like me. I need your friendship, Elisabeth.

Jimmy

~~~~~~~~~

155

I was in tears after seeing this letter and knowing I had not read it. All I can recall are the ominous looks I got from Jimmy around the time he wrote this letter. I had more things on my mind. I was with Jake and the envy of all the other girls in school. Jake knew how close I was to Jimmy, and he kept telling me to leave the "slave" alone. I obeyed my king as he wanted me to call him. Now I feel I was stupid.

When Pat introduced me to Jimmy, I was sure he would remember me. He stared into my eyes as if something connected. But that cheerleader he was sitting with seemed interested in him. Maybe they are dating. As I drove my car down Main Street, Jimmy was walking close beside her, almost holding her hand. Why wouldn't he have a girlfriend? But Pat said he didn't. I feel jealous. Do I still love for him? I hope so!

Chapter Fourteen

On Saturday morning, December fifteen, I arrived at John's for counseling. I told him, "I feel as if an inner spirit is trying to tell me I had a bad game. Just as the experts predicted I would. It felt as if I were shutting down."

"I remember some sports writer writing that in the paper. But I know it was only his opinion."

"I know, and it fired me up when I couldn't make my shots. The thought worked on me and made me believe it. Out of the blue, a thought came to me, 'Use the backboard.' I did, and everything turned around. Could that be God talking to me? Was it Satan trying to tell me I was going to have a bad game?"

"It could be. No, I think it is. Remember, you used to have very low self-esteem, and you still suffer from low self-esteem. Satan uses that to get you down. He isn't happy with you. He had you all to himself, but now you're a Christian, and he doesn't like it, so you need plenty of prayer and confidence. Why weren't you shooting at the beginning?"

"I was trying to get into the flow of the game and thought maybe my teammates would score. I guess that's why, but I'm not sure."

"Jimmy, you see how your fellow teammates work?"

"Yes, it wasn't until I hit those outside shots, that they started scoring. I know that's the point. When Satan is working on me, I have to start scoring to get my teammates going, or we will lose. I knew it!"

"Jimmy that's honorable of you to want to get into the flow, and most coaches would honor that attitude. I know our coach preaches that all the time, but our team is different. We need you to score right at the start. Fire away from outside, if you miss, make the adjustments. Make sure, at the top of your jump, before you push the ball towards the basket, use fingertip control. With your height, you think you can score inside, and you can, Jimmy. You will probably have a good average there, but our team wouldn't be as good."

John paused for a breath, then he added, "You're a great outside shooter. Even though you practice, it is a gift from God, and your height makes it hard to stop you. One thing you do that other shooters never do is to follow your shot, even the shots of your teammates. That's why you get to score inside. First, you have to establish your outside shot."

I agreed with everything John said, and I replied, "I think I've found the girl I was close to in school. My sister says I was in love with her, but she wasn't in love with me. Saturday night, at Keller's, Pat Ender introduced me to Elizabeth Hasselback. She awoke a memory from my past. If she wanted someone to introduce her to me, she must have wanted to talk to me. I couldn't speak to her on Saturday night because two cheerleaders wouldn't leave me alone. I think one desperately wants me. They asked me to walk them to their car, but my sister, Sandy, was right behind me. She asked me earlier if I would walk her home, so I did. I don't know what happened after

158

the girls got into their car.

After a short pause, I confessed, "I sure would like to dump those two cheerleaders and see if I could talk to Elizabeth, but if I do, Judith will leave me."

"How does it feel to be popular?"

"I guess it's okay, but I can't convince these young girls I can't date them because of my age."

"Most boys wouldn't think that way. I'm glad you do."

~~~~~~~~~

Tuesday afternoon, I was in History class when Superintendent John Shumer came into the room and motioned for me to go with him. When I reached the hall, he told me to follow him to his office. I asked what was going on, but he wouldn't answer. It felt like he was mad at me, but I couldn't figure out why.

We went into a conference room that was full of people. Lois Havion was sitting with a big man who scowled at me. I figured he was her father. Ruth Drown was sitting with whom I assumed was her mother. My parents were there, too, along with John Wood, my coach, and counselor. Superintendent Shumer asked me to sit with my parents and gave me a letter to read.

~~~~~~~~~

Dear Superintendent Shumer,

I saw something alarming on Friday night. Your basketball star, who is a mental case and who shouldn't be allowed in our school, got into Lois Havion's car. They drove into the country and went parking. I sneaked close to the car, and he was having sex with her. He is a pervert. Maybe that is the reason he ended up in the mental institution. If not, he came out being one. He should have stayed in the nut house. He doesn't belong in a peaceful school, where girls and boys know very little about sex. This kind of activity is disgraceful, and he should be run out of town on a rail. I'm not the only one who has seen him leave with girls, walk to their car, and drive off together. Ask around. I have added a list of

159

people who also saw him go with them.

Concerned Citizen

~~~~~~~~~

It hurt that someone would lie and say this incident happened. Who could hate me that much? Maybe it was Sessions or someone I couldn't remember. I didn't know how many enemies I had from my past who hated me so much; they would write a lie like this.

Superintendent Shumer said. "I called the people on the list. They all claim to have seen Jimmy walking with Lois and Ruth as they left Keller's, and going to her car. That was all. No one said Jimmy got into the car with them, except the concerned citizen who wrote the letter."

Both girls were crying, and I felt like doing the same thing.

The man sitting beside Lois looked at me and announced, "I'm Art Havion, Lois's father, and I want an answer from you!"

I don't know why I answered like this, but somehow I felt it was the right thing to say. Instead of giving Mr. Havion an answer, I asked him, "What did Lois say?"

"He wouldn't listen to me, Jimmy. I'm sorry!" she blurted out. Her father gave her a dirty look, so she lowered her head and continued crying.

"I want your answer!" Mr. Havion growled angrily.

I sure wouldn't want to meet him in a dark ally. Fear gripped me to a point I felt like crying. How could anybody write those lies about me?

Very emotionally, I answered Lois' enraged father. "Sir, I walked your daughter and Ruth to your daughter's car, parked at the end of my street. Then I told them good-bye, and I went home."

160

"Who saw you?" he snapped. "How do I know you went home?"

I didn't know what to say to him. Should I tell them about Sandy walking with me? Why hadn't his daughter told him about Sandy? It might be too much for my little sister. I decided not to say anything about Sandy, but Ruth took that decision away from me. "He walked home with his sister, Sandy."

"Is that true?" Snapped Lois's father."

I thought Father would say something about Sandy and try to protect me, but no, he wasn't acting like a good father. I had to handle this all by myself.

"It's true, but I don't think you should bring Sandy in here so that you can yell and scream at her. She doesn't need to hear all his crap your hanging on me. Ask my mother," I shouted as I looked at Mother.

"I have told him, Honey, but he won't believe me," Mother cried. "Ruth is right, Mr. Havion. Sandy walked home with Jimmy."

"Maybe she is right, but he could have sneaked out of the house and met my daughter later on. I want to interview the sister."

I could see my father was finally going to say something, but I stopped him. I had heard a mistake in Mr. Havion's response.

"That isn't what the letter said, Mr. Havion. The person who wrote the letter claimed they followed us."

"Ok," Lois's father said, looking at me. "What did you do when you left my daughter, and what time did you get home? I still want to talk to your sister. I have a right to talk to her."

It was time for Father to speak up, but he didn't. Lois and Ruth had been in tears since I had entered the room, causing me to wondered how many times they had told Lois's father the truth, and he didn't believe them.

161

"Mother and I watched the news and a movie. After that, I went to bed at one or one-thirty."

"Okay then," Superintendent Shumer announced. "Whoever wrote this letter is lying and trying to get Jimmy in trouble. Jimmy did nothing wrong, so let's dismiss this meeting."

"I have more questions I want to ask the kid. Why did you go to the insane asylum? Was the letter right that you are a sexual pervert after you went to the nut house?" Mr. Havion accused.

"No, That is a lie! I had a feeling of worthlessness and had absolutely no confidence in myself. I was afraid of girls. There is no way I could be a pervert!"

My father spoke up for the first time. He had an angry tone of voice. "That's enough about what happened to him and why he had to go to an institution. It is none of your business. It's a family matter."

Father wouldn't tell the truth that I was never in a mental institution. I almost said, "Father lied. I was never in an insane asylum." But for some reason, I didn't. Maybe it was respect for Father, or perhaps it was fear of him.

"Yes, it is." Lois's angry father stated. "But I don't want your perverted son around the rest of the girls in the school. Okay, how many girls have you dated since coming back to school, Star?"

"Don't answer him, Jimmy. He doesn't need to know your business."

I was happy my Father was sticking up for me, but he didn't need to. So I answered in a stern voice, to let him know I was handling a situation, "Father, I can talk for myself."

I turned to Mr. Havion, "First of all, Mr. Havion, I was never in an insane asylum or a mental hospital. I stayed with my uncle after I came out of my coma. He is a psychiatrist. Either he or his wife was

162

with me most of the time, especially when I was the most vulnerable. I came here to school for two things: to finish my Senior year and to play basketball. Girls are a no-no, not because I am a recovering sex pervert, which I'm not. I suffered from low self-esteem, and I would have hurt myself before I would hurt anybody else, let alone any girl."

Father finally got to say something. He was trying to cut in all the time I was telling Mr. Havion how it was.

"Jimmy, that is none of their business!" my Father growled.

I cut my father off, knowing he wouldn't like it, but I didn't care. "Trust me, Father, I don't date girls in school. They are minors, and I'm eighteen. I will be nineteen in February. So the answer to your question of how many girls I've dated so far is NONE! If I wanted to date one and she agreed I would ask the parents first."

"You weren't in an insane asylum? It's all over town that you were!"

My father blurted out, "That's none of your business!"

"Everybody in school knows what caused his problems," Lois blurted out. "He was lonely, and the bullies picked on him. A lot of girls I knew, thought he was a sweet guy. That's why I wanted to be his friend. A lot of the girls in school would like to be his friend. But our parents don't trust him. I can't understand why."

"So you liked him before?"

"No, Dad, but I always thought he was a nice guy, and still do. Before he had his problem, he liked Elisabeth Hasselback. But she didn't like him. I felt sorry for him because he would have been a much better boyfriend for Elisabeth then that arrogant Jake Bickhart, who thought he was King of the school."

"That is enough, Lois. I have to get back to work."

Without saying another word, I quickly stood up to leave the room. I knew it was over.

"It sounds like the letter was a hoax. Somebody is out to get this Bass kid, but I'll be watching him closely, and my daughter will not date him."

"Of course," I said. "I don't want to date Lois or any other girl in my school. After all the things said about me, I feel like a fool."

After a pause to calm things down, Superintendent Shumer declared, "What I see here, people, is somebody trying to accuse Jimmy of awful things he, Lois, and Ruth supposedly did. I suppose why this person tried to create this lie, was to hurt Jimmy and ruin the reputation of these two girls."

I said good-bye to my parents and headed back to class, wondering who could have done this. Was it Session? Would he be that hateful to me? It had to be him. I should tell Shumer. No, I couldn't accuse Session unless I was sure. Then a thought came to me. It had to be my past that I couldn't remember. Maybe it was Jake. Everyone was talking about him. I heard he hurt me, but why would he want to bother me now. I should be the one who would want to hurt him. I am confused.

~~~~~~~~~~

At three-thirty, the last bell rang, signaling the end of the school day, and players began heading for the locker room to dress for practice. Coach Chumbly was in his office with John Wood. As soon as John sat down on the chair across the desk from Jerry, he asked, "Well, what happened?"

"The letter was all lies. Somebody saw a situation and tried to create something immoral out of it. Jimmy didn't do anything but walk a couple of girls to their car, parked at the end of his street, then he went home, with his sister. His alibi was his mother. She said the same thing, they watched the news and then a movie together. The girls agreed that they didn't go anywhere with Jimmy."

"Did the girls have an alibi?"

"It was never brought up. Art Havion was the one who brought up the complaint from the letter. I guess duplicate letters got sent to Havion and Shumer's office. He didn't want to hear the girls stories he wanted to hear from Jimmy."

"He didn't believe his daughter?"

"I don't think so."

"You think the rest of the players know.?"

"Probably they only know that Jimmy got called out of class."

"Go, bring him here, and talk to him."

But I have one more question. Do you think this lie was aimed to hurt Jimmy and not the girls?"

"I think you are correct; but who knows."

Could this be Session? I know he hated Jimmy with a passion. That's the way he acted and said when he departed from the team."

"It could be, but I don't believe he would do that."

"I'm going to Shumer and suggest Session."

After a quick pause, Jerry stood and said, "Go get Jimmy."

Five minutes later, John and Jimmy were in the coach's room. John sat behind the desk with Jimmy in front.

"What did you think after that meeting today?" asked John. "I want you to know I am proud of the way you stuck up for yourself today. You told them the truth about the insane asylum. I'm glad you did. That clears the air. I suppose your father will get on your case later, but I think you can handle him. So, what about the meeting, Jimmy?"

"I didn't learn much in school after that meeting. I've felt for

165

a while that somebody is after me. Now I wonder if Jake is the one, but why would a former bully go after me. It should be me going after him. If I could only remember, and know what I did, so I can make amends or know why he is after me."

"Maybe there are no amends to make, Jimmy. It's an evil world, and what I have heard about Jake, it seems he is arrogant and thinks he is the greatest person in the world. His Dad spoils him and backs him up if he gets in trouble, so it may be he is afraid you will break his record in scoring. Perhaps it could be an issue of pride for him. When a person's pride gets to them, evil isn't far behind."

After a pause, John asked, "Are you afraid?"

A thought for a bit, then answered, "Afraid? I don't know. Maybe. Cautious, yes. But I'll just put it into God's hands."

"Good answer! The only answer you could give. You have to watch where you are going, be prepared for trouble, and avoid it as much as possible. I think you will be fine. If anything looks suspicious, call or tell somebody. You can call me any time, day or night."

I agreed, and we both headed for practice. As we went to the gym, John suggested I tell the team, and I agreed.

When I came home that night, Father was angry with me. He got on me for disobeying his command and not saying anything to Mr. Havlon. When he finished, I snapped at him, "Father, why didn't you tell them the truth? I was never in a state mental institution, but you told everybody I was."

Mother looked at him angrily but didn't say anything. If looks could kill, Father was dead. He quickly got up from the table and headed outside toward his shop, and Sandy scurried to her room.

Mother stopped me before I left the table. "I didn't know your father told everybody that. Nobody asked me a thing, except a few busybodies in town and I told them it was a family matter and

166

left it at that. I can't believe your father told the town people you were in a state mental institution."

"Believe it, Mother, he did. I won't tell you who told me, but I know they aren't lying. I'm afraid of what might happen if Father blows his top. He might go after that person. Of course, other people told me the same thing. To be truthful, he told quite a few people in town. If it were before I came out of my comma, it wouldn't be a lie. Possibly he thought that was where I was going. Maybe he thought I was insane. If it was after I came out of my comma and was living with Uncle Walter, then who knows what he felt about me."

I was now sure Father would not have taken me home like I was before. The height alone might have changed his mind, but with the shooting, it was a difference.

"Jimmy I can't believe you think your father is violent and would tell lies when he knew you were alright."

I wanted to tell Mother more about what I expected my father had done to me before and what I was suspicious of him doing now, but I just couldn't, so I countered, "That's all I'm saying."

Surprisingly she said nothing more on the subject. I was silent as I finished eating, staring into space. I did that a lot lately.

I was sure Mother knew more secrets about me. Or maybe not. Father never told her anything, except to give her commands and subservient wives always listen, no complaints, they do what they're told. Sadly, she's a slave to Father. Maybe that's what Father wanted to make me. I knew he had Sandy under his thumb. But could he make me a slave? There was no way because I would leave first.

~~~~~~~~~

Wednesday morning, at ten o'clock, Allen Jamison entered Ender's Hardware Store in downtown Tiffin and asked if he could talk with Hazel Ender. Jamison was lead to the office at the end of the store

167

where the open door revealed a woman sitting behind a desk.

Hazel looked at Jamison as he entered the room. "I'm Allen Jamison, a reporter for The Advertising Tribune." he introduced himself.

"I know your name. You the sportswriter, who writes about basketball games in the county."

"Yes, I am."

"Please sit down and tell me what's on your mind."

Sitting on a chair in front of the desk, he began, "We got some calls to the paper that your star basketball player was in a mental institution?"

"That is none of my business! Talk to Arnold Bass, the boy's father, if you have a question."

"I'm not trying to cause any trouble, but somebody is accusing Jimmy Bass of terrible things. They say he is a sex pervert, and that was the reason he went to the mental institution. I want to talk to someone who knew him before he was institutionalized. I heard that you and your son, Pat, were, and are, friends with Bass. I hear there was a complaint about an incident that happened last Friday night. It involved Jimmy Bass and two of the cheerleaders."

"Okay, but this has to be off the record. That incident was a hoax that somebody manufactured from circumstantial evidence. Jimmy Bass has an alibi. He was with his mother, and both girls claim it never happened. As for Jimmy before the hospitalization, he was a sweet, confused kid with a father who put him down all the time, leaving him with little self-esteem. It was fear and not believing in himself that drove him to the hospital."

"Okay, so the phone calls we have been getting are a hoax?"

"Or some fool is trying to make up something that doesn't

168

exist. You know how people make a mountain out of a mole hole on a rumor."

"I understand. Are you sure it is not true?"

"I wish you could talk to Jimmy, but I think his father will block any attempt. He's a home-boy and is there except for school and basketball. Once in a while, he comes to our house, and he goes to church at St. Matthew for activities at the church. So there you have it. If you want to know more about him, see if Reverend John Wood. Perhaps he will talk to you."

Allen Jamison gave her a surprised look. "Isn't he an assistant coach as well as the coach for Junior Varsity?"

"The same person. He is also a part-time teacher and Jimmy's counselor."

"Really!"

~~~~~~~~~~

At noon on Wednesday, Session came to me while I was sitting with Marsha in the front row of the auditorium. He stood in front of me and began shouting, "You told Shumer that I was the one who wrote that letter to him, about you out parking with Lois and Ruth and all those dirty things you did with them."

He pointed his finger at me and continued, "I didn't do it, Bass, but I wouldn't put it past you to do something like that. You are nothing but a worthless nerd. Who knows what they taught you in the mental hospital where they sent you."

At first, I was shocked and afraid to say anything. Sam's confidence grew when he saw the nerd was fearful, so he continued with his put-downs. I tried to keep a couple of steps away from Sam, whose fists were ready. He planned to put the nerd down with two quick punches.

I was still in the same mold, acting as a fearful kid. All at

169

once, I snapped out of it. Anger took over, and I was about to lose my temper when I thought of Joe Cline, who said when possibly entering into a fight, "If you have time survey the scene before you react."

As I did, I realized Sam was taunting me to take the first swing; then, his quick hands would go to work. I slowly stood up in front of him, waiting for his punch, but I got none. Now Sam was quiet, waiting for my move.

Quite a crowd was beginning to surround the area. At the end of the row, sat Lois and Ruth. His continued comments that it was probably not a hoax were humiliating them, and both girls began crying. Standing fully erect, I asked in a calm voice, "Why do you hate me? I did nothing to you? And why are you embarrassing Lois and Ruth by implying that they did those horrible things you said? I didn't go to Shumer. It never dawned on me that it might be you who wrote that letter. Coming to me and accusing me of something I didn't do shows, everyone, that you hate me that much. I have never said a bad word about you or caused you any trouble. Your playing time and the Coach not letting you do what you wanted, is not my fault. I only do what Coach tells me to do. So I'm asking you again, why do you hate me?"

Sam just stood their seething, I had said my piece and was waiting for him to comment.

Then a comment came from Tim, who was standing close by, "Yeah, Sam, why do you hate Jimmy?"

Marsha also asked why, as did several other students in the crowd. Sam shook his head, knowing he was out-numbered and realized that if he did anything, he did would be the loser, so he filtered through the crowd and left the auditorium. The bell rang, and it was time for us to go to class. I felt I had won without fighting, and it seemed most of the high school was behind me. That felt good.

Walking home from basketball practice, I wondered how safe I was on the dark street. There weren't any street lights on side streets of Cutler Ridge. Each house had some kind of light on the front porch. I guess it was out of respect for the neighbors that these lights were on until a reasonable time of the night, about ten o'clock.

I was troubled by the letter which told lies about Lois and me. It was no joke and proved someone was out to get me. The confrontation with Session today made me believe he might be out to get me for humiliating him. But something told me that someone else was out to get me and I didn't know who it is.

Calling me a pervert in the letter was just like a few notes in sealed envelopes that I had found taped to my homeroom desk. They called me a pervert, too, but I never told anybody about them. I thought someone in school, was playing a prank, trying to scare me, or trying to rattle my brain, so I shoved them aside, believing, "No harm no foul." Another note said I was crazy and didn't belong in this school. I could understand students trying to provoke me, but maybe this was motivated by a parent.

Those notes started coming a month or two ago when I first entered school. At the same time, I got the cold shoulder from a lot of students. It seemed to dwindle when the basketball season started, and we started winning.

The notes have returned, only this time they're taped to my locker, and are telling me to go back to where I came from because this school and our team doesn't need a selfish, arrogant gunner.

I found messages tapped inside my locker and figured that someone must have gotten the combination for my padlock, so I changed the lock, but the notes kept coming. Then I got a key-operated lock for my locker, and that stopped the notes. At first, I believed it had to be someone on the team, maybe a Freshman or a Sophomore who was watching me when I opened my locker or even someone with experience in finding a combination for a lock,

171

perhaps a safe-cracker. I think the reason they're doing this is to scare me. They must have believed I was a weakling.

Very few people knew I had trained in marshal-arts. The former bullies wouldn't believe it. They had learned that a person of a particular personality, like a nerd, would always be that personality. I'm sure Jake and his gang, even though I'm a lot taller with a somewhat muscular build, would still think of me as a weakling, even if they were standing right in front of me. They probably believe I'm still afraid of them, and they have no fear of me.

I had to be careful; bullies never fight one on one. They always have their buddies with them. Maybe I didn't remember being on the short end of the stick in a fight, but I feel it had happened in my past. A voice seemed to tell me, "It will never happen again!"

This hoax had turned a new corner, and someone was now trying to frame me for something that wasn't true. It took careful surveillance and planning.

Jake Birkhart seemed to corner my thoughts. I had heard he was my enemy and feared I was taking his glory from him. I heard comments around town about me being a gunner, a frequent comment by jealous people. Would Jake go so far as to create a hoax with me as a pervert?

If my memory came back and I remembered Jake, maybe I would agree. The fear of me breaking his scoring record seemed a little far fetched, even though I had a twenty-seven and a half point average. Bickhart scored an average of twenty-four and a half points for his Senior season. We had played six games and had fourteen regular season games left, with at least one game in the tournament. If we got beat, a lot could happen.

~~~~~~~~~

Our coach got a letter from the principal of Old Fort High School apologizing for how some of the players acted toward me, but he felt something was wrong. When he saw the letters, he knew he

172

was right. The opposing team players were planning to start a fight with me at the end of the game. Two of our players learned about the plan at our local gas station, a local hangout for some of the kids in school.

Our coach heard that a man who was getting gas made threatening comments about Jimmy Bass and gave money for someone to beat him up, but no one knew who he was.

The students will get punished, and the sheriff is looking into who the guy who paid them. Randy talked to me about kids being paid to fight and told me to be careful. In his spare time, he promised to look into it.

There was more to the letter. The coach who wrote the letter kept saying how good a player I was, and on and on with apologizes about what had happened. I was glad for the apologies, but to think someone would pay money for somebody to beat me up was unreal. Who had I hurt so badly in my past that they would want to have me beaten? Oh, how I wish my memory would come back.

I made it home with no problems, so maybe I am safe, at least in the town. I need to be cautious because I have a price on my head.

That last thought sounds stupid for anyone living in our small country town, but after the threatening notes, the hoax, and the pay to beat me up, I'm worried more is coming. Before the incident, I would have been scared to death, but now I'm not afraid, I'm cautious. I don't want to get blindsided, and I want to praise God that He is with me. The demons and bad dreams are gone; again, I praise God.

~~~~~~~~~

On Friday, December 21, Cutler Ridge had a home game with Bloomville and Elizabeth arrived late. The JV game was ending, in the crowded gym, and she knew the balcony would be a better

173

place to find a seat. Spotting one in the front row, Elizabeth sat down and began to stress on the hoax about the two cheerleaders and Jimmy. She couldn't believe Jake would stoop that low.

Elizabeth knew some guys that used to hang around with Jake, at least one of them is still around, and he hated Jimmy, but she didn't know why. He and a buddy were down-right crazy. Would they stoop this low? They might!

These two guys backed up Jake, and now the nerd, who Jake always called a slave, was scoring a lot of points. If Jimmy continued this pace, he would break Jake's record, hands down. Could Jake's pride mean that much to him?

How low would he go?

Elizabeth feared for Jimmy if Jake and his guys got violent. Somehow she had to get close and warn him. A long talk with Pat might be needed. She knew he was watching out for Jimmy, at least she hoped so.

Elizabeth stood up and cheered when the team came out of the locker room. As she looked at how big Jimmy was, she realized he could take care of himself. Cursed be the person in Jake's crew who tried to take him on.

~~~~~~~~~~

Bloomville played a tight two-three zone. From the scouting report, they were no taller than us. Their offense and defense mostly included the run-and-gun. We couldn't stop them from running, but it wasn't ending our lay-up. They shot a lot of outside shots on run-and-hit. Then they jumped to a ten point lead in the first quarter.

We cut into their lead, but they seem to rebound. A lot of our scoring came from me. I started shooting my long shots from the start of the game. I knew I had a lot of points at halftime. The rest of the team wasn't hitting their shots, and Bloomville led thirty-five to twenty-five at half-time.

174

~~~~~~~~~

"Jimmy needs help," Elizabeth yelled to some of her friends sitting with her.

An older guy heard her and said, "Bass is nothing but a gunner."

Elizabeth was about to say something when some other people told him how stupid he was, and she heard no more comments from him.

She was right; Jimmy had eighteen out of a total of twenty-five points. It wasn't that the other players weren't shooting, they just couldn't hit their shots.

Joey Bell must have taken five outside shots and missed them all. The same with Tim, at high-post. She wasn't sure how many he made, but all were misses. Brad had the rest of the points, seven, but no one else scored. The outcome wasn't looking good.

~~~~~~~~~

No one said much during the short halftime. Coach told us we needed more time to work on our shots, and Jerry asked, "How do we stop them?" as the home team entered the gym.

"That's a great question! They have a high percentage of shooting from the outside. You'd think they would cool down."

"Somebody might say the same thing about Jimmy. He hasn't missed many shots!" one of our players commented.

"The rest of the team hasn't hit anything. I looked at the stats, and Jimmy has eighteen points, hitting nine out of thirteen shots. Bell is zero for five, Ender zero for six. Brad got seven points, but he still missed a couple of easy shots. Rendles and Glen are both zero for two. I guess we've met our match," Jerry sighed.

"Don't give up yet, Jerry, maybe they'll come around."

"I hope so, but doubt it."

I was determined, and I was going to give it my all. We got the tip, Brad tipped to me, and I quickly drove to our end of the floor. A step from the top of the key I hit another long shot. Then I caught four more straight. That gave us ten points, and their lead was cut to two points, thirty-seven to thirty-five.

Bloomville called time out, and I could hear our fans going wild. In the huddle, everyone was yelling. I knew I had just shot a good stretch, and the excitement was for me. Still, I didn't want them to get too carried away. Bad things could again go my way.

"Quit thinking that way, that's the old you. Now you have confidence and can handle anything that comes your way. Give praise to God," I thought.

Coach had other things on his mind, like calming the huddle down. He went over how we should set up for a box-in-one, the same way we did against New Reigal.

When we left the huddle, I called, "You need to keep shooting like I just did or pass it around."

Coach shouted, "Keep on shooting, Jimmy, anywhere you can. Your teammates won't let you down, but they can't hit a thing. Jimmy, you have to bail us out!"

I got the message, loud and clear, but Bloomville changed their defense strategy. At first, they used the same defense and the same the old run-and-gun offense. They guarded me heavily in whichever area I was. Joey could still get the ball to me, but he had other ideas. He had three straight outside shots that went in. With the guard in the front of the two-three kind of over guarding me, it gave Joey the outside shots.

To my surprise, Rendles, on the right-wing, had been open all night long and now hit a couple outside shots. Then at high-post,

Tim got in the scoring column. Still, Bloomville didn't fold, for they had a four-point lead going into the last minute.

After scoring the first ten points of the half, I had a couple of rebound shots, going into the last minute. I had a couple of missed outside shots, but that was it. I didn't need to shoot. The rest of the team was doing fine. By over guarding me, it left me some good passes to Brad for inside shots.

You would have thought Bloomville would have stalled. I blocked the first shot, and they were sure they had it at the foul line. Joey got the ball and headed down the court for a lay-up, but he froze, as sometimes happens. I watched him shoot; it was like a prayer. One defender was on him, but I was right behind and got the rebound over to a smaller player who got fouled as he put it in the basket.

~~~~~~~~~

Elisabeth screamed as Jimmy got the rebound and made the basket. The crowd calmed down, waiting for Jimmy to shoot the foul, a man behind her said, "That was simply a hustle play on defense, down to the rebound shot." She agreed with him, and told him so.

Jimmy had made the foul shot, making the score eighty-four to eighty-three, Bloomville's favor. The next time he was going down the floor, Jimmy got a steal, drove the length of the court, then got fouled; but twisted his body and got the ball up to the basket and in, landing against the mat at the end of the court. The crowd stood in awe when he didn't get up right away.

~~~~~~~~~

An elbow in the stomach knocked the wind out of me, and I laid there trying to get my breath. John was beside me as I got up slowly, but my breathing didn't come back so quickly, and John had to take me to the bench as Sam Alt, the guard for the JV, came in for me. Alt took my foul shot but missed.

177

With the score eighty-five to eighty-four, our favor, Bloomville made a basket. There were only five seconds left on the clock when Coach called a time-out, and I slowly went to the scorer's table. I was ready to play, but I was slow to get to the scorer table and get back into the huddle. My stomach was a little sore, but it was mostly an act to catch the Bloomville guard off.

The Bloomville coach wasn't buying it, and he had me double teamed. We had to bring the ball full-court. Tim took the ball out of bounds and made a long pass to me, just past mid-court. I caught the ball, came down, then went straight up to pass an alley-oop to Brad like Coach had diagrammed the play in the huddle. Bloomville fouled me, thinking I was shooting.

"That was stupid to foul, Bass. He's just inside the half court line. I don't think he would have made it." someone yelled.

Another person around Elisabeth commented, "Bass was passing to Weiden for an alley-oop."

I was just glad Jimmy was alright and hoped he made the foul shots. He already had thirty-seven points; two foul shots would make it thirty-nine and a win. Oh, how I wished I could get to know him again, and I hoped he would forgive me. I knew I still loved him.

Where did that come from?

~~~~~~~~~

I was on the foul line and had some pressure. I took the ball and bent my knees going up to a standing position, and released the ball toward the basket with my hand straight in front of me. The ball went in, tying the game. As I was making my second shot, I didn't follow through correctly. Adjusting, I pushed the ball too hard and saw it was going to hit the back of the rim, so I quickly took two steps in the key toward the basket. I believe God was on my side because the ball came to me. Getting the rebound, I promptly went up and pushed the ball to the backboard behind the rim. It was so

178

quick no defender laid a hand on me.

~~~~~~~~~

Elizabeth watched the ball go over the rim to the backboard and back into the basket, making the final score eighty-eight to eighty-six. Jimmy had forty points! She started screaming, "Bass, has forty points!" over and over. The rest of the home crowd chimed in. It became a chant that the fans picked up and changed it to, "Jimmy Bass forty, and we win!"

~~~~~~~~~

Pandemonium broke out through the town as it had after all the other great wins we had. The whole town celebrated my forty points quite a bit. Even father was at Keller's restaurant, bragging up his son. He even sat with me as we ate. He never said anything to me but was bragging me up to everybody. This didn't bother me because I felt this was where he should be, not in the bar across the street. That came later.

~~~~~~~~~

Elisabeth was back in her pajamas and sitting on her bed, reading the fourth letter from Jimmy, a note she had not read before.

~~~~~~~~~

March 7

I'm glad basketball season is over. There was a party at the Park on Ruffle Road for the team. I didn't want to go, but Pat, Carl Evert, and Jerry Cane talked me into going.

Everyone was drinking but Pat and me. Jake was his usual self, picking on me, calling me names, saying anything he wanted to say. I guess the stupid nerd, or his slave, was the brunt of his jokes.

Then he started talking about you and how easy you were with sex. The more he spoke, the madder I got. So I went up to him and told him to shut his mouth. He put his beer down on the truck bed, stood in front of me, and acted

179

like he was going to grab me to teach me a lesson. I knew I was in for a beating, and if I swung at him, it would be even worse. Two guys grabbed me from behind, and Jake started to have a field day with me.

Somehow Pat, Carl, and Jerry saved me and got me out of there before I got beaten too severely. I wish I were brave enough to hit Jake and defend your honor. Fear came over me, and I froze. I felt I got the beating from Jake because I deserved it. I don't know why I respond this way. I'm scared that more thrashings will come. You know Jake's anger. Probably not by him, but John Alter will probably make my life miserable now until the end of school. After that, I'll try to stay away from him. But that might not work because they will find me.

Father keeps putting me down about being a coward, sometimes he hits me. Jake and his boys taunt me for fun. I don't know where to go.

Elisabeth, run from Jake. He isn't the guy for you. I wish you could love me as I love you, but that will never happen. A slave, nerd, like me, doesn't deserve a Queen. All I want is to be your friend. I could take all this pain if I have your love. That would be heaven.

Your friend always, Jimmy

~~~~~~~~~

Tears were again rolling down her cheeks, and she felt sorry that Jimmy had stuck up for her honor, even though he knew it was going to result in him getting beat-up. She didn't deserve that him. Jake had stretched the truth, a bit. She wasn't easy for him, but she had relented to his aggressiveness. Love-making isn't performed like an animal as Jake did. She hoped to find true love with the right person. Maybe Jimmy still had that love for her, tucked deep in his memory, and perhaps he could forgive her. His passion was pure and gentle. He had a love that could last forever.

Oh, Jimmy! Oh, Jimmy! I'm sorry. Thank you for trying to protect my honor. I know, somehow, we will finally get together. If the memories don't come, maybe we can rekindle a new friendship. Perhaps it will develop into a real romance.

Was this only wishful thinking? No, love like that could come to her! If it didn't, she would never love anyone—no puppy love, like the animal Jake, a crazed beast that would devour a woman.

"Oh, dear God, let Jimmy love me as he did in school. I'll do everything I can to make it up to him."

Chapter Fifteen

Saturday Morning, three days before Christmas, I went to John Wood's house.

"Did you hear that Allen Jamison wants to interview you, Jimmy, especially about the forty points you scored last night."

"No," I said, shaking my head. "My father wanted me to talk to some reporter this morning. Maybe it was him. The reporter told Father he wanted to interview me, but I told him no. When Father hung up, he was angry, saying 'You never get a chance to be on top like this! You need to grab the moment.' But I still said, "No."

"What did he say then?"

"He told me I was a fool for" not getting interviewed. You have been nothing all your life. Here is a chance to stick it to those who put you down before. This interview is your right."

"When I made no response, he stormed out to his shop grumbling that I didn't know what I was doing and that I never listen to him. But, John, if the truth be told, he isn't looking out for my good. He loves all the glory I'm getting and bringing to him, the father. He is so full of pride that it makes me sick!"

After a quick pause, I added, "I remember something he told me after the Old Fort game, that made him so proud. In the balcony, some woman was yelling, 'Go, Jimmy!' They couldn't believe it was Arnold Bass's son. It seems that most of the people there, work for my dad. They reminded him of it on Monday morning. They said he strutted around the factory for about a week."

"Why does that bother you, Jimmy?"

"Somewhere, I was taught to be humble, not to boast about myself. It had to come from Father or maybe the Lutheran Church. I'm leaning toward my father, but I know it comes from Jesus. I never knew Jesus the way I know Him now. I'm sure Father used it as a tool to control me with fear. We were never to be prideful. Now he's acting the direct opposite as he told us."

"So, now he has changed his word?"

"Or he was always was prideful, and as I said before, his stressing us to be humble, was a tool of fear. That's how he controls the family. Both my mother and my sister fear him. There's no love in him, or at least I haven't seen it."

"Jimmy, you're probably right, about your father. But you can't let him get to you. Remember, Jesus wants you to forgive your enemies. I think you are making your father your enemy. I believe what you say is right about your father, but you have to forgive him and try to get along with him the best you can. A child of God is loving, not resentful like you are showing him. If he wants you to do what is against God's will then tell him you won't. If he demands you to do something you now know is against God's will, say, no, and explain to him why."

"You're right about how I feel about my father. Loving him is not easy. Respecting him will be difficult, but I'll do it because it's the will of God."

"Why didn't you want the interview?"

I thought about how to answer this question. I wasn't timing, but it had to have been over thirty seconds before I came up with the answer. "You may think it's funny, but one of the reasons why is Father's drilling into me about being humble. Now he is on the pride issue. It's a backward twist."

After another pause, I said, "I'm sorry, I'm back on my father, but I believe it's the truth. I suppose it was good. I was taught to be humble by my father."

I needed another pause to think, then I continued, "Another big reason is that if I did the interview, it was like telling everybody that I won the game single-handedly, which I didn't. I just made a lot of the points for the team. I could mention the team a lot, but I'm sure the reporter will only be interested in me, and that's what the newspaper article would be about. I'm sure they would act differently, and some of my teammates would be hurt."

"That is very smart of you, and I'm proud of you for thinking of the team. Why didn't you tell your father that?"

"He would disagree with me. In the games I scored in the low twenties, he told me I didn't score enough. So I figured he doesn't care about the team but only the points I score, to give him glory. I felt I was better off not telling him. I could have reminded him about the part where he taught me to be humble. I don't know why I didn't bring that up. You probably can't forget a feeling like that, and attitudes drilled into you as a child."

"That happens, Jimmy, and I agree with you about not saying anything to him."

John didn't know what else to say but prayed for Arnold and his relationship about his son. Then he approached a subject he wanted to talk about ever since Jimmy came.

"What about what happened this week? Can you tell me about what everybody is calling 'the hoax?' I know we talked about it

184

before practice in the coaches office."

I thought for a few seconds and then said, "Somebody is after the girls or me, and I think it's me."

"We talked about that before. What I want to know is how is the hoax getting to you? Is it you affecting your thoughts or fears? Don't act macho on me, Jimmy."

"I want no part of fear because I know that in my past, I can't remember just how I know, but fear was a big deal, and I think it came mostly from my father. I will not live that way anymore. My nightmares were from fear, but God took that away. I will not accept fear again."

"Okay, Jimmy, that's good."

"Another thing, my father kept the lie going. In that meeting about the hoax, when Mr. Havion kept referring to me about my being in an insane asylum, that angered me. I didn't want people in town to think I've been in an insane asylum when I wasn't. So I answered Mr. Havion's question about my being in an insane asylum. Now everybody should know it was a lie. Of course, I had told several people before."

After a quick pause to think, I said apologetically, "I know, John, I'm sorry. I guess in my father's rule, about not defying the father, I should have kept the lie going."

"No, Jimmy, you were right in telling the truth. Your father was wrong to keep the lie going."

John wanted to change the subject, so he asked, "Any new memories, Jimmy?"

"Bits and pieces, I told you about Elisabeth Hasselback. I don't remember her much in high school, but when we were younger, around Junior High, she brought me something to drink while I was working in the field. I remember a little bit in High

185

School, too. I haven't had a chance to talk to her, yet, but when I do, maybe a lot of memories will come back."

There was a long pause in the conversation, then John divulged, "I heard about the incident in the auditorium during your noon hour. Session confronted you accusing you of blaming him for the hoax."

"Yes, but nothing happened. I think Session was trying to make me blow up about what he was saying to me, and it was bad! At first, I froze and gave no reaction. Fear took control like I must have acted before. Then I realized I wasn't the same person. Fear had no control over me. I stood ready for him to try to hit me, and I asked why he hated me. I denied that I told Shumer. I continued to ask him, again, and again, why he hated me. Then other students began to ask the same thing. He felt ashamed and left. That was it!"

"You handled that very well. You stood up to Session and never went after him aggressively. Then you asked him why he hated you. The fact that other kids in school stuck up for you is a tribute to the attitude you have towards them in school."

"I'm told that I'm Mister Popular, especially with the girls. That probably is why everybody stuck up for me." I laughed, meaning it as a joke.

The last words John told me stuck with me as I went home. I realized I was liked in school, even more than a want-to-be-bully like Session. Because of the way I stood up to him, the way it gave me strength with no fear, I now know how the majority of the kids in the school think about me. A lot of it is the way I play basketball and the success of our team. I don't flaunt my glory at them. Instead, I am humble. I am not bragging. It's the way I feel. I want my relationship with the kids in the school to stay the way it is. It feels good the way the kids perceive me. I am no longer a good-for-nothing-nerd as I was before. I probably am mister popularity.

186

Maybe the kids before the incident didn't think of me like I thought they did, a worthless good-for-nothing slave. I remember the statement Lois and Ruth said about me in the meeting about the hoax. It made me feel good to think about myself before the incident. People liked me and cared for me. They didn't look at me, like I thought everybody did, the worthless nerd, that everybody was looking down on.

Jack Victory told me how I helped him with his car, and Randy Diller said I helped with his car, too. But my thoughts keep wanting to put me back to who I thought I was.

Yes, some of them thought of me as a nerd, but not all of them. I wish I could remember the depths of my past, and see into all the confusion of the bad things that have occurred and into the right actions. There have to be some of those.

Chapter Sixteen

Christmas would be fantastic with Uncle Walter and Aunt Helen coming from Tennessee. They stayed in the guest bedroom at the end of the house. Uncle Walter did some counseling with me, and I told him I was starting to remember things. He continued to stress, not focusing on the past. I knew this was my father's desire after the outburst at the meeting about the hoax.

I countered, "What should I do if a memory comes out? I'm not trying to bring the memories out, Uncle Walter, but they keep coming, piece by piece. Should I suppress them, shove them deep down into my brain, and keep pushing them away when they return? Or should I deal with them? You're the doctor; I'm your patient. I think it would be better to deal with them. If they come to me, I'll tell John. So far, all the memories that have returned are ones I've been able to deal with. I learned that in my past that I had many friends. I didn't go around begging people to like me. They came to me. I have a lot of friends here now. That's something my father didn't want me to know. Maybe he thought I didn't have any friends. Every friend I have told him about, he said I should stay away from them. Father says I am here to play basketball. The rest of the time, I'm to spend at home. He says not to mingle with people, especially people that were my friends in my past."

Uncle Walter was quiet. He didn't say anything for quite a while. Then with his lower lip like he was in deep thought he said, "I taught you about self-esteem and self-love, and it seems you understand. When you confront your past, it makes you believe positive things about your past."

After a pause and what seemed to be more in-depth, he declared, "I was wrong, Jimmy. When memories come out, you have to work through them. Memories are your father's biggest worry. He's afraid you can't handle them."

Uncle Walter scowled and shook his bead, then he said, "Your father is wrong! You look and act happy and confident. You found out you weren't as bad as you thought you were. Just a few people in the school didn't like you and enjoyed pushing you around. Have you run into any of these people?"

"No they're not around, and after the incident, they were told to stay away. But with the Lord on my side, I can handle anything. He guides me through my daily life."

"It's good to have faith, Jimmy. I believe you are doing well and there's no more I can tell you."

That was the end of my counseling with Uncle Walter. I heard he had a long talk with Father about me. I don't know if Father agreed with him or not, but he seemed a little more reasonable after that.

I believe my memories are slowly revealing a past. A strong feeling I have involves Elisabeth. She was in the center of it, and sometimes I feel she is a negative memory. Then sometimes I think she is a positive one. It's like my memories are playing ping-pong. One hit is good, and the next one is bad. Maybe this is one of the reasons I'm sure about seeing her.

I still can't remember anything about Pat and not much about his brother, Tim. I remember his face and know he was a year behind me in school. But that is it and nothing more.

My teammates are real friends to me. It's like we are a family. That's a perfect atmosphere for a successful team. I've never heard of teammates encouraging someone the way they do for me. A lot of athletes are selfish, but it amazes me that none of these players act that way. They have the same goal as me--success for our team. If I have to score thirty or forty points for that to happen, that's what I do.

Father surprised me during Christmas by being pleasant to me. It was probably because Uncle Walter and Aunt Helen were here. I didn't care what the reason was, I was happy.

Both Father and Uncle Walter made a big deal about how I was the tallest in the family. Before, Uncle Walter had been the tallest at six-foot-two. Father was close at six-foot-one. Uncle Walter said it was in the genes.

That was something I already knew, for I remember meeting cousins of my father and Uncle Walter at a family reunion. One was six-foot-six, and one was close to six-foot-eight. So I knew my height came naturally. I was glad. I didn't want to be a short guy, who does?

Christmas Eve was the greatest. Mother, Aunt Helen, Sandy, and I went to John's church for the 7:30 Christmas Eve Service. Mother left the service in tears over John's sermon on how Jesus loves us. Aunt Helen was almost in tears, too. Both gave their lives to Jesus at the altar call. Their tears weren't those of sorrow, but joy. Oh. How wonderfully God works. I never thought I would see this, especially with Aunt Helen. Would Uncle Walter give his life to Jesus?

I was thrilled, especially for Mother. She had not looked like she was happy for quite some time. But now I could see the joy on her face. I started praying this wouldn't be a negative thing for my father. How would he react to her being born again? He should be happy for her, but, somehow, negative feelings could quickly arise.

190

No, I'll choose to think positive of Father."

Later on, that evening, when we gave out gifts, I received a small box. When I opened it, there was the title to the fifty-seven, in my name. Turning over the title was something I figured Father would never do. Oh, he promised, but somehow I was uncertain of that promise. I don't remember him ever breaking a promise to me, but I was surprised. The license plates on the car were not legal; they were in Father's name. That was okay. New license plates didn't come out for a couple of months, and I didn't want to drive it until the snow was gone. So my car would stay stored at Uncle Fred's.

He also gave me a whole box of tools. There was almost every tool a mechanic might need. If Father mistreated me before, I think he is trying to make up for it, now. I hoped and prayed joy and happiness would always continue between us. In the distance, though, I saw a dark cloud.

~~~~~~~~~~

Two days after Christmas, at nine o'clock in the morning, there was a meeting at John's office only this time he had my Uncle Walter there.

"What is the report on Jimmy? How is he progressing? He told me he is starting to remember his past. If he does, you want him to keep it quiet."

Uncle Walter stopped and shook his head. "No, that's stupid. That would mean stuffing his feelings. John, he can't do that! He told me that when we had our counseling sessions, and he's right. I won't push for the past, but he needs to let it come naturally and handle it slowly. I hope he comes to you the significant memories, like who it was who beat him. In the locker room, have you ever seen him naked and seen the scars on his back and thighs?"

"Yes, I have, and a lot of the players noticed it too. He doesn't seem self-conscious about it, but he never says anything

191

about them. I'm pretty sure none of the kids are asking questions about it. Whoever did that to him wouldn't want to be around him now."

"I know, he knows martial arts and street fighting, too. He never told me this, but my next-door neighbor trains a lot of people in martial arts in his basement. I know Jimmy took some training their."

"Yeah, I know. Jimmy told me. He also told me the future scares him a little bit. But if his memories come out, he'll be able to handle them. Everything seems to be under control now, except his father. But Jimmy stands up to him if Arnold crosses the line."

Walter smiled, then said, "That is one thing about which I worry. My brother is trying to dominate Jimmy. Arnold always has to be in control, but that's not good. I know Jimmy won't let his father control him. My brother has many things to learn about Jimmy. He's not going to take any more of his father's bullying. Oh, Jimmy will show respect. I don't think Arnold will try to beat him or kick him out of the house, he knows better. I believe a lot of people in this town can't stand Arnold Bass. If he did that his name would be Mud."

"There are a lot of people who like Jimmy and did before. If Arnold tries to kick him out of the house, he can come here. I know Hazel Ender would take him in, too. She's got a son that plays on the basketball team, and her older son lives at home. They're good friends with Jimmy."

"If my brother does that, Jimmy has plenty of money. His dad doesn't know that. I put it in a bank account for him in Tiffin this week when I came up to visit. He earned money working for my wife and me, as well as doing odd jobs for people. He did mechanical work for a few folks, too. So money is no problem for him. If his father knew he had this money, he would probably demand that he have control of it. But he has to go through me. I have a joint membership on his account. When he came here, he had some money that he brought with him. It wasn't a lot, but it was enough to tide them over."

"I'm glad he's got the money."

After a brief pause, John thought, "I've only given good reports. Maybe I should tell Walter about Jimmy's enemies. I should say something. So he asked, "Do you know about his secret enemies and the hoax?"

"I heard some things about it. And the threats Jimmy received in his desk, and locker. I know he was beaten up pretty badly before by the scars he has, but why would those people want to come after him, now? It seems that after they have looked at him, they'd be scared. I'm more worried about the safety of the people who try to beat him. If he remembers them, he might go after them with a vengeance."

"Jimmy told me that you aren't a Christian. I don't know if you'll be offended by what I say, but I think you should know. Jimmy realizes that vengeance is not part of God's plan. If he remembered, he'd say, 'Let's go for justice.' He would try to get the boys arrested and put in jail for what they did to him."

They both agreed that they wanted the best for Jimmy.
When Walter left John's office, he was confident that John had everything under control. He was sure he didn't have to worry about Jimmy anymore.

Chapter Seventeen

Thursday, the afternoon of Christmas Break, I left practice and went out the back door of the school, heading home through the baseball field until I came to an area everyone used as a walkway, between two houses. At the sidewalk, I noticed two men in a car parked across the street. As I walked toward my street, I saw the car make a U-turn and head toward me.

I knew there was going to be a fight. If it was fair, I might have participated, but it seemed this one wasn't going to be that kind. I wanted to confront these guys in the worst way because I'm not a coward. Instead, I turned toward the walkway between the houses. That caught them by surprise.

By the time one of the guys got out of the car, I was running down the walkway, toward the school. One of them ran after me, while the one drove down to my street turned right and headed to Main, hoping to get in front of the school and block me off at the small parking lot beside the school.

I hoped I could beat them at their game and get to Clyde's Gas Station. It was four in the afternoon, full sunlight, and nobody was around. I made it to the sidewalk in front of the school, and halfway to Clyde's when the car hit Main Street.

Now it was a race to Clyde's, the only place that was open. The rest of the town had shut down, even Kellers.

Since nobody was driving, except the maniac trying to get me, I cut across Main Street and made it onto Clyde's lot when the car pulled up behind me. The door to one of the bays at Clyde's opened as the car pulled to a stop.

I ran by a guy who must have been six-foot-four and weighed close to three-hundred pounds, mostly muscle. I knew he worked here and claimed to be an old friend. We now became new friends, and I prayed he would help me. With my friend at my side, I was no longer afraid to fight. I stopped just a step behind the big guy. If I had kept running, I would have run into a car on the lift.

"Stop, Jude, your not touching, Jimmy!" The big man said to the guy exiting the car. Jude, a man around my age, five-foot-ten, and somewhat muscular, was no match for the big guy, so he stopped. The man who had been running pulled up beside Jude and bent over, trying to catch his breath. He was about the same size and shape as Jude. They were about five feet from me, so I positioned my legs for my first kick.

"Leave him alone, Randy. He's our meat!"

"No, Jude, he's a friend of mine, always has been. So you'll have to tangle with me. Did you notice how big he is?" the big guy snarled.

"If he's so big and tough, why did he run? He's a stupid, worthless nerd. I don't care if everybody in town thinks he's a hero. He'll always be a worthless jerk. He'll never change. I've always hated him, and now I can get even with that worthless slave."

I wondered if I should run from a fair fight. I had never been in a row before and had some fear. But I said to myself, "No fear! No fear!" Then the words that Jude said brought back memories I never wanted to hear again. Looking at the man that was catching his

195

breath, a flash of memory exploded.

The more I looked at him, the more enraged I became. I could see the torment he had been to me in school. Jude was saying I didn't belong in this town. Over and over, he kept putting me down. There was no fear now.

Whatever else Jude was saying, to get my attention, my thoughts were on the man standing five feet in front of me. I stepped toward him, pointed my finger at him, and was close to losing what control I had when Joe Cline's instructions came to mind. "Be alert for any movement of your opponent," and this thought kept me from losing it.

A loud voice suddenly erupted from my mouth. "I remember you! I don't remember your name, but I know that face. I remember how you treated me. You tripped me on purpose at basketball practice! In the hallway, in front of everybody, you tripped me while I was carrying my books! Then as I laid on the floor, you kicked me and laughed at me, saying I was a fool, a worthless fool!"

I almost swore at him to provoke him and call him nasty names. I wanted to, so badly, but I didn't. Maybe it was because I'm a Christian.

Then he reacted, probably thinking one good hit with a roundhouse punch and he would own me again. I was waiting for this reaction. His fist went by my face. Then, just as Joe Cline had taught me, a quick jab to his midsection, just below his ribs, knocked the air out of him.

I could have jumped in the air and kicked him in the jaw. I'm sure it would have knocked him out, but I didn't do it. Maybe he thought my fighting was over, as he staggered toward me, then tried a quick jab that glanced off the side of my face. It stung, but that was all.

I quickly grabbed his right arm, twisted it backward until I pushed it behind his back, and jammed his arm as high as it could go. That gave me control, so I pushed his upper body and face onto the hood of the new 1963 Chevy Impala they were driving.

I had complete control, and it felt good. "Now who is the fool, the worthless nerd?" I yelled at him.

There was no reply from him. He was stubborn and wouldn't say uncle no matter how much I hurt him.

"I could break your arm right now, you fool. Maybe a few fingers. You know that?" He tried to kick me, and I shoved his arm up harder. A cry of pain and a curse came out of his mouth.

Do you think I'm still a nerd? I'm bigger than you, and I know fighting moves you've never learned. I could tear you apart piece by piece. Do you still think of me as a nerd? You're a fool. When my memory comes back, and I find out you had something to do with all the scars on my body, I'll come looking for you.

It felt good, having control over a guy I know had tortured me before.

After some pushing and shoving, the guy named Jude tried to get to me, but Randy hit him in the jaw. He was dazed and fell backward.

All at once, there was a friend beside me. It was John. "Jimmy, don't let your rage hurt him. There are plenty of people with you. He won't retaliate. Back off, Jimmy. Please, Jimmy, back off." he said.

I was surprised that John was there, but I did what he said. I didn't want to. I was having fun getting revenge from a guy who hurt me so badly in my past.

Was it revenge? I didn't start to fight. I was defending myself, and it was over, for the time being. As I stepped back, I released my hold on my enemy, whose name I couldn't remember. I kept an eye

197

on this enemy as he quickly got into the car, shut the door, and locked it. Then I notice more men were milling around the gas station.

Jude was behind the steering wheel as he started the car. Randy and his buddies, one a big guy they called Bull, told them if they come back to town they would end up in the hospital. The two pursuers left in there car.

I was stunned. My first row and I won. I wanted to jump in the air and scream, telling everybody how tough I was.

More memories began coming to me, not only from the guy I just beat up but the other one, too — the one called Jude.

I was about to ask John a question when the people around started talking. A couple of other guys, around Randy's age, said they were friends mine from my past. They promised to watch for those guys if they came back.

More guys, in their forties, said they knew me from the past, too. I had mowed their lawns and didn't charge much. Another man said I did extra work for them, trimming and other things. More people said the same things about my relationship with them.

"If we needed something, Jimmy was there to help." a guy in his fifties announced.

"Jimmy, we are going to spread the word around. If anyone sees those two goons in town, we'll start calling phone numbers. The whole town will get them, and they won't be back."

It was unbelievable when they told me that. It made me feel like my past wasn't worthless. No names were said. They knew I wouldn't remember them. Maybe they wanted to talk to me a long time ago, but with my memory loss, they felt awkward. Now was my chance to open up, and it felt good.

Randy grinned, "The way you handled John Alter, I don't

think he will be back."

Everyone agreed with that as they started leaving. So the guy I beat was John Alter. I still didn't remember the name, only the face, and what he did to me. I asked Pat, "So that was John Alter, what is he to me?"

"I heard you yell at him about not being a nerd anymore, so I figured that memory came back."

"Only some brief memories of him tripping me and kicking me when I landed on the floor."

"He was one of your enemies."

"So he was a bully and hurt me, a lot. Why is he after me, now? I should be trying to find him, not him waiting for me on Rice street."

"I don't know why they're after you, Jimmy. I haven't seen these bullies for a long time, not since after what happened to you in the incident. They were blamed for what happened to you and were told by the people to stay away from our town. And they stayed away until today. Jake comes back once in a while and brags about how great he was in basketball, but the people mostly ignore him."

"Do you think it's about Jake's record and the fear that Jimmy might break it? "Randy questioned.

"You wouldn't think so, but you know how arrogant Jake is! It could be that when your memory comes back, you will remember something they don't want the public to know. If they can intimidate you a give you the message that they are still in control, they could scare you into going back to Tennessee. He sees your size, but no matter how big you are, he still looks at you as a nerd."

"It has got to be something important to go after Jimmy in broad daylight, especially here at the gas station with lots of people around."

199

"It's their pride and the nerd thing. That didn't interfere with him before. It's always been that way; why should he be different now?" Pat argued.

I hadn't noticed Pat was there until then. I turned to him and replied, "You're telling me, Pat, that they have no fear of me, even though I'm bigger than them? I'm still the same old nerd I use to be?"

"Until today, but now they know you are different. Maybe you hurt John's arm, and he will always remember that you put that pain on him. I don't think he'll bother you again." Pat grinned.

"Unless it's more than beating a nerd, and its some secret I have in my memories that they don't want to come out. Maybe they were planning to grab me and take me to some deserted place to beat me, hoping to scare me. When I ran, he thought I was, the same old nerd. Well, I sure surprised them, and it felt good."

Suddenly a negative thought came to me; "It isn't over."

I looked around, and almost everyone had left, except Pat. Randy was still closing up the shop. Pat volunteered to take me home, and I accepted. We didn't talk much, Pat had somewhere to go, and he was in a hurry. I got out of his car and went into the house.

My parents were gone, Uncle Walter and Aunt Helen were seeing some of his high school friends, and Sandy was staying with one of our cousins in Tiffin, so I was going into an empty house. John called me as soon as I got home and asked me to come to his house. He knew I was alone. I told him I would be. After that, I took a shower.

When I got to John's house, we went to the kitchen. Kathy made us a couple of hamburgers as John, and I talked at the kitchen table.

"I was so mad at him, John, I wanted to swear."

"Did you?"

"No, I guess because I'm a Christian,"

"You were yelling at him, remembering things he did to you in the past. But what I saw was self-defense. He swung at you, and you reacted."

"Mostly, John, but I have to confess; I wanted him to swing at me, so I could react the way I did from the training Joe Cline taught me. I know that was wrong, but it felt good to have control over him. I enjoyed it; maybe too much."

I paused, then looked John in the eye. "I know it was a wrong feeling to get revenge, John."

Then pausing briefly, again, I added, "If it wasn't for you and Pat, I might not have backed away."

"Look into my eyes, Jimmy. No matter how mad you were, you didn't lose control. I understand revenge is wrong. But they started it, and most of it was self-protection. If this was revenge, ask God for forgiveness, but thank God for Him guiding you."

I nodded my head.

"Are more memories are coming back?" John questioned after a short pause.

I took a bite of my sandwich, chewed, and swallowed before I told John what I remembered.

"It's funny. You didn't remember John Alder's name."

~~~~~~~~~~
Friday night, December 28, 1962

Attica's gym is quite large width seating on both sides. I believed this was the best design for a gym. I remembered being on

201

this floor in my Junior High and Junior Varsity days. I don't know how much playing time I got, but I got to practice before the game and at halftime. Now I was one of the main attractions. I was averaging twenty-nine points each game. That's not bad for a nerd, no, a former nerd.

Maybe I'm acting a bit overconfident, but this is overwhelming. I can't let it go to my head. My teammates are a significant part of my success. They play as hard as they can, as a team. That's why we haven't lost a game. If it weren't for their points, my scoring would mean nothing. I would merely be a player scoring for pride.

I'm playing for the town of Cutler Ridge, especially after the fight I had at Clyde's yesterday afternoon and finding out how many friends I had.

I didn't tell my parents about the fight; it just didn't seem like a big deal. And I didn't want Uncle Walter to find out. He might get excited and try to drag me back to Tennessee. I wouldn't go, but it would create a hassle. Why should my family worry? I won the fight, and I beat the bully. That's it.

My concentration is on the game as we are about to enter the floor. The JV game is over, and we are waiting behind the door at the end of the gym. Attica's players are beside us, and out of the corner of my eye, I can see some of the players looking at me. I guess they are sizing me up. I'm sure they know who I am, and they probably remember my teammates from the past. But I was the new kid on the block. Of course, I was one of the tallest players, especially for Cutler Ridge. I'm sure I stick out like a sore thumb. But that's better than being a little nerd.

Another incentive I have to play one of my best games tonight is that Uncle Walter is in the audience, bringing the excitement up a notch. I had a dream of playing Varsity for Cutler Ridge on this floor. It has a mystery about it. Attica was one of the

202

first schools in the county league to have glass backboards. Our school installed them just this year. Some schools in the league still have metal ones.

As we enter the floor to warm up, I calmed down. We are at half court, at the entrance. Fans who are coming into the gym see our team first. Chills went down my spine as I realized the home town fans were looking for me, the player so much has been written about.

Another reason that playing at Attica is exciting is that when Uncle Fred was alive, he had beef cattle and showed them at the local fairs. I wore white pants and shirt when I displayed the cows for him and made friends from other schools, even some from Attica. I hoped they remembered me and came to watch me play. I don't understand why I know their names, but I don't know people in my home town.

When they announced my name in the lineup, the Cutler Ridge crowd gave me overwhelming applause. As I turned toward the bench, the Attica crowd gave me a curious look as if they were thinking, "So this is the guy setting all kinds of scoring records."

The game started, and I automatically went to my zone and didn't hear a sound from a defender or fan, but I saw most of the Cutler Ridge fans on their feet cheering. I felt it was for me, and it pushed me to play better.

The defense hardly double-teamed me, but had three different guys guarding me; one every two or three minutes. But with all my moves they couldn't stop me. I was hitting shots from the start. I made most of the tries and got some of the rebound shots. Again, I scored most of the points for our team in the first half. But Attica had us by three points, thirty-three to thirty.

We played an excellent first half, especially on defense, and we seemed to have the inside locked, but their outside shooting and ball control was killing us. It seemed that nobody could hit but me and I wondered if it was a good defense. We were running our

203

regular offense with picks and cuts to the basket, and sometimes Tim would break to high-post and get an open shot. The same with Joey, from out front. He couldn't hit, either. Brad had an excellent first half, maybe eight or ten points and Rendles had a fast-break lay-up.

The second half went the same way, but there was more double-teaming against me and more shots for my teammates. They made a few shots, but it wasn't enough. Attica pulled away and led by ten points at the end of the third quarter.

In the fourth quarter, Attica had a lock-down defense. They played straight man-to-man defense, and they scored a quick eight points to our none. Coach called time out and put us in a spread with me at point guard. I prayed to God to let me turn it on, but I couldn't penetrate their defense. A sagging defense made me shoot outside; God hadn't answered my prayer. I was able to make some shots, but not enough to make a rally. We had met our Waterloo, and we lost.

The final score was eighty points to our sixty-six. I had made thirty points, should I cheer about that? I felt good about what I did, but still, I had no bragging rights. It was a team effort, and the team lost. Maybe I should be ashamed because they all expected me to score the points. They were afraid to shoot. Perhaps they believed the defense was too difficult. My teammates had shots, but they were afraid to take them. It was as if they were saying, "Here, Jimmy, you shoot."

If it had been Jake, he would be walking around, all cocky and not caring about the team as long as he made all the points.

All at once, I realized, "Am I remembering Jake?" I guess I was a little bit. I remember seeing his arrogance, but that's all I saw, no face, no body, nothing. That was weird; maybe God doesn't want me to see how he looks. It seems that's just the way it is with my memory.

There is no way I want to be like him, a king that wanted everybody to bow down before him. I remember Jake, but I can't remember how he looked. I only remember his attitude.

I want friends, and I want to play basketball with my friends. I'm not a star all by myself, that's selfish.

Now, how do we handle this loss? People will say, "Jimmy Bass did all he could, but his team failed him."

I might even hear them say I'm a gunner and didn't let my teammates have a chance to score. That would be a bald-faced lie, but if it comes out, I have to accept it.

After considerable thought, I knew I had to keep the joy of the points I scored, to myself. I could never hold it against my teammates. If this happened when I was playing for coach Summerall, I might I have acted differently, maybe even show up Jake.

Just then, my train of thought was interrupted, and I was sitting on the bus with Joey.

"Jimmy, this loss isn't your fault; it's us. I had times where I knew I could drive on my man to the basket, but I was afraid. What if I missed? I would look like a fool. The other players felt the same way. It's like we wanted you to do all the scoring. We were afraid to try, but you're calm and collected. How do you do that? I don't want to quit shooting. I know I should help you score, but their defense made us look like fools."

I wondered what kind of response I should give, and suddenly it came to me. "Jimmy, you shoot good outside in practice, and you're super at driving, especially if somebody shuts you down. You can pass two big men for an easy lay-up. You need to trust what you do in practice. If you can do it in practice, and you can do it in a game. I can shoot outside because I practice outside shots over and over again. And I'm tall enough that no one can stop me. Attica proved that all they had to do was to stop my teammates, and they would win the game. The team could score against them, but you

205

were afraid."

I paused for a second to look Joey in the face, then commented, "I'm not trying to put you down, Joey, and I'm sorry if I did, but I want you to enjoy scoring, too."

"You're right, you're right," Joey grinned.

That was the end of our conversation. There were people at Keller's restaurant and some on the street to console us. But they still wanted us to eat with them at Keller's, so we did. Some wanted a brag about me and my points, but I humbly thanked them and shook my head, saying it was useless to praise me when we didn't win.

All of this humbleness came from my dream. I had wanted people to praise me, and I enjoyed it, but being humble was crucial.

Praise be to God.

Chapter Eighteen

Dear Elisabeth,

When you get this letter, I will be in another world. The pain is so intense I can not survive. My memory is fading away, and last night, something terrifying happened. I was in the country, running for my life. Was it real? Maybe the pain was causing me to believe somebody was after me. That is all I can remember. When I woke up, I was in my room, on my in bed, fully clothed, but covered in dirt from head to toe.

My father has gone on a business trip, Mother went with him, and Sandy is staying with a friend. This day has been a haze. I am writing this letter before I go to the skating park at Tiffin. When I woke up, I took a shower and found cuts on much of my body. It looks like they came from a belt. I washed my bedding and my clothes.

I don't have to worry about Sandy; she is going home with that same friend she was with last night.

I should be in school, but I don't understand what is happening. I am writing to you the only person I love.

The pain is coming, and it is unbearable, Elisabeth, help me. I'm scared! Who is going to help me? My father beats me whenever he gets a chance. I know some of the marks on my body are from his belt.

Help me, Elisabeth. Help me!

Your friend,

Jimmy

~~~~~~~~~~

John was in his office on Saturday morning, talking to Elisabeth Hasselback. She revealed the situation she was in with Jimmy and the letters he had written to her. She explained that she had paid no attention to the last two or three letters and asked John to read them because she thought they could be helpful to Jimmy's recovery of his memory.

When he finished reading, she confessed, "I was cruel to him just before the incident. My problem was pride, trying to be popular, and I hurt Jimmy horribly. If we meet and start talking, he may remember what I did to him. How do you think he will react?"

"Do you want to be friends with him again?" asked John.

Elizabeth looked down as tears formed. "Yes," she answered. "I most certainly do! I made a big mistake with Jimmy and want to make it up to him. We may never become lovers, but I want his friendship."

"Okay, when you meet, tell him how good a friend you were in the past. Be truthful and tell him how you hurt him. It's better to tell him, then to hide it until he remembers. You don't have to tell him all of the details; just let him know that you think he cared for you very much, that you walked away from him, and that you know you hurt him deeply. You don't need to tell him all of the grim events of his life."

"You don't want him to know a lot of offensive events of his life? I thought the more he knows in advance, the better it would be when he finally remembers."

208

"Your logic is sound, but that's not the way his doctor wants it. And don't let him know about these letters, especially the last two."

"Okay, I understand. Since you're Jimmy's counselor, would you keep the letters and show them to him when you think the time is right?"

"Let me ask about the last letter and his run in the country. Do you think his father whipped him with a belt?"

"I'm sure he did! His father was very ashamed of him, especially the way Jimmy was acting before the incident. He wanted his son to be a man and beat up the bullies. I know Jimmy was small, but I believe he could have fought back because of his quick hands."

"You're right. Jimmy does have quick hands, but he got beaten down so much, he didn't believe anything good could happen to him."

"That describes Jimmy, to a tee."

~~~~~~~~~

When Elizabeth left John's house, she was hungry, and it was close to noon, so instead of going home to an empty house, she drove uptown and parked close to Keller's.

As she walked into the restaurant, she spotted me sitting alone in one of the front booths, and debated if it was too forward to step up to my booth and ask to sit with me, so she stood between the door and my table, feeling embarrassed. She was about to leave, or maybe find another place, but I had seen her come in and knew that she was trying to figure out where to sit, so I shouted, "Elisabeth Hasselback, do you remember me? I'm Jimmy Bass. We used to be friends, and I want to talk to you." She looked at me and walked over to my booth.

"Can I sit with you?" she asked.

"Sure I would enjoy that."

As she sat, I asked, "Have you heard about my memory?"

She nodded as she took off her jacket and laid it on the seat beside her.

"It's strange. There are very few people I remember in this town. It's like I'm making all new friends, then I find out they were my friends before. However, when Pat introduced you to me, I felt a connection. Then the night when someone came up with that horrible hoax, I recognized you here in Keller's. As time goes on, I remember more and more about you."

She changed the subject by saying, "I didn't realize how tall you have grown. Seeing you playing on in the game is one thing, but up close is different. Before the..." She was going to say, "the incident," but she stopped herself.

"I was five-foot-ten, and now I'm six-foot-four. It's hard for me to believe I'm this tall, but I enjoy it on the court. Height is in my genes. I have cousins who are six-foot-six and six-foot-seven. My uncle, the psychiatrist and my doctor, is six-foot-two."

"That's amazing, Jimmy. I bet you surprised a lot of people when they first saw you."

"Ya, they were amazed. Some recognized me right away and said my face hasn't changed."

"They're right. It hasn't. You have the same facial expressions, the same blue eyes, and the same blonde hair."

"I'd like to get back to the subject of our childhood, if that's okay, with you."

"Okay." she grinned and thought to herself, "He's cute, and his height seems to give him a mature masculine look. He probably doesn't know it, but he could sweep any girl off her feet."

"When we were around ten or twelve, I was old enough to help Uncle Fred on the farm, and I remember you would bring a cold drink out to me while I was running the tractor. We became closer in school and stayed friends until the last half of the basketball season, the time everybody calls 'the incident.' I'm not supposed to ask anybody what happen to me at that time or even where it was. And I don't want to know because it scares me. I don't know why, but it does!"

Elizabeth didn't waste time and did what John had just told her. "Well, Jimmy, during that time I hurt you."

When she said that she hurt him, a memory suddenly returned. I could feel the pain she had caused and didn't know what it was. I just wanted to run. All that I had imagined I would feel for her wasn't there. The pain she had caused returned. I had hoped it might be love at first sight, but that was stupid, it wasn't going to happen.

As the pain pounded at me, I knew I had to get away, but I wanted to be polite, so he lied, "You did? I don't remember."

I knew she had dumped me and had humiliated me, telling me to leave her alone. The embarrassment and pain she had caused me at that time made me want to run from her.

Wait! That was the old me. I used to run from anything that felt like rejection, especially girls. That's what Elisabeth did to me. I realized I had refused all of Marsha's advances for fear of a brushoff. Now I had to forget how Elisabeth had discarded me and try to make a new friend.

Elizabeth knew I remembered something about our past, especially the pain she had caused me. I looked sad, and she wondered if she should she open up to me?

"Maybe I should leave," Elisabeth thought. "Jimmy has a good life now, and he doesn't need the pain I caused or the hurtful memories that messed him up."

211

I changed the subject to basketball, and after a pleasant conversation, we left the restaurant as friends and promised to meet each other for lunch at Keller's next Saturday morning.

Elizabeth suggested we could meet after a game, and I nodded, "If it works out."

When we departed, the pain she caused me was gone. I hoped it would stay away and prayed fervently about it.

~~~~~~~~~

On Sunday night, in a Tiffin bar on Washington Street, John Alter was drinking a beer with someone he considered an old acquaintance, not a friend. The only alcohol that one could drink on Sundays was three-two beer, the strength a person under twenty-one could drink. John took a drag on his Chesterfield.

"So that was Bass that took me down?" he probed Randy Diller, as he lowered his head in shame.

"Yes, he is the former little guy you used to pick on. Now he's grown into a man, bigger than you, and he knows martial arts, too. You are stupid to think you can still get him."

"No, Randy, I want nothing to do with him," Alter stated as he took a drink from his beer. "I saw firsthand how tough and mean he can be. He could have busted my arm, and I wouldn't blame him, after the way I treated him in school. I want you to tell him I'm sorry, and I won't bother him again."

Randy could see Alter's hands shaking, so he let him have it. "He is got you scared! Are you afraid he is going to come looking for you and take revenge?"

"Listen, I want no part of him. You're his friend, so you tell him I'm sorry."

Randy knew Jimmy would never come looking for John. Jimmy Bass was a Christian, and it wasn't his style. But a little more

212

fear for John might help to keep him away. "Your right, John, stay away from him. What I saw in his eyes when he had you on the hood, was pure hate. He could feel the pain you caused him, and if that preacher friend of his hadn't told him to back away, a broken arm would be the least of your worries."

Taking another drink, Adler answered, "I know." Then using a couple of swear words, he said, "When we left the gas station, I told Jake and Jude the same thing. But Jake has Jude convinced that whoever we saw wasn't the real Bass. Jake still believes Bass is a *%^#@&* nerd. I told them I'm done, and I am! I didn't care what they call me. I left vowing to never hang with them again. I told them they should grow up. But it's Jake and his record; he doesn't want a nerd to break his record. It's a matter of pride!"

After a short pause, he swore again, followed with, "Stupid! Stupid! Stupid!"

"So Jake is going to replace you in stalking him?" Randy asked.
Alder laughed. "Are you kidding? Jake doesn't do any dirty work. He hires it out."

"Jake paid you to go after Bass?" Randy asked as he lit a Lucky Strike, then took a sip of his beer.

"Ya, but he wouldn't pay because I didn't do the job. Of course, I didn't ask him for it. When I left, I called him a fool."

Alder lowered his gaze, shook his head, then announced, "You tell Bass and some of the tough guys in town to look for Singer and somebody else. They will be after Bass, I guarantee it. Jake's pride is at stake.

~~~~~~~~~

We had two practices before our next game, on Friday, January the forth, at New Reigal. Brad and I always practiced as long as we could, until Coach Chumbly had to leave. We dressed quickly

213

without taking a shower and left in Brad's truck. Brad, like Joey, had become close to me. He understood why my sister didn't want to see him anymore. I had explained to him about my father and the age difference.

He found out about the trouble that might come from Tiffin from Jake Bickhart. But being from the big city, he knew how to fight, so he took me home after practices, in case we ran into trouble from Jake's people.

Randy told everyone he could in Tiffin about Singer and the thugs. He informed me that John Alter had apologized for all the wrongs he had done to me and that he was scared to death of me. That made me feel good, maybe powerful. No one had ever feared me.

Alder also said that Jude Singer and another of Jake's hired guns were out to break my right hand so I couldn't make shots and break his record.

"That's stupid," I declared. "A lot of things could happen through a season, and if I get hurt, everybody will know who did it."

"But Jake is always clean, letting other people do his dirty work," explained Randy.

I understood what Randy meant, but I couldn't believe the way Father reacted when he heard this. He wanted protection for me. I told him I could handle myself, but Father wouldn't accept it. It's funny how he worries about me getting into a fight when he used to hate me because I wouldn't fight. I guess Father has to protect his property, and that's me. I told him about Brad Weiden and the rough life he had lived in the big city. Father told me to ask Brad to look out for me, and he agreed, saying, "We can't let our leading scorer get hurt!"

So after practice, I'd be safe. In the morning, when father went to work, he said he would drop me off at Clyde's. But Father

214

left for work an hour before school started. I objected, but it was like protesting to the wind. Father had determined that I needed protection. Believe it or not, Clyde agreed with Father, and so did most of the people in town. They didn't want hoodlums hurting their star player.

Our school didn't have lockers, except in the gym, so on the first day back in school, Wednesday, the second of January, I found a message from my tormentors in my homeroom desk.

"If you didn't leave town, a certain nerd will get the worst beating of his life. There are guys after you that are far greater fighters then John Alter," they wrote. Of course, nobody signed it.

I didn't know if I should make a big deal of it or not. I chose not, figuring it wasn't a big deal. My enemies must have thought I was a coward, and threatening me would cause me to run like a coward. But I'm a man, now, and I can handle it myself. I assume I was a coward in my past, but not now.

Thursday's letter was different. It said if I didn't leave, they would reveal my sexual past in Tennessee. Where did they get the idea I had a sexual history or that I was a pervert? I've never had sex. I'm a virgin.

This person had to be the Jake, everyone tells me about, pushing the sexual pervert angle. I figure it's Father's lie, that I was in the state mental institution, that made him think I learned to be a sexual pervert there. They went on to say soon they would reveal damaging evidence to prove their case.

This letter crossed the line so I showed my homeroom teacher the letters and she sent me to the Superintendent.

In a small school like Cutler Ridge, the Superintendent was in charge of discipline. We had a principal, but he was also a teacher and only disciplined as back up.

Superintendent Shumer was furious, and he understood my

215

anger. He ensured me he would find out who had done this. All day long, he or the principal pulled Seniors out of their classes, questioning them about who had been around my desk before school started.

The end of the school day as Brad and I were heading for practice. The Superintendent stopped us and told me he didn't find anything, but would keep looking.

Friday morning, Father left for work at six-thirty, like he did every morning, and dropped me off at Clyde's to wait until school started. As I did before basketball, I helped out by pumping gas since self-service stations didn't exist in those days.

A brand new red Impala Super Sport pulled into the station, and I recognized it right away as the one that had been staking our house. Last night, after Brad dropped me off, I saw the car with its engine running, parked a block from our house. I thought that was odd. Who would park their car and leave the engine running?

Maybe it was legitimate. Somebody may have stopped for a quick visit, and left the car running so it would be warm when they returned. Then I saw what looked like two cigarettes glowing in the front seat, but I didn't say anything because I wasn't sure.

Later on, when Father was working in the shop, Mother was in the living room, and Sandy in her room, I sneaked out the back door. Using neighbors back yard lights to illuminate my way, I crept up on the car without anyone seeing me. I got close enough to touch the car, but I didn't. I wanted to see who it was, and my questions had answers. It was Jude with some guy I had never seen before.

Randy was beside me when he saw the car came into Clyde's and told me he would take it. As soon as they saw Randy, they peeled out of the gas station, and Randy walked back to the office.

"The one replacing John is a guy I know. He's not as tough as John, but he thinks he's strong. In reality, he couldn't fight his way

216

out of a wet paper bag. I heard that Jake is trying to get some seriously tough guys to work for him, but they all told him to go fly a kite, especially after they heard what you did to Alter. So that's all Jake can get. He's scrapping the bottom of the barrel."

Looking at me with a smile on his face, Randy declared, "Singer is all show. He tries to make you scared of him by looking mean and talking tough. But he is scared to death of you!"

~~~~~~~~~

When I went to school, I expected another letter, but I was disappointed. There was none. Shumer's questions must have scared whoever it was away. I began to think it might be a classmate.

The talk in town was about our loss to Attica. Could this be the start of our downfall? The people in town had never seen the success we had so far, and they didn't want it to go away. Losing was something they had gotten used to, but now that they had tasted winning, they didn't want to suffer again.

Clyde talked to me about what the people were saying, and I told him to tell them the team, and I would not let them down.

I'm sure Clyde told me how the people felt to get a reaction from me. When I gave it to him, he seemed pleased. Then I did something I don't usually do with our team. I told them what Clyde said and kept firing them up during practice. They were surprised by the way I acted, but I got no complaints.

That night was the game at New Reigal. Their gym has stands for the fans on one side, and a stage on the other. It's the same size as ours, with the entrance at one end and doors that lead to the locker rooms at the other end.

Although this was the first game of the New Year, a memory suddenly came to me, and I felt the pain of going to this gym and knowing I wasn't going to play. I was sure people were staring at me, thinking I was worthless. I don't understand why the pain hit me so

217

hard as I was warming up. I had to convince myself that I was a starter and a good one at that. I kept pumping myself up for the game, so when it started, I was ready to play.

I figured they might play a box-in-one, like when we played them before, and our coach thought so, too. We worked on it a lot in practice, but it was for nothing. They had a reasonably good team, only losing four games out of nine, and probably felt their regular two-three-zone was strong enough. But they didn't do so well against me when they played the box-and-one.

Again I was in a zone, blocking out any crowd or opponents sounds. I kept thinking, "The game and only the game." It worked, too, along with prayers to God.

It was an outside shooting game for us with New Reigal packing in the zone defense and taking away any notion of an inside game. They were good!

We used the high-post-offense, passing the ball around to get a shot. Almost every time, down the court, Rendles and I would switch sides on the wing, instead of using a rotating offense. With my height, their players couldn't block my shots. Good passing by Joey and occasionally from Tim playing high post got me plenty of chances in the first half, and I made a good percentage of them.

My talk to Joey on our bus ride home from Attica had worked. Joey shot from the point guard position and missed the first two, then started connecting. Towards the end of the first half, he hit three or four of them. Rendles learned to use the backboard for an outside shot. He had asked me if I would teach him, and I did. Now he was hitting them.

We had only a few stick-backs by Brad. They had him pretty well boxed out. Tim didn't score, even at the high post, because of that he got packed in. In their game plan, they were boxing me out with their guards, making sure I didn't get close to the basket for an offensive rebound and they made sure we didn't fast-break.

No matter who shot the ball for the home team, their center was the only one staying inside. The rest the team made a beeline down to the other end of the court. There was no possibility we could fast-break. As for steals, there were none. The home team handled the ball well, with only two turnovers.

New Reigal's big men, in a double low-post, were getting most of the points for their team. They both had moves that avoided Brad's high jumping ability. Tim had no luck with the other one. Maybe I could stop one of them, but I didn't think Coach would let me because he was afraid I might get in foul trouble. So I didn't ask him. It also might make Brad or Tim angry with me, thinking I could do there job and they couldn't. Another reason was that it had never happened. I obeyed the coach and didn't give my opinion.

At halftime, the score tied at thirty all. As we went to the locker room, Coach told the guards to gamble. Drop down when the ball gets passed to one of the big men. They have a habit of taking at least one dribble before they shoot. This order was given to Joey and Jack, to try to get a steal, but not me. Coach was afraid I would get into foul trouble.

Their offense was three guards and the two big men, with the big guy getting most of the opportunities. The guard sometimes used a weave, but our defense kept their guards from scoring, except for a couple of times. When their guards were anywhere near me, they wouldn't shoot because of my reputation of blocking shots. Neither Brad nor Tim would front the big guys, for fear of passes over there heads would become a basket.

As we entered the floor to warm up for the second half, some of my teammates cried, "No, Attica!" Meaning we didn't want another loss. We kept pumping each other up. I felt shy at the start of the second half.

Coach's idea about the guards worked. We started getting some fast-break point steals from their big guys leading us to a ten-point lead.

New Reigal made adjustments throughout the quarter. Their big men started looking for our sagging guards. A quick pass to their guards gave them shots, and they made some of them. They played a two-person game, giving them enough scoring to stay within ten points of us. Joey got in deep foul trouble with four fouls and had to sit out parts of the third quarter as well as the forth. Can you believe it? Coach made the tallest man on the team play point. Yes, that was me.

After passing the ball around, the team again relied on me to do the scoring. I didn't disappoint them, especially in the fourth quarter, at point guard. So we kept our lead at ten points. Joey came in around the middle of the fourth quarter, and I was back on the wing.

The home team had a new play to their offense, and I got suckered away from my player on a pick and rolled. Their guard scored a lay-up, making the score fifty-five to forty-seven, with around three and a half minutes to go.

As I brought the ball down the floor, a man was guarding me. At first, I thought box-and-one, but instead, it was a man-to-man. Coach called out the spread is an offense we will play at times. The wing-men went almost to the side out of bounds line, and the big men went to the corner so I could go one-on-one with my defender. I blew by my man for an uncontested lay-up.

On offense, the home team tried to play the same play, that they suckered me with before. A pass to the wing-man and a pick got by one of two big men. I moved around the pick of the player with Brad guarding him. And set, there was a big argument layout, and I stole the ball. Brad saw what was going on and broke down the floor as I passed it to him knowing I was trailing him and probably
220

knowing I had the rebound if he missed as he went in for a dunk.

These days, basketball teams, especially in a small school never dunk in a warm-up, let alone a game. With my height, it wouldn't be such a surprise. Even though Brad jumped the center, his six-foot height, nobody would expect it from him. Most coaches would allow it, but Coach never told him not to try it in a game. I had some dunks in earlier games, and both John and Coach Chumbly never said a word. They knew what was coming and I think half our fans did too. With his right hand, he slammed the ball through the hoop, and the place went wild. Even some of the home team fans enjoyed it. With the score fifty-seven to forty-seven, the home team called time out. Only two minutes and forty-five seconds were left.

When time resumed, we shut them down. Then I, on a pick, got switched to a big man. I showed my jumping ability and blocked his shot, but the referee saw it differently and called a foul. It was my third, and Coach pulled me aside, telling me not to try to block a shot again. These referees would always call it a foul except when you block a guard's shot. I didn't say a word but nodded at the coach. I agreed because some referees were like that. Earlier in the game, Brad found out the same way. Tim had four fouls all on tried blocks, but I was sure I had it clean and had to go for it. I'm sure I did, but men in striped shirts have the final say. Their player made one of his shots, and the score was now fifty-seven to forty-eight.

The home team was back in their two-three-zone, looking like they would use it as a trap. Coach Chumbley called a time out. He figured they would do this. With Tim at high-post and Joey on the wing, he moved me back to point, telling us to move the ball and stall, but if somebody had a bunny shot take it.

On offense, we moved the ball around, and we did an excellent job knocking thirty seconds off of the clock. Then they intentionally fouled Jack, figuring he would be the worst foul shooter. In practice, he was fair but now, with the pressure on, could he hit

221

them?

I knew when he released his shot; it would be nothing but net. His follow-through and his arch were both excellent. He made both of them, thus raising our lead to a fifty-nine to forty-seven edge.

With close to two minutes left in the game, I completely took over. On the home teams next possession, we held them to a contested shot from outside a deep rebound that I retrieved and drove the length of the court, then took a ten-foot backboard shot, giving us a sixty-one to forty-seven lead.

Our defense held again, and as I tried a fast break, I was planning to slow it down, but Coach screamed, "Go, Bass, go!" meaning to push the fast-break. I did and got fouled on a short shot, but with an acrobatic shot, I reached out with my left hand and made a backboard shot. The visiting crowd roared as I walked to the foul line. I made it, bringing the score to sixty-five to forty-seven.

The home team made one more basket, I made three foul shots, and Brad had a stick-back. With twenty seconds left and a seventy to forty-eight lead, I got taken out of the game.

The crowd roared as I looked up at them. I even saw some New Reigal fans applauding for me. Two of our fans were standing with the group, but they weren't cheering. It was Jude Singer and a tall, lanky guy beside him. Both were staring at me, glaring with hatred and sending a chill down my spine.

I look away as I was coming to the bench. Just before I sat down to be congratulated by the players and the coaches, I took one more look at the men, and they weren't there. I stood up to get a better look and see if they were leaving. They had to go through the fans to leave. I sat back down, wondering what that was all about.

In the locker room, I heard I had made thirty-four points, but I hardly said a word. I acted excited, like the rest of the team, and I was. The sour feeling that we had after Attica was gone.

The feelings now came from the sight of Jude and that other guy. I'm sure it was Jake. No, it had to be a vision from my past. I'm sure they weren't there. Thoughts of those two started to push me into a haze.

"The King" with his glaring eyes started to control my thoughts. I never saw so much hate directed at me. "The King," why did I think that? But the daze seemed to stay with me. Their evil stares wouldn't go away.

Suddenly, I was heading home on the bus, but I had no smile on my face. Everything seemed to look different. I was wearing clothes that I hadn't worn for over a year. It was an outfit like every player wore, but something about it wasn't something that would come from my closet anymore.

I stood up and realized I was sitting on the back seat. I usually sat in the middle. The people were different, too. I didn't know the players or cheerleaders, except for Pat Ender, Bill Kumar, and Glen Hass. The others seemed to be kids from my class. I remember their faces but not their names. What are they doing on the bus? They were classmates from my Junior year. Then I understood that time had rolled back, and Coach Summerall was sitting in the front seat.

The trio walking down the aisle toward my seat was another surprise. I was ready to fight, but I realized I didn't know how to fight. My body wasn't as big or strong, even though I was the same height as Alter. Maybe he wasn't as strong as me, but there were three of them. I was no match for them. Fear controlled me, and I felt like a sitting duck.

All at once, Jude sat down on the seat and pushed me against the side of the bus. Then John sat on the bench and pushed hard against Jude, and I was shoved harder to the side of the bus. I was sitting in the back seat for a reason, and I didn't want anybody to see me. No one but my tormentors saw me.

223

Who was my protector? It certainly wasn't the Coach. Nobody would turn around to look at me and the trio. They were glad the trio were picking on me and not them. If I screamed for help, nobody would respond. The trio had everybody scared of them, even my friend Pat was scared. His friendship was the only thing that made up for how he let the trio torment me.

Jude kept punching me in the stomach and asking me why I didn't play tonight. Their words and punches in the stomach, on the arm, and some in the chest left me in misery.

I realized this was a memory, not a fantasy, and I wanted it to go away. I was on the bus ride home from a game in New Reigal. That's when it happened.

I shook the memory out of my head, and I was back in the present world, sitting towards the front of the bus with Joey like I always did. Neither he nor anyone else noticed I had been out.

The thought of what the trio had done to me sent chills down my back, just like those eyes I saw at the game. My hands were shaking, so I clasped them together. I prayed that God would help me relax. After a few minutes, I calmed down.

~~~~~~~~~~

I got a call from Jake, at least I thought it was Jake. If anyone else had answered, he would have hung up. All he said was, "Let my boys break a couple of the fingers in your right hand, and all will be even."

I tried to tell him what I thought of his idea, but he hung up. I wasn't afraid, or was I? Those eyes still shook me up and scoring my thirty-four points stirred his anger.

I have to get over it. Jude and Jake weren't at the game. I beat one of my enemies, and now he was scared. I realized I could fight, and I'm ready.

224

I wanted vengeance! I deserved it! Then a voice seemed to say, "Vengeance is the Lord's."

Then another voice, beside me, said, "What are you thinking, Jimmy?"

I wanted to say, "I was thinking about my enemies and how I would like to tear them apart!"

I wanted to say, "I thought I saw Jake Burkhart and Jude at the game. When I came out of the game, their stares were deadly."

But I couldn't say that or talk about my nightmare. Only John would know about it. So I said nothing.

That was another intentional lie. I asked God to forgive me again, but I still didn't want to say anything about the vision of my depression.

We started talking about the game and my scoring. Joey was bragging me up, and as always, I reminded him it was a team effort. I meant it, but I also liked him bragging me up. I told him how good he was, too. It was corny, but it was also enjoyable.

The bus rolled into our town and stopped in front of the school. I could see there was a crowd in Keller's. As we left the bus, a voice behind me whispered, close to my ear, "We can get you any time, fag."

I quickly turned around and saw the back of a person running away. He was dressed entirely in black and pushing people out of the way as he ran away. People around me, mostly fans, asked what was going on. I explained, "He threatened me."

They wanted to know what he said, and I told them Several men took off to find him. People around me asked if I was okay. I nodded, but inside me, I was scared.

"He could have put a knife in my back," I thought, and it

225

shocked me. Would it go that far? Maybe they would try to cut my hand.

When I entered the restaurant, Marsha grabbed me, asking where I had been, and led me to a table where the cheerleaders and team were sitting. The crowd gave us a cheer, and I saw Elisabeth looking at me from another table. She looked sad, and I began to feel the pain.

Then I remembered I had told her I would see her after the game. I broke away from Marsha's hand, excused myself, and looked toward Elisabeth. She looked so beautiful. I couldn't get to her fast enough. She smiled when she saw me coming. It took a while because there were so many fans who wanted to talk to me and shake my hand. I knew Elisabeth understood.

As soon as I sat beside her, she took my hand, and I felt electricity go through my body. Even if she had hurt me before, love had given me a second chance. Gone were the nightmares. Gone was the man who whispered at me. I was in la, la land. When I glanced toward Marsha, she looked like she could kill me.

Chapter Nineteen

On Saturday, January 5, I went to John's office for another counseling session. We didn't meet every Saturday anymore, only twice a month.

"This guy said we could get you anytime, fag?" John asked.

"Yes, but I think it's from someone besides Jake and his buddies."

"Who could that be?"

"I don't know, but I have a feeling I'll find out soon."

"Could it be Sam Sessions?"

"It wasn't Sam that gave me the message. He's too small and is still trying to get me to lose my temper in school. Every time he get's close enough to say something to me, it's something bad and mostly when nobody can hear but me. When he makes an unkind remark to me, he always has a big smile on his face, so everyone thinks he's nice to me."

"Do you think the notes you get are coming from Sam?"

"I can't say, John."

"I'm sorry somebody is out to get you. But by what you say, it might be three different people. How are you dealing with this? Are you scared?"

"I don't want anything to do with fear. I continually ask God to control me and keep me from fear. I am watchful and cautious, and I feel safe in school, at home, in church, or here with you. I also feel safe while we are practicing and when we're playing a game. I have no fear while sitting on the bench, but I was afraid when we were warming up last night."

I explained about the fear I felt when we were warming up and the evil stare I thought was Jake and Jude.

The dream on the bus brought back a lot of anxiety!" I admitted.

"Some of your memories are coming back, but they're not good memories?"

"I guess."

"You have to stay close to God and pray."

I agreed with John by nodding my head.

"Are you trying to suppress your past as your Father wants you to?"

"I can't; they come out quickly. I might be talking to someone, and instantly, a memory comes. I always think, 'Where did that come from?' There's no voice saying, 'Jimmy, here comes another memory.' So I can't do what Father wants. I don't know what to tell him. I know it's not what he wants, so I try to keep it a secret. I don't know what he would do if I told him I remember things. He might go berserk."

"If he does and you can't handle him, come to me. I'll help you, all I can, with him. Better yet, do you want me to talk to him?"

That comment scared me, and I blurted out, "No, John, at least not yet, I think God wants me to wait and cross that bridge. when it comes."

"I don't want you to get into a fight with your father. If it gets physical, I have no doubt you could take him, but you might hurt him. In our conversations, Jimmy, you have not shown, any anger or resentment towards him. If you lose your temper, you could hurt your father. I know you are praying about it, but sometimes Satan stirs things up."

I accepted what John said, knowing I could tear my father apart. If that situation came up, I would run to John. He also told me to be careful with everything on my plate. I understood what he meant and agreed with him.

As I left John's, thinking over the situation around me, I realized trouble could jump out at me anywhere. If my truck didn't start, I would think someone got under the hood and messed things up. What is the matter with me? I am safe, in John's neighborhood, yet I keep watching, feeling that at any time, trouble could come.

The truck did start, and I drove to Keller's to get something to eat and have another date with Elisabeth.

I parked in front of the restaurant and went inside. Elizabeth's Buick was outside, so I knew she was already there, sitting in the same booth we did the week before. I hesitated before going up to the booth because all I could feel was that pain, again. I have forgiven her, but the fear remains, even after our time together last night, and the kiss she gave when she drove me home.

I sent up a quick prayer before I walked to the booth and sat across from her. "Hi!" I greeted.

She looked so cute, and I was attracted to her more now than last night. But the fear of rejection was so intense that I felt like running away. No, I had to be strong. She is my friend, but I had to

229

shove her attractiveness away. It was so difficult, but I had to do it. After last night I was afraid I couldn't. I wanted to love her with all my heart. However, the fear of rejection rose its ugly head. Last night, I felt no hesitation, so why now?

Elizabeth broke my train of thought with a question. "What happened last night? I mean the romance we felt towards each other?"

Her inquiry caught me entirely off guard. I thought everything was real last night. Was this rejection already? She didn't ask the question with an irritable tone, and she was smiling. Well, that was something! But what did it mean?

I was curious about how I felt about her. Maybe being dragged into the restaurant by Marsha is what made her curious. I didn't know what to say. I was confused.

Elisabeth understood Jimmy. He was still as bashful as she remembered. The boy had never had an attraction to girls, except for her, and she had rejected him, causing total confusion. He was innocent when it came to girls.

"I don't know what to say about last night, Elisabeth. I've never had a girlfriend. Marsha's not my girlfriend. She would like to be, but I won't let her. She's too young for me. I'm an adult, and she's a minor. It's pure and simple. But after last night, you seemed to like me, maybe more."

I started to say more, but she waved her hands in front of her and said, "I don't know why I asked that question. I was treating you like some of the jerks I dated before. You aren't like that. You're the same nice boy you were before."

She waved her hands in front of her again and said, "Sorry, I didn't mean it that way. You have grown from a boy to a man."

After a pause, she continued. "I know, I'm on the subject of how I hurt you. But, Jimmy, Jake was good looking and very popular. I fell for him, and his lines caused me to lose my…"

She stopped talking, and instead of looking down, she looked me square in the eyes. "You know what I mean, Jimmy?"

Yes, I knew what she meant. She lost her virginity. That was something I didn't need to know. I guess this Jake was a fool. He didn't care who he hurt. He took and took and didn't care who he hurt, just so long as he got what he wanted. What I had, heard about what he did to me wasn't very good. I wish I could remember, but maybe that wouldn't be so good.

"The reason I asked the question was to know how you feel about me? Forget about that Jake thing!"

I paused for a second to think but knew I didn't want to play games with Elizabeth's feelings, even though I knew how to play games. So I said, "I like you very much." I don't know why I couldn't say, "Love."

"Thank you, Jimmy, that's what I wanted to know."

"But, I have a fear of being rejected."

"I understand. At school, you could be like Jake."

I glared at her.

"Jimmy, I don't mean about you being a bully. But I'll bet you are the most popular boy in school. I saw you with Marsha James. She the most popular girl in school and the way she was so close to you last night, I thought maybe you were a couple. When you came over to me, I didn't know what to think."

"Last Saturday we agreed to meet on Friday night after the game. As soon as I came into the restaurant, I looked for you. But Marsha grabbed me, and before I could respond, she dragged me to the table where the team was."

231

"I understand, Jimmy."

~~~~~~~~~

We played Green Springs that night, a school north of us, close to Fremont. This school is a little bigger than us. I don't know how many more kids they have than we do, but that is what they told me.

It was time for the game. I was fired up and in my zone. The home team's gym, like ours, has a stage and an auditorium. Their record was four and three because their school had football, and they didn't start playing basketball until December. We had played three more games than them.

Green Springs was also fired up, especially wanting to keep me from shooting from the outside. They not only had a box-and-one on me but every section I went into, the men were in the zone in that section and cut me off into a double team, leaving three defenders to guard my four teammates.

We changed our offense and played the box-in-one as we did against New Reigal, the first time we played them. With me moving from corner to corner, too much over guarding of me set up beautiful inside shots for Brad and Tim. And Joey got hot from the outside.

I was a forward and scored no points in the first quarter. I set picks for Tim and Brad, but with the home teams defense, I was just a decoy for my teams to score. In the second quarter, I got a few offensive rebounds but got fouled a lot and missed the shots. One time, on an offensive rebound, I went up so powerfully, I almost slammed it through, but instead, I just pushed the ball in the basket. There were very few points for me, a couple of rebound shots and the rest were foul shots.

I made only eight points in the first half, but my defense was great. The referee let Brad and me block shots. The rest of the

232

players were doing their job, so our team held Green Springs to only eighteen points in the first half. The halftime score was twenty-seven to eighteen.

Our lead increased as Green Spring kept using the box-in-one. I got a few inside shots and a few points when we pushed the fast break, but most were assists from me. I made two out of three long shots when I got open from the corner. All in all, this was my lowest scoring game at fifteen points. However, we shone in defense, allowing them to only forty-eight points to our sixty-six.

Brad was the high scorer, with twenty. Joey got sixteen. Tim had twelve points, and Rendles made four. I was happy for my teammates and showed it in the locker room by trying to instill in their minds that I wasn't for winning for the points I scored. Two stats I enjoyed were my fifteen rebounds and five assists.

After the game, when our bus rolled in town, fans were shaking our hands and thanking us. I quickly hurried to Elisabeth's car, and she took me to a Fremont restaurant to eat. She didn't believe I could trust Tiffin. Singer was still on the prowl. There was a little fear, but I knew that whoever came, I would be ready for them.

If they beat me and broke my fingers, I would continue to play, even if I had to be a power forward. I showed tonight that I could play inside.

I wanted to forget all about this and think about how I had ended up with Elisabeth. I knew I wanted no part of Marsha, and Elisabeth was taking me to Fremont!

~~~~~~~~~~

Sunday morning, Elizabeth went to church with me and loved John's preaching. She told me she wanted to come here with me every Sunday. I spent the afternoon at her house, and she cooked for me. We had a great time.

As I drove home in my truck, I felt I had found true love. I guess it was what I was looking for. Then I told myself to slow down. She is just a girlfriend. There is no reason to get carried away.

When I got home, neither of my parents said anything about Elisabeth. I was surprised. I thought Father would have said something after what Elisabeth did to me in school. Then I thought, 'Why would he?" I'm sure I never told him how I felt about Elisabeth, or how she hurt me. I'm sure he would never offer sympathy; it would be something about me being a man.

~~~~~~~~~~

Getting up early every morning wasn't just to please Father or for protection. I liked helping Clyde and Randy open the station. Clyde tried to pay me, but I refused, saying they were my friends and I enjoyed helping them. Oh, I got an occasional free drink, and that was enough. Since I had my school clothes on, I didn't do much in the shop. Mostly, I ran the gas pumps and the cash register to sell items in the station when Clyde was busy selling kids candy and Cokes before school.

Red Barber worked part-time for Clyde every Monday, Wednesday, and Friday. Afternoons, Red worked in a factory and would be gone by two. That gave Clyde time for a hair cut at eleven o'clock.

This Wednesday morning, Clyde was getting his hair cut at Fred Stalling's Barber Shop. Old Jim Dillin, Randy's grandfather, spent a lot of time either at the barbershop or at Clyde's. They enjoyed gossiping about people in our town and Clyde was getting an ear full from Fred while Jim was nodding in agreement with him.

"Think, Clyde, if Bass hadn't come back as the star he is, we would have a statue of Jake Bickhart on the sidewalk in front of our gym. Old Bob Bickhart was planning on it until Bass came along and broke all of his son's records."

"Ya, we sure wouldn't want that. That would be an

embarrassment."

Suddenly, Fred asked, "He isn't still planning to?"

Clyde responded, "He used to talk about it over at Wall's, and I heard him tell that he asked the school board members about it. Since Jimmy Bass came along, Arnold's bragging about his son after the games at Walls. Bob has kept his mouth shut." Fred commented.

"Isn't it weird? Arnold never talked about his son before. If he did, it was his shame. Now he's the greatest son a man could ever have."

"I know, "Clyde said, shaking his head.

"Don't count your chickens before they're hatched, Fred. Jimmy hasn't broken the records yet, except the part of winning more games. That is the only thing that matters. At the Green Springs game, he only scored fifteen points, and we still won."

"That's because Green Springs was worried about Bass scoring and did everything on defense to stop him. That left the rest of the team open for easy shots," Jim Diller stated.

"Jimmy didn't act as if he cared."

"Your right! He's that way, Fred. I think, sometimes the coaches have to push him to score. There is no arrogance in Jimmy. Once I asked him about his shooting, and he told me that before he left, I mean, before the incident, even though Jimmy was small, he could pass, rebound, and dribble. He could hustle on defense, too. But scoring was not a skill the boy had; so the coach didn't let him play. Now that he can score, he's allowed to play. Jimmy loves playing inside like when we played against Green Springs. He told me he never dreamed of scoring a lot of points and never felt he would be tall. He said that putting them together is one big dream come true."

After a short pause, Clyde continued. "Jimmy says he is happy to play and will do whatever he can to help the team win. Whether he scores forty points or just ten, he's happy. You saw him Saturday night. He wasn't disappointed that he only scored fifteen points. I don't think he cares about that record."

"That is true, but Jimmy has beaten Jake's single-game mark with forty points in the Bloomville game. If nothing happens to Jimmy, the way he is scoring, he will easily beat Jake's season record."

"Okay, Fred, what is Jimmy averaging and what did Jake average?"

"Jake averaged twenty-five-point-two points in twenty-one games. Jimmy is averaging close to thirty, right now, and it's only halfway through the season. If Jimmy only averages close to Jake's average for the rest of the year, he will still beat Jake's single-season scoring record."

"Your wrong, Fred," Jim Diller spoke up. "Bass is averaging less than twenty-nine points a game."

Fred gave him a dirty look. "One point, Jim, that's neither here nor there."

"You sound like you want Jimmy to beat Jake's average." Clyde declared.

"Yes, indeed, I do. For two reasons, Clyde. If he doesn't, we might get a statue."

"And we don't want that!" Clyde answered with a chuckle.

"If Jimmy fails and Jake gets his statue..." Fred started to comment.

"I don't want to think about that."

"So he has got to break the record!"

"Your acting as if all we think about is breaking a record.

236

What about winning a league? "

"Let's be realistic. We won't win the league even though we have a one-game lead. One of the bigger schools will beat us. Oh, everybody knows we are having a winning season. We'll most likely beat Thompson here on Friday night. We are guaranteed a winning season."

"First time in fifteen years." Jim Diller smiled.

"That is something to celebrate, but league champs is a pipe dream."

"Your right, Fred, a pipe dream," Diller acknowledged.

"How many games do you think we'll win?"

Fred went to a bulletin board that had the schedule on it. Then he commented, "Thompson on Friday night, Townsend a little over a week from now, and Republic towards the end of the season. That's three more games, Clyde. Our luck is about to run out on Saturday against Vanlue and the following week against Bettsville. Now, if Jimmy breaks not only Jake's record but also pushes some league records, our school will be something. That is what you, a friend of his, should be pushing him to do."

"I believe your wrong, maybe two more loses is all, Jim. Bass has got a great determination to play his best to win. He won't let us lose many more games."

They both stared at the sober-looking Clyde. Then shook their heads.

Jim announced, "Your crazy, Clyde. I guarantee you, that will never happen."

"We'll see, guys," Clyde said, smiling. "We'll see."

Chapter Twenty

Monday, during the noon hour, Marsha stormed into the auditorium and stopped in front of me. I could see she was angry!

"Saturday Night, I saw you with Elisabeth Hasselback, and you left town with her," she snapped.

I didn't know what to say. Should I tell Marsha that Elisabeth was my girlfriend and we were dating? Someone told me never to tell a woman the truth. I knew enough not to tell her a half-truth. That would be another lie.

Then I thought, why not play the game? I'm dating Elisabeth, but Marsha is a pretty girl that I enjoy being around. Should I string her along? No, there is no way I want to play that game. I'm sure God brought Elisabeth to me. I have always treated Marsha honorably in our friendship and have never shown a romantic interest. So with as gentle a voice as I could, I said, "Elisabeth and I are dating."

Some of Marsha's friends and several other students were watching us and when I said Elisabeth and I were dating and everyone became quiet, waiting for another outburst.

"You're making a fool of me!" she screamed.

Calmly I replied, "I don't see how. We were only friends. I always treated you as a friend."

"Well, maybe I want more," she whimpered.

I couldn't believe she said that but I wasn't going to argue with her. I didn't know what to say.

I had never had a girlfriend, except for Elisabeth, and she was the only one I wanted. I knew my emotions weren't ready for this, so I stood up and left her standing there with her hands on her hips.

As I left, the auditorium was quiet. I hurried to my homeroom and went to my desk, knowing Mister Popularity was gone. I felt terrible, but what did was not wrong. I was so sad that tears almost began to spill down my cheeks. I should feel overjoyed that a popular and pretty girl wanted me. I knew she was too young and didn't know what she was doing.

My lost memory, the confusion, and my enemies, some worse than Jake and his buddies were swirling around in my head and making it difficult to think. Elisabeth knew what was happening, and I knew she could help me in this confusing time. I think I love her!

Marsha is not in my world. I need to keep a low profile and not get close to any girl at school. But I can talk to Elisabeth!

I had a long talk with Joey while we were warming up for practice. He agreed with what I had done.

"I was concerned about you being a friend with Marsha. I wanted to say something, but I felt it was none of my business," Joey commented.

He stood still for a while as if he had more to say, then he explained, "She's a man-eater, Jimmy. When she was a Sophomore, lots of the guys were attracted to her, just like now. She dated any guy that made her look good, then when his usefulness was over, she dumped him. I know you don't want to hear this, but you are a star, and that's what she wants. She wants to be with you because you are the star. When basketball season is over, she'll be gone. She did the same thing to Bill Kumer last year. He fell for her hook, line, and sinker, but when the season was over, she dropped him."

The rest of the week went fine. Some of the girls said hi to me and even carried short conversations with me. Of course, Marsha and her friends didn't, and I was glad they didn't.

Wednesday night, I went to see Elisabeth at her place. When I told her what happened, I know she was pleased by the way she showed me that she was the girl for me. She didn't want to be near me because I was a star. Oh, she like watching me play, and she was glad the school was finally winning, but she wanted to be with me. When the basketball season was over, she would still be there.

As I drove home that night, I knew I had a girlfriend, and I felt I was on Cloud Nine, a feeling I never felt before.

~~~~~~~~~

Friday night, the eleventh of January, we had a home game against Thompson. They gave us all we could handle with their slow-down game. It was nick-and-tuck all the way. They had been successful this year and won more than they lost. With a minute and fifteen seconds left in the game, the score was forty-one to fifty, Thompson's favor. I had scored the most of our team's points, and now we were passing the ball around to get a good shot.

The team told me to go for it, so I went for my favorite backboard shot, from the left side, and praised God as I went down on defense. Thompson made a mistake on a pick, on offense. I stole the ball when the big guys of Thompson where both playing high post.

When Brad saw me get the steal on the right side, he ran

240

down the floor to receive a quick pass from me, and a slam through the hoop. The crowd woke up with a roaring cheer.

The score was now forty-four to fifty-one, Thompson, with forty-five seconds left. They had to take a quick shot, which was out of there nature. They missed and crashed the board hard as Tim held on for a rebound, quickly getting the ball to me. Thompson was pressing now and double-teamed me. I saw Rendles on our court, all alone in the corner. I promptly passed to him, and he drove to the basket. But the lone defender cut him off. I passed to Joey and got a lay-up and a foul. Joey got three points, making the score fifty to fifty-one.

Thompson fell apart as I made another quick steal and passed down the floor to Joey, who made a basket and a foul, another three points.

Getting steals towards the end of the game was easy for me. Thompson continually ran the same play over and over. I saw how it ran and where a gamble could get a steal. I caught them by surprise, and their players froze briefly leading to a fast-break basket. A couple of failed shots, in the end, and we pulled ahead. I scored against their zone defense all over the floor, and they made no effort to stop me. The final score was fifty-three to fifty-one.

~~~~~~~~~~

I went to John's office on Saturday morning, January twelve. After talking about the game, John asked, "How do you feel, Jimmy?"

"Other than being stuck in town, I'm okay. Oh, I can go to another town, as long as it isn't Tiffin. I'm always looking over my shoulder."

"Do you still get intimidating notes in your desk?"

"Not many threats this week, but Session is still making comments, and they aren't friendly. He makes sure nobody around us can hear him, but that is all."

241

Suddenly I remembered something I wanted to tell John. "I had an incident with a girl at school." Then I gave him the details about Marsha and Elisabeth.

"Are you happy with your relationship with Elisabeth?"

"Yes," I responded. "One thing I'm sure about is that Elisabeth understands me. We were together last Wednesday night, and when I drove home, I felt like I was floating on a cloud. I am thrilled that I have a girlfriend. That's something I always wanted. Now I know how it feels, but it still doesn't seem right, and I don't know why."

"You drove out of town alone to see her in your truck?"

"I thought it was safe to drive out in the country. Behind Father's shop is a stone driveway that goes to Uncle Fred's farm. We very seldom use it, and nobody knows it exists. Since there isn't much snow on the ground, Father and I figured it was safe. I have a lot of weight in the bed of the truck so that it will go through a lot of snow."

"Okay, I understand. But let's get back to Elisabeth."

"Being involved with a woman is something that terrifies me. Deep down in my memories, I feel a horrible hurt and rejection from girls. When I think about this fear, it is sometimes so bad that I want to cry."

I paused, then with a shaky voice, said, "I don't want to go there yet, John. I can't think about rejection, even though Elisabeth told me she would never leave me."

Then looking John in the eyes, I asked, "Do you think she'll ever leave me?"

John grinned. "At one time or another, everybody has to take a chance on love. I understand what scares you about Marsha, and I think you made the right choice with Elisabeth, but in the future, you

242

might decide not to date her. Just take it one day at a time and enjoy it.

I let that sink in and realized John was right. "Okay, here is another thing that bothers me, John. I came to this school as a mystery. In my mind, I wanted to be a normal kid, not a nerd like I thought I was in the past. Surprisingly, it turns out I am one of the most popular kids. I don't know if I want that, or if I can handle it."

"Jimmy, you're popular because of basketball. Do you want to quit playing basketball?"

"No!"

"Are you walking around school puffed up with pride?"

"I try hard to guard myself against acting like that. I think I should be a loner, but I like to talk. Talking to Marsha, as a friend, was a treat. It's good to have a girl as a friend. I'm beginning to learn how girls feel. When I think I'm ready to date, I'll have some idea how to act. Girls are a mystery. I want to know what they want and how to react. I know how to act with Elisabeth, or at least I think I do."

"Well, Jimmy, there are no answers to those questions. Each woman has a different personality and is physically different than we are. Guys are strong, and they are often not, but there are exceptions. Their feelings and emotions are different from ours. Their likes and dislikes are often different, too. A lot of things they want to talk about are varied. The only explanation is, they are feminine, and we are masculine."

"I think I understand what you're saying, John," I interrupted.

~~~~~~~~~

After my visit with John, I drove uptown for a date with Elisabeth and parked in front of Keller's. Exiting the truck, I walked down the sidewalk and saw two men whom I recognized walked

243

toward me. I figured a fight was coming.

"John Beckman and Icky Sager," I acknowledged. "I remember you two, but I don't understand why you want to fight me. I have done nothing to you."

John was just over six feet tall with a muscular build. Icky was short like I was when I was younger.

We used to talk about fixing up cars. I didn't know John very well, but he was always kind to me. They were both in the same class as Jude.

"Singer says that you raped some girls!" Icky accused.

"Let's get him!" Jude yelled when they were only a few feet from me.

All at once, a voice came from beside me. "You take on Jimmy, and you take on me." Randy Diller warned.

"This guy says he knows Icky and me but I don't know him. Why are you sticking up for him?" John demanded.

"I'll be darned! He is right, John." Icky exclaimed. "He's taller, possibly stronger, but that is Jimmy Bass."

"No way, Bass was a short guy. I would never beat up on him."

"Icky is right. Jimmy grew up while he was gone. Other than that, he is the same guy, and Jude wants to beat him up as he did in the past. Of course, the orders came from Jake. Jude and Alter, came here a few weeks ago to do what he wants you to do, and Jimmy kicked his butt. Alter almost got his arm broken. Why did they come after Jimmy, and why are you here to take him on?"

John and Icky looked at Jude, then Icky asked, "Why are we here, Jude?"

244

Jude pointed at me and snarled, "He's a rapist!"

"That was proven to be a hoax, and you know it, Jude! You probably set it up," Randy countered.

"Well, he came here from a mental institution and, you know, only crazy people come from those places. He should be beaten up and sent back there. Come on, guys, let's get him!"

John stepped towards Jude. "I remember Jimmy Bass and you, Jake and Alter, deserve to be beaten the way you hurt Jimmy."

"Jake won't Like that!"

"I was afraid of you and your gang back then but not now, Jude. You're nothing but wimps who act tough, so everybody is scared of you." I glared down at Jude.

"We're out of here. Sorry, Jimmy, for the trouble we caused you."

"Wait a minute." Before Jude could say more, John had a grip on his arm and was dragging him to the car. That was the end of the fight that was supposed to happen.

I had remembered two people from my past, no make that three. I finally remembered Randy.

~~~~~~~~~~

By halftime, at the Vanlue game, we were behind thirty-four to twenty. One of the statisticians told me I had twelve of our twenty points. The reason we were so far behind was because of their two quick guards who were creating havoc with Joey and Rendles and had several steals to create fast breaks from them. If the guards got the ball to me, their forward couldn't stop me. So I got most of my points from dribble-driving in the middle. After a couple of passes to Tim or Brad and they both made baskets.

In the second half, the coach wanted me to be the point guard, and I was told to shoot. That changed one thing, their quickest guarded had me, instead of the forward who had me the first half. He was faster than me, but I knew how to dribble and keep the ball away from his eager hands. My desire to play the best game I could and in my zone made me dive into an offensive explosion, with outside shooting that amazed even me. With no one able to block my shots, and my ability to get in position, I scored eighteen points in the third quarter.

Vanlue's coach got tired of me scoring, so he had their guards double-team me as soon as I stepped across the timeline. The two quickest guards kept busy with me, so it was easy pickings for Sam Alt, who was subbing for the foul-troubled Joey's or Rendles' shooting and their driving to the basket to draw attention from Vanlue's big men. Then there would be a quick pass to Brad or Tim for an inside shot. Our team was adapting to scoring when I got double-teamed.

It was a wild third quarter with the defense going south. Vanlue was leading fifty-six to fifty-two, giving room for an even hotter fourth quarter.

Joey, who had four fouls came in for Rendles in the fourth quarter. I felt the reason Sam Alt stayed in the game was that he hit a couple of outside shots in the third quarter.

Vanlue's coach figured double-teaming me was a mistake, so he let me shoot. They stopped the rest of our team from scoring, but he had the forward back to guarding. We got the tip at the start of the fourth quarter, and I saw the set-up.

I knew any pass to the guards would be disastrous, so I sent up a quick prayer and went to work. When the game was over, we had won eighty-four to seventy-nine. In the locker-room, the statistician claimed I had made forty points. I had been in my zone and knew I scored a lot of points, but forty was unbelievable.

Everybody was congratulating me on my excellent game and

how we won. We still had only one loss. I smiled and thanked everyone who congratulated me, but I was stunned forty points was beyond my dreams. Who scores that many points? Me, I guess. But how?

As I looked back on our past games, I wondered what was different. We had played the same kind of game that we played tonight, the same minutes in this game, and we used an identical stage floor. The difference was that tonight I needed to score a lot more points to win. I couldn't slow down because they were always ahead.

Then two inside shots from Brad and we had the lead. Some foul shots by me and an outside chance for Joey and we had the win. Other games were different; the team had to score. Tonight I made forty out of eighty-four points. That means forty-four points had to be scored by my teammates. I couldn't score all of the points.

In a daze, I took a shower, dressed, and walked with the rest of the team to the bus. The cheerleaders and junior varsity players were already on the bus and cheered as I entered. The cheering was for me! I mean they called my name.

I sat in a middle seat, and somebody sat with me. I looked over, and it was dependable Joey. I thought he would hate me for scoring forty points. I don't think he scored many points. He smiled at me, and we didn't say anything until we were a mile or two out of Vanlue. Then I looked at who I thought was still one of my best friends and said, "Forty points! How does a person do that twice in one season?

Joey gave me a strange look and answered, "So we could win. You did it for the team, the town, and the community. That's why you made forty points, Jimmy."

"Okay, how do you feel with me scoring that many points?"

"Do you think I'm jealous?" Joey answered with an angry tone. "If you do, you don't know me as you should. I played a bad game tonight. Was that my fault? I don't think so. Those guards were quicker than me. They made me look like a fool. Are you putting me down because of that? I know you aren't. You probably wish I could have had a better game, and maybe you feel guilty because I didn't have a better game."

I knew I was wrong getting into this kind of talk, but I did feel guilty. "I suppose I do," I answered.

"Well, get over it, Jimmy. If it wasn't for you and your great shooting, I mean great talent, we would have only won so many games. If we were lucky, we would have won half of our games. I'm so happy we only have one loss, and I'm proud to be able to play basketball with you."

Joey stopped and thought before he added, "Didn't you tell me the other night that scoring points to break a record wasn't right. It's scoring so we can win for the town and the community. That's the difference."

"Yes, I remember that, and I feel the same way."

"Enjoy the victory and enjoy the points you scored. It was a thing of beauty."

What Joey said was right. "Enjoy the moment and praise God."

After I raised my head, ending my prayer of thanks and understanding, Joey asked, "How tall are you now?"

"Mother measured me tonight, just before I left for the bus. I'm still six-foot-four."

"That is amazing! "Then he surprised me, saying. "You should dunk more."

"I will if you pass the ball to me when I'm going to the hoop," I grinned.

248

"We will have to work at it in practice on Monday."

"Agreed!"

~~~~~~~~~

Jake Bickhart was sitting at the bar in his usual beer joint, listening to the Vanlue game on the radio. He was livid. That weakling had scored forty points in one game and broken his single-game scoring mark for the second time this season. It wasn't right. Only men should be able to that, not little weaklings.

Everybody tells me he is tall and not skinny. They say he has a lean build, but I think they are all lies. He's still the little pervert he used to be. I'm supposed to be the star of the town. I did all that work, perfecting my shots, knowing how good I am. Summerall set the games around me so that I could get most of the shots. And I came through, giving the town a thrill. Then a nerd comes around and takes my glory. It isn't right. I'm the star, and I deserve a statue proving it. Some people will say I was a gunner, but if I had better players around me, or if the league was weak like it is this year, we could have won more games.

Now, this worthless little squirt is taking away my stardom. I won't have a statue unless I make the Nerd look bad. The answers have to be in Nashville, where I have a guy working on it now. If Bass was in a mental institution, there have to be secrets the Nerd doesn't want to be known.

"I'll get you, Nerd!"

The radio announcer cut into the music that was playing, saying, "Now, we have an interview with Jimmy Bass!"

Jake screamed, "No!" a few times then threw the money he owed for his drinks on the bar and left.

"How did it feel scoring forty points?" Mel Wilson, one of the announcers, asked.

249

There was silence for a few seconds, then an answer. "I don't know."

A young man, alone in a booth in the bar, imagined, "He's just nervous making sure he says the right thing. That's what I would do if I were in his position."

"It was like the team needed me to score and shooting from the outside was the best opportunity. With Brad and Tim inside, I had great back up."

"Your talking about Brad Weiden and Tim Ender?"

"Yes, Sir.

My shots seemed to fail, and Vanlue kept scoring. They held the lead. It was something I had to do for our team and our fans. At the end of the game, we went around them and won. Somebody said I had forty points. I figured I had over thirty, but forty was unbelievable. That's all I can say, except thanks for the support of the team and all our fans. It's all unbelievable, just unbelievable."

After a lull, he repeated, "Unbelievable!"

"I guess that is the end of the interview. As, Jimmy Bass says, 'It's unbelievable.'

The young man in the booth concluded, "Bass deserves it after the way my partners and I messed his life up. Good things should happen to him. I feel guilty for what I did to him. It makes me sick. I need to do something right for Jimmy. I can't let Jake and Singer get to him. I just can't! Beckman told me what Jude did, trying to get Icky and him to help Jude beat Bass this afternoon. When Randy told them who he was, they were both shocked. John grabbed Jude, and they were gone.

That is the only way Jude will face Bass, with at least two people with him. Jude is scared to death of Bass. Oh, Jude acts tough, like he can take him on by himself. But we know he can't. He's a coward, and so

250

is Jake. Both of them are all mouth, but Jimmy is the real thing. I'd hate to see those two jerks, get somebody who might hurt him. I owe Bass, and I'll keep watch."

John Alter left what he owed on the table and headed out the door to follow Jake.

~~~~~~~~~~

I didn't know what else I could say. The interview was inside Keller's, and there were people all around me. I knew the announcer wanted more for the audience, but I was sure I had said all I could. I walked away before I said something stupid, or something I felt I was wrong.

As I left the interview, I saw one happy person. The way his chest stuck out showed his pride. I could hear him say, "That's my son!"

He had tried to teach me to be humble. This action was a mockery of the way he taught me before when I was a nerd. Now, everything is different. I'm not a nerd, anymore. What about before the incident, Father, when you thought I was a loser? But I'm not going there. Now is a happy time.

The rest of the week was routine, between school and practice. One night, Elisabeth took me to a concert at Heidelberg College, in Tiffin. I felt safe being on the east side of town, not near the downtown area.

Father, who liked Elisabeth, agreed. Elisabeth played the piano and even had a small solo part in one of the pieces. She did an excellent job, and I enjoyed the whole concert.

After the concert, we went to a quaint coffee shop near the college. Elisabeth got a coffee, and I drank a Coke. Some of her friends came around and congratulated her on her solo. I figured they were orchestra members. The girls asked who I was and she introduced me. They all acted like I was cute. Who, me, the Nerd? It made me feel good, but nobody recognized me as a famous high school basketball player.

I wonder if she was embarrassed to tell her classmates, I was a high school student.

On our ride home, she opened up to me. First, she asked if she could talk about the incident. I agreed but asked her not to tell my father. She knew how my father wanted to keep it secret from me, but I felt it was time to find out.

"When I saw you at the incident, I felt ashamed of how I hurt you, and the way Jake was putting you down in your weakest moment. It made me sick. I knew I had lost someone who cared for me, not the big jerk who wanted me for sex. It's a wonder I didn't get pregnant. I hurt so much after that incident. Many nights, while going to school in Chicago, I cried myself to sleep. Going to school was a way of escaping and starting a new life. I didn't know if I would ever see you again, because, with your family, especially your father, everything was hush, hush. Your father even told me you would never come back, and I should forget about you."

It was silent in the car as we rode along. When Elizabeth continued, she said, "I dated one guy in Chicago for a couple of dates and all he wanted was sex. I thought if that's all men want, I can do without them. When I heard you were back and playing basketball, I had to see you. Then when you didn't remember me, I prayed that God would help me to be friends with you again. I did, and I'm holding on to you until you push me away. I want to be with you; anyway I can."

I got caught off guard. I hadn't known the pain she felt at the incident or after. She mourned for me and left town because of the way she was hurting."

"Okay, Elisabeth, I understand. But I care for you a lot and want it to be serious. I don't want to hurt you as you did me. I want to enjoy dating you, and do things together. I want to tell the world I have a girlfriend and you will be there for me."

She didn't say anything, so I said, "I guess that is acting seriously."

Smiling at me, she whispered, "I guess it is, and I understand the dating thing, Jimmy, I do. That is what I want, and I'm ready to march down the aisle in church. But I want you to know how I feel, and I won't change. You're the one for me, Jimmy Bass."

Then she smiled and said, "I like the way we are open with each other."

"Me too, and no games."

I wanted to get off this subject. "Tell me more about the incident," I urged.

"Okay, Jake and I were leaving when we saw that you were the only one on the floor. You were skating in circles that were becoming smaller and smaller until you were in the middle of the floor. Then you sat on the floor, crossed your legs, and just stared into space. Pat tried to talk to you, but there was no response. Then Pat said that your entire back was bloody. That's when I knew the boys had gotten to you big time. The skating rink attendee called an ambulance. You were like a zombie as they put you on the stretcher. I could see you were bleeding. And that was the last I saw of you until I went to one of your games. I was surprised at your height and the way you played basketball."

"My father wasn't at the incident?"

"No."

Then why is he afraid? Why doesn't he let me know about the incident? That is confusing to me. I thought that by now I would remember the event, but I didn't.

Chapter Twenty-one

On Friday night, January 18, 1963, we played Beltsville at Bettsville. Playing at Bettsville was a big treat. They have one of the biggest floors in the league. Colleges and most big high schools have the same size floors, but Attica's floor has more room on both sides, and the fans aren't next to the floor. Their gym is like a stage with a small drop from the gym floor to the floor in front of the seats.

The seating is only on one side and is so large that it only got filled once, and that was during a holiday tournament with four schools. Of course, we are talking about a small school. Most big schools have seating this size. Playing on a floor with this much room is a dream.

~~~~~~~~~~

"This is Mel Wilson and Jorge Billings announcing the game between Bettsville and Cutler Ridge. Cutler Ridge has the leading scorer in the league, and in the area, with a twenty-nine point average, as well as an eleven and one record overall. Cutler Ridge is nine and one in the league. Bettsville has a seven and five record overall, with six and four league record. You might think Cutler Ridge would win because of a better record. But the last time they played, it was a last-second basket by Jimmy Bass that made the difference."

"Mel, you know Jimmy Bass is becoming a household name in the area. By the looks of this crowd, it isn't only Cutler Ridge and Bettsville fans here. I bet a lot of people are here to see Bass for the first time. I am one of them, Mel."

"I saw him once. He was a joy to watch!" commented Jorge.

"I see Allen Jamison, from the Tiffin Newspaper. Jamison says Bass is poetry in motion."

~~~~~~~~~

Sam's Bar and Grill in Tiffin had the radio turned up loud enough for the patrons to hear the game. There were small slips of paper in a big pickle jar, along with five-dollar bills for a pool to guess how many points Jimmy Bass would score tonight and the final score of the game. If someone guessed right on both, or the closest one to it, they would be the big winner.

Jake Bickhart was a regular customer, and none of the other patrons liked him. Even the establishment barely tolerated him. The pickle jar was to irritate Jake. All he did was brag about how he was the hero of Cutler Ridge, not this nerd Bass.

"Bass isn't worth the powder to blow him up!" mumbled Jake.

Another pickle jar sat on the bar, which had ten-dollar bills and slips of paper. This pool was for predicting the game Bass would break Jake's record. Entries contained the guesses for Jimmy's average and total points at the end of the regular season. Jake's account included a one tournament game, but the patrons and workers were unanimous; Bass would beat Jake's record in the regular season.

Whenever Jake looked at the pickle jars, he wanted to smash them to pieces. He had been warned many times not to touch them. If he did, he would go to jail for destruction of property. The establishment didn't want him at their bar and often told him so, but

255

the law stated, "No one can refuse service to someone unless he is a nuisance to the patrons, inebriated, or guilty of destroying anything at the bar." So the establishment could not keep Jake out until he made a mistake.

Sitting at the bar, drinking his beer, and trying to figure out a way to stop Bass filled Jake's time.

Everybody in the bar knew that Jude Singer and John Alter had walked out on Jake and refused to beat up Bass or break two fingers on his right hand to hinder his scoring ability. He could probably still play but wouldn't score as much.

"That's all I want," Jake insisted. "Is that too much to ask you to do, to stop a stupid nerd? It's not like Bass is a person who deserves the record."

"If your goons accomplished your purpose, wouldn't that be like cheating? Don't you want to have your record fair and square?" somebody asked.

"No!" Jake snarled. "That mental pervert doesn't deserve it. The record is mine!"

When he said things like that, everybody in the bar decided he was an emotionally sick person. Whoever heard of someone breaking a person's hand to maintain a record? Perhaps Jake belonged in the nuthouse, but he kept saying he was the greatest, actually believing everybody around him was a fool.

When a player from Bettsville bragged, on the radio, that he was going to stop Bass, that night, Jake howled in glee. "I bet anyone in the bar that Bass will score fifteen points and Cutler Ridge will get buried. It's time for the nerd to get what's coming to him, and I'm sure tonight is when it will happen!"

~~~~~~~~~

Allen loved to watch Jimmy play, and in the first half, he was

256

not disappointed. Not only was Jimmy scoring but also passing. Both teams were in a running game, which was right down Bass's avenue. Jimmy put on a show demonstrating how to pass and shoot in a fast break. Joey Bell set him up with one pass on a fast-break, which was just above the basket, called an alley-oop, as Bass Jammed the ball through the hoop. The basket brought everyone to their feet, except the Bettsville fans.

The announcer couldn't help but notice some people were fans of neither team. They just wanted to see Jimmy Bass play. The most significant part of watching Bass had to be his beautiful outside shots as he scored eighteen out of the thirty-four points by halftime to Bettsville's twenty-three.

Jake was beside himself as his bet on Bass's points grew to be more than he had predicted for the whole game. As he listened to the second half, Bass poured in more points, and Cutler Ridge held on to their ten to twelve point lead. It made him sick to hear everyone cheering every time Bass made a basket.

He wanted to scream to Bass's teammates, "Why don't you score? Don't you want to make points?"

Suddenly it dawned on him, how he could get to Bass, through his teammates. "I could make them jealous of him. They must have some pride. Some of them had to be sick of Bass scoring all the time. Maybe I could confront them as they celebrate at Keller's," Jake decided. "I could pour it on and make that nerd look like a fool. I'm pretty good at making people look like a fool."

Would it work? It had to. "If not, I'll beat him up. Maybe I should take a hammer or a knife. No, that would be a weapon, and I would end up in jail. I won't try to kill him, even though I like the idea. No, I better not go there, even though he is a worthless nerd. But I could cut up his hand."

Shaking his head, Jake wondered were he was getting these

ideas. "If I have a knife, they might charge me with more then assault and battery. I could get him alone, but people could still construe my actions as attempted murder. It would be better if I have Singer do it. Then the authorities couldn't arrest me, because I wouldn't be with Singer. I'd deny I paid Singer."

Suddenly he knew what he had to do. "No, just Bass and me, one-on-one in a man's fight! First, I'll make the teammates jealous. Maybe they would save him the trouble of fighting. But if I have to fight Bass, the first thing I'll go for will be his right hand. If two fingers get broken, it'll be called a good-old-boys' fight. Man on one man is perfectly legal."

~~~~~~~~~~

Allen thought this was one of the best games Cutler Ridge had ever played. The whole team was involved in scoring, and Jimmy loved to set up his teammates. No one man got shown, even though Jimmy scored over his average because Joey Bell set him up. That point guard deserved a Most Valuable Player award. He not only passed to Bass but he also gave some perfect ones to Weiden, and Ender had a lot of defensive rebounds to set the fast break in motion.

"Well, that's the end of the game," Mel Wilson announced. "The final score is Cutler Ridge eighty to Bettsville sixty-six. And for Bass listeners, he scored thirty-four points tonight."

Sam's bar and grill patrons were ecstatic as Sam opened the pickle jar to check the slips and determine the winner. Jake was long gone, on his way for his encounter at Keller's.

He got ahead of everybody in Cutler Ridge. The downtown area seemed deserted. Wall's Bar and Keller's had closed. All of the residents must have gone to the game.

"That didn't happen when I was playing. Businesses never closed, especially Wall's. And hardly anybody came to meet the bus.

Maybe a few parents of Freshman and Sophomores who lived in the country. If you lived in town, you walked." Jake reminisced.

Jake made a new scheme. He would wait until Bass started walking home, then corner the weakling and beat him up, breaking a few fingers on his right hand.

Cars started parking uptown, and as people left their vehicles, they milled around on the sidewalk. Even though Keller's and Wall's were now open, most people stayed on the walkways. The temperature was below thirty, and ice meant they had to watch where they stepped.

The people outside, waiting for the bus were either dedicated or, as Jake called them, stupid.

"They never waited for the true star, me, the star and the man. Why are they waiting for a worthless weakling?" he wondered.

Soon, the downtown area was packed, making Jake even angrier. When the school bus parked in front of the school, people crowded around it to welcome the team. More and more, he saw the players getting off of the bus, and his anger increased. He looked for the little nerd but couldn't find him. Several small players then some tall players got off, but none looked like Bass. One of the taller players looked like Bass in the face, but, no, that couldn't be him.

Jake kept looking at the smaller players and still didn't see Bass. With all the fans crowded around the players, maybe he missed him.

Or maybe Bass was that tall player. He had blond hair like the nerd, but he couldn't get a good look at his face. Both Singer and Alter had said he was tall and well built.

"When I paid the guy I hired, a couple of weeks ago, to walk up to Bass and give him a message, he refused to beat up Bass for two reasons. First, Bass is big and has the quickness of a basketball player, which gives him quick hands. Second, they say he knows

259

martial arts. Quite a few men chased him a good distance before he lost them. If he had slipped and they got him, he would have been dead meat." Jake recalled.

His rage was slipping away, and fear was replacing it. "That guy I hired was supposed to be the toughest person around. What am I getting myself into?"

After a few seconds of dwelling on that thought, he began to reason, "Bass is nothing to fear. He is still a weak nerd, no matter how tall he is."

With everybody off the street and either in Wall's or Keller's, Jake pulled out of his parking space and drove quickly out of town, toward Tiffin. A man stood on the sidewalk, a few feet back from the spot where Jake had been parked, waiting for Jake to make a move toward Bass.

Alter was surprised that Jake drove off. Wondering what Jake had up his sleeve, he decided to wait around and see If he came back. He was too far away from where his car was parked to catch up with Jake now.

~~~~~~~~~~

Saturday morning, January 19, 1963, Jimmy was at John Wood's house.

"You had a nice game against Bettville last night, beating them the way you did. I think it was sixteen points."

"Thirty-four!" I blurted out.

"So, you're keeping track of your points," John stated jokingly.

"I guess, wouldn't you, John?"

"I would, and I think it's normal. How many points do you have to score before you break Jake Bickhard's record?"

260

"I don't know. I don't want to get caught up into that. Some people have said that's why Jake and his gang are after me. It's hard to believe. But if someone were to break my finger, I would be done. A person would have to be arrogant and selfish to want to do something like that. If it happens, I would have to believe that Jake's life would be miserable, even if they can't prove he had any part of it. The public would blame him, and that could hurt the dealership."

I don't think Jake is thinking that far ahead. His ego controls him, and something is trying to rip that ego away from him."

"You're saying the ego from that record controls his personality."

"It could be. Also, what does Jake think of you?"

"Since he was my biggest tormentor, at least that's what someone told me. Jake looks like a jerk to me. In my mind, that is the lowest form of a human being, and now a nerd is beating this jerk's record. Jake thought of me as a slave, his slave. So he can't let this happen. That's scary."

"Remember, Jimmy; you have God on your side as well as a lot of good people are watching out for you, too."

"I think the best way to handle this situation, is to confront Jake and beat the tar out of him, instead of waiting for somebody to jump out of the dark and get me. I've convinced myself I am ready for the fight no matter where it happens. I wasn't going to be afraid as I was before. No more fear!"

"I'm sorry, but you shouldn't talk about Jake like that."

"That's okay; I'm not afraid of him or anybody who comes after me. I won't be reckless. I'll be cautious everywhere I go. And I've got God on my side. So how could I go wrong?"

John knew that Jimmy expressed a lot of times that he had no fear, but he knew, down deep in his heart, he had some. He hoped

Jimmy was ready if trouble came.

"I hope you are trusting God if trouble comes," John prayed.

As if suddenly trying to change the subject, Jimmy declared, "John, I almost forgot, I have a new memory trying to come out. It isn't a dream, but it isn't a nightmare, either. It's at night, and I'm running through fields and woods to get away from people who are chasing me. Then the dream turns so that one single person with a rifle is after me. He shoots me several times, and it hits me, but it only stings a little.

I outran him, and he was gone. But I kept running and screaming. That's it. It doesn't come to me in a dream anymore, but bits and pieces come back throughout my day. The memory doesn't bring fear with it, only curiosity. Do you think it could be a memory trying to escape?"

"It could be, but be careful. It may come out with a bang. If it does, try to get hold of me and pray to God about it."

"I have been."

"Good!"

~~~~~~~~~

The same morning Jimmy was meeting with John Wood, Clyde entered Fred Stallings crowded barbershop, but he wasn't there to get a haircut. He was listening to the comments people were making, especially Jim Diller's.

Diller was unusually quiet because his predictions were going down the drain. He was still a pessimist, believing we were going to lose a lot more games, but we were going to win the league. Everybody else kept telling him he was wrong.

All he would say was, "You'll see, you'll see."

The rest the people in the barbershop were celebrating, especially after last night's game. They had all the confidence in the world that we would continue on the way we were going. Some said we have to watch out for Jake and his buddies, but everybody agreed Jake wasn't going to get their star.

Clyde was thrilled as he left the barbershop. Seeing so many people who agreed with him made him almost giddy. He was so proud of his buddy, Jimmy, and how the team played. It sent goosebumps all over his body, and he wanted to scream, "Jimmy Bass, you're the greatest!" But he didn't. He quietly walked back to his gas station.

When he got back to work, Randy asked him, "What was the gossip in the barbershop?"

"Everybody was positive, except for one person."

"That would be my grandpa. He's always negative. Oh, he wants you to break Jake's record, but doesn't believe we'll win many more games, especially not the league championship."

"I know I have to put up with his complaining all the time, but as I told my grandmother, he is Grandpa, and I still love him," Randy grinned.

~~~~~~~~~~

I was reading Saturday's Advertising Tribune in Keller's restaurant. There was a remarkable story about how our team sets me up for my shots, written by Allen Jamison. He told how we played as a collaborative team in all aspects of the game.

There was nothing about me trying to break Jake's record, except a little about my scoring average. Mostly the article was about my teammates and what they averaged in points, rebounds, assist, and steals. Jamison even interviewed Joey and Tim to get their opinion of the team. Their comments were excellent, with a lot of bragging about me and how I didn't want to score as I did. They explained that the team convinced me I had to score for them. The whole article was well written, and I was glad that Allen praised the

263

team, and not just me. He mostly told how my teammates felt about me.

Elisabeth was eating with me and asked how I liked the article. She had read it when I was talking with John. I told her it was a great article, and I loved how Allen wrote the truth.

Just as our food arrived, Randy came into the restaurant and sat at our table. He had just gotten off work and was hungry. As was often the case, we ate together about this time every Saturday. He was a good friend, and it was better now that I remembered him.

That night we played Townsend, a country school, northwest of Bellevue, at their gym. It was our first blow-out of the season. Everybody on the team got their turn to score. The effort that Townsend put forth to stop me left more open shots for my teammates. Most of my points came from outside shots when I could get free. I shot a good percentage, but most of the fast-break points went to my teammates as well as some offensive rebounds, or what we call stick-backs. I got twenty-two points in the game, out of eighty points for the whole team. Brad had twenty points, all inside shots, while Joey Bell had fourteen and Tim made twelve. The rest of the players shared the last twelve points. We won eighty to fifty-eight.
~~~~~~~~~~

We were celebrating our thirteenth win and one lone loss at Keller's. The crowd was smaller than most of our victory nights, so the restaurant's extra room wasn't open. The team sat in the middle of the room, with the regular tables pushed together to make one big table. As we were eating, five big guys, all at least six feet tall, came in. I had never seen them before, and I wondered if maybe they were hoods that Jude Singer rounded up around Tiffin. I'm sure Jake's father paid the bill.

As soon as they came in, I saw someone leave and thought he was a coward who was afraid of a fight. In truth, he went to Banks Bar to let their patrons know about the visitors in the restaurant.

Most of the men left Bank's and made some phone calls.

The phone calls drew attention to a lot of old men into the restaurant, including Randy Diller and one of his closest friends, Bull, whose real name was Sam Kell. Everyone called him Bull because he was six-foot-four and weighed at least three hundred pounds of mostly muscle.

Jude wasn't afraid of losing the fight because his gang included some of the strongest men around, at least that was the impression he wanted. What could these old men do? A rumble was about to happen, and it looked like the thugs were going to win. The nerd or at least his hand would be busted.

Bull and Randy in the middle could cause a problem. The main interest was to humiliate the nerd big time. Jude's gang stopped at the side of the basketball team's tables, across from me.

Jude tossed a newspaper article on my plate and shouted, "Jake got this article in the mail from an investigator he hired in Nashville, Tennessee."

He and Jake were sure this article would end Jimmy's career, and the people in the town would send the nerd packing.

"Folks, this article from a Nashville, Tennessee Newspaper is about a gang of youths in a state mental institution who raped and beat women in the hospital. Our great star was one of them. His name is in the paper."

I knew, before reading the paper, that this article was all lies. I was angry and scared that this would be a gang war. Would everyone end up in a big gang fight? My first concern was to keep the women and children safe. Aggression like this shouldn't happen in a small country restaurant.

"Okay, Nerd, you read the article. What do you have to say for your self?" Jude roared arrogantly, staring at me.

265

I stood up calmly. Everybody in the room wanted an answer, and I had to give it. But first, I needed to tell everyone about my father's lie. I didn't care what my father thought. He was in the bar across the street. I was going to plead that there wouldn't be a fight, but I thought, if they believed me, the truth would take care of that.

"First, this incident happened on April 12, 1961. At that time, I was still in a coma, in St Luke's hospital in Nashville, not, a mental hospital, a regular hospital.

Again, I repeated in a commanding voice, "I was NOT in a mental hospital!"

"I can vouch for him," John Wood stated, standing up beside Randy.

"I talked to his psychiatrist over Christmas break, and I have the record about his stay at St Luke's, in my office. The school also has these records.

"We were told that the hospital he was in was a mental hospital. But it doesn't make any difference. We accepted him as he was with the knowledge that he suffered from depression!" John Dempler, a citizen and a fan from Cutler Ridge, exclaimed.

"I can clear that up. It's true. I suffered from depression. Almost everyone said I was worthless, so I began to believe what I heard. I eventually gave up on life and fell into the comma. I still don't remember a lot of my past, but it is slowly coming back."

I looked around at the people before going on. "My Uncle Walter Bass is a psychiatrist, and he was my doctor. St Luke's had a psychiatric ward, but my uncle refused to have me admitted when I woke up from my comma. After recuperating in the regular hospital, I moved to Uncle Walters house, where I lived until I returned home."

As soon as I finished, I saw my father standing at the back of the room, and he didn't like what I had said.

"We were told you were in a mental hospital," Mary Martin, a resident of town insisted.

"It was only a rumor and never happened. People thought that is where I would end up when I was in the coma, but things changed when I woke up."

"But that is what your father said."

I knew this would come up, but I just shrugged, like I didn't know, and looked at my angry father.

"Notice, this article says J. Bas, with one's'. Jimmy's name is Bass, spelled 'ss.'" Elisabeth affirmed.

Jude was frustrated and started screaming, "It's all lies! Lies, Lies, Lies! The article is the truth. Do you people believe him instead of the truth?"

On and on, he screamed cussing and swearing at me, ready to jump across the table at me. He turned to his buddies to give the command to attack, but Bull and Randy were talking to them. Their choice infuriated him even more, and he said to the new guys with him, "Don't listen to them! You're with me, and I command you to take them."

"You're nut's, Jude. We're not messing with anybody in here. We didn't know the guy you're after was a friend of Randy and Bull, as well as the star of this town. I've never heard anything bad about him. Now leave us alone. We're out of here. You certainly don't expect us to fight with women and children around! Your nuts, Singer. Look at the people in the restaurant and outside. I don't want to hurt old men or women and children."

Then they turned to leave.

"Where are you going? You guys get back here, or you won't

267

get paid."

There was a hush in the restaurant.

Randy stopped one of the guys from leaving, and Bull prevented the rest from leaving.

"What is this about getting paid?" Randy asked.

"Don't say a word," Jude cried out. "It's none of their business."

"Jake Bickhart was paying us fifty dollars apiece to beat up, the one he claimed was a rapist and so filthy that he doesn't deserve to live. He was outraged, and we felt we should get this guy."

"When we came into the restaurant, I knew something wasn't right. another guy blurted out. "Now that we know the whole story, we won't cause you, fine people, any trouble."

The guy who spoke first countered, "When I saw Singer was after Bass, I knew this was messed up. I've seen him play, and he's good. I knew then; it was Jake or his father trying to preserve a record Jake has at this school."

Another man added, "When we walked in the restaurant, Singer said something about breaking the guy's right hand. At the time, I thought it was weird. Now I know why. As my buddies said, there will be no trouble from us. Now, you Tiffin people have found out what Jude Singer and Jake are capable of doing."

As they left the restaurant, Jude was furious. He screamed and swore more. Then, standing between Rendles' and Joey's chairs, across the table from me, he started to try jumping across the table at me. Randy grabbed him in a bear hug from behind and started dragging him out of the restaurant. Jude went kicking and screaming, calling me all the names he could.

Somehow I had no anger, but I was so sad that I had caused

so much hate to be directed at me, hate I didn't deserve, hate derived from jealousy over who they felt was a nerd. They had it all, and I had nothing. Now I was fulfilling my dreams, and they hated it. In their minds, it wasn't right. I was a slave and should stay as a slave.

God, I want to hate them, but I know I have to forgive my enemies and pray for them. That's hard to do, but with your strength, I will.

Chapter Twenty-two

The Advertising Tribune covered every angle of Jude Singer's arrest for giving a false report about me being a rapist. The article's headline read, "Attempted Gang Fight At Keller's Restaurant," and told everything that had happened, along with the truth about the rumor of my hospitalization in a state mental institution. The Tribune article explained how my harassment in school, the abusive notes which gave no proof for their accusations, and the imagined ideas of what I was like or threats of what would happen to me caused my depression. Then the paper described the kind of person I am and finished with my accomplishments in basketball. No one interviewed me, so they must have received their information from questioning other people in town.

Jude was the only one arrested; the rest of his gang was found and taken to the sheriff department. After explaining their part and how they were acting on pretense, they were lectured and released. When asked where the money was, they said they hadn't been paid and wouldn't be until the job gets completed. Since the matter didn't get finished, they didn't expect to get any money.

At Clyde's, Monday morning, Randy told me that since Jude

arranged the business, Jake left him out in the cold, denying he knew anything about what happened or that he had any part of Jake's so-called gang.

I don't know if anyone in town cornered Father about his lie, but when I saw him the next morning, he never said a word.

I didn't expect to be such a high scoring player with a record-breaking average or drawing attention from people in our local area and beyond for our county league. Cities like Norwalk, Fremont, Bellevue, Sandusky, Fostoria, and beyond sent reporters to write about the high scoring player from little Cutler Ridge.

As the week went along, kids began asking me who was writing the hate notes to me. I told them I didn't know and asked them to watch and let me know if they saw something suspicious. They agreed, but I didn't expect anything. Squealing on a fellow student was considered to be a big no-no.

Lately, I have been spending the lunch hour studying in the library. The librarian, a chubby woman with an outgoing personality, was always there. If any student messes around in her jurisdiction, she isn't afraid to confront them with her sturdy wooden ruler. A smack on their hand or their behind put them in their place. Rumors said that Jake and his gang feared her. However, she was sweet to students who behaved.

I figure I must have spent time in the library in my past, to get away from the bullies. The librarian never asked me why I was spending my noon hour with her now. But I needed to stay away from Marsha.

That's funny. I am trying to stay away from a girl. I know I wouldn't do that in my past. The truth is I am afraid of getting close to her. I know the only reason she wants to be my girlfriend is my popularity as a basketball player. A pretty girl acting like she is interested in me may sound good, but I don't want any more

271

confrontations with her or her friends.

What do you say to a girl, when she may be out to get you? I dumped Marsha for Elisabeth, though I never asked Marsha for a date. It was a confusing mess, something I wanted to avoid. Now I have Elisabeth, and things are going to be okay.

At church, a few Sundays ago, she turned her life over to Jesus, and now we are dating as a couple in God's eyes. Our relationship has taken on a newer meaning. Walking together with God has taken my doubts away. We are close to loving each other as one, as the Bible talks about marriage, but we were not married or having sex.

On Friday, in the auditorium, during the last period of school, there was a pep rally for the Old Fort game which would take place that night. The basketball team was to sit on the stage with the curtain drawn, closing off the gym. We sat in folding chairs, while the cheerleaders ran through there series of cheers between the stage and the first row of seats.

Coach Chumbly and Captain Tim Ender were supposed to give speeches to inspire the audience. I was never asked to present a talk, nor did I desire to do so. These pep rallies didn't happen before a game every Friday night, only before the home games. With our success, parents and other fans also came to our assemblies.

Soon the whole audience was standing and moving with the cheerleaders. Most of those in the auditorium were girls. Guys stood around and acted macho. The girls, mothers, and cheerleaders made enough noise.

I sat on the stage, feeling like a fool. Why were people cheering? It didn't affect how I would play. But I felt everybody in the auditorium was staring at me.

~~~~~~~~~

"You good for nothing fool, why are you up there? Summerall will never play you, you worthless piece of junk."

I looked at who was sitting on the stage. I recognized some, like Pat Ender, John Alter, and Jude Singer. Then I saw the arrogant Jake Bickhart sitting proudly in his seat. I knew it was him. He called himself, "the King.

Looking at him brought feelings of the pain he caused me. I had no memory of what kind of pain, but I could see evil in his eyes, an evil that sent chills down my back. I looked down at the cheerleaders doing their routine for a team that couldn't win a game. It felt worthless, and I was not part of it. I was wearing a uniform that was part of my misery. I knew number six would not see action, no matter how bad we got beaten.

I looked at the small body with a number six uniform and knew he didn't want to be here. But I don't have that body anymore. I am a tall, well-proportioned man, and not that worthless kid.

Panic came over me, and I wished I could run away, but a force held me. The horrifying pain continued. I wanted to find a hole and crawl into it. How long can I stand this pain?

I was about to the end of my ability to stand the pain when there came a chant from the players, the cheerleaders, and the fans were yelling Jake's name over and over again. I had a hard time looking at my tormentor's beaming countenance as the mantra went on. I had reached my limit and was about to scream when the chant slowly changed from "Jake" to "Jimmy Bass."

What is happening? Is this another dream? I looked at my teammates. Gone were Jake and the old team. Joey, Brad, Jack, Glen, Tim, and the rest of the group were in their places chanting my name, with the cheerleaders were leading the audience!

A chill ran down my back, a feeling I never expected to have.

273

Past dreams sought this moment, but I never supposed it would come.

I was the only one sitting, feeling embarrassed, so I stood up quickly. Then the chant changed again, from my name to "Speech! Speech!"

I stepped forward slowly as Coach adjusted the microphone to my height. When he stepped aside, the whole auditorium became silent. I said a silent prayer, asking God to guide me. I was at a complete loss to know what I should say.

Then a thought came to me. "I thank you for the cheer you gave me; I didn't expect it. I thank you for the support you give our team."

The words seemed to flow from my mouth. "Without you, the fans, and the cheerleaders leading us on, we wouldn't be much."

I paused for a second, wondering what else I should say. Then raising my voice, the words seemed to come out naturally. "My teammates and I play for you."

I pointed at the audience and asked, "Who are the fans?"

Answering my own question, I declared, "You, the people of this town and our community are the fans. You are with us in all our success. I will do everything in my power to play the best game I can for you."

I pointed to the fans again, and they yelled my name again. I was about to step away from the mic when I saw my girlfriend, my partner, standing in the back, cheering for me.

Elisabeth had said she didn't think she could make it, but her presence brought joy. As the pep rally ended, I thanked God for giving me words to say and for Elisabeth to hear it.

~~~~~~~~~

274

When we ran onto the gym floor, to warm up for the game, the noise was so loud the gym seemed to vibrate. Our fans roared when the announcer called the starting line up, especially for my name. I enjoyed their applause, yet it was unbelievable that people would cheer like that for me. It is one feeling I will never forget.

Both teams were pumped up, causing several missed shots in the first quarter. Some people yelled, "Good defense!"

I knew it created pressure. Old Fort was playing man-to-man, yet double-teaming me to keep me from driving and making sure I was boxed in to keep me from making rebound shots. Mostly, I took what they gave me and shot from the outside. At first, I didn't take any chances, but I connected on a few as the game continued. Shooting wise this game was an off game, but again, double-teaming me led to my teammates scoring on open shots, keeping us in the game. The shots were not easy, as Old Fort was ready for that game. They sagged off the double team quite quickly, but always had one man guarding me, at all times.

Our defense kept the game closed, and we kept Old Fort from doing much damage. Their outside shooting was the reason they were ahead. The score was forty-three to thirty-seven with Old Fort ahead at the end of the third quarter.

I was bound and determined that this would not be our second Waterloo. Uncle Walter told me there would be games when my shots wouldn't work, and this seemed to be one of those times. Then, walking onto the floor from our huddle it came to me. Why not shoot my backboard shot from the outside, where I could get shots. In practice, I worked on them from time to time. I had tried this method before, and it was successful. So that's what I'll do.

~~~~~~~~~~

Brad tipped the ball to me, and I tried my backboard shot from the left-wing, but I missed and was outraged, and I went back

275

to defense. Our defense was tight and wouldn't give an inch. I blocked a shot from the inside, and the referee called a foul on me. I was furious. I never touched the other player. But I didn't want to lose my cool and say something that might get me in trouble, so I walked to the other end of the court to calm down, and quickly sent up a prayer, asking God to guide me through this trial.

I watched the player I supposedly fouled make his first attempt, making the score forty-four to thirty-seven, Old Fort. He missed the next foul shot, and Brad got the rebound. I don't know what processed him to do it, but he threw a long pass toward our basket. The closest defender to me was a small guard, and he stepped back from the foul line. I retrieved the ball in mid-air, and in the same motion, I dunked the ball.

As I landed on the floor, there was an explosion from our fans. I could hear the Old Fort coach screaming about why I was left alone. Then a defensive guard ran into me, almost knocking me to the floor and causing the visiting coach to yell again.

I gained my balance as the whistle blew and the same referee who called me for a foul was calling a none-shooting foul on the defensive guard, but we weren't in the bounds, I was underneath the basket.

I was going to take the ball out of bounds, but Coach called a time-out. In the huddle, he explained a play for me to get the ball. The first option put me at the point, Tim was to inbound the ball, and the rest of the players where to line up at the foul line. As soon as the referee handed Tim the ball, Joey and Alt, who was in for Rendles, broke to the wings and Brad went to the corner and with a quick move, I broke around my defender. He stayed close to me, but I was ahead of him.

I received a pass from Tim, directly under the basket, and took a couple of steps away from the basket. Then I took the ball one big step toward the basket and went high in the air for a dunk, again I was fouled, but this time it was in the act of shooting. The trick made the score forty-four to our forty-one and a foul attempt. I made the foul shot putting us two points down, forty-four to forty-two.

As I was heading down the floor, for defense, I saw the home fans standing, and the auditorium exploded, yelling, "Defense! Defense! Defense!"

Old fort took their time on offense, working for a perfect shot, but they missed it. Tim rebounded and passed to me. I quickly went down the floor on the left side. When I came to my spot, I shot as I did before. The wing position went for the backboard, and I made it, tying the game. Our defense held again.

Joey hurried down the floor and up the middle where he was cut off. A perfect pass to me on the left-wing gave me a successful shot. Again, the defense held. Joey passed to Tim and broke to the high post then a quick pass to me, and another backboard wing shot went in. We now had a forty-eight to forty-four lead with the halfway mark of the quarter.

Old Fort called time out, then scored on their next possession. The next time we got the ball, my defender tried to deny me the ball, but a quick break towards the basket and a bounce pass got the ball to me. Brad's defender switched to me, leaving Brad all alone. A high pass to him breaking to the basket created another dunk. Home fans erupted with a roar. It pumped me up, and I knew we would not disappoint them.

Our tough defense created another semi-fast break down the floor. Joey drove down the middle with me on the left side. I thought he was going to the basket. Instead, he passed the ball to me. I was too far in the corner to shoot a backboard shot, so I took my usual long shot. I could feel it leave my right hand in the proper position and was relieved to see it go through the net.

277

With the score fifty-two to forty-six, our favor, Old Fort called another time out. Two and a half minutes remained on the clock.

John pulled me aside and told me to watch for a pick by their best forward at the foul line. If I slipped in front of him, I could easily block the shot. John didn't think the referee would call a foul on me after seeing me dunk the ball twice.

John was right. Rendle grabbed the ball, driving the length of the court for a layup making the score fifty-four to forty-six. Suddenly, Old Fort exploded, the last minute of the game and we couldn't stop them. But Joey had a couple of outside shots go in to keep us ahead.

After I made the last shot, the score was fifty-eight all, but Old Fort had one last chance, sending disappointment throughout the home crowd. We met our second Waterloo. They won sixty-two to our fifty-eight.

Our team was down in the dumps, as we quietly showered and got dressed. There were very few people and no excitement at Keller's. My sad feeling changed when I saw Elizabeth. She consoled me. "We now have thirteen wins and two losses."

~~~~~~~~~

Saturday night, we played York High School, a few miles west of Bellevue, on route twenty. They were considered to be an outstanding team, losing only a couple of games so far this year, but that was typical. When the schedule got drawn up, York probably figured this would be an easy game. But now, my scoring ability and the rest of the team playing very well made things look different.

Even though we lost, the publicity I got from our last game

brought attention to my scoring average and the two dunks I made. The Toledo Blade dubbed me as the leading scorer in Northwest Ohio, at twenty-nine points per game as well as my seven assists a game, eleven rebounds, and two steals. My blocked shots didn't get recorded, as no recorder kept that information at this time.

By the third quarter of the Junior Varsity game, York's gym was packed, mostly with York fans. We were sitting with our fans, a small group compared to the home team. York had a large gym with the seating for the fans on one side, just like Bettsville, but Bettsville had a larger seating capacity.

The benches were at each end of the floor with visitors on the west end. We left for the locker rooms and traveled an aisle between the seats leading to a hallway. To the right was the lockers for the visitors, with a stairway leading under the stands.

As we entered the aisle leading out to the hallway, the fans leaned over the rails from the stands and pointed at me. Some called out my name, acting like I was a celebrity. It pumped me up and gave me a sense of pride like I was someone important. I thought this popularity would give me more incentive to play better. I couldn't disappoint my fans after last night's loss.

Suddenly a thought came to me. These aren't my fans. They are the enemy and would like to see me go down against their home team. I thought, "Why should we be proud? There was no way I was going to get caught up in an ego game as Bickhart did. Our team and what I could do for them was what was necessary.

York was a larger team than us and had both inside players and outside shooters. On paper, Coach Chumbly felt there was no way we could stay with them. They had a big front-court that could score inside and guards that scored from the outside. They used a three-two half-court press after they made a basket. Coach Chumbly had Jack and Tim splitting the pressing out front, which was the

279

center in the middle, with two guards on the side and lined up on the timeline. The middle guy was big. Tim was out front because of his height and could pass high over the big guy.

Jack's quickness and ability as a good passer, especially with the bounce pass, meant he could fake a bounce pass then pass high over the guards head. With the high jumping Brad Weiden at the high-post, me on the left-wing, and Joey on the right-wing we worked the ball through the press, scoring points around the key.

We used a pass breaking to Brad for a layup and sometimes for me. Joey and I collected outside shots, so their coach called a time out and pulled the press. Then they played a strictly two-three zone.

After the first quarter, we had a six-point lead, mostly from beating their half-court press. As Bettsville's two-three defense set in, Joey's and my outside shooting kept us in the game, but they dominated the boards on defense and somewhat on the offense. That was where I got in foul trouble again. The referee didn't think my blocks were clean. Coach convinced me to back off in a time out. It was hard, but I did. I got some deep rebounds, and acrobatic shots for baskets and fouls and Brad got a stick-back or two.

I knew I had a bundle of points, mostly from the outside shots. With all that, York led by six points in a high scoring game of seventy-eight to our seventy-two points with one minute to go. They had the out of bounds at our offensive end, so they had to go the length of the court.

After a time out, Coach put in a full-court press a diamond-and-one, making me the one. It was the only chance we had. If we didn't get a steal in a trap, we had to foul them. I was the player furthest down the court guarding our opponents' basket. I had four fouls, and Coach was trying to keep me from fouling out.

An experienced team like York should have beaten our press,

but Joey and Jack got two steals and a quick pass to Brad to connect on some inside shots. The second one was a foul. The York coach called for a time out to set up a play and break the press. After the time out, Brad was on the foul line.

Coach let me line up on the foul line. Brad, a bad average foul shooter, missed, but the ball careened deep off the rim, and I quickly slid in the middle, jumping higher than anyone else and retrieved the ball. When I landed on the floor, I kept the ball high above me, going up for a shot. I could see their big man was about to stop me. It would be a foul, but I wanted more.

Twisting my body acrobatically to the left, I released the ball toward the backboard, and it went in. I would have fallen to the floor on the body of the defender if Brad hadn't grabbed me. To my surprise, the ref didn't call a foul.

The score was tied at seventy-eight points each with no time out called. I hurried down the floor for fear York would inbound the ball quickly then take a long pass down-court, to easily make a basket.

I was right and made it down the court in time to jump in front of the guard, who was to receive the ball. Since I out jumped him, I got it and brought the ball down quickly, for I didn't want York to set their defense. I made it before they did as I went up for the shot. York was confused on defense and left Brad wide open on the baseline, next to the three-second line. With a perfect pass and Brad had a dunk.

York called for another time out. As I walked to our huddle, I looked at the stands and saw our fans going crazy. The York fans were shocked. The score was eighty to seventy-eight with ten seconds left.

Maybe this was a miracle, but I'm not counting my chickens before they're hatched. In the huddle, the first thing Coach said was, "Pull off the press and play a regular man-to-man. York quickly brought the ball up the court, and after two missed shots, the miracle was intact. We still had only two loss-making it fourteen wins with two losses.

When we entered the locker room, our statistician announced that I again had a forty point game. A little nerd turned into a big scoring machine was unreal. My father and mother were both at our big celebration at Keller's to commemorate our win. My father seemed happy and didn't go to Wall's that night.

At home, as I was heading for bed, he told me how proud he was of me. It was a great moment for me. I'm not sure this was the first time he said he was proud of me, but somehow this time it connected, leaving me to believe it was real. A Father's love for his son is unique.

The Toledo Blade, our Sunday paper, had a big write up about the game against York, even a picture of me shooting from the outside. Then the story about the game and the forty points I scored, saying I now had a thirty point average and claiming I was the best player in small schools in northern Ohio.

I didn't read the paper, but a lot of people told me about it. It appeared like I was at the pinnacle of my glory, and pride started seeping into my thoughts. Quickly imagining arrogant Jake, I decided that wasn't for me. I would be humble and happy for the success of our team. A lot of people think this was weird and I should be walking around crowing like a rooster, but no, I won't do it. I will be humble.

One guy in town was pleased about me scoring all those points, but he wasn't happy with the team and still thought we would fail, yet Randy's grandfather wanted me to break Jake's record.

I knew I was getting close with the last forty points, and Randy's grandfather was excited, like me, but I wanted to score for

282

the team, and that was all.

The Advertising Tribune's Thursday Edition had an article on the sports page about Cutler Ridge's basketball team and their upcoming games. It mentioned that I needed only fifty-five points to break Jake's record as well as the comments from the disagreeable Gene Sanders, who predicted Old Fort would win the league.

I lost hope thinking about Old Fort, but with the loss of Cutler Ridge on Friday night, it made everything closer than it was before. Rest assured, Cutler Ridge would not win the league. The nearest team to Cutler Ridge was Bloomville and Attica, each with three losses. Cutler Ridge has one or two more losses coming. Bloomville, Hopewell, Loudon, and Attica are the four last teams they have to play. Then their Cinderella year would be over. The article went to brag about some of the teams we had to play.

Not one kind word told about us in this article. The opinion was that we were the luckiest team in the league. Not one word, good or bad, mentioned me. I wondered why. Did I do something to the reporter in my past, and now he hated me? Was this another of Jake's ways to get to me? He probably had some control over Gene Sander.

If I was to break Jake's record this weekend, I had to look over my shoulder everywhere I went because I expected trouble. If Jake wanted his scoring history to be safe, this had to be when he would get me. He would have to get me completely out of control. I knew I would go down fighting, but I was scared.

No matter how much I prayed, my fear wouldn't leave. I can't say it was a fearful feeling; maybe It was just me being overly cautious. I don't know what it was, but it was scary. I believe it wasn't God's fault. Even though I prayed to Him, maybe I didn't trust Him to keep me safe.

Maybe there was another reason; the feeling Father drilled

into me, I had to be a man, and men are strong. They don't let anything bother them and never show vulnerability or fear. That's why he beat me in the garage. It was because of my weakness.

How did I know that?

A vision, a part of my memory, came to me. I was leaning over a bench in father's garage. My pants and underwear were down around my ankles, and he had a whip that he used to whip my butt. I wanted to scream for mercy, but I didn't. If I did, the whipping would be worse.

Anger welled up in me while I was in the kitchen reading the paper. Father was out in his garage, Mother and Sandy were in the living room watching TV. I didn't say a word to them. I just walked out to the garage without saying a word and went to a metal barrel in the corner. I didn't have to look very long before I found the whip. When I saw it, my anger exploded. I took the strap and walked over to a bench a few tools on it. Pushing the wrenches aside, I slapped the whip on the empty workbench a few times.

Father was working on one of his cars and didn't pay any attention to me until he heard the slap against the bench then he turned and looked at me. I could see a shocked expression on his face as I pointed the whip at him and shouted, "You want to pull your pants down and lay over the bench? Let me thrash you without crying out like you told me!"

Father just stared at me, not knowing what to say. His expression changed to pure fear.

"You are not a father. You are like Adolf Hitler, saying you're the head of the family. That doesn't give you a right to beat me with a strap. If you try to touch me again, I'll beat your brains in. I have no respect for you. You can kick me out of the house, fine! I have plenty of people in this town who will let me stay with them."

284

I stormed out of the garage, into the house, and down to my bedroom. Quickly changing into my sweats, my running shoes, and a light jacket, I walked out of my room and told Mother, "I'm going for a run."

"Why?" she asked.

"Go out to the garage and talk to Father about the whip he used on me," I shouted.

"Why are you angry?"

I left the house and started running. I didn't care where I ran. I need to get my thoughts and anger under control. I felt I deserved to be angry because I could still see the vision of him whipping me!

I wanted to scream, but I didn't cry, that was the old me. I just ran and ran. There was no worry about somebody trying to attack me. If anyone did, that person would have been an angry animal on their hands. I ended up running in a park on the south end of town — a considerable distance from my home.

As exhaustion took over my body, I headed home. The anger was almost gone, but my respect for my father was utterly gone. I kept praying that God would help me with the problem I had with my father. I knew I had to forgive him, but I needed time.

When I got home, I went directly to my room, not looking for my father. I took a shower and went back to my room. There was a soft knock on my door. Then Mother's voice asked, "May I come in?"

"Okay," I agreed.

She came in and sat on my desk chair as I sat on my bed.

"Father told me what he did to you. He did more than the horror of whipping you. Your father was angry because he believed that you were not a man. But he was wrong. Your comment of him being like Adolph Hitler struck him hard. He said you were right."

"That's why Father didn't want me to remember the past. If he had apologized earlier, it wouldn't have been so bad. Why did Father keep lying about me being in a mental institution? Why keep that story going? It was a way to stab a knife in my back. People would think less of me. They were all shocked the other night at Keller's when I told them the truth. He was angry because I told the truth. Father always told me to tell the truth, but the rule doesn't count for him. I would rather people know I wasn't in a mental institution than to think I was. That was not fair!"

There was a long silence, then I said, "I have promised God I will accept Father's apology if he asks me for one. If he doesn't and thinks that's a father's privilege, well, let him think that."

"He has asked me to accept his apology. But he's too ashamed the face you. He doesn't even want to drive you to school tomorrow."

"I agree with him, Mother. I'll make it to school, no problem. We both need some time to clear the air."

Mother left my room, and I knew she would tell Father. After we smoothed things out, maybe we would be able to have a better relationship.

When I was at Clyde's, before school, three of my teammates came into the office to talk with me. They showed me something I had never thought I would have to face. They showed me three duplicated letters, all saying the same thing.

~~~~~~~~~

Dear players,

Bass is a cocky, arrogant player, thinking he is better than you, his teammates. You have a right to score. Why don't you shut him off and make

286

baskets yourselves? In Cutler Ridge, it isn't the winning that counts.

It is who scores the most points. Don't let him get away with this. Stick up for yourselves and become the scorers you want to be. Tell Mr. Big Shot Bass that you are going to shoot tonight and have the fun he is having. You have that right to do it. I'll be listening to the game on the radio and laughing when you score points and the totally arrogant, nerd, fool doesn't.

Signed, a Concerned Citizen.

~~~~~~~~~

Brad, Tim, and Joey showed me their letters. "Don't pay attention to these, Jimmy," Tim said.

"Don't get shook up. Do what you do when you hear somebody calling you a gunner. We have some big games coming up, and we need you to shoot whenever you can."

"We're your teammates, and we're not jealous of you or what you score. No, we want to win, and whatever it takes, we want to do it. You're our teammate, Jimmy, and our friend. Always remember that."

"We know the letters were from Jake. It sounds like him and his last-ditch effort to get into your head. Don't fall for it, we didn't!" said Joey.

We walked to school together. The fellowship with my teammates is excellent!

287

Chapter Twenty-three

The non-league games were over, and there were only four games left. We played Republic on Friday night, the first of February.

We started at Bloomville's gym, on Saturday night, which was my birthday. I hoped I could celebrate with a win. Friday, the eighth, we would be home, against Hopewell Loudon. The following Friday night, the fifteenth, Attica will be on our floor. The next week would be the Seneca County Tournament at Seibring Gym on Heidelberg College campus.

The weekend started successfully. We beat Republic's team by twelve points, but they were no pushover. There was no trick defense, just a two-three zone, and their big men made it rough for Brad and Tim to score inside. They had us beat. Tim got only four points, and Brad got six. I had another big game so our team could stay ahead of them. I scored everywhere, but mostly outside. Joey helped with fifteen points, also mainly from the outside. Sam Alt had six points from the outside, and Glen Carl made three points. I scored thirty points in a sixty-four to fifty-two win.

Saturday was my birthday. My parents, my sister, and Elisabeth gave me clothes for gifts. It's nice having a girlfriend, but fear continued to push me to prepare for rejection and doubt made me believe this wouldn't last. Fear kept telling me that after all the excitement was over, I would drift back to being a nerd, and Jake would control me again.

Where did I get that thought? That will never happen!

I will never doubt Elizabeth's love for me. Her promises are genuine and show me how much she loves me.

Then I began feeling that I didn't deserve her and should leave her. Elizabeth deserves somebody better than me. Take away all my wrappings, and I am a worthless nerd. I had to push these feelings away and pray for God to help me.

Most of Saturday I stayed with my family at home. Mother made a great meal, and some of my teammates came to celebrate. Father was friendly to my teammates and me. Even John was there. Kathy stayed home to take care of their baby; she was too cautious her to bring the baby out in this weather with the temperature in the teens and a brisk wind. But I was with my family, my teammates, and Elisabeth. It was a great day!

That night, we played Bloomville on their court. As Elisabeth left me at the bus, I started looking over my shoulder. This night had to be the time.

If I scored over twenty-five points tonight, I would break Jake's record, and he didn't want that to happen. Even on the half-hour bus ride, I feared something might happen.

Maybe a gang would hijack the bus and get me. The bus went down some lonely country roads, and my imagination went wild around every corner.

Fear seemed to control me, and I had no control over it, except to be ready to fight. I had to get hold of my fear and doubt. I

289

couldn't play a game like this.

Nothing happened on our ride to Bloomville, not even while I was walking from the bus to the school, but the fears were still with me, but not so strong in the school watching the Junior Varsity with the audience.

Going to the locker room to get dressed for the game, I was cautious. When I entered the gym to warm up for the game, all my fear of Jakes retaliation was gone, and I was zeroed in on the game.

Bloomville had us from start to finish. They played a two-three zone just like Republic, and they shut us off, inside. The difference between the two teams is that Bloomville had a lot better offense.

They didn't try to use a particular defense to stop me from shooting as long it was outside. I made it somewhat close, about ten points, with my outside shooting and some inside shots from Brad.

With four minutes to go, the score was sixty-eight to fifty-six, Bloomville. Our coach encouraged us not to give up, but to play harder on defense and for me to shoot more. The defense held and I went on a wild shooting streak, but it wasn't enough. We lost by three points.

There were some questionable referee calls. The fans, the coaches, and some players thought that was the reason we lost. One of there questionable calls fouled me out of the game with thirty seconds left. I knew it was part of the game.

We lost seventy-five to seventy-two, and I made thirty-five points in the game. It was more then I expected, but Coach kept yelling at me to keep shooting, and I rarely missed.

With Bloomville knocking off the leading team in our league and putting them one game behind us in the league, this was defiantly a big game for them. So their fans rushed the floor, and we left the floor quickly letting them have their celebration. We'd had plenty.

I was happy the way I shot; I was pretty good on defense; I hustled, probably too much, trying to block too many shots. That's how I got fouled out of the game. I'm sure I didn't touch the body on those blocked shooters. It was like the referees didn't believe I could jump that high without touching an offensive player. I felt like saying something to Chumbly, but what could he say? The referees weren't going to listen to him, so I had to live with it.

As I entered the locker, I saw everybody with there heads hung down like they were ashamed or mourning over a deceased loved one. We're fifteen and three, the best record Cutler Ridge ever had. I know it's normal to feel sad over a loss, but I was never in this position, with a team who suffers a dramatic loss like like this. The Attica game hurt me more, but after getting over that game, I expected more damages, so I saw each win as a blessing.

My Junior year in basketball was nothing but terrible memories, but not because we lost a game. I don't remember much about my Sophomore year. I played some, but that was it. I never played in my Freshman year. So wins and losses in those three years were not in my memory.

I was the leading scorer on this team after our third loss. How should I feel? I had a great game, but I can't tell the players that. It would make them feel as if they were defective, so little emotion was best for me. Coach gave us our final speech as he did after every game.

"Believe it or not, I think we're still in the first place. Attica has three losses so we may have tied with them. Bloomville has four losses, and so does Old Fort. So hang in there, guys. We have two games to play."

No one looked up, so Coach went on, "Next week we go against Hopewell Loudon, the following week it's Attica. Both will be on our home floor. I know they're big games and there are no Saturday night games the rest of the regular season. Each week we prepare for only one team. This week it will be Hopewell Loudon and next week will be Attica. Forget this game. It's over! We played our hardest to win, but it just didn't go our way tonight. Some say we have a weak league this year, but I think it's the opposite. Everybody's beating everybody; even Thompson has won half of their games in the league. We beat all of the teams we played outside of the league, and the rest of the league has done the same things. It might not be as good as our record, but they have a good percentage of their wins. We're more successful winning games outside the league, but within the league, we're beating each other. Don't get discouraged. Let's concentrate on the next two games, but only one game at a time."

I had broken Jake's record by ten points and now have five-hundred-forty points while Jake had five-hundred-thirty. Nobody told me, but I knew how many points I needed. I read about it in the paper this week. I thought nothing of the number of points and what it represented. Now on the bus ride home, it dawned on me, I had beat Jake's regular-season record by ten points.

Knowing this gave me pleasure. No, it gave me a lot of joy. I wanted to scream, "I beat Jake. I beat the bully. This stupid nerd beat the bully."

I wanted to tell Joey sitting beside me or Tim and Brad, who sat in the seat in front of me. Then I realized I couldn't. I wanted to tell them, but I couldn't. I always said that I scored for the team, not for a record. Bragging would make me a liar.

When we got back to Cutler Ridge, there weren't many people to greet us. Most of the team went to Keller's, but Elisabeth and I went to a restaurant across from the Ritz Theater in Tiffin. I didn't think Jake would be there; he was probably in a bar getting angry enough to kill me. I didn't feel guilty, because I didn't intentionally try to beat his record. So why was I so quiet as we sat in the restaurant waiting for our food?

Elisabeth asked, "Are you bummed out about losing?"

I was hurt. Elizabeth, my girlfriend, forgot about me breaking the record. She knew how many points I needed and she was going to keep my points straight so she would know.

Before I said anything, she reached for her purse and pulled out the little notebook that she used to recorded all my stats and looked at it. Then smiled, "You did it! You beat that old bully's record!"

"Yep!" I grinned.

It felt good when she said that, but it gave me mixed feelings. Was it pride or revenge? Some people would be screaming it from the rooftops.

"Is that why you're so bummed out?"

I smiled and answered, "I know, but I'm supposed to be humble."

"Forget it, Jimmy. Breaking the record is something you should be proud that you did. You beat your enemy, the old bully. I was so bummed out over the loss that I forgot. I'm sorry."

"That's okay. I'm glad you remembered without me telling you."

"Did the team, the coach, or John say anything to you?"

"No, they forgot, but Coach made a good speech after the game."

293

I told her what he said, and she agreed the speech was good.

As the man in the booth in front of us was leaving, he looked at me and asked, "Are you Bass, that player from Cutler Ridge? I thought I heard you say something about Hopewell Loudon."

He had to know I was from Cutler Ridge; I was wearing my red and blue Cutler Ridge jacket with "Indians" written on the back. My height made me stand out like a sore thumb. I was afraid we would get in an argument, and I didn't want that. I knew I had to be polite when I answered him, but Elizabeth beat me to it.
"He sure is." Elisabeth smiled.

Another man across from us, sitting on a swivel seat at the bar exploded, "Are you the famous Jimmy Bass?"

It went around in the restaurant people talking to me about my team and the loss that night. Mostly they talked about the fact that I beat Jake Bickhart's record it was all over the radio. Some of the people were Hopewell Loudon fans, even the one who first recognized me. He gave me some friendly banter, asking who we were going to get beat next Friday.

There were more Hopewell Loudon fans and more friendly banter over our next game. I enjoyed it immensely. The rest of the fans there were from Tiffin. They were glad to meet me. Most of them shook my hand, praised me for my accomplishments, and acted like I was a celebrity. All in all, it was a happy time.

~~~~~~~~~~

Joey and his girlfriend, Jill, as well as Tim and his girlfriend, Beverly, were in the first booth at Keller's. Pat and Clair sat with Randy and his girl, Sue, at a table next to them. They weren't the only ones in the restaurant; the central section was three-quarters full.

Jake Bickhart walked in the front door, stopped a few feet inside, and looked around. It was the first time he had been in this

294

restaurant since he was in high school when people used to like him.

Now Bass was their hero, and he was here to meet the nerd, not to hurt him, how could he with all these Bass loving people around.

Was Jimmy Bass, the nerd he knew in the past? Was he trying to torment him or was he a ringer? As he looked around, he couldn't see anybody who looked like Bass, only cheerleaders and what looked like Junior varsity players.

He saw a kid who might be Bass. It had to be him, "How could a little shrimp beat my record?" Jake fumed.

As he started to walk toward the kid, his thoughts accused him, "Don't make a fool of yourself. Everybody says Bass is tall." But he couldn't get that straight, not wanting to believe Bass was taller than him.

Scanning the restaurant's patrons to his left and those at the tables and booths in front of the restaurant, he spotted Pat Ender and Randy Diller, a guy he didn't like. Diller was with his girlfriend and shouldn't give any trouble. A lot of people were looking at him, making him feel like turning around and high tailing it out of there since he was getting a lot of evil stares. No, he came here to see Bass, and it looked like Pat was the person to ask.

Pat saw Jake come in the door, looking around like he was looking for somebody. Now he was walking towards his table.

In a soft voice, he told Randy about Jake. Randy turned to see Jake just as he stopped in front of them. A big smile was on Jake's face as he looked past Randy and stared at Pat.

"Pat, I'd like to meet Bass and congratulate him for his big accomplishment. I'm not here to cause any trouble."

"What accomplishment are you talking about?"

"Your hero didn't brag to you about beating my record, tonight?"

"That's Jimmy, Jake," Tim replied from his seat in the booth.

"He is nothing like you. You always brag about your self. He is very humble."

"Is he still a nerd?" Jake wondered. "Maybe he'll be a pushover in a fight."

Then he remembered how Jimmy had handled Alter. "So, he's not here?" Jake asked.

"No, Jake, he went somewhere with Elisabeth."

"Hasselback?" Jake asked, surprisingly.

"Yes, they have been dating for a month or so."

Jake just shook his head and said, "So your star isn't here. That's a shame. I bet he felt like he didn't want to eat with you boys."

"Teammates," Joey corrected him. "Or were you thinking peons? He is nothing like that, Jake. We are a team, and that is why we win." Tim declared.

Jake laughed. "You're all fools, letting a nerd take advantage of you. The only thing that counts in Cutler Ridge basketball is how many points you make. What do you think you're going to do, win? That's a pipe dream!"

Tim was surprised, and everybody looked at him with a confused expression. "You don't know our record, Jake?"

"I know you won a few games, but that's nothing to cheer about."

Three middle-aged men were standing behind Jake. One, about Jake's height but weighing a lot more, said, "How about our fifteen and three record? We are still in the first place, even though we lost tonight."

Jake turned to his side, smiled. "Hello, Mr. Bush. What did you say?"

"With this team, Jake, Cutler Ridge has fifteen wins and three losses. Even with a loss, tonight, we are still in first place."

Jake didn't know what to think. When he read the paper, all he looked at was what Bass scored. Cutler Ridge had a winning season, and that was so shocking to him, that he turned to leave, but the three men weren't going to let him.

Joe Bush raised his voice and shouted, "What you did to Jimmy Bass was shameful, Jake. I thought you would have matured a little. Your twenty-one or close to it, but you still act like a kid. You had somebody plant all those evil notes in his desk and his locker. You arranged a hoax that made him out to be a sexual pervert."

"You sent guys to beat him or at least break his fingers," somebody yelled angrily in the crowd scattered around him."

Other people said the same things, then Joe said. "I know you're going to deny it. You've never owned up to any evil thing you did. Never, Jake, never!" It seemed everyone was reminding Jake that he had been cruel to Jimmy Bass.

Jake didn't know what to do, but he knew he had to get out of there. Slowly he pushed towards the door, but people pushed back, making it difficult for him to get through. His only thought was fear. It would be okay if he were in charge of this mob, but the tables had turned, and he was the victim.

As he made his way through the door, more men were waiting for him. Where did they all come from? It seemed like all the men from the town were there. They continued calling him names

297

and even women were yelling the same thing, "No, hero! You're just a bully, a stupid bully who is turning into a nerd, a worthless nerd!" Jake screamed as loud as he could in anger.

"I am not a nerd! I am a man!" Jake countered.

The next thing he knew, he was laying on the sidewalk. A couple of guys had tripped him. He tried to get up, but a few people's feet were on his chest, and others were pinning his legs to the sidewalk. Nobody kicked him like he used to do.

The crowd kept shouting. One person yelled, "How does it feel? What we are doing is just like you did to Jimmy, over and over. But, you kicked him, too."

"You deserve it!" another man declared. "We won't kick you. We're civilized."

Laying there, he felt the end was coming, and he remembered what he and his gang had done to Bass. They said they weren't going to kick him, and he hoped they didn't go back on their word. He didn't want to feel that pain. No one had ever kicked him, but he could see and feel the pain he did to others.

Hands grabbed hold of him and brought him to a standing position. One of the men in the crowd remarked, "I have a rope. Why don't we hang him? Not by his neck, but around his shoulders. Tie him to one of the light poles, and let him swing for a while."

Jake was scared. As the man came towards him with the rope, Jake was crying and pleading with them to let him go. He promised he would leave Bass alone. As the line slid under his shoulders, he was pulled down the sidewalk and under a street light. He started screaming and begging for mercy. Then he heard Clyde demand, "Let him go!"

They let the rope drop, and Clyde stepped in front of him.

298

Almost nose to nose with Jake, Clyde yelled, "This is a lesson for you Jake. We know where you live, we know where you work, and we know where you hang out. We might stalk you as your boys did to Jimmy. If anything happens to Jimmy, I mean anything, even a threatening letter, we will come after you. Do you hear me, Jake?"

Jake didn't say a word. His whole body shook with fear, a fear he had never felt before. He nodded his head in agreement. Then Clyde and some of the rest of the crowd escorted him to his car. When they released him, he hurried to his front door, opened it, and quickly slid into the front seat. Jake was so nervous it took him a while to fish his keys out of his pants pocket, put them into the ignition, and start the car. Shifting the Chevy into first gear, he drove quickly out of town.

Once he had finally made it out of town, he relaxed and felt wetness on his thighs. He was so scared he had peed his pants.

Chapter Twenty-four

Another of Jimmy's enemies stood in the shadow of a building across the street and watched the whole incident, waiting for trouble that Jake might cause. He was glad he wasn't with Jake and felt the humiliation Jake should have felt, knowing he deserved the same. Although surprised with the outcome, he was pleased to see the fulfillment of the old country expression, "Ride a man out of town on a rail." Well, it wasn't a rail, it was a new Chevy.

Life hasn't been good. The horror of Jimmy's dreams hit me hard, and all I could think of was the fear I had caused him, the names I called him, and the mean ways I hurt him. Why, because it made me feel powerful. Now I felt nothing but shame and wished I could talk to Jimmy, begging him to forgive me. Jake would tell me I am a fool, the nerd got what he deserved, but don't think so. I wonder how Jake feels after what happened to him tonight. He doesn't have a single friend in the town where he grew up, and it's the same with me.

I am staying deep in the shadows between buildings so no one will see me. All the good things I had growing up in this town will be only memories.

Before I became an arrogant bully, I felt like I was powerful, working as Jake's muscle, and I enjoyed it. Now I'm ashamed I did those things. My downfall was the night Jimmy Bass endured what everyone refers to as "the incident."

People who knew how our gang hurt Jimmy told everyone all over town. There was a meeting in the auditorium, and the truth came out. That's when the Superintendent, principal, and Coach Summerall got fired, and the community disciplined our gang. When my mother found out what I did, she was so angry at me, that she kicked me out of her house. I'm still not allowed to come home because of the shame I caused her and the family.

I left without graduating and joined the Army where I lasted a year and a half before getting kicked out for fighting. I spent time in jail; then I went to work for Jake, the only one who would hire someone with a dishonorable discharge. Then he fired me when I didn't fulfill my mission for him.

I wanted to get the nerd again. I blame all my failure on him. Jake said Bass is crazy. I was home for only three months and didn't know what was happening. I believed what Jake said. What a fool I was!

Even when I faced Bass, I didn't realize how big he had become. I still saw him as that little nerd I had enjoyed teasing. The next thing I knew, this nerd had me in a hammerlock, bent over the hood of the car, and I felt like my arm would break. That was my turning point. I'm not as tough as I thought I was! Then the dreams came. They scared me. When the streets cleared, John Alter rushed down Main Street to his car and quickly left town.

~~~~~~~~~

There was a small article in the paper reporting how I broke Jake's record. People in town congratulated me when I ran into them, as well as my teammates, and the coach at Monday's practice. Of course, my mother, father, and sister congratulated me, too. At the beginning of the year, Father was always congratulating me about the game I played, making me feel like a hero, but not so much lately. He quit going to the bar after the game or any other time. He seemed moody, but he never said a cross word to me.

My memory was slowly coming back, and there was nothing I could do to suppress it. My mind would eventually show how badly Father had treated me, and that scared him.

I didn't have to say that something terrible came from my memories. I could keep it quiet, but my father knew, and since I came home, he acted as a father should.

But the memory of the way he beat me with that whip wouldn't go away. I knew it would take time, and God was on my side.

Until I met John, I didn't know God. Now, after all the turmoil I've gone through, I'm glad I do. It's easier being on God's side.

Memories are coming back about how Jake and his gang treated me in school. Sometimes I would accidentally overhear a conversation. Sometimes people told me what happened to me.

When people started explaining, I thought the pain was under control, and I was a man who could handle it. Surprise! The memories brought the horrors of the pain I felt before. I thought that self-esteem and believing I was beyond the hurt would take care of it. Wrong again!

Fear and depression were pushing me toward despair. The horror of that pain, brought me to my knees, pleading for God's mercy.

The demons fled, and so did the pain. Still, I could feel it in the distance waiting for me. Sometimes an inner voice would try to draw me back into my former world, but I rebuked it, in Jesus name, and it seemed to disappear.

It gave me comfort to hear what the folks did to Jake. When I first heard it, I was happy, knowing so many people in the town cared for me. Some would say it was because I was a star, but I didn't believe that. I was one of there own. They had watched me grow up, and when they found out what Jake and his gang had done to me, the people of my town felt guilty, or sorry, for what happened. When I came back to town as a tall basketball player, even though I couldn't remember some of them, they drew me in, as one of their own and were with me emotionally on every move I made in the games.

The whole week, everyone was excited about the upcoming game. Rally signs telling what we were going to do to Hopewell Loudon were everywhere.

The patrons in Fred Stalling's Barbershop were skeptical, but Jim Diller was on the bandwagon. At the Friday afternoon pep-rally, the auditorium was packed, not only with students but also with an abundance of fans who were able to get out of work and, of course, the usual Mothers who didn't forget that I broke Jake's record.

Before the Hopewell Louden game on Friday, I was the last person to be announced. As the host called my name, he said, "Our all-time Leading scorer in Cutler Ridge history, for one season, with five-hundred-forty points and counting, and averaging thirty points per game..." Then the announcer paused before finishing his introduction: he shouted, "I present, Jimmy Bass!"

When I exited the huddle, the fans let out an enthusiastic cry, and every one of my teammates grabbed and shook my hand. Some patted me on the back as I stood with the starters in the middle of the floor. I was in awe, knowing the fans were cheering for me, and the Hopewell Loudon fans also stood, giving me acclamation. I felt honored.

303

The ovation pumped me up, but it didn't help me. Hopewell decided not to double-team me in their attempt to check me but played straight man-to-man, attempting to stop my teammates, so Coach put me at point and told me to work out front for my shots. I hit only part of my shots, some of their success was a good defense, and I was cold, missing even some of my backboard attempts. I was very disappointed and stopped shooting. Then Coach called a timeout and told Joey to play point guard. He said we should go on the motion offense.

It was a good move. We were getting pics, and people were open for shots. We went around Hopewell, but they came right back and ended the half by leading us, twenty-four to twenty-two. Hopewell might have scored more, but we had a strong defense, and they missed a lot of shots.

Elisabeth was sitting with Sandy in the upper level and went down to the concession stand to get some refreshments while Sandy stayed in the balcony to hold their place. Everywhere she went, people asked, "What's wrong with Jimmy." But she didn't know what to say. Then when she got to the concession stand, it was so crowded that she decided to go back to her seat.

Elizabeth was frustrated and told Sandy what she went through. Sandy asked, "What is the matter with my brother? He seems so confused out on the floor."

"I don't know, other then he's having a bad day. Everyone has one of those every once in a while."

Elisabeth knew it was more than that. Even though she tried to act strong, she knew his memories were coming back, the ones reminding him of the horrors he went through. Maybe they are affecting his game. He told her he prayed a lot about it. She did too.

I probably had six points in the first half, Joey and Brad had

304

the rest. Going to the locker room, I felt ashamed as if I had let the team down, but the new strategy Coach had for the second half pumped me up.

Coach told us that even though our motion offense was working, he wanted to try something else. He wanted Joey and Jack to split the point guard position as we played against New Reigel with their box-in-one. I would roam the baseline to get open with picks from Brad and Tim who played both low-posts on each side of the key. It worked, not only for me but also for Brad and Tim, when I got my defender picked, and broke open on the side. The defender that broke out on me didn't get set as I drove around him. I got a close backboard shot or a pass to Tim or Brad for an easy shot. Sometimes, on the set-pick, both the defender, who was the pick and the defender guarding Brad or Tim followed me, leaving Brad or Tim open for an easy shot.

With this offense, Hopewell Loudon's coach made adjustments in the middle of the third quarter after we pulled ahead by eight points. The player guarding Jack sagged back toward the wing to stop me, leaving Jack wide open. At first, he was afraid to shoot, but I encouraged him when one of the Hopewell Loudon players was on the foul line. I knew Jack could hit the outside shot. He had worked hard to develop it, with me teaching him what my uncle taught me.

The game was tied at thirty-five points when Jack took the first shot and hit nothing but net. Then he made two more in a row, putting us ahead, forty-one to thirty-five. So they covered Jack and left Joey open. That was a mistake! He made two more baskets when Joey's defender hesitated just a little, and I had the player on the left-wing well covered. When his defender sagged, Joey drove around him for an easy short backboard shot, and no defender could react to stop him. They were all worried about the two big men or me getting open.

305

Playing much the same strategy, Joey had a good game, and so did Jack when he was open. With a sixty to fifty lead and three minutes to go, Coach had me go to point and try to stall. He placed Brad in one corner and Tim in the other with Joey and Jack deep on the right wings. I controlled the game and was comfortable doing it. I kept dribbling the ball back and forth out front, trying to penetrate towards the basket. When I was in position for a backboard shot, I took it and made it, knowing the man guarding me couldn't block my shot. I got the center tip all night long, and if he came at me, I was ready with a quick pass to Brad or Tim for an open shot.

I thought we had the game in hand, but Hopewell had other ideas. I had to run off the clock over forty-five seconds before I made my shot.

There was a time out called by Hopewell Loudon, and in our huddle, Coach Chumbley told us to look for traps and spread out so we could use the offense whenever they double-teamed me.

Hopewell was hitting their shots from outside, or we would have had a more significant lead. They made a basket and set up traps when I got the ball on an inbound pass. We had worked on this passing game to perfection in practice. It was a lot of work, but it paid off, getting either a layup or foul shot winning the game, seventy to sixty-one.

Elisabeth and Sandy cheered excitedly throughout the second half. Elisabeth hoped this would cheer me up and help me forget about my troubling memories.

In the locker room, I discovered I had only eighteen points. I had a high score, but Joey had tied with me. The rest of the scoring got distributed around. I stood up and cried the words, "We want Attica!" over and over, and the rest of the players joined in. It was a glorious moment for our team, and I wanted to enjoy it.

We had a fabulous celebration at Keller's. The biggest surprise came close to an hour after the game. Mr. Keller got everyone's attention, and the crowd became silent. Then he said, "Bloomville seventy-eight, Attica seventy-four." Everyone cried out, "Champs!" We weren't champs, because we lost the last game to Attica. But we were at least co-champs, and nobody could take that away from us. I wondered what Randy Dillard's grandfather thought about that.

The town's celebration was unbelievable, and I was a big part of it. To think, five or six years later, the small school and their connection with their community would slowly dwindle because experts said and demanded, "Bigger is better."

The headlines on the front page of Saturday's paper read, "Cutler Ridge, Seneca County League Co-champions. Under the caption, also in big letters, it said, "First Time In Twenty-four Years."

The rest of the weekend was perfect. Elisabeth and I went to a movie at the Ritz and afterward to the same restaurant, across the street. Everybody knew me, now, and congratulated me, even the Hopewell Loudon fans that I met the week before. Sunday, we went to church, and there was plenty of praying and thanking God.

I spent part of the afternoon at a concert hall watching Elisabeth playing the piano. It was the second performance I had attended. The first time I was afraid, but after what the town did to Jake, I was sure I was safe.

Attica played us at home on Friday night. Again, like Hopewell Loudon, they didn't try to double team me. Our coach had us play the same offense we played in the second half against Hopewell Loudon. I got some shots from the outside and drove off of the picks. It was either a backboard shot for me or a pass to Tim or Brad. Again the guard would sag on me after Joey or Jack passed me the ball to cut me off from driving, giving Joey or Jack an outside shot, and they made a good percentage of there shots.

Sometimes Joey faked a pass to me then, as his man took a step toward me, Joey drove to the middle and got a backboard shot. Joey used the backboard shot a lot, always pushing to an angle where he could use it. If the big man came out on him, Brad or Tim had a shot.

This offense worked perfectly, and we scored thirty-three points. But our defense had a hard time holding them down, especially from the outside, and they scored thirty points.

At halftime, Coach went to our regular motion offense. I lined up on the baseline with Jack, and we broke out to a wing position after some unreliable picks. This play was a decision Jack made so he could move to one wing position and I could take the other. Sometimes I would go to the corner, leaving Tim to take the wing position.

In the second half, Joey played point, and I went to the corner. On our first try, Joey drove around his man for a clear shot, making a layup. Brad saw what was happening and stepped towards the edge, drawing his man with him so he couldn't block Jimmy's shot.

We stayed with Attica the whole half. First, they would lead, then we would. There were no fast breaks because both teams shut them down with good defense.

I thought the game would go down to the wire, but I was wrong. We pulled away, midway through the fourth quarter, because I was on fire with my outside shots and Attica had cooled off. I started to run more and get some close backboard shots before the defense set. We ended up beating Attica by thirteen points in a high scoring affair, eighty to sixty-seven. I made thirty-three points with twelve rebounds and five assists. I was happy with my output, as well as my teammates' scores.

Now we were eighteen and two for the season. I ended my regular season with five-hundred-ninety-one points giving me an average of twenty-nine and a half points. Not bad for a nerd.

People didn't rush the floor because there were plenty of security guards to keep them back. I asked our announcer if I could have the mic and said, "We are truly Seneca County's champions."

I got a big cheer, then I said, "I thank all of our fans, everyone in the stands who supported us this year. You are awesome. Winning the championship was a great accomplishment for us."

Then I walked to the middle of the floor, as far as the cord would allow, and pointed to the fans as I said, "We did it all for you! Without you, it wouldn't have been worth it. We enjoy the loud noise and cheers you give us. I thank God that I was able to come back here and be part of this. Thank you, fans for everything. Now I'm going to walk into the audience and try to shake everyone's hands. I invite my fellow players to do the same thing."

The whole team walked among the fans shaking hands with them. Women hugged me, men shook my hand, and I got a lot of pats on the back. When I came to my parents, my sister, Sandy, and Ben, her new boyfriend; Mother hugged me and Father gave me a good handshake congratulating me. As I left my family to greet some other fans, I saw my father trying not to cry. There was a lot of emotion in the auditorium. I don't know why I came up with the idea to do this. It was a spur of the moment thing, yet I felt it was something I ought to do. We left the auditorium as one, fans and team together.

After the game, there was another celebration. Elisabeth had to go to her brother's house in Chicago for the weekend because her mother had been staying with him since Christmas and now she wanted to go home. I wouldn't see Elizabeth until Tuesday, so I didn't stay at Keller's very long, and I walked homeward.

I was cautious, glancing at every corner for somebody to jump out at me. If someone did, my watchfulness would save me. I felt like somebody was watching me at a distance, but if there was, no one came after me, and I made it home safely.

~~~~~~~~~~

I was watching Jimmy. I wanted to talk to him and tell him how sorry I was. I got hired back as a mechanic because I needed to earn money to keep Jake's father's business afloat, and Jake couldn't afford high priced mechanics. I knew about as much as one of them.

I wouldn't work for Jake if he didn't promise to leave Jimmy alone. He promised he would because he had too much to worry about with the dealership. His father wasn't around much. A weak heart had him staying home, especially when it was cold. Jake even left his apartment and moved back with his father to keep a better eye on him. Jake's father had an older woman who watched over him, was his housekeeper, and cooked for him. But she left him alone at five in the evening. So Jake felt he had to move back home.

I knew what happened to Jake because I was there when the whole town disowned him. At first, I was shocked, but I knew it was a reality and that it would hurt Jake's business. People from this town wouldn't buy cars from him again as they used to with his father. He was still too proud to make up with Jimmy or the townsfolk, so his advertisements went to another area. Lately, he spent a lot of time on that. So Jimmy didn't have to worry about Jake.

Singer left town after he got out of jail and didn't want anything to do with Jake. He never got paid the money Jake owed him, even when he confronted him. Jake promised, "If you touch me, Jude, you'll go back to jail."

It scared Jude, and he left swearing he would get even.

As John walked backed to his car, he knew there would be a time he would make amends with Jimmy.

Chapter Twenty-five

Saturday morning, the sixteenth of February, I had another counseling session in John Wood's office at ten o'clock. John opened the meeting by saying, "Colleges like Bowling Green and Toledo are interested in you."

"What are you talking about, John? I'm not good enough for a school like Bowling Green or Toledo."

"They have been scouting you and asking questions. Nobody has said anything to you because they want to watch you play more. Isn't that good?"

I just stared at John, in a daze, and began telling him the story of what happened.

~~~~~~~~~

I was in the country, and saw a fire in front of the doors of an abandoned barn and went over to check it out.

I know the country pretty well, so I'm sure I could find the place again.

Suddenly Jake and his gang showed up and started to say they were going to beat me. I thought I could get away and lose them, but there was no escaping. They hung a rope from a beam in the barn and tied it around my hands above my head. I was stripped down to my underwear with my pants around my ankles.

I was blindfolded so that I couldn't see anyone, but I know there were three girls. From what I gathered, they wanted to see a completely naked man. I could feel them touching me all over my body, and I mean all over! Then they left with Jake. I was sure it was him by his voice. I think Alter and Singer were with him.

I felt a whip crack on my back and screamed for mercy, but the person with the whip wouldn't stop. He called me a nerd fag, saying the girls didn't affect me, because only boys turned me on. He kept yelling, "I'm going to kill you, Fag!"

With each word, he hit harder and harder. I thought he would kill me right there on the barn floor. The pain was unbearable, and I screamed after each hit, hoping he would stop.

Then I heard Jake and Alter come into the barn and stop him from beating me. The one with the whip kept saying, "I want to kill him. I want to kill the stupid fag!"

When someone untied the rope, I pulled up my pants and fastened my belt. Alter threw my shirt at me, and I put it on. I could see blood on my chest and belly. I knew my back had to be bloody. Then Jake gave me my jacket, stating, "This is your get out of jail card; Run, nerd, run!"

He didn't have to tell me twice. I started running as hard as I could. I moved slowly, at first, and nobody tried to stop me. They laughed at me and called me names. Running was difficult because of the pain, but the noise of the camp was getting further and further away, and that gave me comfort. I thought I was safe; then I felt a sting on my back.

I knew it was from a BB gun and I wondered if it broke the

skin. I ran faster. Then another pellet hit my back. I quickly headed towards the woods because I was sure I could lose him there. There were two more hits on my butt before I entered the woods. I could hear BB's flying around the woods, but they were hitting trees instead of me.

I found a hiding place where the ground was dug out in front of a lot of brush. I laid on the ground and slide under the brush.

The shooter didn't see me, but I saw him. I was sure I could surprise him and knock the BB Gun away then give him some of his own medicine. That was wishful thinking. I didn't have the courage, and I just froze as he walked by. Then I wondered what gave him the courage to come after me. I was taller than he, and could probably beat him if his buddies were not with him to protect him. Then I saw what had given him courage; he had a pistol in a holster strapped to his belt. This kid was out to get me!

He disappeared, and I went slowly in the opposite direction. I ran home and never saw him again. I remember entering my house, as the demons started pounding on me.

The next thing I recall, I was laying in my underwear, on my bed. I looked at the clock on my nightstand and saw it was eleven in the morning and I wasn't in school. Then I remembered my parents had gone on a business trip and Sandy was staying at a friend's house. So I was all alone.

I took off my underwear and took a shower. There marks all over my body; some had broken the skin, but the blood had dried. I was still bleeding in other places, too. I used gauze and tape to stop the bleeding.

I washed my clothes that were lying on the floor next to the bed, the bedding, and anything else that had blood or dirt on it in our new washer and drier.

Throughout the day, I stayed in the house fighting the demons. My ribs hurt, and other places where they beat me. I struggled to walk.

The demons controlled me, saying, "You're going to Hell. No person like you should live. Death will release you from pain. Make them feel sorry when you're dead, especially your father, who is mad at you all the time. He whips you with the whip he hides in the garage. He doesn't love you. He wishes you were dead. Show him."

I kept screaming, "I will not go to Hell," over and over. I felt the battle going on all day.

~~~~~~~~~

"Can you feel the pain now?" John asked, bringing me back to reality.

I stared at John, realizing, for the first time, I had been in a trance. It felt as though I was in the barn, getting beaten. I could feel the kid running after me. I could feel the pain I felt in my house as if I wasn't in John's office. I was at home, feeling the pain.

John's voice started pulling me back to reality, but I didn't want to go. The stupor had a hold on me that I could not break. The pain owned me and tried to control me, but somehow, I remembered his question.

I realized he was praying for me, and I knew those prayers. God's love pushed me away from the demons, and I came back to reality. I looked at John. I declared, "It's unreal; I feel like I'm there, but I'm not. I was in a trance, yet I knew you were here."

I paused for a moment, then went on, "John, I know what I told you was real. There was something horrible in those memories that scared me."

"I believe you, Jimmy. You look like you are in pain. Do you want to continue?"

315

"I feel I should, but not in a trance, just by memory."

"Go on, Jimmy."

Somehow I got through the day, then drove to the skating rink. The demons were on me, wanting me to wreck the old Chevy my Father gave me to drive. They commanded me to drive head-on into a tree or a pole so that the pain would be gone. I was tempted, but wouldn't do it.

Only Juniors, Seniors, and a few Sophomore from our school were in the skating rink. I saw Jake with Elisabeth, and he gave me an unbelieving look as if he couldn't believe I was there. Then kissing Elisabeth, he smiled at me. He knew how much I liked Elisabeth. She smiled at me, hoping I would understand. She was popular with Jake, and that was all that counted. I hurt so badly that the pain drove me into a stupor.

I began skating around the rink as my thoughts slowly drifted away. Then they were gone. There is nothing until I woke up at St Luke's Hospital in Nashville, Tennessee.

John gave me the letters Elisabeth had given him. The last letter described a lot about my last day before the incident. I forgot about Jake beating me at that party for the basketball team. Of course, I asked for it by expressing myself over the way he talked about Elisabeth.

I put the letters on his desk and said, "I remember writing them."

"You just now remembered this?"

"Yes, it came to me when I first sat down. I barely remember what you said. I think it was something about Bowling Green University being interested in me."

"Now that you remember that, what are you going to do?"

316

"I don't know. Jake and his gang deserve to go to jail for what they did to me, but that will never happen. Who is going to believe me after all this time? After all, I have mental problems."

"How do you feel now? I mean, emotionally."

I thought for a second. Even though I am a Christian, anger, and revenge could control me. So I said, "I'm alright with it, except the way they beat me. They should get punished. As for Elisabeth, I understand why she acted the way she did. She told me everything she did to me and the things Jake did to her."

I had to pause for a second or two, then I continued, "She broke up with Jake that night. After that, she couldn't get me out of her thoughts. She says that for the first time since the incident, she feels happy because she's with me. I believe walking with God helps her a lot."

"What about Jack and the boys? Now that your big and strong and know how to fight, will you go after them?"

"Defiantly, not! I've got to finish school and basketball, and I don't want to ruin that. I'll fight only in self-defense. I will have to fight the desire to get revenge. The pain and scars are terrible. I feel deep inside someone has to pay, but God's words are with me, "Revenge is Mine."

"One last question, Jimmy, who is the guy that beat you and followed you with a BB gun?"

I tried to remember him, but nothing came to me. I finally said, "John, I don't know."

Then he asked, "Do you know where the barn is where they beat you?"

"I don't know for sure, but I think if I search around a little, I could find it if it's still there. It was dilapidated and may have

317

collapsed. I remember it was north of town, somewhere around my uncle Fred's farm. I think Jake's father lives around there somewhere, but I know it wasn't on his father's farm. I'm confused, but I know that area quite well. Do you think I should try to find it?"

"Why not? If you see the place where they beat you, it might help your closure with these bad feelings."

"Okay, when I leave here, I'll go look for it."

When I left John's place, that's what I was going to do, but then I remembered Randy wanted to eat dinner with me, so I went to Keller's.

Randy was sitting at our usual place, the last booth in the front. He was facing the door, and another man sat across from him. I sat down next to Randy and looked at the man across from us, and was shocked. It was my archenemy or at least one of them. Now he was sitting across from me. I felt like jumping across the table and beating him. Instead, I glared at him.

"Jimmy, do you know who is sitting across from us? He used to be one of your tormentors, and he wants to apologize."

"Yes, Jimmy, I am deeply sorry for all the terrible things I did to you. When I faced you a couple of months ago, I knew you were different, and I heard that you did a lot of wrong things. They convinced me you needed to be beaten up."

"Since you were a weakling when you were here before, I thought it would be easy. But when I saw you walking from school, I thought that's odd. I figured you were out of school. Jude said you were the one. After my first good look at you, I told Jude you weren't Bass. He told me you were and that you had just grown a little. He convinced me you were a rapist who got away with it and needed to be put down."

318

"When I ended up facing you at Clyde's, I knew you couldn't be Bass. You were too tall, but I wasn't backing away from a fight, and you surprised. Me"

He paused to think as if he didn't know what to say. Then He went on, "When I heard that I was supposed to beat you up because of you breaking Jake's record, I was angry. I almost tore them both apart. That's the last time I saw Jake until he hired me as a mechanic. I needed a job, and I am a good mechanic. Will you forgive me?"

I was engrossed in his story, and my anger subsided. Still, it was hard to forgive him, even though that is what Jesus would want. I had a question to ask him, "Why did I get beat and whipped in that old barn. I just remembered this, and it makes me angry!"

He shook his head and stated, "Jimmy, you have to believe me. I wasn't there."

With a fearful look, as if he was afraid I wouldn't believe him, he responded, "Jimmy, I swear I knew nothing about it, until after your incident at the skating rink."

I didn't say anything at first. I could see Jake was afraid of me. He wanted nothing negative to come out of this meeting. Then he said, "Later I heard you squealed on Jake, and that convinced him you needed a beating. Still, Jimmy, you've got to believe me. I wasn't there. I admit I did a lot of mean things to you. I know you remember things I did to you in school when you had a hammer-lock on me. I realized you had to be Jimmy Bass, and I thought you were going to break my arm. Please forgive me?"

Again I stared at him, remembering the ways he tormented me in the past. It was horrifying to think of the pain he caused. Why should I forgive him? Then a few thoughts came to me. "What did, Jesus say to the people who put him on the cross? Forgive them for they know not what they do?"

Steven said the same thing when the Jews were stoning him to death.

Other thoughts came to me, things that I read about forgiveness. Finally, an impression came to me, "I forgave Elisabeth," and I knew what I had to do.

In the Bible, it talks a lot about forgiveness. Peter asked Jesus, "How many times should I forgive a person?"

"Seven times," Jesus answered. "Seventy times seven."

I think that means not to keep track of forgiveness.

"I am a Christian, so I will forgive you and try to forget all the misdeeds you did to me," I replied. "But I want one favor from you?"

"If I can do it, I will."

"Keep Jake from bothering me again."

"I don't think Jake is after you anymore. First of all, no matter how much he wants to pay, nobody will have anything to do with him or hire out for a hit on you. After the town people chased him out of town, Jake is scared. He knows if something happens to you, he is dead meat. The men in this town will find him and do a big, bad beat down on him. He will never forget it. He is petrified of them."

After a pause, he chuckled, "I guarantee; I'll keep him away from you. Thanks for forgiving me. It releases me from the pain I've been feeling."

He was about ready to leave when I commented, "I know your pain, and it isn't easy to get rid of it. Maybe the reason for your pain isn't the same as mine, but pain is pain. Only Jesus Christ, our savior, can take that pain away."

He looked at me strangely, but I went on, "Today, I remembered everything that happened when someone whipped me. I was so confused that I was sure you were at that barn. I thought I heard your voice, but it must have been somebody else. I was about to see if I could find the farm and the barn where the beating happened. When I came here and saw you sitting across for me, I didn't know what to think. I wasn't going to take you on here in Keller's, but that's what I wanted. God made sure I didn't say anything until after you told your story. Then I knew I couldn't be angry with you. God has set this up so I could feel your forgiveness. If you keep feeling the pain, go to Jesus. Do you know John Wood?"

John shook his head. "Do you know St. Mathews church?"

"That's the old Baptist Church, right?"

"Yes, he's the pastor, also my counselor, and the assistant coach. You can come to service there on Sunday or call his number." Then I wrote John's number on a paper for him and commented, "He'll help you with the pain."

I paused for a wile before continuing, then I told Alter, "I believe you when you say you were not at the beating in the old barn. Do you know where the barn is, and who else was there?

"I don't know everyone who was there except I know Jake and Jude were there. I think some Tiffin kids were there and they brought three girls. I remember them bragging about how they stripped off your pants so the girls could see you naked. I heard the girls touched you, and even played with you."

John tried to remember more, then continued, "All I remember is that Jake and Singer were there and the Tiffin kids. I don't know of anybody else who was there."

"Okay, thank you for telling me."

After John Alter left, Randy whispered, "Do you believe him about not being at the beating?"

321

I thought for a second or two and then said, "Who cares, Randy? There's no way I could prove he was there. I thought I heard his voice, but I could have been wrong. There was only one person who beat me with the whip, and I can't remember him."

Randy thought for a while before he said, "I'm sorry you had to go through that. Of course, if I'd known, it never would have happened, but hindsight's always better than foresight."

"Have you ordered?"

"Yes, and here it comes, now. Are you going to order? If you do, I have an idea. When we finish eating, let's find that barn together."

I ordered and ate with Randy. After we finished, we got into my truck and drove north out of town. I was sure it was close to Jack Bickhart's father's farm. Maybe it was on that farm, I didn't know, but I was sure it was around that area.

It didn't take us long to find it. It was down the road and across from Jake's father's farm. The barn stood out in clear sight. Some of it was collapsing.

It was one of the old barns where the bottom section is where you keep animals. The top section of the barn is where you keep your equipment and the hay. To get to the top part of the barn, you had to follow an incline, that ran the length of the barn.

To the right of the barn was a house that had seen better days. It was so dilapidated and falling apart; you wouldn't try to enter the place. Nobody had lived here for a long time. The driveway from the road to the barn was still there. There wasn't much snow on the ground, so I drove the truck up to the base of the incline. Randy and I were wearing boots, so we got out of my vehicle and followed the slope to the closed doors of the barn. We were able to open one of the big sliding doors.

We had to use a shovel in my truck and cleared away the ice and snow that held the bottom of the door. Once we broke it loose, we got both doors open.

As soon as the doors opened, I started walking into the barn. I could see where the beating took place. A long rope hung from a beam in the barn. There were a couple of crates that somebody used to stand on while they tied my hands, making sure my feet barely touched the floor.

A vision came over me, almost the same one I had in John's office. I could see myself, almost naked, hanging from the rope. My pants and underpants were hanging around my ankles. I had a blindfold on and couldn't see anything, but I could hear and feel the girls around me touching my body all over. They didn't turn me on because I felt so humiliated and embarrassed by what they were doing.

When they left, and I thought the whole ordeal was over, but that's when the beating with the whip began. I could feel every crack when it connected with my back. The pain was terrible, but I didn't want to scream. I wanted to take it like a man, but too much pain and the anger of the guy whipping me made me cry out.

He cried, "Nerd! Nerd!" with each slap of the whip. Then he started saying I was nothing but a nerd, fag. I was such a filthy person I didn't deserve to live. The words, he said, seemed to make him angrier, and he hit me harder. I started screaming at the top of my lungs. That's when Jake and Jude were beside me, and the whipping stopped, and they untied me. Even though I was in excruciating pain, the embarrassment of being naked was stronger. I quickly reached down and pulled my underpants and pants up. Someone threw me my shirt and jacket, and I started to run.

That's when the vision left. All I could feel was the pain. How could a person hurt another person so badly? I felt the person who

323

whipped me had so much hate for me; he didn't want to quit whipping me. But Singer stopped him. If I find that person, will I want to hate him, and beat him so severely that he would feel the pain I did?

I had to figure that out, but with the County tournament coming up, I wanted to forget all this mess. After that, I could pursue whatever God wanted me to do. I wanted God in this picture. I wanted to do it all on my own, but I had a lot of praying and talking to do before I made a rash judgment.

As we closed the door of the barn and walked back to my truck, I told Randy what I saw in my vision, but for now, I would leave it there.

Chapter Twenty-six

Seneca County League plays tournament games at Seibring's gym on the Heidelberg College campus. Every team gets one hour of practice, and our time was four o'clock, Sunday afternoon.

As our team was warming up, I looked at the empty stands and seemed to see a thirteen-year-old boy sitting with an older man. It was a game between Cutler Ridge and Hopewell Loudon, and the gym was packed. As the boy watched the teams play, he dreamed that someday he would be on that floor leading Cutler Ridge to victory. But the result of the game was the same as always, Cutler Ridge lost.

That boy was me, and the man was Uncle Fred. My dream wasn't over. I had to satisfy the young thirteen-year-old boy who was suffering from the torment that drove him into fantasy land four years later. I remember the pain and suffering that boy went through; he deserved all the success he could achieve. Motivation grew strong within me. I had to please the memories of that boy.

Then I thought of the fans who, year after year, came to the tournament and saw nothing but failure. If they were lucky, maybe they saw a close game, but that was all they could expect.

Gene Sander wrote, "Cutler Ridge doesn't belong in the winners' section. They should float away, and we should all forget them." That was a horrible thing to say, but it was a motivation for our team.

I'm sure these memories came from dreams I had in the past and my desire to be good enough to play for Cutler Ridge on this floor. I remember practicing in this gym. Summerall had us scrimmage with twelve players, but as always, I didn't get to play one bit.

I asked him why, and he said, "You're not good enough to play, and I wished you would quit."

"My father won't let me quit!" I yelled. "Why can't you give me a break?"

"Shut up and go stand where you were!" he growled.

Then Jake and his boys pushed me around on the ride back home. How cruel can people be?

I would like to see Summerall or Jake and show them how foolish they were. Of coarse Summerall would say I wasn't that tall back then and what I've heard from Jake he still doesn't believe it.

The pain keeps erupting over what those two did to me. I want revenge, but would that make me feel better? No, I knew it wouldn't, so I need to stay close to God and pray when those feelings come. What I have accomplished this year is a gift from God. He let me succeed, so I praise Him.

Since as it was a gift that God gave me, I would be spitting in God's face, if I looked for revenge. It seems like God is blessing my teammates and me to succeed. I pray His blessing lasts so we can win the tournament. We practiced hard for our hour's practice, and then we went home.

The first game in the tournament was Thompson and Republic. They played at seven-thirty PM on Tuesday, February nineteen. The winner played us at seven PM on Wednesday, the twentieth because we were top seated in the tournament and we were the league champs.

Think about it, Cutler Ridge, one of the worst teams was in the league was the league champs and top seated in the tournament. Fans told me it was unbelievable when I saw them in town. The words pumped me up. They deserved the championship.

Everything went well throughout the week, and on Wednesday noon, in the auditorium, I was sitting with Marsha and Ginger, in the first row. They both had boyfriends who were out of school, and each thought their boyfriend was more mature. That's why Marsha said she was after me. Am I more mature? Not according to Jake and Session.

Elisabeth came home on Tuesday afternoon, and after I ate at home, I drove the truck to her house, where we had that talk. Some of what I said, we had talked about before, but now that I remembered, it was different.

Why was it different? I didn't know, and then it hit me. It's different now because I know it's real, not just something she told me, and I realize what she went through after seeing me at the incident.

Then I told her about a new memory that came to me. I was in a coma when I went silent, but that was for only a short time. I saw you, Elisabeth. You were staring at me as if you were thinking about how you were wrong and how you hurt me. Your thoughts were crying out about your undying love for me. It was so strong and real, and I wanted to reach for you. I tried so hard, and your affection was reaching towards me, but negative thoughts were fighting all the way. I can't remember what the ideas were, but they were winning.

I continued to keep my eyes fixed on you, but you drifted away from me, and that's all I recollect. Next thing I knew, I was waking up at St Luke's and didn't remember you.

Elisabeth and I were sitting on the couch in the living room. She gave me a passionate kiss and said she had the same feelings and was sure she had lost somebody she loved, forever by being stupid. Now she was glad I accepted her. There was no doubt, we were together as one, as God wanted it.

~~~~~~~~~~

When I came out of the trance, I saw Sam Sessions sitting on the gym floor, staring at me as if I was his pawn. He yelled, "Hey, ladies, and anyone who can hear, your hero, Jimmy Bass, used to run in the fields and woods howling at the moon. The last couple of nights, I heard that same howl, so I think he's about to go off the deep end where all nerds go."

I became furious and wanted to lose control. Then another memory came; Sam was telling the truth. When I first came home, I did run whenever the pain was extreme, but not in the fields or woods. I ran on the sidewalks around town. A lot of times I ran in the park in the middle of town where there are a lot of trees around the picnic tables. And I had never howled at the moon. I screamed and cried for mercy, but that was before, not since I came back. He made that part up.

As he was yelling, these things about me, I heard the other

students, telling him to shut up. Their words made him more annoyed, and he looked straight at Marsha, saying, "You think he's a man? He's not. He is nothing but a nerd fag, and he doesn't even like girls. He prefers boys. So, Marsha, you couldn't turn him on."

Some of the people in the area, mostly girls, began to put me down, but the words "nerd and fag" hit me like a ton of bricks. With his voice and those words, I seemed to be back at the beating.

Suddenly I saw the face of the kid shooting me with the BB gun. When he came into the woods, I got a good look at him. It was Sam Sessions, a freshman. He was the one whipping me and also the one with the BB gun.

I tried to keep control and determined to ask him about the night of torturing me and his BB gun escapade.

I stood up as he was walking in front of me, ranting about the howling. He saw me stand and stopped walking, glaring at me. Then he said, "Do you have a comment?"

"I won't deny that I used to run at night, not howling, but screaming and crying over the pain you, Jake, and his gang caused me."

He was about to reply, but I cut him off, yelling with a louder voice. "The night before my incident, I was captured by Jake, his gang, and you, Sam Session.

He started screaming, "Liar, Liar!" But Joe Harber, a big kid who didn't play sports, Tim, and Brad came up to him and told him to shut up. They wanted to hear what I had to say.

Sam tried to leave, and the guys grabbed him so he couldn't move. "Go on, Jimmy," Tim said.

Before I said anything, I saw Superintendent Shumer standing by the door, nodding for me to continue.

"They took me to an old barn and tied my hands with a rope above my head. I was stripped naked. They had some girls there. I think there were three of them. I couldn't see them because I was blindfolded. They came over and touched me all over. When they finished with me, Sam took his belt and started to whip me on my back and my stomach.

I turned around and pulled up my shirt so the students standing around could see the marks on my back. They were shocked, especially the girls. I pulled my shirt back down and looked at Sam.

"You did it, Sam when Jake and the gang took the girls to their car. You kept beating me and beating me, calling me names over and over. The more you beat me, the angrier you got, calling me a nerd and a fag again and again."

"Then Jake and another dude came back and stopped you from beating me. They untied my hands and gave me my clothes so I could get dressed. Then Jake told me to leave, and I started to run. The fear of getting beat again gave me energy, and I was running at a good pace."

"Somebody followed me and shot me several times with a BB gun."

I stopped, feeling nothing more needed to be known. Then God led me to my next response. I looked him square in the eyes and said, "I forgive you for all you did to me, Sam."

Sam, with hatred in his eyes, was prepared to say more hurtful words to me. But when I said I forgave him, confusion came over his

330

face, and I saw a shocked expression over a lot of people in the crowd.

Again I said calmly, "I completely forgive you, Sam. But I want to know why do you hate me so much? I have never done anything to harm you with words or action. So why do you hate me?"

"Because you thought you were going to be a star, the top man in school. You wanted to be another Jake. But Jimmy took that away from you. Isn't that right Sam?" Tim challenged.

Sam didn't comment. So I countered, "No, Tim, I think it goes deeper, back in my early years."

Sam blurted out, "If you are such a Christian, why are you gay? Being gay is against the Bible. It says we are supposed to stone gays to death. I don't know why we don't do it now. If anyone did, they would get arrested for murder. The country should go with what the Bible says!"

"You are misquoting the Bible, Sam. When Jesus came to earth, His crucifixion for our sins fulfilled most of the Old Testament laws and eliminated them. In the four Gospels, Jesus tells us how to live, even in the epistles of Paul. Jesus commanded us to love."

"So you admit it. You're homosexual, and you think it's okay to be one?"

"No, but God doesn't want you to stone them. However, they can't enter the kingdom of God if they live in sin. They need to repent and follow Jesus. They have to give up their sin."

"So you're saying you were gay."

"No, I've always liked the opposite sex. I'm not attracted to men." I shook my head in disgust. No way!"

"Your lying!"

"Have you ever seen a man and me in an inappropriate position?"

"You mean having sex?"

"Kissing, holding hands, or anything that would be inappropriate."

"No, but you used to ride around with Carter Tillman, and he's as gay as a two-dollar bill."

"I don't remember him, Sam. I'm not lying to you."

"Carter is not gay," Tim added. My brother knew him well. I don't remember Jimmy hanging with Carter. Maybe you saw with Pat and Carter. But you better not say Pat is gay."

"That is what I heard about Jimmy!"

"Probably lies from Jake. I wouldn't put it past him. He called Jimmy all kinds of bad things."

Sam saw he had no way out, but he wasn't giving up, yet. "You're all taking his side, but remember how Jake and his gang slammed him to the floor and how guys used to beat and kick him and he never fought back. Jimmy was a coward, a nerd. He wasn't a man. No man lets people laugh at him, tease him, and call him all kinds of names; but Bass didn't do anything about it. Now he comes back, all tall and big and you think he's something else. I should be the star, not you! I earned it, and no fag, nerd should have it."

Most of the students in the group started yelling at Sam, telling him he should say he was sorry for all he did. But the bell rang, and we headed toward class.

Mr. Shumer caught me before I went to class and told me my

words were powerful, and he was going to talk with Sam.

Sam was suspended from school for two weeks, for his language and trying to instigate a fight. His father agreed with the school and took his son to a counselor. Sam didn't want to go, but his father was strong, and Sam relented. I hope the counseling will help him because I don't want to hear his words against me anymore. I hoped it was over. But I had more things to worry about than thinking about Sam.

The problem was with my father. He wanted to press charges against Sam, Jake, and the rest of his gang. But he rejected the idea that I had forgiven Sam. He said that wasn't justice, for all they did to me. But Sandy, Mother, and I argued this is what Jesus would want. He knew the Bible and what Jesus said about vengeance, but he kept saying what about justice?

I answered him, "That's okay, Father. Maybe we can pursue justice, but for now, I am only interested in the tournament."

He agreed and not another word was said after that. Well, maybe later.

Chapter Twenty-seven

Hopewell Loudon played Attica in a game right after ours. If we won, we played the winner of that game on Friday, the twenty-second, at seven PM, Thursday night, the twenty-first of February, Old Fort and New Reigal played at seven, and Bloomville and Bettsville played right after them. Friday night, the two winners of each bracket would play. Then the winners play for the championship on Saturday night, the twenty-third, at eight-thirty. At seven o'clock, the two losers of the Friday night game, play for third place in the tournament.

We had two practices before Wednesday's game, and I worked hard, asking to stay later to get in some shooting. I wanted to be at the top of my game for Wednesday night and win this tournament. Republic was the winner over Thompson, so Republic was the team we would play.

When we entered the floor to warm up, I knew all eyes were on me. In the paper, the reporters wrote about our team in the tournament as well as about me. We weren't the favorite to win the championship, some media claimed we would only win tonight's game, and the rest of the tournament would be a downfall. Critical comments claimed most of our past success was luck, and we had run out. They said our school would retreat to being bottom feeders.

"This tournament will separate the boys from the men," Gene Sanders, our most prominent critic, maintained.

Allen Jamison was still on our side, but he was drowned out by the others who agreed with Gene. It seemed the media was trying to intimidate us so we would lose. They had their favorites and were not going to give them up.

My teammates and I discussed the reports given on the radio and written in the paper. They didn't intimidate us. The direct opposite happened.

I was pumped up, focused, and in my zone. Nobody was stopping me! But it wasn't a walk in the park. I knew there would be no thirty point averages in these games. In a tournament, it's single elimination, and every team does there best to win. You will never play for a bigger crowd all season, and you want to look your best. Plus, in most games, the score never gets to be over fifty points.

The biggest problem for me was that they were denying my getting the ball outside for my long shot. Again I had to face a box-in-one and a running baseline. The first half, I only made twelve points because they kept denying me the outside shots, but my determination kept them from stopping me inside. I not only got rebound shots, but high passes from the guard gave me baskets. We had a twenty-two to eighteen lead at half time.

Republic made a big mistake in the second half tip-off by trying to stop me from getting the ball. Brad tipped towards me, at the top of the key. Players were so worried about me; they forgot Joey was close to the baseline. I saw him immediately, and instead of catching the ball, I tipped it to him, and he had an easy layup. At half time, Coach told me to take over at point and try to get some shots from out there. The defender guarding me would probably pick me up around a step or two in front of the top of the key.

Our defense held them, and I brought the ball up the floor. The defender picked me up, where the coach said he would. Still not sure of my long shot, I took a quick dribble to the left, the spot that had enough angle to use the backboard. I shot, aiming for the sweet spot on the backboard and everything worked. When the ball swished, I felt confident that my shot was back. The next one was dead center, a few steps back, for the top of the key, another swish, gave us a twenty-eight to eighteen lead.

Republic called for a time out, and Coach told me to go back to the baseline, then directed the guards to take their time and try to push it inside.

"No wild passes. Take a shot only if you are wide open," Coach directed.

Republic had the ball after the time out. They worked their offense and took an open outside shot. As soon as the ball went through the hoop, the defender assigned to me was guarding me. His purpose was to deny me a chance to receive the ball, but he was surprised when I went down the floor not wanting the ball. The defender was a small guard, unlike the taller player, before. Joey caught me breaking to the corner as he was dribbling a fast pace down the court. I was briefly open in the dead corner.

After a quick pass, I went up for the long shot, one of my favorite shots through the season. I hoped it would work. In the first half, I missed a few. This time I could feel it was right as the ball left my right hand.

I watched the ball's flight as it went through the net and the defender fouled me. So I had one foul shot coming.

I made the shot, making the score thirty-one to twenty. The rest of the quarter, Republic had me clamped down. They scored from the outside, and we scored inside, it was mostly Brad. He had a big quarter because all the attention got directed to me. Sometimes they left Brad completely open, and a couple of rebound shots went to him. It was a slow-paced game, like Coach Chumbly wanted, with the score forty-two to thirty-two, our favor.

At the start of the fourth quarter, Joey hit a couple of outside shots to give us a forty-six to thirty-two lead. They scored, then a lob was passed to me for a ten-foot backboard shot, and they fouled me. I got the pass because the defensive guards were worried about Joey and couldn't drop down to double team me. I went up, twisted around, and dropped the ball off of the backboard before the defenders could foul me on the arm so I would miss the shot. However, his body connected me, giving me a chance at a foul shot. With that, the score was forty-nine to thirty-four, and we had under four minutes to go.

Republic kept hustling and cut our lead to seven points. We tried to stall but with them fouling us, and our foul shots, we pushed the lead back to ten.

We won fifty-seven to forty-seven. There was tumultuous cheering for our team. It was the first win in many years and meant that even if we lost to Hopewell Loudon, we would still play for third place.

In the locker room, after all the cheering, the stats were read. Brad made thirteen points with thirteen rebounds, and Tim had four points with ten rebounds. Joey earned twelve points with three steals.

Rendles was four points and five rebounds. I had twenty-four points and eight rebounds with two blocked shots, just like Brad, and four assists.

We watched the Hopewell Attica game that played after ours. At the third quarter, we left when Shumer reminded our coaches it was a school night.

In School, Thursday, we found out about Sam's suspension from school. It was quiet in school, but not a slight to me. During the noon hour in the auditorium, I sat in the back row, wanting to be alone.
~~~~~~~~~

As soon as I sat down, I went back in time. I was sitting in the same spot I always occupied in the past to keep away from the bullies. Nobody would give me any attention, except Pat Ender and Bill Kumer but they were with there girlfriends. I wished I had a girlfriend, somebody to love me. That wasn't happening, especially since the girl I love was Elisabeth Hasselbeck, and her boyfriend is bigger and better than me.

I was a worthless nerd. I didn't want to be, but people kept telling me I was, so I guess that's what I am. I tried to be friends, but everybody put me down, making me feel like a worthless failure. Maybe I should run away and find a new life where people would like me. I could go to another town and attend a different school, where they might let me play. I could be a point guard and set up their star players. Girls would like me, and I would be happy.

But that won't happen. My father told me, if I ran away, he would get me back, no matter what I did. So I'm stuck at home and have to face Jake and his buddies, with more trips and kicks, while I try to get away crawling across the floor. I couldn't stand up, because one of them had his foot on my back to hold me down. I didn't think they would bother me today. They were with their girlfriends, and I was slumped down in the back row. I was sure that if they couldn't see me, I was safe.

I sat there hoping for peace, yet I had nothing but fear. The pain slowly engulfed me, trying to convince it wasn't worth living. I tried going into a fantasy world where everything would be happy, and people would like me, Elisabeth would be in love with me, and nobody would want to hurt me.

I was fighting to get in that world and not think of the present world, and my head was hanging low when I heard a noise. No! I'm not safe. They're coming after me. I froze, afraid to move. Jake and his buddies were about to attack. I was ready for the pain.
~~~~~~~~~

Instantly I was sitting in the same seat, but it was another time, and nobody was around me. I remember the feelings I had about myself in the past. The fear I felt from the bullies made me want to find them and show them who this nerd is. What a relief it was! That was then. This is now!

I believe these memories will always be with me. The best way to avoid them is to think positive. I do have a girlfriend, the same one I wanted before, and I play basketball. With God's help, life is good.

I decided to do my homework before going to the Thursday night game. Elisabeth had a concert out of town, and wouldn't be back until late. My mother and I were home, but Father and Sandy went to the game. I listened to it, off and on, on the radio. Old Fort beat New Regal by seven points in the first game. There was an upset in the second game, Bettsville beat Bloomville by two points.

These games didn't matter to me, because we had to beat

Hopewell Loudon. In the long run, we would have to play the winner or loser of the Bettsville, Old Fort game, either in the championship game or in the third-place match. I wanted the championship game and would do anything to get it.

My thoughts went back to the memories I had at John's, the events of the beatings, and the time before the incident, which was the remembrance I feared the most. I had released many more memories, and now everything was there. I knew what my father did to me. I knew how it felt as he beat me and knew I had not imagined it. The memories were real.

I could still feel the pain, and sometimes, his anger remained intense. I hoped he would never lose control again. He came close to picking up the whip a few times, but he didn't use it. He used to hit my body with his fist, but not my face. He only slapped me for fear of leaving a mark and having people ask questions. There would be a lot of yelling and calling me names, mostly "coward" and "weakling" with colorful adjectives.

When I confronted him, before, he would whip me with the strap. At first, I had only one memory of him beating me. Now I remembered everything, especially when he said, "You ought to be strong, and make me proud. I am ashamed of you, boy. I wish you were never born!"

I could feel the pain and anger he projected toward me, and it scared me. I didn't say a word, I just stood there, shaking. Sometimes that would make him furious. What was I supposed to do? I felt hopeless, wanting to run, but I knew I shouldn't. If I did, he would eventually get to me, and it would be worse.

My father blamed me for not playing basketball. His chief complaint was that I didn't try hard enough. I pleaded with him that I did try. But he didn't believe me. I begged him to talk to the coach and ask him why I didn't get to play, but he never did. He blamed me for everything.

Now I knew what Father had done to me, and the story wasn't complete. More memories came, like the dream or vision I had at school today. I knew there were more, and I wanted to quit remembering them. If they continued, I couldn't let them control me like they did this afternoon.

I just wanted to forget the memories of my father. I didn't see the purpose in confronting him. One time was enough. I knew a situation would come up that I wouldn't be able to control, and the pain Father gave me would come out.

I have to keep remembering that I'm not like I used to be. I'm a calm, humble man who is a good basketball player. Thanks to God, my dream is now!

All day, Friday, my attention fought between listening to the teachers and thinking of the game. This year, I had an excellent grade point average, almost all A's. Before, I had only a C average. I was concentrating more and more on my studies, now, with no depression pounding on me like before.

Soon, game-time arrived, and I was back on Heidelberg College's Seiberg Gym floor. Jake Bickhart and John Alter stood against the wall, in back of the baseline at the entrance of the gym. John had talked Jake into coming to the game. They agreed not to sit in the Cutler Ridge section, for fear of an incident that some of the fans might cause. They had no desire to sit with any other fans while their teams played tonight.

When the Cutler Ridge team warmed up in front of them, Jake looked for Bass but said he couldn't find him. Just then Bass had a thunder dunk in a warm-up layup, right in front of them. John leaned over to Jake and said, "That's Bass."

Jake's mouth dropped open, and he denied it. That couldn't be Bass! He became silent, just shaking his head.

When they announced the starting line and called, "Jimmy Bass," he knew it was true. Again he shook his head. John didn't know if it was Jake's firm belief that a little nerd couldn't possibly be so big, or if it was merely a surprise.

Hopewell was as fired up and intense on winning the game as we were. Our defense was up for the game, but so was Hopewell Loudon's. We had beat them twice, the first game on their floor. That was enough to get them fired up. When they got close to us, they kept chanting, "No third time."

It was a battle through the first half. Hopewell Loudon got a six-point lead and held on to it, but hey didn't try to double team me. They had two men guard me, one player for five minutes, then another, back and forth.

I had no trouble getting shots in the spread. The coach had us playing this offense from the start of the game. John told me Coach was going to ride his horse, and that was me. I was hitting a good percentage from the outside, but my teammates were almost shut down. The score at halftime was twenty-eight to twenty-two, and I was sure I had seventeen of the twenty-two points.

It was the same in the second half. Again I was scoring from the outside, but Hopewell kept their lead. I knew I had over thirty points. Towards the end of the game, with two minutes to go, we were down fifty-three to our forty-six. At that time, I had thirty-two points of our forty-six and would not score another point.

Joey had two steals where he picked the guards pocket, making it a fifty to fifty-three, Hopewell lead.

With a minute to go, Hopewell stalled. The player Tim was guarding was between the foul line and the top of the key when Tim stole an inbound pass and drove the length of the court for a layup that got fouled. Both of their guards were caught on the wing, leaving the two big men almost at the top of the key.

Tim made the foul shot giving us a tie game. With twenty seconds left, Hopewell Loudon called a time out. All Chumbly could say was, "Play good defense and try not to foul. Play for overtime."

Overtime wasn't for this game. On the inbound pass, from the side which our defense contested, Brad jumped high to tip a Hopewell pass. Joey cut to the ball and started to our court, but they fouled him with fifteen seconds left. On the foul line, for a one-and-one, he made the first one, putting us up by one.

He missed the second one, but it bounced toward Brad's area, and Brad out jumped the players around him, and got one hand on the ball, tipped it towards the basket, and the ball bounced off the backboard. The ball then went in, and the place went wild. You could say we were lucky, but I'll take it.

We were ahead by three, and Hopewell Loudon called a time out, with twelve seconds left. Again Chumbly stressed no fouls. Joey and Rendles were told to full-court press so Hopewell couldn't roll the ball on the floor to get a couple more seconds before the inbound player picked the ball up.

Well, that didn't work, and the Hopewell player tried to pass the ball from out of bounds to the half-court. Again Brad's high jumping ability stole the ball, and a quick pass to Joey lead to a layup. Hopewell Loudon quickly in-bounded, got a shot off, which they

343

missed, and we won fifty-eight to fifty-three.

The bench erupted at the end of the game with cheering and players patting each other on the back. The celebrating continued in the locker room.

Jake and John left right after the game and hurried to Jake's Chevy. As Jake drove away, he said. "I know you want to brag on Bass, and probably should, but it's a different time from when Bass and I played. You can't compare the two of us."

That was all Jake said, and I knew that was all he would say. He finally accepted Bass, and I knew Jake would eventually leave Jimmy Bass alone. Never a negative word about Bass came out of Jake's mouth again. Some might say it was due to respect, but I say it was fear.

~~~~~~~~~

In the gymnasium, each of the four teams had a section for their fans — two on one side and two on the other. Since we played the first game, we sat with our fans for the second game. Our section was on the side opposite from the entrance to where the team comes out from the locker room. When the team had showered and dressed, we came out to aisles between the stands. The other game had started, but our fans still gave a cheer.

My mother, Elisabeth, and Sandy were sitting in the third row, and they had saved a seat for me. Mother and Elisabeth were getting close. I hugged Mother first as she congratulated me on my game, then Elisabeth, the woman I knew I would marry. Rather than sit with the family, Father stood against the wall behind the baseline, right behind the basket. His position was at the back part of the court, close to our seating section. While we were playing, I noticed he was there, but it didn't bother me. He was probably bragging me up, so that was alright. He was my blood, but I couldn't call him a father. Father's don't do what he did to me. No, I'm not going there! Pain, stay away, enjoy the moment.

It was a joy to set with Mother and Elisabeth during the game. I wondered how popular I was. If I went to the concession stands, would people recognize me as a star? Oh, boy, what a thought. I tried to stay humble, and now I want to be known as a star? Would people recognize me in a crowded area without my uniform?

Those are crazy thoughts. No concession stand for me. Someone is feeding us a steak dinner at Keller's, so I stayed seated where I was and watched Old Fort beat Bettsville. As soon as the game was over, we went to the bus waiting for us at the back door of the gym.

After the Old Fort, Bettsville game, I learned about the radio broadcast interviewing some Old Fort's players, who said, "We've seen enough of Bass, and Bass is going down."

I was asked to comment to the fans at Keller's, where we went to after the game. I responded, "I'm playing the game and giving it my best. If they stop me, so be it. But I'll try my best not to let that happen."

I meant every word.

The next morning, I had a counseling session with John. "What do you think about the whole ordeal? I know you want to win and Old Fort players have a lot of comments about how they are going to stop you. There is nothing we can say about the game."

"I know you're right, but when people like the Old Fort players make those comments, it hits my self-esteem. I think they are right and they know something I don't."

I thought for a while, then observed, "I guess I have a little doubt there. I can't throw low self-esteem completely away. Something that has been with me for years is bound to creep up on me once in a while. I know I shouldn't let it bother me. I keep telling myself to go to the game and play the best game I can. That is all I can do."

"So how are the memories going."

"My father's punishing me wasn't the worst thing, nor was Jake's gang the worst thing that happened to me. I can feel the pain when the memory comes to me, and it hurts. But you know I confronted my father over what he did to me, and that's settled. That memory doesn't seem to come back to me anymore."

"What about Session?"

"Naw, after the blow out in the auditorium, and the way the students treated him in school, I think he's learned his lesson."

"So you don't think Sessions, will bother you anymore, physically or mentally?"

"I hope not, John, but the main thing about Sessions is that I don't think I'll ever remember him from the past. I know my memory situation, but I don't think he was in my life back then. I might be wrong, if my renewed memory serves me right, I kind I recognized him shooting me with the BB gun, but I wasn't sure. In the woods, when I got a good look at him, I was kind of shocked that it was a freshman. At one time, I was thinking of charging him and beating him up. I was debating if I should, then I saw the pistol, and that changed my mind."

"Those are Satin's tricks. Pray for control."

346

"Yes, I know, John, but it's hard sometimes."

After a short silence, I changed the subject by saying, "I have to confess, the main reason I came back, is because I wanted to play for the school. Cutler Ridge is my town. I feel it is part of me. I am a different person, and I want to show the people in this town. Even though I had lost all those memories, I knew what kind of life I had before, and I felt a lot of people looked down on me. To my surprise, it was the opposite. A lot of people accepted me with open arms. Some didn't, but I think the majority did. That's one of the reasons I love playing for this town and community."

"Your right, Jimmy, a lot of people in this town like you, but they hate how your father used to treat you. Remember what the town did with Jake? What you did this season, put this town on the map. Your attitude is what everybody likes."

John reached his hand toward me. "Now, I don't want you to downplay this comment. You are a star, Jimmy. The town and community agree with this comment as do your teammates. Most stars are arrogant, and walk around as if they think everyone holds them in high regards."

John put his hand on his desk. "Not you, Jimmy. You're humble and kind to people. You talk to them like you're one of them. You're a pillar of the community, and that's something which can bring you pride.

You're a witness for Jesus, proving that a person can be successful, and humble like Jesus wants us to be. If you beat up your enemies, people would think less of you. But it isn't your make up. Everyone knows you believe in self-defense, but not attack."

What John said was right. I probably was a pillar of the community. I had to accept it and be humble. It wasn't in my nature

347

to brag or hurt people, even my enemies. I am a man of God, and I have to continue acting like it.

I believe that if you brag about your self, somebody will make a fool of you. I love the attention of reporters interviewing me, but fear keeps me from talking to them. If I say the wrong thing, it might hurt someone, and I would feel terrible. So I stay silent. I promised I would let Allen Jamison, sports reporter of the Advertising Tribune, interview me after the season and I will keep that promise.

I ate lunch with Elisabeth and Randy, then Elisabeth had an appointment at Heidelberg before attending the game. I went home where I knew the house I would be empty. Mother and Sandy were shopping at Tiffin, and Father said he would be at the factory for a meeting. That was okay. I took a nap and slept without dreams or visions.

Saturday night, February 23, the Championship Game of the Seneca County Basketball Tournament occurred at Heidelberg College gymnasium. The first game was Bettsville upsetting Hopewell Loudon for third place.

Now, at eight forty-five, I was on the west end of the court, the court closest to the main door, the warming-up area. I'm the type of person who prefers warming up outside. When I got to there, I heard fans yelling, "Go, Bass, go!"

I acted like I didn't hear them because people assume the players are to keep quiet. We need to focus on the game, and that is what I was trying to do. If everything worked out, my plan, along with prayers, was to come out firing, and it worked. I know what the Old Fort players said about stopping me. That fired me up, and I still scored for the team. If I didn't, we wouldn't have a chance to win.

The game started and I got my wish. I made the first five

shots I attempted from the outside, giving me ten points to Old Fort's four. After a timeout, they started pressing full court and made a basket, then scored on their next possession.

After the first mistake against their press, Tim took the ball out. They were in a man-to-man press, so Tim passed the ball high in my area at the top of the key on Old Fort's offensive end. If Old Fort hadn't double-teamed me, I could have taken off down the court because I knew I was faster than the man guarding me. I had an easy shot, a short backboard shot.

Our defense stiffened as I received the rebound and quickly drove full court down the left side with a defender beside me. Suddenly I stopped in my tracks, catching him off guard, so he went a step past me. I took a long shot off of the backboard, and it went in. The defender fouled me, so I got a foul shot, making the score fifteen to six.

After that, Old Fort turned it into a rough game, trying to foul me before I shot, trying to keep me from two-shot fouls.

When I was inside, Old Fort players would let me know with an elbow, a push, or even a punch in the stomach. They cut into our lead. Their offense was clicking.

At the end of the half, I was going up for a ten-footer when a defender backhanded me in the stomach. I crumbled to the floor. The pain was nothing new, and I usually popped right up. But this time, I couldn't. I had lost my breath and went into the fetal position, moaning, and groaning.

I heard whistles blowing, players pushing and shoving, and the crowd booing as I was trying to catch my breath. John knelt beside me and asked if I was okay. I couldn't speak, I gasped for air, and John told me to take it easy. Then a doctor knelt beside me, checking for injuries. When I could breathe, the doctor said, "Take him to the locker room." John and the doctor guided me off the floor.

Later, Elizabeth told, me that when they took me to the locker room, the whole auditorium was quiet, wondering how badly I was hurt.

I got my breath back slowly. After the doctor checked me thoroughly, he said there was no reason why I couldn't play. When the team came in the locker room, at half time, they asked how I was, and John told them I was okay.

My teammates told me that Brad went after the Old Fort player who hit me, and both players exchanged blows. Players from both benches started fighting, but the coaches and referees got everyone to back off. When everything settled, Brad and the player who hit me were both ejected from the game. Tim said the player who hit me was the one mouthing off to the sport's announcer about stopping me, and he was one of their better players.

The referees came into our locker to tell us they had just left Old Fort's players, warning everybody that if they had any more rough fouls, more ejections would follow. They walked over to where I was sitting and asked how I felt. When I said I was fine, they said they were sorry that something like this had to happen, and promised that no one would hit me again. I thanked them. As they left, I followed them out to the gym.

Both teams must have been out on the gym floor, leaving me the last one. The fans gave me a roaring cheer on my return. Only a couple of minutes were left to warm up, so the bench players started passing me the ball to get my shots in for warm-up.

The buzzer sounded for us to return to the bench, and I

looked at the scoreboard. I remember when the Old Fort player hit me, we were ahead by five, but now only two. The score was twenty-eight to twenty-six.

With Brad ejected, Glen Carl, a five-eleven Junior, played in his place. Although he played most games, it was seldom that he scored. Playing inside, like Brad and Tim, he would help us on the boards, but he couldn't jump like Brad. That's why I jumped to start the second half.

My thoughts were only on the game. If Old Fort thought that hitting me the way they did would scare me, they were wrong. I was more fired up. I tipped the ball to Tim; nobody on Old Fort's team could out jump me, and Tim passed it back to me. The first half, our court was closest to the main door, but in the second half, we had the far end. I quickly drove to the end of the court. I took a short backboard shot, and no defender came close to fouling me. What the referees said was right. The referees now called the fouls close.

Tight reffing was great for me to score, but on defense, I had to back off on attempts to block shots. We played better defense, and my shooting was on target. It seemed every assortment of shots I took went in. I was on a mission to win this game, and that was my total thought.

After making a short jump shot, I saw Jake Bickhart, standing against the wall and staring at me. My mind went back in time when his gang was beating me, and I felt the fear they gave me. I froze and thoughts of the basketball game that I was in left me. The fear of Jake looking at me like he had control over me, and enjoying it, caused me to shake. My whole concentration was on him. Then John was beside me, guiding me off the floor to the bench. I was shaking so much I might have fallen if he hadn't guided me.

351

"Look at Bass." Mel Wilson, from the radio station, said to his partner, George Billings.

"I see what you mean, Mel. He's just standing there looking at someone standing against the wall."

"It's like he's in a daze."

"Isn't that Jake Bickhart, his supposed tormentor in school? That's who pushed him into a coma. Bass could be experiencing a relapse, Mel."

"He's about ready to collapse, John Woods and a teammate are there to support him and guide him to the bench, George. He's shaking all over, and I doubt if he'll be back in the game."

After I was seated on the bench, I told John what happened.

"Keep praying that his fear can't control you," John encouraged.

I prayed that Jesus would help me, and slowly, the panic subsided. My shaking was gone, and I told John, "I feel good. God took all the fear away from me.

"Look at him, Jimmy. He is still over there against the wall." John directed.

I did, and I could see he wanted me to feel the pain I felt before. I knew by the look on his face that he had put me in a trance and had proved his power as king. I shook my head and whispered, "No more, Jake, no more," as I relaxed on the bench.

John could tell by the expression on my face that I would no longer let Jake get to me.

"When you are ready, Jimmy, come to your coaches."

John went back to sit beside Coach Chumbly, and I looked at the scoreboard. We were in the fourth quarter at the six-minute mark, with a two-point lead. I was ready, so I stood, took one more look at Jake, and shook my head to let him know he would not going to bother me again.

"Mel, it looks like Bass is going back into the game. He's looking at Bickhart and shook his head. Now he's going to the coaches and kneeling in front of them."

"Yes! Bass is going back into the game, George!"

"You folks out there can hear it on your radio. The fans are going crazy! Bass is coming back into the game, unbelievable!"

When I returned to the game, I was motivated. Nobody could stop my teammates or me. I did my best to score and played top-notch defense. I wasn't giving Old Fort a chance.

Occasionally I checked the clock, and we were always ahead by ten or more points. With thirty seconds left in the game, Coach Chumbly took me out of the game.

As I went to the bench, the announcer proclaimed, "Jimmy Bass has set a new tournament record by scoring forty-two points in a game."

The fans roared, and the Cutler Ridge fans started chanting, "Jimmy Bass, Jimmy Bass!"

It was contagious. All of our fans screamed. We won seventy-three to sixty.

Mel Wilson turned to Gorge Billings and stated, over the radio, "Unbelievable, George! that Jimmy Bass is one great player."

"Unbelievable!" George repeated.

Epilogue

Cutler Ridge had plenty to celebrate. I won two individual awards and player of the year, in our league, which was the top vote-getter from the coaches of the league. I was the only one chosen for the first string, and only Brad made second string. I felt Joey should be there too. He would have had third string if they had one, but they didn't. I told Joey latter that I felt terrible for him. He just shoved it off as if it didn't mean anything, but I knew he was hurt.

I also received the honor of being chosen Top Player in the tournament. Everybody on the team got an award for winning the league and tournament, and a trophy for each.

The league is twenty-five years old, and as far back as the records go, there was no record of our school ever winning the tournament. It was the first time on record our team had gone into the district competition.

Everyone picked us as the losers, but they were wrong. We won on both Friday and Saturday night, with more awards presented to our school and the players. I got the Best Player award again, and I had an unbelievable average of thirty-five points in each game.

In our first game of the Regional, we again met our Waterloo getting beat by seven points. Walnut Grove was an excellent team, and they were better than us. We hung in there all the way, for we had no desire to lose. Walnut Grove loved to run and play a fast game, but that was our Achilles heel. A zone team's defense gave me ample opportunities to shoot, and I was hot, shooting all over the floor. But no matter how good I was, they stayed ahead by five points or more. We never had the lead. My teammates had a hard time scoring, so it was left up to me. Thus I racked-up another forty point game. I would rather have won the game, instead, but we lost seventy-six to sixty-nine.

That was my last game in my high school basketball career. My final stats were thirty-one, and a half points, twelve rebounds, five assists, and two blocked shots a game.

Another award I received was when I made first-string on the all-state team. Some people said I should be player of the year.

I had struggles with my emotional status, but Elisabeth was with me all the way and, by the grace of God, became my wife.

When the season was over, my father wanted to press charges against Jake for ganging up on boys. He said, "I am not getting revenge for my son; I want justice."

I looked down at him and said, "What about you, Father? The accusations all come from me, and I have forgiven you. Don't you think Jake and his gang knew what you did to me? You told me that nobody in this town knew what you did to me. No one, before the incident, and no one after I came home, remembered it. So let's leave it alone."

He didn't say anything, he just turned and went out to his garage, and that was the end of that.

~~~~~~~~~

This book was not about basketball, even though it shows that God rewards people who suffer; it's about bullying, how it can get carried away, and the harm it can do.

If it wasn't for the right psychological help, giving his life to God, and walking with God, Satan could have controlled Jimmy Bass. We must stop the bullying of children and provide them with the knowledge of how to get help.

Those who tend to take control of others must be made to realize how important it is for them to help those who are different or weaker. We must eliminate bullying in our schools and help our young people to understand love.

Many children grow up feeling the pain bullies give them. Often, their fear is so intense that they can't succeed, and have a difficult time accomplishing the talents they have.

Some who experience bullying, develop a desire to get revenge. Former bullies get their reward for past behavior, when a weakling they had fun with becomes, their boss or supervisor. Others become bodybuilders fighters and beat their enemies.

However, the best way to overcome the pain you suffer from bullying is to get counseling and turn your life to the Lord, Jesus Christ, who is love and wants to give you peace.

Jimmy Bass

ABOUT THE AUTHOR

Howard Weider grew up in Northern Ohio where he coached boys' basketball successfully for over forty years. After his wife died, he moved to Lancaster County, PA, to be near his son and continues to write Christian fiction.

For more information on Howard or his writing, visit his Face Book page at: www.facebook.com/Christian.fiction

Howard asks you to "like" his Face Book page and leave a comment.